A Study In Flesh

by Wendy Evans

Cover image: Wendy J Evans
Author photos: Donna Swan of Swan Photography

A Study In Flesh

Copyright: Wendy Evans
Published: 15th March 2014
ISBN: 978-0-9924784-2-1
Print Edition

Ivory black: Primitive man knew this pigment, and used it in cave paintings. It was made by placing ivory and other bones in a stoneware container, surrounded by hot coals. The charred residue, consisting of ten per cent carbon, with potassium and other carbonates, was then ground and mixed with water. The modern pigment is a more refined process, but the qualities of ivory black are identical. It is not poisonous and does not fade in sunlight. However, many artists shun its use, preferring to blend near-black from other deep colours.

Fragments of innocence, placed in the crucible of time and heated with the red-hot fires of experience, leave a dark hardness which can mask the colours of a man's life.

It can turn tenderness to violence, passion to apathy, joy to hatred, love to jealousy and empathy to a chasm of mistrust. Yet innocence can be reborn, like the Phoenix which rises from the charred ashes of dreams.

When the dark mood held him in thrall Ronald Norman Turner had a perverse desire to cut and slash. He gripped the knife handle firmly and brought the blade down onto the pearly flesh, leaving a scarlet wound across the pert breasts. He sliced fiercely, watching with pleasure as the brown-red tips were replaced by a smear of red from which an oily tear trickled. There was carmine in the black hair which curled over her shoulder-blades, hair which he knew to be scented with gardenia and redolent of the musk she wore behind her ears.

There was no change in the expression on the face of the woman. She looked at him with pansy-dark eyes, heavy-lidded, thickly-lashed; world-weary eyes in a face graced with a straight nose and nostrils that flared widely in passion. But only the fullness of her lower lip betrayed the sensuality of her nature when her face was in repose.

Bitch...cow...tease...man-baiter. He'd tasted those lips, nuzzled that sweet spot behind her jaw, felt the shape of her breasts in his palms and had responded when her curious hands measured him. "Oh, my dear, sweet wanton," he whispered.

He took a handful of rags and carefully removed the thick paint laid on by the palette knife. He took his obsession's flesh from the easel and replaced it with the version which had been commissioned. He had painted her dozens of times in the past, drawn her in a hundred different poses. In this portrait she was dressed in peacock green silk, the sheen of the fabric casting a turquoise glow onto the matt, golden-brown perfection of her face. He started to paint it in as a thin glaze over the shadows below her jaw, under her finely-arched brows. There was a hint of it flecked into the lust-dark eyes. A tiny rigger brush was dipped in alizarin blended with titanium white for the corners of the eye. He wiped the brush on a rag and chose green and white for highlights that gave her pupils a liquid life.

He mixed turpentine with black and dipped the fine brush into the pool of darkness on the palette. His hand was quite steady as, in bold letters, he painted his distinctive signature, ROMAN, across the bottom right-hand corner of the canvas. It was ironic that the Romans coined the phrase, Art's long, life's short.

He had worked as Roman for many years. He had painted hundreds of portraits and as many again of preliminary nude studies, but few showed his undoubted genius. Portraits of his patron and his royal lover, studies of his godson, and all those of Mercedes, who had introduced him to the bedroom arts, who he could not capture except in paint. As Roman he had achieved fame and fortune, but he still identified more with Ron Turner.

And he knew the paintings he did under his real name had given him more satisfaction and had done as much good as those which had won acclaim for his alter ego.

He was, in essence, the same person as the high school student who had won the State prize for Art in 1979. That had brought him no more joy than a small paragraph in the local paper. It had cut no ice with his family. Nor had anything he achieved since held any significance to the folks at Cootimurra. He was, in their eyes, a dead man. In their dead eyes. They were only ghosts in the skeletal landscape of his youth.

PART ONE

Imprimatura

1

Flake white; the most commonly used white until the 19th century, popular since the time of the Ancient Egyptians and made in those days by burying earthenware jars of metallic lead in fermenting manure with vinegar. Heat and chemical reaction formed a white crust which was scraped off and ground. It is a heavy, dense paint, with warm undertones, but is highly toxic and must be used with care.

"What's it like to walk off the land you call home?"

Ron cocked his head and looked sympathetically at the Downs girl. He'd known her for years. She was in his class and he often sat with her on the school bus, talking of this and that, when she wasn't too busy looking after her brothers and sisters, who were still in primary school.

"To be honest, it's a relief. Dad doesn't think so. He's still seething with anger. Ma's over the worst of it, now. She's being philosophical. She says that at least we'll have some sort of a life. You can't honestly say you like living in the back of beyond, Ron."

"Don't know no different, do I?"

"I thought you wanted to go to art school."

"Fat chance."

She stood and ruffled his fair curls. "Chicken. You're chicken, mate. If you want it, grab it. Gotta go. I've got to help make sandwiches for this mob."

"You're expected to feed them? Dammit, your mother told mine it's hard finding the food to put in your own mouths."

"Bread and scrape. My auntie's cutting the ham real thin and spreading the mustard real thick. She'll be right. Can't expect people to drive all this way without a bite to eat."

It had been a bit of a joke, calling the station Faraway Downs, when the Downs family first came to the shire. They'd come with high hopes, full of ideas, wanting to try dryland farming in an area which had only run sheep in the past. Three years of drought had put paid to their dreams.

When the bank foreclosed, there was a clearance sale. Mr Downs, spitting bile, said he was damned if he'd leave a living beast, a harvestable crop or a stick of usefulness on the station.

His wife dug up the rose bushes she'd tended with devotion. Her old man took a chain-saw to the straggling fruit trees onto which every drop of washing-up water had been poured, and had razed the vegie patch. What they couldn't sell, or give away, would be burnt, he told neighbours.

"That sanctimonious money-grabbing bastard from the bank said we were damned fools to try to make a living out of marginal land," he said to James Turner, who ran Cootimurra Station, on his eastern boundary. "Said I wasn't so much a cockie-farmer as a bloody galah. Ponced up city bloke, with his walk-shorts and long stockings, wearing polished shoes! I ask you! Looked more like a preacher than a man who understood the land. Took the heart out of me. Shite, man! Do you want that tractor or not?"

Ron glanced at his father and hoped he wouldn't buy the old Massey-Ferguson. It was a lemon, had been a lemon from the day Matt Downs bought it, and would probably remain a heap of crap all its rust-bucketing life.

His father shook his head. "No way, but I'll bid for those drums of paint when they come up. Ron here wants to be a painter, so he can start by painting the roof of the house! What the hell were you going to do with it all?"

"Beats me. Came in a job lot with a harrow and a water-tank. I thought there were two tins, not two dozen."

"You can't use that on the roof, Dad," Ron protested. "That's white lead. It'll poison the rainwater."

His father looked bitterly at the cloudless sky. "What bloody rain? We'll carry on using bore water like we always do. Next week you can give your brother a hand with that tank and move it down to the west paddock by number six windmill. The bugger keeps breaking down and we could do with some reserves for the stock. Now make yourself scarce while I talk business with O'Malley."

Ron sighed. He was used to being treated like an idiot but wished his father would keep his opinion to himself, not mock him in front of O'Malley. O'Malley the sheep-shifter. Ron knew that meant they were hard up again. His father always rounded up a load of wethers for the long haul to market when there were bills to be paid. Not that they got much in return by the time they'd paid O'Malley to transport the sheep to the port for export to the Middle East, where they liked their mutton delivered live before they slaughtered them. Most of them were, in truth, half-dead before they arrived but there was no room for bleeding hearts on the land.

"Bloody Ay-rabs!" James Turner often grumbled. "Won't eat their mutton unless the sheep's throats are cut facing Mecca, or some such nonsense. I'd give them O Allah Allah! Costs a fortune to ship them live and then the blood Ay-rabs say they don't want them and send them back. Not fresh! How much fresher can you get than saying Baa?"

The auctioneer was about to swing into action and the would-be buyers, most of whom were present out of sympathy with the Downs family, were wandering off to the stockyards where the livestock was assembled.

"Don't forget to bid for the chooks," Ron reminded his father. "Ma says she could do with another dozen."

There were papers everywhere, fliers advertising the auction, lists of various lots coming up, some marked with a cross by those willing to pay over the odds to help a neighbour in trouble. The backs of the sheets were blank. Ron started to gather them up. His Ma said there wasn't the money to buy fancy drawing paper so he drew on bits of cardboard and on the inside covers of old exercise books which were being thrown out by the school. He drew on butcher's paper and on the margins of newspapers. He sharpened pencils until they were little more than stubs.

He grinned happily and felt in the pocket of his dungarees for a stick of charcoal. It was one of his own making. He'd read about charcoal burners in an old Arthur Ransome book, not Swallows and Amazons, but one in which the plot involved the ancient craft. He remembered little of the story, except that the woodsmen kept adders in a cigar box. He recalled every detail of how they stacked the twigs and covered the wood with turf before starting the slow, cool burn which left pure carbon instead of ashes. He'd had to use mud from the creek to seal his cache and had experimented with many kinds of wood before he'd found a bush vine which hardened into brittle sticks of comparable quality to those the art teacher handed out.

He rested the pile of paper on the bonnet of a ute and began to sketch the face of the auctioneer. He caught the likeness immediately, then looked for other subjects. O'Malley, fat and balding, was his next victim. He drew Matt Downs, catching the worry and fear with a few lines and a fingered smear of shadow around the eyes. He lost track of time as his fingers flew over the pages, his eyes bright with concentration, his mouth soft in the corners with a smile of contentment. He didn't realise the sale was over until the auctioneer snatched the pile of drawings from his hand.

The man leafed through the pages. "I saw what you were up to, young Ron. I'll give you a fiver for the one of me."

Ron's jaw dropped. He made no protest as the auctioneer stuffed a note in his shirt pocket and went off, chuckling, waving his picture. Others drifted over and struck deals. Within ten minutes Ron's pocket was bulging and only the sketch of Matt Downs remained.

"I'd buy it, Ron, but I can't afford it," the cockie said.

"You take it," Ron replied. "And, if you can find some paper, I'll come over and draw Mrs Downs and the kids as well. You've been good friends to the Turners."

"I heard that." The auctioneer patted Ron on the shoulder. "Come over to my car before you go home. There's a ton of paper in the back you can have."

By the time Ron staggered to the Turner ute with a couple of boxes of pamphlets, his father was staggering from the woolshed with other inebriated neighbours.

"That home-brew was off," he muttered. "You'll have to drive the ute. Pull over to the yard and load the paint."

James made no attempt to help. He slouched in the passenger seat and rolled a cigarette. He farted loudly as Ron got behind the wheel and blew a cloud of smoke in his son's direction.

"Smells rich," the smoker muttered. "Rum and molasses. Talking of rich, how much did you make?"

"Nearly fifty bucks."

"Hand it over!"

"No way. I'm giving it to Ma. She can buy some new frocks."

"Have it your own way!" His father spoke with a growl, let the back of the seat down and threw the butt end from the window. He pulled his battered felt hat across his face and settled down for a long sleep.

Ron drove smoothly away. He'd been driving around Cootimurra from the time his long legs could reach the accelerator and had held a special licence from the day he turned sixteen. But in the ensuing year he'd had little chance to practice on the open road. If his father wasn't using the ute, his elder brother was off to town in it, spending his evenings with cronies in the pub, playing pool or taking a hand of euchre.

"No way you're borrowing the wheels," his father'd said. "I'm not having you kissing an ironbark like your brother Phil."

Phil had fallen asleep at the wheel after a game of footie and a riotous celebration in the next shire. They'd cut his body out of the wreckage, but the old Holden was still wrapped around the only bloody tree between Cootie and Faraway. Ron shuddered as he drove past the spot. With James junior dead in Vietnam, Bert would inherit the property. Bert was ten cents short of a full dollar. He'd work until he dropped but couldn't think enough for himself to tie up his bootlaces.

Ron glanced at his father, who'd had four sons to rear and a wife as gaunt as dried leather on a road-kill. Short of money, short of food, short of temper and damn nigh empty of hope. Ron squinted at the far horizon, driving into the sun which blazed from a hot white sky.

Cootimurra...which his brothers called Cootie because, like body lice, it got in your hair and bugged you. The land round Cootie was merciless. He knew its savage places well, the plains where the blue had drained from the sky to lie deep and sinister in the shadows below the breakaways. He knew the feel of sand beneath bare feet, sand that stripped away the paint from weather-board shacks, that abandoned the roots of the wheat which struggled to grow on acreage on the edges of probability. He knew the back breaking weight of sand that drifted across paddocks bare of feed and piled high against the troughs under the windmills, where the hollow-bellied sheep drank only of starvation.

He couldn't blame his father for lashing out when he'd found his youngest son behind the barn, drawing pictures with charcoal on a sheet of cardboard, instead of out at the windmill, shoveling the dirt from below the water tank.

"You no-good drongo!" his father'd yelled. "Scribble, scribble, scribble. What makes you think you could make a living as an artist? Dammit, Ron, it's a wonder you can draw breath! You can forget those fancy ideas about art school your teacher's been talking about. Your place is here, helping your brother and me. Where do you think I'd find the money to put you through college?"

Ron sighed as he changed gears and braked to take the side road to Cootie, the turning marked only by an old oil drum under a grevillea bush. Ron had spent many hours in its shade, sitting on a pile of worn tyres, waiting for the school bus. He wondered if there was any point in returning for a final year if his matriculation was going to lead nowhere. He didn't want to leave. He was a competent all-rounder, but his artistic talent had been like an epiphany to his fat old art teacher. She gave him more than knowledge. She gave her star student encouragement and a deep belief in his innate ability. She introduced him to music and poetry, to good books and other cultures. Her classes were like water in a desert to a man doing a perish.

"But it's all a mirage," Ron muttered the next day, squatting on the hot roof on a pad of hessian bags, an outsize brush in his hand and a tin of white lead paint beside him. He'd done only the northernmost roof and his back was aching. His Ma hollered that it was time for smoko. She tied a billy of tea and bag of bread and cheese to a string left dangling from the eaves. Bert had needed the ladder to fix a termite-rotten beam in the woodshed. Ron had been left stranded aloft.

"Put the brush in turps while you eat," Ma yelled. "And put the lid on the tin!"

"Yes, Ma."

Ron looked out across the purgatory of the station with his cool grey eyes, eyes the colour of the skies when the cyclones streamed moisture-laden clouds down from the Timor Sea and dropped the rain anywhere but on Cootie. There'd been times when they'd been cut off by flood, but the Turner land hadn't felt a drop. Ron knew he would die inside if he stayed there. He thought grimly of the future as he finished the south side of the building. He peed off the western gable at midday and missed the blue heeler dog who was panting under the washing line.

"You can do the woolshed roof tomorrow," said Bert, putting the ladder back against the outhouse eaves.

"Pig's bum I can. I made forty-seven dollars yesterday drawing portraits. And I bet I'll make more at the agricultural show next week. I'm not sticking around here being your off-sider."

"You pull your weight or Dad'll strap you! Who the eff do you think you are? Who earns the real money round here?"

"Any money you earn gets pissed against the wall of the pub."

"Why, you cheeky sod," snapped Bert, pulling the ladder from under his brother's feet, sending him tumbling to the ground, the half-empty tin of paint rolling across the yard. Ron, stunned, got up shakily, holding his hand to a cut on his chin, which was bleeding badly.

"Stuff you, Bert. You could've killed me." Ron wiped his face on his sleeve and picked up the empty tin, the can of turps and the well-worn brush, which was now thick with dirt. He limped off to the store where he cleaned off the mess and made sure the bristles were lying straight. Determined to stay out of Bert's way, he took paper from the boxes he'd dumped under a workbench on return from Faraway and, scrabbling through a toolbox, found a carpenter's pencil. An hour later he strolled up from the dry creek-bed with a handful of exquisite drawings of leaves and lizards.

His father, grim-faced, met him at the door of the shed. "You time-wasting slob," he sneered, snatching the papers from his son and tearing the sheets into shreds. "That's it! No more of your bloody nonsense. Here, Bert, hold the bastard. He can watch while I show him what I think of his bloody art!"

The boxes of paper had already been taken out to the yard and now James Turner drenched them with kerosene. The flames devoured them and the ashes flew like black confetti when they were stirred. Ron yelled in protest as his father ground his box of charcoal under his heel, turned to his son and laughed in his face.

"Sod you!" cried Ron, swinging a fist at his father, who was unbuckling the leather belt from his trousers.

"Raise your fist at me, would you?" James dropped the belt and socked his son in the stomach with his left and broke his nose with a right-hander. "I'll have no son of mine defy me! Piss off, Ron! You're no damn use to the Turner family! You're no damn use to Cootimurra!"

Ron dripped blood all the way to the kitchen. His mother, tight-lipped, found ice for his nose in the kero refrigerator and then, without a word, pulled a battered suitcase from the top of the wardrobe and folded his meagre supply of clothing into it.

"You'd best go to my uncle's place," she muttered, tucking a round of bread and cheese sandwiches into his duffle-bag and adding a bottle of water. "Uncle Alf will see you right. If you start walking to the highway now, you should get a lift with O'Malley when he takes the next load of wethers from Faraway Downs in the morning. Now get out, before your father kills you!"

She opened her purse and handed him the money he'd given her the night before. "You'll need this, I expect." She turned her back on him and took the flat iron from the side of the wood-burning stove, spitting on it to test if it was hot enough to tackle the basket of washing.

"Hard-hearted cow," thought Ron. "Not so much as a goodbye. Well, Ma, I love you as much as you loved me."

He slammed the door behind him and reached under the verandah for the tatty old portfolio given to him by his teacher. It was full of his sketch books, his finest work. Also inside were his water colours of landscapes, his still-life studies, his pen and wash drawings of people with interesting faces.

"You'll need a portfolio of work to get entry to art college," his mentor had said. "Keep this and this. No, that's not your best work, Ron. Never be afraid to discard what isn't first rate."

Ron picked up the suitcase in one hand and the folder in his other, and started the long trudge to meet O'Malley. He was not afraid of the future. He was not afraid to discard what was not first rate and life at Cootimurra was far from perfect.

"What does it feel like to walk away from your home?" he'd asked at Faraway.

"To be honest," the Downs girl had said, "To be honest, it's a relief."

Ron, sitting on his suitcase in the shade of the grevillea, rubbed the dust of Cootimurra off his boots and all his yesterdays out of the pictures in his mind.

2

Sepia; a dark reddish brown pigment obtained from the fluid secreted by cuttlefish. From the Greek, Sepia, a squid. It is used in water colours and the preparation of drawing inks, notably of Indian ink. It is also used extensively in photography to give a range of soft brown tones instead of the more usual black and white images. It can be smelly and highly toxic.

The remains of the crumbed calamari rings went into the waste bin with the wilted salad and the squeezed lemon quarters. Ron sighed. What the patrons of the Delphi wasted in one night would have kept him fed for a week. He scraped prawn shells and congealing lamb with courgettes from the heavy white plates. He sluiced the dishes and stacked them ready to load the dishwasher after it had coped with the discarded platters of the first flush of patrons. The place was busier than he had known it in previous years. The Greek press were in Fremantle, following the exploits of America's Cup yachtsmen.

In the kitchen the chefs were dancing between grills and deep-fryers, the demis were racing to keep up with cold larder demands for entrees and salad ingredients; the sous was throwing a tantrum because they'd run out of field mushrooms. A harried commis-chef staggered into the kitchen pig's domain with an armful of dirty pans. Ron sighed and buried his reddened hands in hot soapy water and began to scour them.

"Hurry! Hurry!" Kostas, the commis, dumped a second load on the draining board. "There's a party of ten just been seated and chef's freaking out. We're running out of basics. When you finish this lot beard another box of mussels, will ya? There's a run on the

Delphi special."

"What? Drenched in ouzo? Soused in tomato and chopped parsley? Tastes like crap."

"Who cares? It looks great and it's different. "

Aristotle Populis set high standards for the Delphi. He was usually to be found at a small table at the back of the restaurant, with a few crooked cronies, drinking retsina and playing cards, smoking his fat cigars and keeping a watchful eye on the front-of-house. Every twenty minutes or so he would rise ponderously and bully his way through the kitchen, shouting instructions and quarrelling with his mother, Agnella, who spent every evening stuffing dolmades. Up to her elbows in mince and rice, she separated the marinated vine-leaves with skill, wrapping them around the filling and laying them in trays, ready for the thick tomato concasse to be poured like gore across the traditional delicacy.

It was a chore she'd taken over when Aristotle's wife, mother of Zoe, had high-tailed it back to Thessalonika, where she remained, deaf to all arguments that her place was in Australia, making good the duties of wife and mother, meeting the threat of divorce with a shrug and the universal Greek gesture for the cuckold.

"If you can't see your face in those pans they're not clean," said Aristotle, stubbing out his cigar in a half-empty dish of taramasalata as he pushed past to the staff toilet in the yard.

The smell of burnt cods' roe made Ron's gut churn. He swallowed hard and took the steel wool to a stockpot which had been used to make egg and lemon soup. Rinsing off the soapy water he could see the wavering image of his long, hungry face, the high cheek-bones and the deep-set eyes of the country-boy doing it hard in the city. The curve of the base distorted the hooked nose, broken by his father in a drunken rage.

His hair, soaked with the steam, fell forward over his brow, curling in an annoying fashion. He'd have to tie back the blonde mop or ask his uncle to chop it off again. He glanced at the pile of pans, seeing a dozen Rons reflected, most elongated like the stick figures of a Drysdale painting, emaciated cockies in parched landscapes, sere in summer drought, scuffing through the dust of poverty. Gaunt men and worn-out women, like his mother, whom he regarded with scant affection.

But better his Ma than Mana Populis, who pushed past him with her arms full of trays of dolmades, taking them to the cool-room next to the staff toilets. Agnella started screeching when she saw her son lounging on the old sofa on the back porch, a space squeezed in between the brickwork of the Delphi and the butcher's shop next door.

"What's she yelling about now, Kostas?" The commis, a Populis nephew, was the only other member of staff who spoke Greek. He'd become a good friend in the past two years.

"Same old," he replied. "She's telling him it's time he divorced his wife and married again so that she could retire and leave his missus to work her fingers to the bone."

"Who'd have him!"

"He don't have to work, Ron. The old fart is rolling in it!"

"Smells like it!"

"You seen his place? Tart's palace! And my cousin plays the effing princess!"

"Yeah! Well, I always wanted to marry the boss's daughter!"

"Don't joke, mate. You haven't met her. Miss Zoe Populis is convinced she was sired by a bloody Greek God. She walks the earth as if she can't stand the smell of her own feet! And hairy! Man, is she hairy!"

Ron threw a dish-cloth at him. Mana Agnella ran out of breath and stormed back into the kitchen. "You, come," she snapped. "Kitchen pig shell eggs!"

She kept him busy until the last customer had left. The chefs piled the last of the dishes in the sink and wiped the work surfaces. Ron glowered at the mess in the sink and started scrubbing. He could see the staff lounging outside the windows on the broken chairs on the porch, drinking beer. Aristotle heaved himself off the sofa and went inside to count the night's taking while Mana watched and gloated. The old lady reached across the table and snatched a handful of twenty-dollar bills. Her son growled but she took off her apron, slapped it down on the table and stalked off, like a carrion crow come fresh from pecking out the eyes of a dead bullock.

Ron, carrying a tray of glasses, hot from the dishwasher, grinned. A new waitress was laying up tables for the next day's trade. She was slow, weariness hanging on her shoulders like sandbags.

"Need a hand?" Ron asked. "You do the cutlery and I'll set the glasses."

She looked up at him with gratitude and he caught his breath. Hers was the most stunning face he had ever seen, Eurasian, honey-gold skin, blue-black hair neatly plaited and eyes of deep violet-brown.

It took him only a few minutes to set out water and wine glasses but it gave him the opportunity to study the girl's figure, hidden under the white shirt, black slacks and long, bartender's apron which all floor staff wore. The androgynous uniform merely emphasised the budding breasts, the sinuous hips, the long-legged grace of her.

"I'd like to paint you," he whispered, reaching across to finish the table she was working on.

Aristotle hissed. "You, Turner, back to the kitchen! Stop wasting time, Mercedes. You think I want to be here all night?"

"It's all right, Mr Populis. I'll lock up when I've mopped the floors. You get off to your poker game."

Not a word of thanks. Aristotle merely grunted. Ron heard the front door slam. The chefs finished their drinks and clattered into the squeeze that Aristotle called a staff room, to change from their dirty jackets into street clothes. They threw their whites into the hamper on top of the used tablecloths and napkins. Ron added the tea towels to the pile and humped the wicker basket out to the back gate, down the sagging wooden steps from the back verandah, past the stinking dustbins and the crates of empty bottles.

He grabbed the mop-bucket on his return and started to clean the floors. He checked the front door and pulled down the blinds which proclaimed to passers-by that DELPHI was open for business for lunch and dinner, Tuesdays to Saturday. He switched off the lights and picked up his duffle-bag. Kostas had left a large screw-top jar beside it, filled with moussaka which had been on the menu for three days and hadn't proved popular. Ron hated aubergines but he was starving hungry and glad of the left-overs.

He locked the back door and stepped outside, turning off the yard light as he did so. The flare of a match took him by surprise. He snapped the light on again and stared with bewilderment at the new waitress, who was stretched out on the old sofa.

"I've missed the last bus," she said. "You don't mind if I kip out here?"

"It's not safe. There's all sorts come sniffing around the back at night, down-and-outs going through the bins for scraps. Winos looking for dregs in the wine bottles."

"They won't find any tonight. I've scored them myself. Fancy a swig?" She waved two half-full bottles at him. "Red or white?"

Ron laughed and held up the still-warm jar. "I'll share if you'll share. You like moussaka? I'll get plates and forks."

When he returned she was sitting up, rubbing her feet, which looked swollen around the ankles. "I won't walk far on these," she said ruefully. "Have you got a place I can sleep?"

Ron flushed red. "I've only got a single bed."

"I don't mind sharing. I'll snuggle up real close."

"It would be a tight fit!"

"But I like tight fits, don't you?" The invitation was obvious, the touch of tongue to lip a definite invitation.

Even Ron, green as they come, understood instantaneously what was being offered and felt a tingling all over. He sat down and busied himself dividing the food, hoping that his hard-on did not show under his old footie shorts. She poured red into glasses and passed him one.

"You're Ron, aren't you? Cheers. My name's Mercedes. Like the car. And spare me the jokes about how many miles an hour I go and do I fire on all cylinders."

"Classic lines and high-powered engine?"

"Yeah, and built to drive men round the bend!"

"We're made for one another!"

"What makes you say that?"

"Because I live in a garage!"

Mercedes burst out laughing, a rippling gurgle as musical as a bird at dawn. They were quite merry by the time they finished the wine. Ron took her hand and helped her down the steps to the yard gate.

"Is your car out back?" she asked.

"Hell, no," said Ron, ducking behind the cool-room and unlocking the chain from his old bicycle. "I'll have to dinky you on my deadly-treadly."

She hiccupped as he eased her rounded butt onto the cross-bar and wobbled down the lane to the road which ran alongside the railway. He could normally get up the hill to Uncle Alf's place but the extra weight defeated him...that, and the huge bulge in his pants where her body rested against his crotch. She slid off into his arms and walked barefoot by his side, swinging her shoes in one hand and tucking the other into the back of his belt.

"We'll have to be quiet. Uncle Alf's a war veteran and doesn't sleep well."

Ron unlocked the garage door and wheeled the bike inside. There were few comforts, not even an electric light. Candlelight revealed the old iron bed. It stood in the middle of a space cleared among the cans of paint and stepladders, next to a workbench heaped with tools, the corners of the garage dark with piles of junks such as broken furniture which needed fixing, old flower pots and lamps with broken shades. There was a lawn-mower at the head of the bed and, on a lop-sided chest of drawers...one leg missing...a bowl and a jug of water which Ron used for washing.

"Tasteful decor," said Mercedes. "Where's the bathroom?"

"There's a dunny round the back, but its next to old Alf's room."

"Don't worry. I'll pee in the garden." And she did so, all over a patch of petunias. Ron grinned and watered the lemon tree.

"You can use this washing bowl. I'll hose myself off in the garden."

Mercedes nodded and left him to it. Ron grabbed a towel from the clothes-line and shivered as he played the sprinkler-hose over his sweat-drenched body. He grabbed a handful of mint and rubbed it on his skin, chewing a few leaves to freshen his mouth. He wrapped the towel around his hips and stepped inside.

Mercedes was naked, languidly soaping her body. She was poetry to his eyes. He sat on the bed and watched her hands caressing herself. She turned her head and smiled, quite unabashed at his obvious appreciation.

"Up," she purred. "I need your towel." She flicked it from his loins and laughed as he tried to cover himself. "Don't worry about that," she chuckled. "I've got just the thing to fix that."

And she had, and she did, and it wasn't she that yelled aloud in ecstasy.

"Holy cow!" Ron gasped.

"Hey, I'm no virgin, and neither are you, now."

"Is it always like that?" Ron, in wonderment, looked at his bed mate.

"Sometimes it's even better," said Mercedes, busying her hands. "Try it again, but slowly."

And he did, and it was, and this time Mercedes begged for mercy.

***

She was gone when he awoke the next morning. He glanced at his alarm clock and groaned. He'd forgotten to set it and had missed his first lecture. He washed quickly, smelling her scent on soap and towel, feeling worn-out in unaccustomed places and remarkably invigorated in others. There was no time for anything bar an apple for breakfast. He slid the strap of his portfolio over his shoulders and wheeled his bike down the path.

"I heard yer last night!" Uncle Alf leered at him from the front porch. "Had a bird in there, didn't yer? Goin' great guns, yer was. I know!"

"Do you mind?"

"Half yer luck, that's what I said. Half yer luck, young Ron, and if I was your age I'd have come in and joined yer!"

"She's gone."

"I know. Saw her walkin' down to the station. Good looker, for a slope! Mind, she's not half the looker of the bints I had in Tunis. There was one time in El Alamein..."

"Yair, I've heard the yarn! Her with the dancing snake. See you tonight, Uncle Alf."

Ron rode like the wind but the life-drawing class was already under way by the time he arrived at the College of Art. He sidled in and took his place at a spare easel. The model was pretty ordinary, a plump housewife with sagging, doughy breasts and a roll of stomach fat. He made a moue of distaste and took up his charcoal.

"I don't want a composition in light and shade today," said the tutor, at his elbow. "Today we're concentrating on line, like an Ingres drawing."

"She's no ballet dancer!"

"She was once. Look closely and you can see the muscle below the fat. Look below the surface, Turner. Just as you need to understand what's under the clothes to paint a good portrait, you need to know anatomy, to know what muscles are under the flab, Turner, and what bones are under the muscle."

Ron stripped the model down to the bare essentials in his mind. As eye and hand worked together to catch the pose on paper, so his mind probed that of the subject. He grew to like her, to empathise with a blithesome thing grown heavy with the years. He read her loathing of herself and her nostalgia for her youth. He looked at the trunk-like legs in understanding of how she must feel to be trapped in a mass of blubber when she had once floated gracefully across the stage, on full pointe in the corps de ballet. He could hear ballet music in his mind and imagined she had once been beautiful and much desired.

He drew her as she was now but within that sketch he caught the essence of what she had been and it was there, too.

"Remarkable," the tutor said at the end of the class. "How did you do that, Turner?"

"Dunno."

"Come and look at this, Mrs Darcy," the tutor said.

The model, now dressed and ready to leave, crossed the studio to look at Ron's work.

"Thank you," she said simply. There were tears in her eyes. "I know you need your work for the end-of-year assessment, but when you've been marked, could I buy that sketch from you?"

"I'll give it to you. I enjoyed drawing you. You were beautiful when you were young, but you're more interesting in maturity."

"Well, so your tongue is as clever as your fingers, young man. You should go far." She opened her bag and took out a business card. "Come and see me. I think I have a proposition for you."

A couple of fellow students made lewd gestures behind the woman's back and joshed Ron furiously in the corridor outside.

"Proposition, is it, Ron? She wants you to hump her?"

"Yeah! Rent-a-Stud. Be like bouncing on a rubber mattress."

Ron grinned in high good humour. He sensed Mrs Darcy wasn't in lust. He'd been propositioned by enough bored housewives to know the difference. He wondered what it was she had in mind.

"You've made a good impression there," the tutor said,

heading for the staff room. "Quite a patron of the arts is Pru Darcy. Owns a couple of restaurants. She may have a job for you."

Ron's heart sank. Kitchen pig was kitchen pig, no matter who owned the greasy spoon. Still, if he wanted to get a good training, he had to work to support himself. He had to earn money to survive, with scholarships few and far between.

Then he reminded himself that life could be worse. The Delphi meant seeing more of Mercedes. He could get no closer to her than he had already been, but was ready to travel a very long distance on the well-sprung hips of his first lover. He couldn't wait to hear the throaty purr of her engine, to open her clutch, work up through the gears and put his foot on her accelerator. He wanted to drive her to the limit, to explore with her the far horizons of experience.

Damn. He was hard from simply thinking of her. He moved his portfolio from his back to his front and headed for the pottery studio, wishing his hands were about to rest on her form, rather than on a lump of clay.

3

Raw Umber; a brown earth permanent pigment, darker than ochre or sienna because its iron content is supplemented by manganese. It is greenish brown in the raw state but dark brown when burnt. It takes its name from the Latin, umbra, a shadow. It is permanent, non-toxic and has been used since pre-historic times. It is essentially an iron-stained clay.

Browned off. That was Ron's state of mind for the next four days when he learned that Mercedes was on the morning roster. When he arrived after classes she was on the point of leaving. She brushed past him in the doorway and, had it not been for the quick thrust of her hips against his, he would have sworn she hardly knew him.

"You won't miss the bus today," he mumbled.

"No, but I've got a date I mustn't be late for. See you." And she was gone.

"Fancy her, do you?" said Kostas.

Ron blushed.

"Classy bitch, that. Was at a posh boarding school until her dad went broke. Shot himself, or got shot. Dunno which. One day she's rich bitch, the next just another poor cow!"

"Big deal. How do you know?"

"Had smoko with her this afternoon. Bit of a come-on, isn't she?"

Ron swallowed hard. "Is she? I wouldn't know."

Somehow the dishes seemed greasier and the pans heavier.

Mana Agnella slapped him with a wet dishcloth when he was slow fetching her another tray from the cool-room. He broke six plates and Aristotles ranted that he'd dock his pay if he wasn't more careful. The chef gave him left-over stuffed green peppers which had been burnt on the top. They gave him indigestion for two days and a miserable night with the runs.

"Serves you right, eating that wog food," said Uncle Alf. "You got the rent for me?"

It was only five bucks a week, but Ron was expected to pay on time. The old man cackled and showed his great-nephew the racing pages. He had marked his favourites and the amount Ron was to lay out on bets at the TAB.

"We'll have a tenner on Mistress Golightly, shall we? 33 to 1 but she's got good breeding. She's a stayer. Yer want a filly that's a stayer, Ron. What happened to yer dolly-bird? She's a non-starter, eh?"

"Looks like it, Uncle. Got her over the first furlong but she's run out on me."

"Didn't like the stables, I expect. Can't ride a thoroughbred in a garage. When are yer going to get a proper place to live?"

"When I can afford a month's rent in advance."

"I suppose yer thinks I'm a mean old bugger to put yer up in the garage instead of in the spare bedroom. Have I shown yer the spare bedroom?"

Ron shook his head.

"It's me art room. I paints when yers at college. Learned at the Senior Citizens Centre. Come and look."

The war veteran's home was a small, fibro-cement house, with minimal comforts. There was an old gas stove in the kitchen and a porcelain sink in which Uncle Alf washed his undies. The laundry was used as a brewery, full of bins of dark, frothing liquid and a stack of full and empty bottles of various vintages. The old man sank a couple of flagons every night, sitting in the old armchair on the front verandah, picking the horsehair out of the torn leather and tapping rollies into a bucket of sand and beer caps by his side.

The sitting room was a pig-sty, racing papers piled high on all surfaces, along with baskets of unironed washing and a dog-basket filled with logs for winter fires. Ron had never dared stick his nose into his uncle's bedroom, which he expected, from the smell, to be in similar disorder. Now he followed the old man into the back room and waited, in amusement, while the door was unlocked.

The familiar smell of turpentine and linseed filled his nostrils as he was ushered into the room. The walls were hung with unframed pictures which appeared incredibly bad.

"I don't do originals." said Uncle Alf. "That's a Van Gogh and that's a Manet. See that? That's from a Renoir. Made a good fist of the Rousseau, didn't I? But I like Gaugin best. All those tasty little Polynesian crumpets. What do yer think, Ron?"

"I'm gobsmacked. No one told me you painted."

The old man cackled. "Shocked, ain't yer? My brother, that's yer grandpa, went in for sign-writing and his father made a living painting pictures of the nobs. Runs in the blood on yer mother's side of the family. That's why yer've got the talent."

"Ma never said."

"Yer Ma ain't said anything worth listenin' to since she married that miserable git and went bush. Now, seein' as how yer a real Norman, yer can come in here and paint when yer wants to. But yer'll have to buy yer own paints. Cost a fortune they do, even the students' oils."

Ron looked at the tortured tubes, many without caps, most

squeezed in the middle or leaking pigment at the ends where the lead foil had been unfolded. There were dirty brushes everywhere and palettes crusted with many colours. Uncle Alf was not merely untalented, he was messy. But he was kind-hearted and generous in his own way. He hadn't been at all dismayed when a lanky youth had shown up on his doorstep and begged to be put up for a few days. The days had turned into months. Nothing had changed in two years.

"Yer drink beer?" Uncle Alf had said. "Yer sit down at the kitchen table while I fry yer a plate of bacon and eggs. Our Peggy's boy! Well, there's a turn-up for the books!"

Uncle Alf had run him through a crash course in city life, sheared the wild, sun-bleached curls from his head and given him a decent Army cut. He'd shown him how to shave the bum-fluff from his face. Then, satisfied the youth looked something like decent, had found him the job at the Delphi through a mate of a mate. He'd crowed with delight when his young relative had been accepted at the art school. He was enjoying the company, pleased that Ron was willing to work in the back garden at weekends, relieved that someone was there at night in case he threw a funny turn. Uncle Alf knew his heart was grinding to a halt, that the windmill of his life could stop pumping the good red stuff at any time.

He'd rigged a line from his bed out through the window and across to the garage, and had tied an old ship's bell to the rafters.

"If I calls yer, run down to the telephone box on the corner and get an ambulance," he suggested. "If I throws a wobbly it'll be no use yer holding my hand and getting me an aspirin. It'll be a hospital job; too right it will, mate."

Affection for the old war-horse kept Ron by his side. After months at the Delphi, he could have easily afforded somewhere else to live and had, in fact, turned down several offers to share houses with fellow students. He knew that Uncle Alf was comforted by his nearness and, in offering an affection he had never known, was binding him in chains more tightly than any felon.

On afternoons when Ron had no classes, Alf dragooned his young relative into walking down to the river and casting a line for tailor, though they caught more blowies than edible fish. Ron listened to the old man's memories of the war, to tales of the race-track, to home-spun philosophies on how to handle the female of the species.

"But you never married," Ron protested.

"Hard to settle for one peach when there's an orchard full of them. Don't do it, young Ron. Women are all the same. First they wants yer body, then yer wallet and then they takes yer soul!"

"Can't think why any bird would want my body."

Uncle Alf glanced at him, then started reeling in as the float bobbed on the water. "Yer not that bad. Bit stringy but yer'll flesh out. Pity yer nose is bust but women like a man who's not afraid to use his fists, as long as it's not on them. Yer never to hit a woman, Ron. Promise me. And pass me that crab-scoop so we can lift this beauty out of the water."

"I'll never hit a woman. Cut my throat and wish to die!"

"Yair. We'll see. Yer Dad hits yer Ma?"

Ron dropped his head.

"Thought so. Bad blood in yer, Ron, from his side. Yer temper'll make a jackass of yer before it makes yer an artist!"

Ron went to work the next morning full of fried bream and good intentions. Mercedes was on duty.

"How was your date?" he hissed, jealousy dancing in his eyes.

"Wasn't so much a date as an interview. They offered me the job."

"What as?"

"Topless barmaid."

"Dammit!"

"What's wrong? Pays more than waiting on tables. I've got nice tits. You know that."

"Yeah, but to have old men groping at them. You wouldn't."

"Ron, old men have been groping me since I was nine years old. Starting with my father!"

"That's sick!"

"The world's sick. Didn't you know?" She picked up an order pad and prepared to go through to greet the first customers. "I'm not ashamed of my body, Ron. It's something I use."

It was a busy night. Ron scrubbed as if the very devil was in his hands, punishing them as if they had violated Mercedes' flesh. It was irrational that, having felt her body in wonder and innocence, he now felt as sullied as those who had pawed her as a child. It was a sickening realisation that the very thought which turned his stomach was accepted by her with complacency, if not indifference.

"Your place or mine?" she asked, at the end of the evening.

Ron groaned. He was ashamed of his background. "There's time to catch the last bus," he murmured.

She gurgled with amusement. "But I want to make love to you, you silly boy. I can't do that on a bus!"

Ron felt the blush starting at his toes and burning through to his ears. "My place, then. Uncle Alf's got a bad heart and likes me home at night. That is, if you don't mind the mess!"

"Who looks? I don't."

"Do you make love with your eyes closed?"

She chuckled. "No, but I'm very short-sighted. And I'm very hungry. Did you score a meal tonight?"

"You like dolmades?"

"We don't eat vine leaves in Java," she mumbled, her mouth full. "Rice and curries, yes. I'll make you nasi goreng some night when we stay at my brother's flat."

"You live with your brother?"

"Mmm. If you call it living. He's a fat slob. A globe-trotting slob. Runs the family import-export business from Jakarta."

"Don't you like him?"

"I don't like the company he keeps. Hugo's got all the vices of the Dutch and none of the virtues of the Indonesians."

"Is that what you are? Indonesian?"

"Hell no, I'm a dinky-di Aussie. Born in Melbourne."

"I didn't know." Ron went red. "I mean, I knew you weren't a Pom!"

Mercedes poked him in the ribs. "You're blushing! Haven't you met anyone like me before? Coloured, I mean."

"I thought you might be an Aboriginal at first but you're prettier."

"Dad's family were Dutch, stubborn as they come. My mother's Javanese. She's beautiful."

"So are you."

"Not when I stand next to my mother. She's a stunner."

"My mother's an old boot."

"You've left home?"

Ron smiled painfully. "I got kicked out."

The girl laughed. "Well, there's a thing. The Australian government kicked my parents out. Said they were illegal migrants and all that heavy stuff."

"Were they?"

"Hell, yes. They got shot of Dad as an undesirable. He went back to the village where his folk used to grow coffee. He was still fighting to get the land back. Silly bugger!"

"Land's worth fighting for, isn't it? Uncle Alf and his mates helped liberate the East Indies from the Japs. They take an interest in what goes on."

"So you know the story? It drives me crazy. Dad's family fought the Sukarnos to the bitter end; then the poor duffer was daft enough to fall in love with the new president's second cousin twice removed, or whatever. He was on the nose with the Suhartos as well. He eloped with my mother to Australia."

Ron sighed. "It's like an adventure. All my Dad fights against is the bloody bank."

She wiped her lips on a serviette. "You're a country boy?" She unwrapped a honey-soaked pastry and broke it in half. "Tell me."

"About Cootimurra? There's not much to tell." He described his childhood and she looked at him with amazement.

"You think that's not much? At least you know who you are and where you belong. You've got your feet on the ground. What have I got? I belong nowhere. I don't fit in here and I don't want to be there. I wouldn't live with my father and my mother's shacked up with an Indonesian General. She ditched my father for this big swank, General Ihza Dinegoro."

"Who the hell is he?"

"Rich. Powerful. What's it to you?"

Ron's face was red. He wanted to know and he hated to ask. "Did your mother know your father was molesting you?"

"Yeah, Ma said if he wanted young girls he'd better find them some place other than Australia because they'd crucify him if the police found out. And they did. So she packed me off to boarding school with the nuns and they went back to the islands."

"Kostas said your father died recently."

"Yes, he did. That's why I'm broke. The General got Dad a government job but he blew it. The company he worked for was big time in debt. They figure my father had something to do with it."

"And did he?"

"Hell, no. He was just a dirty old man but they needed a scapegoat. I expect he groped one of the Suharto kids. They had him shot."

There was a long, thoughtful silence. She patted his arm. "Don't worry about it, Ron. I had no affection left for him. And not a lot for my mother."

"I thought it was hard enough walking away from my home. What did you feel when they walked away from you?"

"I felt as if I needed someone else to love me."

Ron watched as she ran her finger around the plate, sipping the thick tomato sauce from its tip. She licked her lips then gazed at him intently.

"Take me home," she whispered. "I don't mind your hands on my body, Ron. At least I know they're effing clean!"

***

"Wake up, lover-boy," she said. "It's Saturday and we should go to the beach."

Ron groaned. "I've got no bathers."

"Who cares? Get out of bed. I'll make tea."

Mercedes pulled a length of batik from her bag and wrapped it around her like a sarong. By the time Ron found his shorts and a shirt she was sitting at the kitchen table, talking to Uncle Alf. The racing pages were open in front of them and the old man was buttering toast.

"She'll go well at Randwick," he said, passing Ron the Vegemite. "Don't forget to collect me winnings on yer way back."

"Mistress Golightly," Mercedes said with a grin. "Uncle Alf's got a hunch."

Uncle Alf threw a tube of zinc cream at Ron. "Mind yer don't get sunburnt, young feller. And don't let yer young lady frazzle, neither. There's towels in the linen cupboard."

They bought fizzy lemonade and doughnuts at the corner shop near the bus stop. Mercedes led the way down the hill and through the sand dunes to the small beach. She kicked her shoes off and ran barefoot to the water's edge.

"It's warm enough to swim," she called. "Come on in."

"I told you, I've got no bathers."

"Ron, it's a nudist beach. No need for cossies." She unwound her sarong and threw it at him. "Get your gear off."

Sheepishly, Ron undressed and, folding his clothes neatly, wrapped a threadbare towel round his waist.

Mercedes dived through a breaker and came up wet, gleaming like a bronze statue. She splashed towards Ron and tweaked the modesty cover from his hips. She pressed her cold wetness against him and kissed his lips. "Come on, it won't hurt you."

"But I can't swim!"

"Run, jump, splash. Have fun. Don't you know about having fun?"

Ron shook his head but followed her into the waves, shivering with the shock of cold water on his groin. He took a deep breath and plunged into the ocean. They romped in the shallows like a couple of frisky puppies, then she took his hand and led him deeper so that their joining was a secret thing.

Satisfied, they headed for dry land and stretched out on the towels. Mercedes spread zinc on the narrow band of bare flesh on his hips, the only part which the Cootimurra sun had not burnt brown. She was tanned all over.

"Was that good?"

"The best. But I look at you and wonder, why me? You're so beautiful. Why me?"

"I like corrupting innocence," she laughed. "And you're going places, Ron Turner. I know it. And I'm going with you."

"No topless barmaid job?"

"No. You can have exclusive groping rights, for now."

"Forever?"

"I don't do forever, Ron. I live in today, not tomorrow."

"Would you pose for me? And at college? We need models for life-classes."

"Does it pay?"

"Yes. You said you wanted to be a model."

"I'd rather be an actress. I've got an audition next week."

"Drama school?"

"Maybe."

"Good luck." Ron rested his head on her thigh and dozed off, savouring the feeling of salt prickling his skin as it dried, breathing deeply of the sweet musk of her body.

Mercedes rested on her elbows and looked out at the sparkling ocean. She smiled at the essential and simple nature of her new lover. He had much to learn and she would enjoy teaching him.

They missed the bus and had to wait an hour for another. There was barely enough time to dress for work. Mercedes went into the Delphi while Ron chained up the bike and slipped across the road to the TAB. Mistress Golightly had won by a length. The roll of notes was thick and he stuffed them deep in his pocket. His grin of delight survived even the wrath of Aristotle, who yelled at him, reminding him kitchen pigs were two-a-penny and he'd better not be late again.

The euphoria lasted all evening. He hurried Mercedes home and, as expected, found Uncle Alf still awake, dozing on the verandah with a clutch of empties at his side.

"Your hunch paid off," he said, pressing the Mistress Golightly winnings into the old man's hand.

"Good-o!" The old man kissed the small fortune and handed it back to Ron. "I don't want it. It'd stuff up me pension," he said. "Get yerself a nice place to live. It ain't right havin' ter sleep in the garage."

"We don't get much sleep."

"Me neither. That's a damn noisy bed. Me ticker can't take the excitement. Now bugger off."

Moonlight shone through the window high in the garage wall, bathing the bed with a silver light. Hours later Mercedes rolled onto her stomach and came up into a crouch.

"Try it this way," she suggested, guiding Ron.

Ron threw his inhibitions away and lost himself in sensation, driving Mercedes wild, so that she buried her head in the pillow to muffle her mews of pleasure. Ron looked up and froze.

"Damn it!" he said. "Uncle Alf's on the stepladder outside the window! He's watching us!"

Mercedes sat back on her haunches, her butt hard against Ron's thighs. She looked the old man in the eye and deliberately ran her hands up her body, to cup her breasts for his enjoyment.

Uncle Alf, whose eyes were already signalling a jackpot, gave a strangled cry. His arms waved in a wild semaphore. There was a great metallic crash and the sound of breaking glass.

"Keerist! He's fallen through the cucumber frame!" Ron pulled on his shorts and ran outside.

"Ring for an ambulance," the old man groaned. "I've broke me hip."

"Let me get the ladder off you."

"Right, but don't yer move me, young Ron. I'll just lie here quiet until yer gets help what knows what they're doin'."

Uncle Alf, legs across one side of the cold frame, his head resting on the other, chewed on his lip until it bled. He stifled an agonised cry when Mercedes knelt by his side. She had wrapped the sheet around her body.

"Gawd, yer a beauty," the old man gasped. "Yer all silver and sassy. I could die and go to heaven when I looks at yer."

Mercedes stroked the thin hair from his forehead and kissed his brow. The sheet fell away and Uncle Alf sighed with delight. Mercedes reached for his gnarled wrists and lifted his hands to her breasts. Uncle Alf squeezed her, smiled happily and shut his eyes. His hands fell limply to his sides. Mercedes sighed and draped the sheet across his body. She went to the garage and got dressed.

"You're too late," Mercedes told the ambulance men, who had told Ron to stay by the phone box to direct them to the house. "I think he's gone."

"Looks like the glass severed an artery, Mr Turner. Just as well, perhaps. A broken hip is a slow death-sentence at his age."

Mercedes put her arms around Ron and hugged him tightly. "Don't grieve," she murmured. "He died happy. I saw to that!"

Ron pushed her away. "What do you mean by that?"

"I let him touch me. He was nice."

And Ron, who'd vowed never to hit a woman, lifted his arm and slapped her across the face. "You dirty little slut!"

4

Orpiment; ground from a natural mineral, sulphide of arsenic, which is found in hydrothermal areas, such as around hot springs. It is highly toxic and reacts badly with lead and copper-based paints, darkening them. It varies from lemon-yellow to orange and has been used for centuries, though its popularity has waned since the introduction of safer and more chemically-stable pigments.

There was pure poison in the looks Mercedes cast at Ron over the Christmas period.

"Nobody hits me!" She'd screamed at Ron, who'd been standing dumb-struck beside Uncle Alf's body, looking at his tingling hand as if it didn't belong to him.

"I'm sorry," he mumbled.

"You will be! You're yellow! Only a coward hits a woman. There's a big streak of nasty in you, Ron Turner, and I'm damn glad I found out before we got any closer."

"We couldn't get any closer!"

"Bull! You'll never know what you've missed out on. All that bile because I gave the old man a bit of pleasure? What's it to you if he had a squeeze? He died with a smile on his face and a stiffie that would make your eyes goggle."

"You didn't!"

"No, I didn't, but I wouldn't have been ashamed to have gone down. I like older men. Hell, Ron, yours isn't the only one in town, but it's the only one that's a lemon."

"A lemon?" Ron had never failed to rise to the occasion,

despite his inexperience.

"Yeah, a lemon. Suck it yourself! It'll leave a sour taste in your mouth!" She turned her back on him and went to speak to the ambulance men, who were loading the corpse onto a stretcher.

"Taking him to the mortuary, Miss. There'll have to be an inquest."

"Can you give me a lift to my brother's place?"

"You're not sick, are you?"

"I'm in shock," she snapped. "I'm sick as a dog and, if it makes you happy, I'll faint for you!"

Ron, watching her climb into the cab and the ambulance roll away down the hill, rushed to the dunny and threw his guts up. Then he fetched an armful of home-brew and sat in Uncle Alf's armchair, watching the sun rise in an acid yellow glory.

***

"I'm sorry about your uncle," said Pru Darcy, when she met him again. "What will you do now?"

"I don't know. I can't stay on in the house. It's a war veterans' home and he only had use of it in his lifetime. He left everything he'd got to me, but he hadn't got much, Mrs Darcy. Only a room full of home-brew, but the men from the Returned Servicemen's League finished that off at the wake."

"I told you I had a proposition for you," she said. "Come and have a coffee and I'll explain. And for heavens sake call me Pru. Mrs Darcy makes me feel like a grandmother!"

Ron dragged his heels but followed her to the cafeteria, feeling rather like a marionette whose puppet-master was pulling the strings. He hoped she was not going to chat him up. He'd sworn off women, since Mercedes. Since Mercedes...even the thought made him wince as if he'd got lemon juice in a cut.

"I've bought a place in Portside," she said. "There's a restaurant downstairs and enough room for an art gallery on the first floor."

Ron shook his head. "I don't want another dish-washing job." At least the Delphi still employed Mercedes and he could feast on her with his eyes, even if he was ignored.

"No, no! It's the attics. At some time in the past they were turned into a flat, with a toilet and bathroom. They're full of junk and spiders so I can't rent them out. But I thought you could tart them up and use the big room for a studio."

He eyed her warily. "How much rent would you ask?"

"Nothing. You'd be there, like a caretaker. We won't open for business for months but I'll feel happier if there's someone on the premises. When we do open, I've got plans for you."

"I wondered what you'd get out of this."

She told him and Ron burst out laughing. Why, he'd be back to square one, back to the auction at Faraway. She wanted him to draw lightning sketches of the customers.

"You can charge for the service. Look, they'll sell like hot cakes, believe me. Before then, I'll commission you to do big charcoal portraits of celebrities. I'm going to have a black and white theme for the restaurant and your drawings will be the only pictures on the walls of Margett's. You like the idea?"

"I'm stunned. It's a brilliant offer."

"You'll get asked to paint proper portraits. Can you?"

"I've not had much practice with oils, but I'll learn."

"Good, then you can practice on me. You can do one to hang in the entrance of the gallery. And I'll hang your other work if you want me to."

Ron thought of the dozens of canvases stacked in the corner of

Uncle Alf's painting room. The old man's mates had come round and helped him clear the house of rubbish, but he'd not let them in the spare room. Every bad copy could be scraped off, sanded down and a new under-painting given ready for new work. It wasn't fear that the RSL boys would fancy the imitation Gaugins and Monets which made him keep the door locked. It was the work in progress on the easel.

Ron had painted Mercedes from memory, a sea-goddess rising golden from the waves. It was a private painting, one that had come from the heart, one that showed his longing in every brush-stroke. It was a painting which made him hard with desire, a desire he wanted no other man to feel.

"There is one thing, though," Pru Darcy said. "You should change your name."

"What's wrong with Ron?"

"No, not Ron, but Turner. There's only one Turner in my book, and his name is sacrosanct."

"My mother's family are called Norman. That's my middle name. Ronald Norman Turner."

"Fine. Then we'll take the Ro from Ron and the man from Norman and you can paint as Roman. It's snappy, it's smart, it's marketable. You, Roman, are going to get a makeover."

There was something strangely formidable about Pru Darcy, patron of the arts. The former ballerina, he now knew, was on the board of directors of the art school. She posed, not for the fees, but because students needed life-models and they were in short supply. Ron smothered a giggle. He had a vision of Pru as a small, nude steam-roller, flattening all opposition to her ideas. He decided to paint her that way, as a caricature, a wry comment on her personality which would join Mercedes in his private collection.

"Did you say your girl-friend would model for us?" she asked, snapping Ron out of his reverie.

"You'll have to ask her yourself, Pru. We're not on speaking terms any more."

"I see. No wonder you're looking hang-dog. A month back you were wagging your tail and panting with eagerness."

"I hit her."

Pru frowned. "I won't ask you why."

"Jealousy. Arrogance. Ignorance. Take your pick."

"You've apologised?"

"She doesn't want to know me. She looks at me as if I've trodden in cat turds."

"You want her back?"

"I ache for her."

"That's good. An artist has to experience suffering."

"Oh, ha-de-ha-de-hah!"

"Cheeky bugger. Meet me at Margett's tomorrow. I'll show you the attic and you can decide if you want it."

The building faced onto the main street, with wide sidewalks busy with traffic and pedestrians. It had an ornate Federation facade, with 'Margett's, Shipping Chandlers, 1898' incised on the pediment over the front door. Workmen were busy on the renovations. The walls were already painted black and the floors tiled in Italian mosaic.

"The kitchens are out back," said Pru. "It's been a restaurant for years, but we had to strip out all the stoves and refrigerators and replace them with modern ones."

She led him up wide stairs and showed him the spacious, high-ceilinged rooms which would be the gallery. Electricians were at work installing strip-lighting along the cornices. There was another flight of stairs behind a door on the landing.

"You can lock yourself in if you feel you need privacy," she said. "Now, up we go."

The attics were dusty and draughty. There was a wall of windows in the gable end facing south, overlooking the coast and the offshore islands. There was a sheer drop below, down to the yard where the workmen's vans were parked.

"Good light," Ron said. "The studio?"

"I'd think so. There's no window on the street side. The gable butts up to the facade, but if you lean over from the flat roof at the side you can see the inner harbour."

There were smaller windows set into the longitudinal wall, giving light to the kitchen and bed-sitting-room. French doors opened onto the roof, where there was a little courtyard and a view across the historic quarter of the town to the fishing-boat harbour beyond.

"There's no cooking facilities. You'll have to manage with a toaster and an electric kettle. Eat out or manage on sandwiches."

"Uncle Alf had an electric frypan. Could I use that?"

"I'll ask the electrician. I don't know how much power you can draw off this circuit. The bathroom's connected to the hot water system in the restaurant kitchen. You'll be fine as long as you don't use it when the staff are trying to do the washing-up."

"Tell me about it! It would be a nightmare if the kitchen pig found the taps running cold!"

Pru laughed. "Well, I know it's a mess, but do you want it?"

"When can I move in? Veteran's Affairs are dropping big hints about needing Uncle's house for someone else."

"Take the keys. When you're ready."

"It'll be hellish cold in winter and it's hot now, under the roof. How do I keep milk cold?"

"Dammit, Ron. Think for yourself. Scrounge an electric fire, borrow a fan. There's a ice-works down the road. Keep a block of ice in the bathtub!"

It was a good thing Ron knew how to apply whitewash, for it took him a week to chase out the spiders and paint the place from floor to ceiling. Kostas loaned him his van and helped him load Uncle Alf's stepladder and all the part-used cans of emulsion they could find in the garage. The result was pleasing, though a mixture of pastel shades. They unearthed a large drum of matt-finish marine varnish and used that on the floorboards. An RSL member with a truck gave a hand with the iron bedstead, the kitchen table and chairs, a lead-lighted kitchenette and the double bed which he said Alf had bought after a big win on the 1975 Melbourne Cup. Ron was determined to take the old armchair from the verandah.

"That's a wreck," said Kostas. "You can get a better one at the auction rooms."

"Sentimental value. I think of Uncle Alf whenever I sit in it. If I put it opposite the French doors I can look at the view."

"You're not going to have time to sit around mooning. Let's get the painting stuff and hand back the keys to the old boy's place."

Alf's mates had promised to take the rest of the furniture to the Salvation Army, if the incoming tenant didn't want it. Ron had taken his uncle's supply of winter jumpers and a thick greatcoat, and had raided the closet for sheets and towels. A last minute exploration of the garage had disclosed an old ice-box buried under a pile of flower-pots. Boxes of china and other household goods had to be shuffled to one side to fit it in, and the canvases stacked around it.

Ron carried out the sheet-wrapped portrait of Mercedes and would not let it out of his grasp. He held it against his knees as the van rattled along the coast road to his new home. The old man's easel had folded flat but was too long for the back of the van and had to rest between his shoulder and that of Kostas.

He held onto the seat grimly as Kostas threw the van into a tight curve and the whole load shifted. "Bloody maniac!" he swore, unwrapping a packet handed to him by the Veterans' representative who came to collect the keys. Inside were Uncle Alf's war medals. He ran a finger over the bronze and felt tears mist his eyes. He was missing the old boy like buggery.

"He died happy," Mercedes had said. Ron swallowed hard to try to dislodge the lump in his throat. What a prat he'd been to so resent a small act of charity. What had it cost Mercedes to give a dying man a little pleasure? And what had Ron's irrational jealously cost him?

"I am a damned fool," he muttered.

"I know you are," said Kostas, crashing the gears. "So how long are you going to work for Aristotle? You know he's got the hots for Mercedes? I bet you'll not be able to stand watching him grab her arse!"

"You're having me on! She wouldn't!" Ron scowled awfully, but within the week the truth of the remark became clear.

He was already at his bike when he realised the key to the padlock was in his apron pocket, hanging up beside the sink. He had his hand on the knob of the kitchen door when he glanced through the window. Aristotle had Mercedes pinned against the wall. Her shirt was unfastened and he had his hands on her breasts. Her skirt was rucked up and Aristotle's trousers were around his ankles. There was no doubt what they were doing. Her eyes were closed and she was crowing with excitement. She came wide-eyed in climax and saw the face at the window. She screamed and Aristotle renewed his attack.

Ron kicked the guts out of the bike on his way past and walked home. It took him more than an hour, and he staggered along the roadside like a drunken man.

"We thought you weren't coming in," said Mercedes the next night, when Ron arrived to collect his wages and his bike. Mana Agnella was bullying Kostas, who was up to his elbows in soapy water and yelling in Greek and English that he was no dish-bitch and she could wash her own effing pans.

"I came, I saw, I quit!"

"I'm sorry you caught us last night."

"Enjoyed it, did you?"

"Why not? I needed the money."

"He paid you? You bleeding whore!" Ron kept his hands in his pockets, his fists clenched. There was a scarlet fury in his mind. "Why did you need money that badly?"

"For an abortion, you stupid bastard! You've got me pregnant!"

"You lying bitch." Ron picked her up and dumped, her butt first, into the sink of greasy water. "How do you know it's not Aristotle's brat?"

"He's had a vasectomy, you damned fool. And my brother wears a condom!"

"Your brother?"

"Yes, my big fat slob of a brother!"

Ron's lip curled. "Well, you're in the right place now, slut. My God, you're a dirty bitch!"

Aristotle and Mana Agnella pushed past the kitchen staff who were crowded in the scullery doorway, listening as Ron swore and Mercedes screamed back. Ron grabbed his keys and the wage packet which was thrust in his face.

"Get out and stay out," roared Aristotle. "You come back here and I'll kill you!"

Ron punched the Populis gut and brought his knee up into the man's nose. "Now go stick a dolmades up your arse!"

Mana Agnella was yelling for the police and Kostas was doubled up outside the kitchen door, laughing fit to bust. "Nice one, Ron! I've wanted to do that for years!"

"Shaddup!"

***

The first study of Prudence Darcy was finished. Ron had painted her in raw umber, in a monochrome of light and dark. The pose was right, the balance perfect, the likeness unmistakable. His patron was satisfied with progress on the portrait and with the celebrity drawings, which were already framed and ready to hang.

"It'll be a week before it's dry enough to continue. Go and have a holiday. Spend some time at the beach. Relax. Have fun."

There was no longer any embarrassment at exposing his entire body to the sun. He was a familiar figure at the nudist beach, sketchbook in hand, enjoying the biggest life-drawing class in Australia. He always asked permission to draw sun-worshippers, and once they realised he was no pervert but a true artist, he was regarded with affection and a kind of pride.

He introduced himself only as Roman, and tried to shed the Ron personality like a snake casting its outgrown skin.

"You've got that wrong." said the balding blonde with the eagle tattoo on his shoulder. The man flopped down on the sand next to the artist and pointed to the line of the vein Ron had just sketched. "You need to know your anatomy better, old son."

"You'd know?"

"I'm a surgical registrar at the Royal. Mike Carney. You're the one they call Roman."

"That's right. But my friends call me Ron."

"Well, Ron, me old mate, it's not enough to get the surface detail right. Look, where does that vein go? You've made it look at if it ducks under that muscle, but it doesn't. Look closer at the old boy's arm."

"Ah, yes. There's a shadow that distorts it."

"You want to know my theory about the great artists? Men like Michelangelo and Leonardo Da Vinci? Donatello and Durer? They knew their anatomy. You need to know how the skeleton is put together, how the muscles work, where the great blood vessels go. You need to understand what's under the skin before you can start a life-study. You'll be here tomorrow? I've an old Gray's Anatomy I can let you have. See you, young Ron, Roman, whatever you like."

Mike took Ron on a crash course in the workings of the human body. Gray's became his text book and, in the weeks ahead, Ron reached a greater understanding of what he was doing. He also found friendship; intelligent, undemanding friendship. Mike was a man who couldn't draw worth a damn, but who knew more of the history of painting than most of the lecturers at college.

"It's not enough to simply look at a landscape and say it's good. You need to know why it's good, what the artist was trying to achieve, why he used the pigments he did, how his work compares to that of his contemporaries. If you want to paint portraits, as you say you do, go and look at other people's work. You've got to have a yardstick against which you can measure your own ability."

Uncle Alf had acquired a stack of art books, most ex libris, bought at sales of discarded State Library books. Ron sat in the old man's armchair and really looked at the illustrations. He glanced at the study of Pru and decided it was amateurish.

All his preconceived ideas about adding colour to achieve a fine result went flying. He propped the monochrome on a kitchen chair and screwed another canvas into the clamps on the easel. Loading his palette with artists' oils, bought from the Mistress Golightly winnings, and filling the clip-on cups with turpentine and linseed, he gathered the new brushes in his hand. He shut his eyes for a moment and prayed for inspiration. He experienced an intense drive, as potent as making love. Glancing from the old to the new, he began to paint, not the carefully considered line of the student, but with the free-flowing vigour of the genius. He stopped only when the light died and stood back to assess his progress.

There was work to be done, but Pru Darcy's persona glowed from the canvas.

"Renoir, eat your heart out!" Ron stretched like a cat which has caught its prey. He opened a bottle of wine and took it out to his roof-top garden, gaudy with pots of geraniums dug from Uncle Alf's garden. He'd moved the old iron bed outside, for it was too hot to sleep indoors. He flopped onto the mattress and watched the sun go down in a blaze of gold and orange, reds and the soft purples of night.

He knew in that moment everything was possible, every dream could be fulfilled, and that there was magic in his hands.

5

Aureolin, or cobalt yellow, a compound of potassium and cobalt which came into use only in the mid-nineteenth century, in Paris. It enjoyed great popularity among artists for its brilliant colour and lightfast quality, but it was too expensive for general use. It lacks covering power but mixes well with all other pigments. Known as Goblin yellow in Germanic mythology, as miners believed it repelled silver.

"It's brilliant. I love it, but it won't sell," said Pru Darcy. "Finish the other one. The market likes conventional portraits. This is too avant garde to make your name. It's too, well, exposing! Look, Ron, people who'll commission you want an image which matches their perception of self. That's why your charcoal studies are so good. You don't have time to do deep and meaningfuls."

"You mean, pretty them up? I won't do it, Pru."

"You won't have to. A Roman portrait will be pure class. Recognisable, but with the strong technique you're developing. At this stage aim for Rembrandt, not Renoir! You'll never make a Rembrandt because you're an artist of light, not of dark, but you're too immature for Renoir. You haven't fondled enough bums yet."

"I should throw it in and buy a camera!"

"No way. Cameras can't get the feel of flesh. Be a mirror, Ron. Reflect back what sitters think they are. You'll not be the first to make the mistake of painting your interpretation of the sitter. Look at the Graham Sutherland portrait of Winston Churchill, glowering, sombre, ugly. It's the best study ever done of the man and he hated it."

"So you don't want this one?"

"I didn't say that. I'll hang it in my bedroom and enjoy it." She looked around the room with interest. "You're comfortable here? You've got everything you need? The bed's better than that iron monstrosity."

"I wouldn't know. I've been sleeping outside on the monstrosity. It's too hot at that end of the attic. It's cool in the studio because I can throw open the big windows for the sea breeze."

"What do you do when it rains?"

"Throw a tarpaulin over the top. I'm a country boy, remember." He picked up the palette and began to stroke flesh colour onto the canvas. "This will take much longer than the Impressionist style."

"I don't mind. People expect several sittings before the work is ready. It makes them feel they've got their money's worth."

Ron simply grunted, deep in concentration, coaxing the paint to lie as he wished. "Enough," he said, eventually. "I'm bushed and I've a class this afternoon."

"Can I see what you've done?"

He grinned and shook his head. "Nobody sees a Roman until it's finished."

"Cheeky young scamp. I can spare an hour tomorrow at nine."

"Fine. The light should be the same."

Cleaning his brushes took time so he had to race for the bus, cursing the portfolio as it slipped from his grasp. He sat entranced through a session on pigments and their properties and went eagerly to life-studies. There was a buzz of excitement in the room.

Then Mercedes, wrapped in a sarong of golden yellow, stepped onto the dais. She adopted the position suggested by the tutor, unfastened the cloth and let it fall across her thighs. Her eyes scanned the room and, when she saw Ron, she gave an unmistakable wink. Then she lowered her lids and looked downwards, in a pose of sweet modesty.

"Why, she's not ashamed of what she's done," Ron thought, taking his pencil between fingers which were trembling with emotion. "She's as amoral as a bitch in heat. Any dog will do. She just loves it!"

He made a poor fist of his drawing and closed his sketch-book before the tutor had time to do a critique. "It's crap," he said, tossing his work onto the desk.

The man grinned. "Everyone produced crap today. You all wanted to tie your pencils to your dicks, that's the trouble!"

"Not funny!" Ron gathered his things and strode down the drive, seething with irritation.

"Wait for me, Ron!" Mercedes was running after him. "I need to talk."

"There's nothing to say."

She pulled at his wrist and dragged him to a bench in the garden. "There's plenty to say. I still need the money."

"Aristotle piked out on you, did he? Cheapskate."

"No, but Mana Agnella sacked me. The Athens police have bust my brother for drug running and the landlord's thrown me out of the flat."

"You're a bloody disaster area, you are! What do you expect me to do about it?"

"You've got a place. Kostas told me."

"Oh no! Oh no! You're not playing me for a sucker again."

"Please, Ron. Please." She grabbed his arm. "Ron, I'm

frightened!" Tears streamed down her face and she sobbed, her face covered by her hands.

Ron's anger evaporated. The cries were those of a small child, bewildered and betrayed. He thought she might have cried like that when her father first abused her, when her brother forced her, when her mother abandoned her. She might have cried that way until she accepted her role, until she stopped caring, long before the time when she became so accustomed to abuse that she learned to enjoy the act.

She's taking you for a ride again, boy! Ron sighed. His inner voice was stilled. He knew Mercedes was as wanton as she was treacherous, yet he could not harden his heart to her. He did not think this was what the poets meant by love. He wasn't sure what that emotion really was. What he did know was an urge to protect, to possess, to plunder. Hers was the face he saw when his eyes were closed. She filled his mind with a desire that came close to being obsessive. Yet he knew he had to fight against it because she could ruin him.

"Just for a few days, then. Until we work out what to do."

She flung her arms around his neck and kissed him. He shook her off. "Not that, Mercedes. I'm not having any more of that! Where's your gear?"

"In the back of Kostas' van. He's giving us a lift home."

"The hell he is. Why didn't you go and shack up with him?"

"He lives at his mother's house. She'd have thrown a fit!"

Kostas kerb-crawled from the car park and stopped beside them. "Get in. Some people still have jobs to go to. I'm not being late again with the mood the old cow's in. She's been on and on at Aristotle to get shot of his wife and he might just do it, now he won't have to pay out in a divorce settlement."

"How come?"

"Aunt Clemnystra wants to go into a nunnery! Hey, it's not bloody funny, Ron!"

"But it is! It is! Aristotle cuckolded by a wimple and a set of rosary beads? It's effing hilarious!"

"No, it isn't. He's ordered his daughter to come home and help out around the place. Next thing Mana Agnella will be trying to marry her off to me and I'll have to run away from home and join the army! Which is crazy."

Mercedes laughed. "Fat chance there'll be of her working in the kitchen! Not after a year at finishing school in Paris. Catch your cousin getting her hands dirty? No way. We shared a room at boarding school and she was my best buddy. They don't come much closer than we were!"

"Hairy! That's what she is. Hairy!"

"She can't help it! Anyway, I thought your pater was trying to match you to a little widow woman."

"Fat chance. If I want Helene Pappas I'll have to go back to Greece to get her. And if I go back to Greece they'll expect me to do military service. Look what happened to Petros. Got knocked off by the Turks when he was manning a border post. Bloody shame for Helene and the boy. He was my best mate, too."

Kostas helped carry some of Mercedes' things to the attic and rushed off after a quick word with Ron, leaving him to take up the last suitcase. "Sorry to land you with her, but the poor bitch was threatening to do herself in."

"Seriously?"

"Yes. Seriously!"

"Oh, damn!"

"You'll have to do the right thing, mate. She's talked to me. If it's your brat, you're going to have to get her fixed up."

"How much?"

"How would I know? Ask that doctor mate of yours. He mightn't be willing to do the job, but he's sure to know who'll oblige."

"I can't. He's away at camp with the Army Reserve."

"More fool him. Then ask when he gets back."

Ron sat on the attic stairs for a few moments, unwilling to confront his unwanted guest. He didn't know what to do. There wasn't much left of the Mistress Golightly money, after paying tuition fees and materials. Pru, with his agreement, had put the money from his drawings into a savings account which would enable him to complete his education in Paris, Amsterdam, London and Florence. It was, she said, vital that he should stand in front of the Old Masters and see great art for himself.

"No matter how you plead, you're not touching your savings," she'd said. "It will do you good to starve in the garret, even if it is pretty plush as garrets go. I'll teach you economy, my lad, if it's the last thing I do."

No, he couldn't ask her and, with a blush of shame, admitted he would be loathe to explain his predicament. There were Uncle Alf's savings, but probate hadn't been granted and he wouldn't be able to access them for months. With great reluctance he'd taken another greasy-spoon job at nights, though it was only a short walk away. It brought in enough to pay the electricity bill and buy food, for the cook was not as generous with leftovers as the chefs at the Delphi. Until Margett's opened its doors and he started earning from his drawing, he was cash-strapped.

"I'm causing you a lot of worry, aren't I?" said Mercedes, who was making a pot of tea. "I'm sorry, Ron. Shall I go away?"

"No. I'll think of something. Bring the mugs outside and enjoy the view."

Mercedes leaned over the rail around the roof above the yard. "Maybe I should jump."

"Don't talk like that!" He could not keep the panic from his voice. He was so vulnerable to her emotional blackmail that he felt the yellow bile rising in his throat.

"No splat?"

"No splat!"

"Where do I sleep?"

"Inside. I prefer it out here."

"I remember that old bed."

Ron groaned. "Make yourself at home," he said. "I've got to play Cinderella again and scrub pans. Don't wait up for me."

She was fast asleep when he wearily climbed the stairs. Her sweat-sheened body was covered only by the golden sarong. She stretched like a sun-warm kitten when he tripped over a suitcase. She blinked at him lazily.

"I'm hungry."

"Fish and chips? They're cold but I'll warm them in the frypan."

"I scrounged a small cable-drum from the electrician. It makes a good table. We can eat outside."

Satiated, she carried the dirty plates indoors. "I'll wash these in the shower. Why waste water?" Ten minutes later she stood at the open French doors. "Are you coming to bed with me?"

He shook his head. "No. Let's not start that again."

"Why not? It was fun."

"Because I'm hot, and sweaty and totally exhausted. Because I need a bath and some shut-eye. Because, if I make love to you once, I'll never want to stop. You're addictive, Mercedes."

"That's not a crime," she whispered, stroking his cheek lightly. "Goodnight."

She was gone when he woke and he knew an unaccountable feeling of loss. But her cases were tucked neatly under the bed and her perfume lingered in the air. There was, Ron realised, barely enough time to wash and shave before Pru arrived for her sitting.

"That's girl smell," said Pru, sniffing like a bloodhound.

"That's Mercedes. Do you mind?"

"The Eurasian girl? The new model? You were fast off the mark, weren't you?"

Ron went red. "We were previously acquainted," he said, awkwardly fumbling for the right phrase.

"So that's what they call it these days. No, I don't mind. I'm not a wowser, not a prude, not a killjoy. The world needs give and take. Give generously, but take care. You know what I mean?"

"I do. Now turn your head just a little to the right. That's it. No...stop talking. When you talk it changes the shape of your whole face, not just your mouth."

"Worse than being at the damned dentist!"

"But I don't cause you any pain."

Pru Darcy screwed up her eyes and regarded him balefully. "No, but I reckon you'll give me grief, one way or another."

The entrance of Mercedes ended the sitting. She carried two shopping bags and a stick of French bread balanced across an armful of lettuce and cucumber. "Hi, Mrs Darcy. Your new assistant's waiting for you."

"Good. Then we can start discussing how to hang paintings in the gallery. You'll get on well with Zoe, Ron. She's just finished a year in Paris, taking a course in Fine Arts. She knows her stuff."

"You don't mind me staying here, Mrs Darcy?"

"You're only young once. If it's fine with Ron, I'm easy. Have you seen my gallery? Dump the groceries and come and take a look. We can have a coffee and talk about life-classes. Did you enjoy it?"

"What's to not enjoy? I don't mind people looking at me. It's the sitting still that gets to me."

"Tell me about it. Join us when you've cleaned the brushes, Ron. There's something I want to ask you."

"Will it keep, Pru? I've got oil techniques this morning."

"I only wanted to know if you can drive a car. I've lost my licence. I want to take a run to my property in the hills. Make sure the fire-breaks have been put in."

"I'm not working tomorrow."

"Fine." She followed Mercedes down the stairs, but turned for a last word. "Just the two of us, Ron. No dolly-birds!"

He looked at her with something so like the expression of a startled rabbit that she burst out laughing. "Don't worry. I'm not planning to seduce you. The most exercise you're likely to get is with a pruning shears."

Her guffaws of good humour were melded with laughter from the younger woman. Ron glanced at the studio as he hurried past, but he could only see the back of the new girl. She seemed an odd shape, big hips and a narrow back. He shrugged. Time enough for the art critic!

Mercedes was in the bath when he got home. "Share?" she called.

"No way. But leave the water. I'll have a cold dip after the restaurant closes."

"There's a ham and salad roll in the top of the ice-box. I've just made it."

"How much do I owe you?"

"Nix. Aristotle gave me my wages."

Ron bit back the tart retort which sprang to his lips. The food was like sawdust in his mouth until he slapped down his jealousy and told himself to be sensible. Money was money. Food was food. A quick turn was a quick turn. No big deal. The little voice inside that protested, whimpering about it ought to mean more than that, got hammered back into his subconscious without mercy. *I can't allow myself to think like that,* he told himself. *I can't go all bitter and introspective. I can't stand the pain!*

Mercedes came dripping and sassy from the bathroom. "I might go out tonight. I won't wake you."

"Good. I've a feeling Pru is going to work me like a dog."

He cycled to the Darcy house, an imposing modern residence on a low cliff overlooking the ocean. There was a BMW in the drive and an old Volkswagen parked on the verge.

"Put your wheels in the garage," said Pru. "There are boys with light fingers around here." She bit hard on a slice of toast and picked up a large tote bag from the porch. "Ready?"

To Ron's disappointment it was the Beetle that belonged to his benefactor. Their destination was miles beyond the city limits, way past quarter-acre blocks, on a side road which meandered along the top of the escarpment.

Her little house was a stunning A-frame, poised high on forty-foot poles rising in front of a sheer granite cliff-face. There was a bridge from the parking area on the road to the front door, spanning a sickening drop on one side, the flat roof of a lower storey on the other. The interior gave the impression that the whole house was airborne, for the hallway opened onto one large room with a wall of glass from the floor to the ridge of the roof.

"I sleep on the mezzanine deck up there when I stay," said Pru, indicating a steep ladder. "There's a toilet and bathroom on that floor and a kitchen and dining area under here. Guests use a couple of rooms in the basement. It's only the front of the house which is in free-fall. Come and see the view from the balcony."

They were at the level of the canopy. Ron took a grip on his vertigo and joined her on the far side of the wide deck. He gripped the balustrade tightly and saw, far below him, the hillside plunging down to join a stream in the valley. There were black cockatoos feeding off flowering gums, white and scarlet-red, the deceptive stillness of a kookaburra and the elegance of an egret, gazing intently into a lily-pool near the base of the house.

"Silly bird," said Pru, sadly. "There've been no fish in there since the last tenants moved out. He's eaten them all long ago."

"I expect there are frogs. And skinks. How far does your land go?"

"All the way down to the stream and up to the road on the other side. There used to be a path but I expect it's grown over."

"Why don't you live here?"

"I did once. My first husband built it. It was Tamberlaine's studio, you see." There was a long pause but Pru offered no further explanation. Then she pulled herself together. "My second husband says it's too far out for business. Mr Darcy needs to be close to the city. And his golf. Maybe we'll retire here. Maybe not. I just love it. I feel like a bird, standing out here. I feel as if I could spread my wings and fly over the treetops, up, up and away!"

Such was the illusion of a ballet dancer's hands that Ron could see in her the gliding sweep of feathers on the wind. She cooed with pleasure as the breeze teased her hair. "You don't like it, do you? You don't care for heights?"

"It takes some getting used to, but now I'm used to it, I love it.

The space, the light, the freedom. It's inspiring. I could paint here."

"It was designed to be filled with colour. I remember when...but no. Ron, I need to be alone with my memories. Do me a favour. Go downstairs and out the back door and walk the boundaries for me. I've got a stitch in the side and it's such a pain that I doubt I'd make it. The fire-breaks are essential. The contractor sends his bills on time but I'm not sure he's as thorough in his work as in his accounting."

Peace enfolded Ron as he tramped along the cleared area towards the watercourse. There were places where it had been impossible to follow the lines on the map, for there were outcrops of rock and stands of timber around which the grader had worked. There was little water in the stream-bed, but he kept his eyes sharp in case there were snakes. He did not go up as far as the distant road, for he could see the bare earth exposed in dozed strips.

From the valley the house looked like a jewel, suspended on a pendant, glinting in the sunlight. He disturbed a kangaroo, which bounded out of the dryandra shrubs on his right. After casting him a look of disgust, it went lollopy-hop down into the thicket of morning-glory which choked the wetter parts of the gully.

He finished his circuit by crossing what had once been a lush green lawn. There were the remains of a tennis net at one side. An empty swimming-pool glared at him accusingly with its one green eye of duckweed and algae.

He locked the door behind him and trudged up the stairs. "The job's been done, but it'd be a fat lot of use if a fire came through."

Pru handed him a glass of iced lemon-juice. "I know. It would leap from tree-top to tree-top. Whoosh! But rules are rules and we try to do the right thing. There are no gutters to catch leaves and there's a sprinkler system on the roof. In an emergency we can pump from the swimming-pool."

"It's empty!"

"Is it? Damn that pool man. We paid to have the leak fixed last year and he's supposed to come and maintain it."

Ron glanced around the main room. The walls were bare, the furnishings spartan. "You don't keep valuables here?"

"No way! The house is covered against fire and I could rebuild, but documents and photographs, things like that, I'd never leave up here. If I were living in the house it would be different. There's a wine cellar in the cliff that we used to use for precious bits and pieces. No, I keep the bare minimum on the hillside and value it for what it is. Did you see the sign at the gate?"

"I was too busy watching to see I didn't drive off the edge."

She chuckled. "I'll bet. The house is called Ephemeral."

"Nice. It catches the soul of the place."

"Refreshed?"

"In every way."

"Good. It's yours when you want to borrow it. The city can cramp your spirit. There are times when you'll need to be alone, to charge your batteries, to restore your vision. Don't bring your dolly-bird. She'll want to party and it's not safe for parties. Keep it a secret between us. Oh, bring a friend you can trust sometimes, but make sure it's another person who will sit quietly and be at one with the environment."

"I'll bring Mike. The doctor who comes fishing with me. The one who collects good art."

"Does he rate you as promising?"

"Yes."

"So do I. By all means bring Mike. You can trust a fishing

buddy. Now take me home. I don't feel well."

They were halfway across the bridge when she doubled up and fell to the decking, rolling in agony as she clutched her stomach. She was in grave danger of plunging into the void before Ron grabbed at her skirts and pulled her legs back onto the bridge. Her face was ashen and her eyeballs showed white as they rolled back in spasm. She groaned piteously and lay still.

"Oh Gawd! Don't you die on me!" He tried to lift her but she was too heavy. He dragged her onto solid ground and eased her into the front seat of the car. He had no idea where the hospitals were in the hills but he knew how to get to the Royal.

He broke every speed limit, and most of the rules of the road. But she was still breathing when he braked hard in the entrance to the emergency department. He watched helplessly as white-coated attendants lifted her onto a stretcher and wheeled her through the plate-glass doors.

Ron's flesh felt as if it had turned to jelly. He rested his head on the steering wheel and let out a great sob of relief.

6

Chrome yellow takes its name from Xpwua, the Greek word for colour. It was invented in 1797 in Paris and was welcomed as a cheap substitute for Orpiment. It is a lead salt precipitated in chromate or bichromate solution. It has good covering qualities and moderate toxicity, but is badly affected by sunlight. When mixed with organic pigments it can turn greenish black, the chemical reaction which is responsible for the damage to Van Gogh's Sunflowers.

"We'll have to operate," said Mike, who'd slipped out to the waiting room for a quick word with Ron. "Mrs Darcy's come round and is reasonably lucid in spite of pain-killers. But we're reasonably sure she's got a perforated appendix. If we don't go in and whip it out she could develop peritonitis and that is mega-nasty."

"What do I tell Mr Darcy? I've got to take the car back."

"She says you're to hang on to it. Her husband's in Sydney but we got through to him. He's flying back tonight. She's signed the consent form for the op so it's only a matter of waiting for a theatre to be freed up."

"Can I see her?"

Mike shook his head. "Sorry. They were giving her the pre-op when I slipped away. She'll be out cold by now. Go home, Ron. I'll give you a report in the morning."

Ron looked blank.

"We've a date with a rod and line, remember?"

"Sorry, Mike. My brain's fried today. I may as well go to work. I rang and they were a bit snarly about me being late. It's a busy night for them. And I need the money, as you know."

There was plenty of room in the yard behind Margett's to park the car, a relief, because the kerbs were bumper to bumper with vehicles. Saturday night parking was a nightmare for would-be revellers. Ron locked the door of the Beetle, found the back entrance to the building open and raced up the stairs to the attics.

"Where have you been? I expected you back hours ago! You're late for work." Mercedes shrilled at him like a fishwife. Then she burst into tears and said, "I'm sorry. I was so worried about you. I don't like people disappearing out of my life without warning."

"I've been at the hospital. Pru's got a dodgy appendix. I stayed until they took her down to theatre. Come on, out of my way. I need a quick shower." He threw on his kitchen gear - baggy shorts and an old shirt. "Got to go. See you later."

"Don't worry about bringing food home. I'm cooking a Malay curry. I've invited Zoe round to keep me company instead of hitting the town. We're going to gossip about our school days."

"How absolutely bleeding fascinating! I'm so sorry I'll miss it!"

"Sarcastic pig!"

Girl-talk was still running strong when he came in. He shed his clothes and slid gratefully into the half-full bath. He ducked his head under to wash his hair and dried himself on the damp towel. The yellow sarong lay in the corner. He wound it around his hips and, with his hair curling damply on his brow, strolled out to meet Pru's discovery, Zoe Xenos.

He had no idea that he looked attractive, his muscles silvered by moonlight, his tall, country-lithe body carrying the drape of the wrap gracefully.

Mercedes handed him a glass of red wine and looked at Zoe.

"See? I told you so," she said. "One hundred per cent

testosterone. And nice with it."

The small, dark girl looked up from the depths of the deckchair and giggled. "How do you do?" she said carefully, her voice plummy with drink. "How do you diddley-do?"

"And cock-a-doodle-do to you," he replied, trying not to laugh. Zoe was what the French call jolie laide and the Poms call pretty ugly. She was Audrey Hepburn gamine but the nose was snub, the eyes set too close together and the short, spiky hair rested above a heavy jaw. Her wide mouth wore a foolish grin.

She waved her empty glass at him. "Ou est le pissoir?" she hiccupped. "Je suis pissed as a newt."

Mercedes pulled her friend to her feet and helped her to the bathroom. There were sounds of a violent chunder.

Ron looked ruefully at the empty bottles and wondered if the frying-pan was still on. It was. He scraped the dried-up curry onto a plate and wandered back to the patio.

"G'night," said Mercedes. "We're gunna sleep."

"Thank God for that," he muttered. "I don't think I could have stood any more of your mate."

The precious pair were still snoring when the morning sun reminded him to get up and head for the briny. It was too early for the Sunday traffic to spoil the appearance of the old colonial streets. It was too early for any anglers other than seagulls and cormorants to be peering into the water below the jetty. There was still night-cool in the air and a pungent odour of dried seaweed in the nostrils.

Mike had found a choice spot where he could lean against a bollard. He was suffering the effects of a night in Emergency. He was dozing, ignoring the tug on his line and the way it was reeling out as a catch took the bait out to sea.

Ron grabbed the rod as it slid towards the edge of the jetty and started to play the fish. It was a nice-sized herring, which he gutted and threw in the bucket by Mike's side. He'd caught three more by the time the registrar realised he was missing out on good sport.

"How's my lady friend?" Ron asked.

"Sore and pumped full of antibiotics. She'll live." Mike rubbed his eyes, red with weariness.

Ron looked at him with concern. "This was a daft idea. You ought to be in bed."

"Need fresh air and exercise."

"What, pushing out the nose music?"

"Walked here, didn't I?"

"Couldn't find a nurse with a handy wheelchair?"

"Who's got the energy?"

"Did you find out about a quack for my bird?"

"Not yet. Give us a couple of days, Ron. I warn you, it'll cost you big time. Couple of big ones, at least."

Ron said nothing. His glum expression spoke for him. Mike sighed. "She could always try gin and a hot bath. Works sometimes."

"You're a doctor. Don't give me your old wives' tales. She won't go to a back-street abortionist. She wants a proper job."

"She wants a bleeding miracle. When did you prong her?"

"October, November...who cares?"

"Cutting it fine, Ron. Nobody'll touch her after sixteen weeks." Mike looked in the bucket and yawned. "Enough for breakfast. Time to hit the sack. Two for me, three for you. Right?"

"Suits me. Who'll cook them?" They walked back towards the town, which was stirring into life.

"I've a date with a physiotherapist who's got a hot frying-pan and an air-conditioned bedroom. Ring me if you want the phone number of that bloke."

"I'll have trouble raising the price of a bottle of gin, Mike."

"Need a loan?"

"I couldn't pay you back."

"You could. You'll be rolling in it, one day."

"Thanks, but no thanks."

Herring for breakfast appealed to neither Zoe nor Mercedes, who were sharing a packet of aspirin at the kitchen table, nursing mugs of black coffee. "Suit yourselves," said Ron, coating the fish with oatmeal and slapping fat in the frying-pan.

"You're stinking the place out. It's disgusting!"

Ron buttered bread and tucked in with enjoyment.

Zoe, turning a delicate shade of green, suggested Mercedes visit her for lunch at her apartment in the city. "We can be civilised."

"Great. I want to paint this afternoon and I don't like company."

Zoe looked around the studio with bright eyes, as if she'd never really absorbed what it was all about. She had been so centred on Mercedes that she'd practically ignored Ron. She snapped her fingers. "Yes! You're the boy who did the charcoal drawings for the restaurant. You're good."

"Pru thinks so."

"You paint." Her eyes fell on Uncle Alf's canvases. "Primitive Impressionism. Are you self-taught?"

Mercedes giggled. "Those aren't Ron's oils. They're going to be painted over."

"Thank God for that. We'd never find a buyer for them. What do you paint?'

"Mind yours," Ron snapped.

"And you said he was nice, Mercedes! He's rude!"

Mercedes raised her eyebrows. "Moody today, aren't you? Come on, Ron. As Zoe's Pru's assistant, she'll get to know your work intimately."

"You can show her when I'm gone. I want to visit Pru this morning."

"Ask her what I should do in the gallery," Zoe said. "The opening is only ten days away and there are many rooms to be hung by then."

"I expect you'll have to do the work yourself, smarty-pants. You do know how to hang an exhibition?"

"Better than you, I expect. Do you need a lift to the hospital?"

"No. I've got Darcy wheels. What have you got? A broomstick?"

"A Volvo."

"Fancy."

Mercedes, dressed for the street, looked daggers at him. "And I hoped the two of you would be friends! Fat chance."

***

Andrew Darcy was sitting beside Pru's bed when Ron made his quiet entrance to the ward. The patient was asleep and the stocky, balding businessman at her side was dozing. Midnight flights played havoc with the system, he'd heard. Hearing Ron, Mr Darcy opened his eyes and shook the miasma from his brain. He put his finger to his lips and pointed to the door. He joined Ron in the corridor and led him to the visitors' cafeteria.

"She's doing well, but she's very weak," he said. "Thank you for your fast action yesterday. You may have saved her life. If she'd been up at that damned eagle's nest on her own, she could have died before anyone noticed."

"I thought I'd lost her when she rolled half over the edge of the bridge, Mr Darcy. I had a hell of a job heaving her back."

"I hate that house. All those drops. It gives me the willies, but she'll not hear of selling it. Full of memories for her. She was desperately in love with Tamberlaine."

"Is that who he was? Frank Tamberlaine? The landscape artist? His abstracts are sensational."

"Brilliant. Pru said he did his best work at Ephemeral. But how their kids never fell over the edge I'll never know."

"I didn't realise Pru had a family."

"She doesn't. Not now. Tam was mad on sailing. He used to crew for me on ocean races. A couple of times a year he'd take Dreamdrift I up to the Spice Islands and spend a month or so painting there. The first year the boys were old enough to go with him there was a cyclone in the Timor Sea. Tragic. Absolutely tragic."

The sense of grief was tangible. Andrew Darcy's eyes were looking far away, seeing the past perhaps. And Ron, sensitive to other people's minds, felt the terror of the towering waves, the panic of the Tamberlaine boys, the helplessness of the father. He drowned with them and, in that instant, knew that he had missed a dimension in Pru's portrait.

No wonder she had dismissed his happy, Renoir-style offering as "Very nice, dear!" He may have caught the essence of the dancer but he had overlooked the tragedy in her life.

"She's never talked about it," he murmured.

"Well, she wouldn't, would she? She's a brave woman. And an obstinate one. It took me years to persuade her to marry me. She doesn't love me as she loved Tam, but I love her very deeply. She was left almost penniless. Tam's paintings always sold well, and are fetching huge prices at auction these days, but he wasn't the saving sort. If she'd sold that damned house she'd have been fine but she said it was all she had left of him and the boys."

"I understand."

"I think you do. She's got great hopes for you, young Roman. In the end I wore her down. I said that, as I was rich, and had no one to spend my money on, she'd better become my wife and spend it for me. That's why she does so much at the college. She's scouting for talent. She's taken three other promising young artists under her wing. One's in Melbourne, another's in Tasmania and the other's a girl from Queensland. You're her only portrait painter."

"I'm honoured."

"You certainly are. You're the first she's taken to Ephemeral. She wants you to go there and paint?"

"Yes. Whenever I like. But I feel bad about it. She's done more than enough for me already, letting me have the studio above the gallery."

Andrew Darcy chuckled. "She reckons you need to have an eye kept on you. She said something about a dolly-bird who could ruin you. Have you been ruined?"

Ron rubbed his ear and grinned. "A bit shop-soiled, I reckon, but I'll scrub up."

"A little experience is a good thing when you're young. Just make sure you hurt no one."

"That's not so easy, sir. Making love is one thing, reading

another person's mind is another. How do you stop hurting someone when you don't know what they really want?"

"When you stop thinking about making love and start understanding what it means to give love, you'll know."

"It won't be easy. There wasn't much of that around at Cootimurra."

Mr Darcy pushed back his chair and, rising, patted Ron on the shoulder. "Keep the car until my wife's better. And tell young Zoe to do as she sees fit in the gallery. A couple of lecturers from the School of Art will come over at the weekend to give her a hand. I'll see to the catering. That's my business."

"Catering?"

"Why not? I've got franchises all over the country. Mind, I can't boil an egg!"

Ron flashed his wide smile. "Nor can I. Shall I finish your wife's portrait? I can work from memory."

"I think you'd better. When she's ill the weight drops off her. After a few weeks on the sick list you'll hardly recognise her and I know she wants that painting ready for opening night."

"It won't be dry enough to varnish."

"Leave it on the easel with a display of brushes and paints around it, as if you'd been interrupted while work was in progress. Hang your smock on the back of the easel and throw some painting rags around. Make it a talking point, like a still-life. I'll get a placard made to stand in front of it...Prudence Darcy-Tamberlaine, by Roman. Sign your work. And Ron...be there! Talk to people, promote yourself and your ability. Book sittings. Take commissions."

"I wouldn't know how...or what to charge."

"Leave it to Zoe, then. I'll have a word with her. But I still insist, you must be there."

"Why?"

"It's a marketing thing. As Roman, you have a great product, your craftsmanship. But your youth, your modesty, your charm will win you as many clients as your art. Hasn't anyone told you you're a good-looking young man?"

Ron went red. "I don't think so."

"Look in the mirror. Paint a self-portrait. You may surprise yourself!"

Mercedes was bubbling over with enthusiasm about Zoe's place when she returned. She chattered incessantly about Swedish design and all the modern conveniences, about the paintings Zoe had bought in Paris and the clothes in her wardrobe. Ron, engrossed in the subtle glazes which added substance to the portrait of Pru Darcy, heard her as if she were at a distance.

Only when the light faded did he smile and turn to watch her busy at the frying-pan, her dark hair tied back for coolness. She wore only one of his old shirts. The rest of her clothes, and his, were pegged on lines she had strung across the patio. They were flapping in a strong sea breeze.

"We'll not be going out tonight; we've nothing to wear," she said, calling for him to join her at the table. "Chicken fricassee suit you?"

It was a night when they slipped back into the easy companionship of their first days, when conversation came naturally and when a simple meal tasted like ambrosia. They skirted the big issues, the looming problems. He washed and she dried the dishes. Mercedes admired the work in hand while he cleaned his palette and prepared to rinse the brushes.

"I'll get the washing in," she said. "I think we're in for a storm."

Ron, breathing deeply of the turpentine as he teased the pigments from the pig bristles and smoothed them straight, was reminded of the smell of retsina, the pine-scented wine of the Delphi. And, like lightning crackling in the distance, the memory of Mercedes with Aristotle flashed across his mind.

Contentment left him. He felt the heavy claws of resentment tearing his guts. Without comment he locked the bathroom door and showered quickly. There were no towels. He didn't care. He walked stark bollocky past Mercedes, who was folding the washing, and closed the French door behind him. He climbed into his bed and buried his face in the pillow, feeling hot tears of anger behind closed eyelids.

"Come to bed with me," Mercedes cooed. Ron opened one eye. She stood, naked and enchanting, in the doorway.

"Piss off," he muttered and rolled his back to her. He could not sleep. It was hot and sultry, the clouds low and lit with an eerie radiance as wild electrical energy set them aglow. There was not a skerrick of wind. Ron threw back the sheets and watched forked lightning score the horizon, and listened to the distant growl of thunder.

He was quite unprepared for a new front which rolled in from the sea, sending bolts of white wickedness onto the roofs around him. He was unprepared for the gust of wind which grabbed his bedding and spun the tarpaulin over the edge of the railings into the yard below. St Elmo's Fire danced around the balcony. Ron, who had never seen anything like the blue flames, was petrified. But it was the torrential rain which drove him inside, shivering.

Mercedes was crouched on the double bed, her hands over her ears, eyes closed tight at every flash. "Hold me, Ron. I'm frightened."

He closed the door, straining to push the bolt home against the force of the storm, and drew the heavy curtains across the glass.

The power was out so there was no chance to make a warm drink to shake the sudden chill from his body. Instead there were welcoming arms.

"You're wet," she murmured. "How cold you are. Cuddle close. I'll warm you."

Oh, she did; she did. She was warm as toast and lit fires in him that he'd thought disdain had extinguished. She teased him and pleased him and briskly exercised him in every way. Neither noticed that the storm had rolled inland, so close were they entwined and so absorbed in one another's pleasure. Satisfied and purring, Mercedes suckled him to sleep.

Morning came with a fresh cool change and Mercedes threw up in the bathroom.

"Early morning sickness is the pits," she groaned. "I'll be glad when this is all over."

He handed her a facecloth and made tea. The milk in the ice-chest was sour so he ran down to the yard and pulled a lemon from the gnarled tree in what had once been a back-garden.

Mercedes had gone back to bed and was curled, in misery, against the pillows. "Mrs Darcy would lend you the money, if you asked."

"How could I, when she's so ill?"

"Ask the man from Veterans' Affairs. He'd advance you what's owing from Uncle Alf's estate."

"I asked. He won't."

She wailed. "Oh, Ron, there must be something you can do! I don't want to have this baby."

7

Cadmium orange; named after the Greek word kadmeia, which is derived from Cadmean earth, a type of zinc ore originally found near Thebes. This ore was named after Prince Cadmus, a Phoenician prince. However, it was not developed as a pigment until the 19th century and was little used because of its rarity. The modern colour, a brilliant orange, is made from cadmium nitrate and sodium sulfide. It is safe and permanent, and has good covering properties.

If inspiration had a colour, it would probably be orange, a hot burning orange as akin to fire as to passion. There'd be none of the cold blues of common sense, the sombre hues of brown, the rationality of green, thought Ron. It may not work, but heck, I've got to do something!

"Pose for me."

Ron ignored Mercedes' protests and fetched his drawing pad and charcoal. He sketched her lying on her side, her head downcast, hair loose over her breasts. He posed her kneeling, her head thrown back as if in ecstasy, then cupping her bosoms and gazing lustfully at him. When his hands grew stiff he tumbled her, so that she was pliant and amenable to his suggestions.

Ron skipped classes and locked the door to the attic so they would not be disturbed by Zoe, who hammered and called insistently all morning.

"Ignore her," said Mercedes, straddling him. "That's good, so good."

He went to work in the evening, leaving her sleeping in

exhaustion. She was extravagantly glad to see him at midnight and showed her gratitude. It was late before Ron woke and realised he'd missed another lecture. He found a public call box and rang the college to say he had influenza. By then Mercedes had finished her ritual chunder and was cooperative.

Three days later the book was filled with drawings, some complete studies, others details of hands and profiles, fleeting expressions and some merely studies in tone, shadows and highlights. He offered Mercedes no explanation of why he was making her pose, for he was by no means certain she would approve of his money-making plan.

***

When he was paid for his week in the kitchens, he drove to the hospital and spoke to Pru. She was sitting up and, while looking pale and weak, was mentally alert.

"I'd like to spend a few days at Ephemeral," he said. "I've a special project and I need peace and quiet. Is there an easel there?"

"There's a store-cupboard behind the main room. I expect there're paints and things that Tam never got round to using, if they're still good after all these years. Use what you need. Andrew said he'd told you about Frank. When I die I'm bequeathing the house to the Arts Council. The Tamberlaine Memorial Retreat. It can select emerging talent to work there and Andrew will set up a trust fund so they don't have to worry about supporting themselves while they paint for a first solo exhibition. Is that what you're doing?"

"It's a wonderful idea but no, that's not what I'm planning. It's much more mundane and, frankly, I don't think you'd approve."

"Then why not paint in your studio?"

"Frankly, because I don't want Zoe butting in. She rubs me the wrong way."

"Oh dear. I thought she'd be a real help to you."

"She's a strange one. She's very possessive of Mercedes."

"Old school chums are like that. Just like old fishing buddies. Here, take the keys. I expect you'll tell me all about it in your own good time."

"If it works. The whole project may be a disaster. I expect you'd call it commercial art."

Pru narrowed her eyes. "There's nothing wrong with commercial art. There's only one thing to remember about it. You've got to have a market. People have got to want to buy what you paint."

Ron grinned. "Oh, they will. I'm betting my bottom dollar on it."

As it was, there was barely enough money left over for food and petrol after he'd bought the supplies he'd need. He chose acrylics rather than oils, for he needed a quick-drying paint. He bought students' boards, fabric stretched over thick cardboard, rather than proper canvas drawn taut on wooden stretchers. He bought brushes of soft squirrel hair and an air-brush, a technique he'd recently studied at college. He left the materials in the boot of the car while he went to tell Mercedes he was going away for a few days.

"I'm doing this for you," he said when she protested. "You can stand in for me at the cafe while I'm away."

"What? Wash dishes? I will not!"

"Then you'll go hungry," he snapped. "There's bread and jam and a few apples. That's all I could afford."

"You've been gambling! Just like your Uncle Alf! You've gone and bet your money on the horses!"

"I'm gambling, yes. But I reckon I'm on a sure thing. Just wait and see."

"You don't care about me! I'll jump off the roof!"

Ron ignored the sobbing and the threats. He reckoned he knew her well enough to be sure she'd not do anything drastic. She was far too protective of her looks to take such a disfiguring way out. She was far too much in love with herself and life to close the door if opportunity knocked.

However, he doubted that Mercedes would willingly play her part in his plan to emulate Alberto Vargas, the King of Pin-Ups. His brothers had always bought Playboy and had a collection of Vargas girls in the room they shared with Ron. He had long admired the sensual watercolours, many featuring Alberto's wife and life-long model, Anna Mae. Ron knew from articles that Vargas was a brilliant painter whose talent had been exploited by men's magazines, which had paid him peanuts in crippling contracts. The old man had enjoyed a revival of interest before his death and his beautiful studies were as popular as ever.

Ron spent four days turning his sketches into acrylics of Mercedes, her exotic beauty shown in poses suggestive yet not lewd. It was, he observed ruefully, a narrow line in some cases. But the technique came to him like magic. He stashed a handful which he judged less than saleable and took the rest away with him. All were signed simply RON, in dark cadmium orange, the R and N intertwined within the O in a stylised motif. He meant to keep this side of his artistic life quite separate from his work as ROMAN. He did not intend to make the same mistake that Alberto Vargas had made in foregoing his ability as a serious artist.

The owner of the city gallery he first approached looked doubtfully at the sample Ron showed him. He whistled softly but shook his head. "We do mainly prints."

"I'm not asking much more than a print," Ron said. "You'd know who'd be in the market for work like this."

"Give you twenty bucks a picture," the man said, tapping his front tooth with a gold pen. "Or leave them and I'll sell on commission."

Ron, glancing at the reproductions of nudes on the walls, realised they were almost pornographic. He had not produced sleaze and had, on reflection, no desire to deal with this cheapskate.

He got another three cold rejections and a suggestion by a rather twee young man that it was boys who were in fashion, not busty birds. Ron felt queasy. Had all his work been in vain? Had his orange inspiration merely covered up his common sense?

He was totally depressed by the time he got back and carried the paintings to the studio. He stacked them behind Uncle Alf's canvases and stretched out on the bed on the roof. A week of sunshine had dried the mattress. He felt at home there, his own self, not the puppet he became when Mercedes pulled his sexual strings. Yet images of her filled his mind.

There was, he saw, only one other way out of the dilemma. If he could not raise the money for the abortion, he would have to do the right thing by her. He would have to marry her and support her and the baby. It would be hard to do that, to take on responsibilities too heavy for his young shoulders. It would mean kissing goodbye to seeing the world, to experiencing first hand the works of the Old Masters. It would mean loss of freedom and an end to dreaming.

There'd be children underfoot, for if there were to be one, there would probably be many, for he was clearly fertile. It would mean midnight feeds and wet nappies drying in the bathroom. It would mean the exhausting business of keeping Mercedes fulfilled, and that, he knew, was a tiring process. Living with a sexual goddess had its drawbacks. He would be expected to worship at her altar even when he felt like crap. And with that profound observation, he fell asleep.

Mercedes, a whingeing Mercedes, woke him on her return from the cafe and burst into tears of frustrated anger. She held out her hands, raw red from the hot water.

"I've been standing over that sink for four nights and my guts are cramping with the work, and you're here, snoring your head off? You're a turd, Ron Turner. You're an utter turd."

She threw a bucket of cold water over him and locked herself in the bathroom. Ron could hear the taps running as she prepared for a long soak. He stripped off and found a dry shirt. He made coffee for her and set out a plate of bread, cold beef and salad. He was apologetic. He was contrite. He crawled. She rubbed his nose in his inadequacies and called him dogs'-breath. He offered to marry her. She almost spat in his face.

"I've told you, Ron. I don't want this baby. Mr Fancy-Effing artist, don't you think I want a career as well? These are the eighties, Ron Turner. I'm not obliged to spend my days as your door-mat. I'm not ruining my figure so some brat can hang off my titties. I've an audition for a good job next week and, if I get it, I'm taking it. Marry you? Thanks, but no thanks. If you can't raise the money, I will, even if I have to whore for it!"

His hand ached with the desire to slap her, but he kept the urge under control. She was, he saw, dangerously over-wrought. A surge of compassion engulfed him and he took her hands, kissing the palms and the chafed knuckles. She started to cry so he picked her up and carried her to bed. He comforted her and promised he wouldn't ask her to do anything she didn't wish for. They did not make love, but he stroked the small swelling of her belly and wished, uselessly, that the unborn child was loved and wanted.

***

He was in no state, mentally or physically, to face the mid-term examinations the next morning. This was the part of the course which did not come easily to him, the details of the history of art, the chemical composition of pigments. Ron was adept only with a pen when it was used to draw, not to write. And today he felt merely like sleeping.

"How's Pru Darcy?" asked his tutor, after the tests were over. "I see you're driving her car."

"Pretty groggy, according to her husband. I'm going to see her now." He promised to pass on good wishes from the staff.

Pru was still hooked up to a drip and was looking washed out. "What I'd give for a hamburger," she muttered. "They won't let me eat solids. They say I'm getting a three-course meal through my veins, but I said it tastes like sawdust. How did your project go?"

"Productive. But I can't find a buyer."

"Tell me."

"You know the work of Vargas?"

"Yes. He's not popular with the feminist movement but he's brilliant in his own way."

"I tried to do some commercial pictures of Mercedes."

"You should send them to a magazine. Or to someone who makes calendars. When I'm out of here I'll look up some contacts for you. You're not thinking of selling them under your Roman name, are you?"

Ron explained and she nodded. "I didn't realise you needed money badly. I suppose that dolly-bird is bleeding you dry." She reached for her handbag and handed him a fifty-dollar note. "You don't have to wash dishes to keep body and soul together. You'll be fine when Margett's opens but until then I'll see you right."

Ron thanked her warmly but, in fairness to Mercedes, defended his house guest. "She worked instead of me when I was at Ephemeral," he said. "She earns her keep."

Pru leered. "I'll bet!" Her face twisted in a grimace of pain. "You'd better go, Ron. I'm going to ring for the nurse."

Any thoughts he might have had of asking his benefactor for a loan evaporated. Sure, she was sympathetic to his need but he had felt quite unable to discuss the abortion with her. She, who had lost two sons in a cruel tragedy, would be unlikely to support the termination of life. And now she had taken a bad turn, a debate on the issue was out of the question.

***

"I've been helping Zoe," Mercedes said, coming up the stairs with her friend in tow. "I'm cataloguing the exhibits." She placed three bottles of wine in the ice-box. "Are you working the kitchen tonight or am I?"

"Neither. I quit for the pair of us. Pru's giving me fifty a week until I start earning by sketching."

"I looked through your paintings while you were away." Zoe lit a thin, dark cheroot and waved a bottle of wine. "You're something else again. Has Mrs Darcy talked about putting together your promotion package?"

"No, but her husband has. He's the marketing guru. He says she's the talent scout."

"You need a manager...an agent."

"Maybe one day. Not yet. I'm not ready. When I am, Pru will advise me."

"It doesn't solve your present crisis though." Zoe filled the wine glasses which Mercedes placed on the kitchen table and told Ron to sit down.

"I've a business proposition for you," she said. "It may sound bizarre, but it's a deal that would solve your problem."

"He won't like it," Mercedes protested. "He'll go all stiff and upright."

"But that's how I want him. Hear me out. I'm a virgin and I'm not happy about it."

A wave of red suffused Ron's face. "Do you always talk like that to men?"

"Yes, if it suits me. I'm not pretty, like Mercedes. Men don't get turned on by me. I haven't got 'it'. I've got brains; I've got taste; I've got money. But no sex appeal. Not a bit of it. I'm missing out, Ron Turner, and you're the man to do something about it!"

"Are you propositioning me? Seriously?"

"Exactly. Two hundred dollars to break me in and an extra hundred if it's good."

Ron went hot and cold at the same time. It was an outrageous suggestion.

"It would pay for the abortion," Mercedes said seriously. "It's a fair bargain." She passed him a plate of cookies. "I made them myself."

Ron bit one and tried not to wrinkle his nose at the herbal taste. "Why don't you ask your mate to lend you the money?"

"I don't do lending," Zoe snapped. "I do business. Shall we dicker or shall we deal?"

"Deal! When?"

"Whenever you're ready. As soon as you've showered. You smell sweaty."

"What? Now? Here?"

"Any reason why not? Can't you rise to the occasion? Here, this will help." She handed him another glass of retsina. It tasted rather odd but Ron tossed it back. His head was buzzing but he held out his glass for a refill.

Mercedes licked her lips. "You can do it, Ron. You know you can! I'll help."

"You're mad. You're both mad! I'll take that shower just to get my brains back." He turned the taps on so that the jets were hard on his face, but the sense of unreality did not diminish. Was he drunk? Or was he drugged? He'd heard of such things. To hell with the pair of them! They weren't screwing him around!

Four soapy hands demolished his resolve. He held Zoe, or was it Mercedes? Or both? His head swam as his body responded to the stimulant. He staggered to the bed, led by his determined seducers. Zoe, the instigator, went rigid under his hands and it was Mercedes who urged her friend to relax, let go, let it happen.

"You need to do this," Mercedes purred. "It will never be right for you unless you know!"

Only then did Ron realise that Zoe's passion was reserved for Mercedes. He did what was expected of him, then rolled over and left them to it.

"Two's company," he muttered and, head spinning and feeling nauseous, took a blanket to the car. He was not interested in observing the variations on the age-old theme. He slept for hours. When he shook the fog of self-disgust from his head and returned to the attic, it was deserted.

Zoe had left three hundred dollars on the pillow. The accompanying note said, "Ho hum! Thanks but no thanks. Mercedes is moving in with me. I'll take care of her."

Irrationally, what Ron felt was not relief, but anger.

8

Verdigris; known as Greek green by the French. The blue-green pigment was popular until the 17th century as it was one of the few green colours readily available. In antiquity it was made by suspending copper plates in the acid dregs left from wine-making. The synthetic pigment is made from copper sulphate and ammonia with acetic acid. It is lightfast but semi-transparent, and is often used as a glaze over lead white.

Retsina left Ron with a mouth like the floor of a cockie's cage and a head pounding from the effects of whatever it was Zoe had slipped into the wine, or Mercedes had stirred into the shortbread. But, as his anger died, he recognised that he was seeing life through a green veneer of jealousy. He could live with Zoe's disparaging "Ho hum," he could live with the shame of what he had done with her, he could live with the duplicity of Mercedes. That, ripe with his child in her womb, she could prefer the caresses of another woman, was the ultimate rejection.

He mooched. He had no energy to do anything constructive. He curled up on the double bed, breathed the scent of Mercedes and yearned for her with an intensity born from a perverse response to her betrayal.

Mike, wondering why his young friend had not been to visit Pru as expected, hammered on his door at midday.

"I expect he's still asleep," said Zoe, her arms full of framed abstracts. "I've not heard him all morning."

"Not at college?"

"Mrs Darcy's car is still in the yard, so I guess not."

"It's not like Ron. He's usually up with the dawn."

Zoe smirked. "He's had a hard night. I expect he's a pretty sick boy! Here, you're the quack who likes paintings, aren't you? Come and tell me what you think."

Hanging was almost complete. Mike was stunned by the array of talent shown by the emergent artists, for Pru Darcy had an unerring eye for what was good and saleable. Zoe, complementing her selection, had an instinct for grouping subjects in a way that enabled each to draw strength from those of like kind. The abstracts occupied the largest walls, the precision of subtlety contrasting with the exuberance of the expressionists. Great glowing canvases challenged him, but easier on the eye were the cool semi-monochromes, with neutral backgrounds enlivened only by wavering lines of colour, or geometric figures which had surprising vitality.

There was a wall of charming watercolours, a room of still-life paintings and flower studies, a corridor lined with pen and wash drawings. Seascapes and marine subjects dominated an area enhanced by a floor display of old cane craypots, nets and sun-bleached driftwood, above which hung a mobile of floats from drift-nets, shining like witches' balls in a spotlight. There were plinths on which rested futuristic sculptures and free-form ceramics.

"Mrs Darcy's portrait will be in this area," Zoe said. "She calls it the Roman Room."

The easel was set up, waiting for delivery of Ron's portrait, the static display Andrew had ordered already in place. The walls were covered in Ron's charcoal studies of figures and landscapes, with fine drawings of animals and plants mounted behind wide borders and framed with non-reflective glass. On the end wall was a striking landscape of Cootimurra, executed in oils, with other paintings of the outback around it.

Mike whistled. "I didn't realise he was so versatile."

Zoe frowned. "He needs discipline. Mrs Darcy says his future is in faces but he's playing at present. While he's a student I suppose he must explore all genres, but he'll have to settle down before we can properly develop his talent."

"Surely he's too young to concentrate only on portraits?"

"Huh! He won't have time for anything else. When I start handling his career his booking list will be full, just you wait and see."

"Yet there are no figure studies here. Why aren't you hanging the oil painting he did of Mercedes at the beach? It's brilliant!"

She shot him a look of pure malice...or that is how he later interpreted it, not understanding at the time the dynamics of Zoe's intrusion into Ron's love life.

"It will not enhance his reputation to exhibit nudes," she said, firmly. "He needs a reputation beyond reproach if people are to pose for him."

"That's crap! There's nothing seedy about life-studies. Even Pru Darcy poses in the nude. Have you some hang-up about studies of the flesh?"

"No, but I detest the way men leer at them. I'm not in the business of hanging pictures that make men want to wank!"

Mike shrugged. "I bet Pru Darcy doesn't share your sensitivity. And she's the boss!"

"But she's not curating this exhibition. I am. If she wants a showing of tits and bums, she can organise a special event. But it won't have my imprimatur."

Mike gave a low rumble of amusement. "Leave you to it, then. I'll go and wake lover-boy."

She glared at him. "Tell Ron to finish Mrs Darcy's commission. I still want to get it framed." She paused and, fishing in her handbag, handed Mike a key. "Mercedes told me to give this back to Ron. She's moved into my place."

The chin was up, the look defiant. What the devil was going on here, Mike wondered. He took one look at Ron and reached for the fruit salts from the kitchen window-sill.

"Doctor's orders," he said sternly. "What's happened?"

Ron told him, hesitantly at first, and then with an outburst of bewildered feelings. "I don't understand Mercedes. How could she do that to me? What on earth does she see in Zoe?"

"Comfort," Mike replied wryly. "Lifestyle. Money."

"Then why did she bother with me? I had nothing."

"I think you had one thing she really enjoyed. Innocence. You said she'd been abused as a child?"

"Or so she said."

"I expect taking your virginity was pay-back time. She was trying to bring you down to her level. Mind, I expect she fancied you, as well. You're not a bad-looker, as men go."

"Good thing I know you're straight or I'd smack you for that!" Ron grinned, sheepishly. "But why does Zoe turn her on?"

"Been at it for years, haven't they? Bosom pals and gymslips? Giggles in the locker-room? Big tits?"

"Zoe's aren't even real! She's had implants. Hard as rocks! And she's hairy. Strewth, Mike, she's got more hair on her belly than an alley cat!"

"I take it you don't fancy her."

"I don't even like her."

"Then who's been a silly boy? By the way, she's nagging for Pru's portrait. Finished it yet?"

"No. I've been busy on other things."

"Show your Uncle Michael."

Ron took the pin-up studies from their hiding place and stood them around the walls. "After Vargas," he said.

"I can see that. They're damned good but you'll not sell them locally. Too stick-in-the-mud here. Send them to Sydney."

"I might just keep them. Souvenirs."

Mike shook his head. "That's sick. Can't stand the thought of you sitting here, lusting after your little Asian bimbo."

"Better than other men drooling over her. Isn't she a beauty?"

"Not my sort, Ron. I like them pink and plump and blonde. I'm a Rubens man, myself. Just don't let Zoe see them."

"I was hoping she could sell them for me."

"She's more likely to burn them. She's got an anti-nude streak a mile wide and, if she's in love with Mercedes, she'd go ape at the sight of these. If you're in a hurry to raise funds, I know a couple of gallery owners over east who'd handle them discreetly."

Ron shook his head. "No hurry now. Zoe's taking care of the abortion business."

"She'd better get a move on, then, or it'll be too late. And we'd better hurry as well. Andrew Darcy is taking us out on his yacht."

Ron, who had never been sailing, enjoyed the afternoon enormously. It was Mike, the experienced crewman, whose complexion went pale green in the choppy conditions and who ended up providing ground-bait for fishing. Andrew Darcy, taking pity on the doctor, tacked back to the harbour and furled the sails of Dreamdrift II. They motored into the calmer river and dropped anchor. The shadows of the tree-dark banks fell across the translucent blue-green water and the captain offered round stubbies of cold beer. Talk was gentle and as inconsequential as the slow lap of wavelets against the hull.

Mike sighed and broached a subject which had obviously been worrying him. "I want Pru to have some more tests," he said. "Andrew, I'm not happy with her progress."

Ron shifted uneasily on his seat in the stern. "If you're talking medical matters, I'll go and drop a line over the bow," he offered.

Andrew Darcy shook his head. "There's nothing Mike could tell me I wouldn't want to you hear. What is it, young Mike?"

Mike sighed. "I shouldn't talk to you at all. Patient confidentiality and all that stuff, but I hardly know your wife. I don't know what to do, and that's the truth."

"Get on with it. You've said too much to shy at this fence. Come on, out with it, man."

"Her abdomen is swollen and we'd expect that. But I felt a hard lump around the ovaries when I examined her last. Has she gone through the menopause?"

"Hot flushes, the lot. Yes. But you'd know that from your clinical notes."

"So I got out my trusty stethoscope and did the usual chest examination, you know, breathe deeply, hold it, cough...all that jazz. Andrew, how long has she had that lump in her breast?"

He smiled gently. "Don't worry about that, Mike. Our family doctor says it's only a cyst."

"It's not. I'm pretty sure it's cancer. I ought to have sent her down to theatre and got a specialist to take a biopsy, but..."

"But what?"

"But if I'm right they'd do a radical mastectomy and have her whole breast off and take the glands under her arm as well. It's a rotten, disfiguring, debilitating operation and, even with chemotherapy, there's no guarantee of getting it all."

Andrew Darcy looked at him grimly. "I know that, Mike, but it doesn't explain your hesitancy. Why the doubts?"

"Because if I'm right about the lump in her belly, it's already spread. She could have dozens of tumours growing away in spots we can't even guess at."

"Let me get this right, young man. Are you advocating we do nothing?"

"It might be kinder. She could keep going for a long time before the cancer hits a vital organ."

There was a long, tense silence. The sun shone as brightly, the water sparkled diamonds over the blue-green depths, but a shadow had spoiled the day.

"I don't want to lose my wife. She's too damned precious to let go without a fight."

Ron looked far away, beyond the land to a greater truth. "But you'd lose her anyway, if you let them carve her up. She'd be a different person. It wouldn't simply be the physical changes but what would be going on in her mind. She'd hate it, wondering if you still loved her, despite the scars, sick as a dog from treatments, stuck in a ward bed, wondering when she was going to die."

"The other alternative's not good either," Mike sighed. "Hey, I'm not even sure if I'm right. Hell, I'm only a registrar. I could be misreading what I found. Maybe you should get her to an oncologist and let the experts advise you."

Andrew Darcy hunched his shoulders and shivered. "The moment I suggested that, she'd guess. She's so much alive, my Pru, eagerly looking forward to opening the gallery, full of plans for your career, Ron. She's busy with new ideas for the restaurant and planning a trip east to see our other proteges. And there's her work for the Tamberlaine Foundation in Indonesia. You're right,

Ron. One hint of this and she'd start to die. She'd wither away and would think her life not worth living."

"Then I do nothing?"

"Give me time, Mike. I need to think this through."

"It's flat calm now. I think we should get back to your moorings. To be honest, I think I threw up more from worrying about how to tell you than because of the chop."

***

Ron still felt nauseous days later. Every time he thought of Pru he wanted to dry retch. He finished the portrait only by divorcing hand and eye from his mind. He painted from the heart...that kept functioning even if fine judgement escaped him. Then he sat back to front on a kitchen chair, his chin on his hands, contemplating the results, heedless of the slow welling of tears from eyes raw with misery.

"Ron Turner, I have simply got to have that painting," Zoe snapped from behind him. She'd come silently up the stairs. Now she was standing, hands on hips, glaring at him. Ron, who had evaded her baleful presence for days, felt like a roo caught in the beam of an oncoming road-train. He felt unable to move except to wipe his cheeks with hands roughly cleansed with turpentine. The turps got in his eyes and made them sting.

He swore mightily and, knocking over the chair, rushed to the bathroom and swilled his eyes with clear water. He took several deep breaths and struggled for composure. He came out. wiping a towel over his face.

"It's not finished," he growled.

"You're playing games. I can't remember which of the Impressionists said it...maybe Manet...that it takes two artists to paint a picture, one to do the painting and the other to knock him on the head when it's finished. Time's up."

"It won't be dry enough to varnish before the launch."

"Who cares? I'll put it behind ropes. Now sign it."

Ron chose a fine brush and mixed linseed into a dark remnant of pigment on the uncleaned palette.

Zoe, tapping her fingers with impatience on the kitchen table, which she had commandeered, lit one of her black cheroots and breathed smoke through her nose. She was, Ron thought, like a small, squat dragon, guarding a hoard of treasure. It was an uncomfortable simile. He had the feeling she was about to sink her claws in his back and singe him with a puff of flame.

"That's crap!" Zoe huffed. "That signature is crap. Make the R big and distinctive like you've done on the charcoal sketches. Keep the o-m-a-n small but bring the tail of the R across in a flourish to underline the other letters! Yes, that's better. Do it like that in future."

"Yes, your ladyship! Anything else I can do for you?" He leered with a lewd gesture.

Zoe's face twisted in revulsion. "You are gross! Men! You think that having that thing between your legs makes you attractive to women, don't you? I hate you, Ron Turner. I hate you and everything you stand for."

He looked at her sadly. "Actually, Zoe, I rarely think of it at all. I don't lust after women, you know."

"Only Mercedes! Look what you did to Mercedes! Look what you did to me!"

"You did ask for it! And, to be honest, I don't remember a thing about it."

He caught an odd look of chagrin in her face. "You couldn't wait to get off me and into Mercedes. You're a wild animal, Ron Turner. You hurt Mercy. It was disgusting!"

"But you watched. How do you know if you didn't watch!"

She howled and beat her fists on the table. "Filth! Filth! How could she let you touch her?"

He grabbed her wrists and held them down as she made to claw his face.

"Now, listen to me, young lady. Your bloody histrionics cut no ice with me. You put me in an impossible position and I did what you paid me to do. You paid me, Zoe! You drugged me and you paid me! What gives you the right to censure my behaviour? At least my motives were good. I only did it to help Mercedes! You put up the money and I covered you. Too bad if you didn't like it."

Zoe spat in his face. He ignored the mucus sliding down his cheek. "I don't even know why you wanted me to make love to you. Why?"

"Because Mercedes likes doing it with men. I wanted to find out why. Because she said I couldn't really love her unless I knew what I was choosing between, her way and mine."

"You silly cow! You poor, silly cow. You can't live the way Mercedes does. She's not far short of being a nymphomaniac."

"And who ruined her? Men! Her father and her brother and her mother's boyfriends! All men with things between their legs. Mine is a better way!"

He sighed and let her go. "Different, perhaps. Better? I wouldn't know. How could I? I've only known her."

"And me! Don't forget me!"

"I told you, Zoe, I don't remember you."

But he did. He remembered the hard breasts, the tiny waist and the wide, stiff hips, her agony at his intrusion and her cries of protest. It had been, in the last moments before he breeched her, little more than rape, with Mercedes holding her friend down and urging him on.

Zoe was crying. He left her to her tears and carried the portrait down to the gallery. He placed it on the display easel and felt reasonably satisfied. "I'll paint you again, Pru," he promised. "You're worth putting on canvas."

When he returned to the attic he found Zoe on her feet, going through the stack of canvases in the corner. She had found the Mercedes pin-ups and had leaned several against the wall.

"I want these," she said. "Sell them to me."

"They're not for sale. I'm going to keep them."

She faced him, her eyes heavy, her tongue licking her top lip, her desire obvious in every gesture.

"Name your price, Ron Turner. Mercedes is mine. I don't want you lusting after her."

"Do you know the difference between love and lust?" he asked. "These are art studies, not pornography. I want to keep them because they show Mercedes in all her beauty, and it's her sheer womanliness that I appreciate."

"Bulldust!" she snapped. "It wasn't art appreciation that got her pregnant! And, in case you didn't like to ask after her health, you can stop worrying."

"You said you'd see to that."

Anger sparkled in Zoe's eyes and she hissed spite through her narrowed lips, "I didn't need to do anything, you bastard. You were so rough that you caused her to miscarry! You got rid of the baby the same way you started it. With your dirty little joystick!"

9

Terre Verte, or earth green, is made from naturally occurring minerals, glauconite or celadonite, which are complex aluminium silicates. The minerals, which are found in various shades of green, are simply ground to a fine consistency and added to a medium. Terre verte is not toxic and covers well. This pigment is permanent and stable, mixing well with all other paints. It is popularly used in under-painting of flesh tones.

Pru Darcy held court. There was no other way to describe her demeanour on the night of the opening. Andrew had brought her favourite chair, an ornate bamboo throne with a fan-like back, which Tamberlaine had brought back from the Spice Islands shortly after that early marriage. It had been re-caned so many times that, in fact, little of the original bamboo remained. But seated in it, Pru always said she felt like a queen.

She was still very pale and weak from her operation, and her plump cheeks had lost flesh. She wore her new wrinkles with disdain. Her flowing kaftan hid the deficiencies in her figure and a silky turban disguised her lank tresses. But her eyes were as bright as ever and her graceful hands, the fingers embellished with rings and her wrists with gold bangles, were as expressive as one might expect from a former dancer. The mind was sharp and the wit pungent. Guests, who clustered around her, were frequently rocked by gales of laughter as she related one of her more spicy yarns.

Ron, with utter reluctance, had been placed under the wing of Zoe. He had been groomed by Miss Xenos, his clothes selected by her. He felt like an actor, dressed in a full-sleeved shirt of soft, creamy wool, which was belted and hip-length. He would not have looked out of place in Renaissance times. The black velvet trousers were tailored tightly to his thighs, and, as he told Mike frankly, nipped uncomfortably in the crotch. He had refused to wear his hair loose, curling over his neck, and had insisted it be pulled back into a pony-tail. He was determined to have it cut short again after opening night, but had bowed to the will of his patron.

"I know you detest Zoe, but she does know what's what," Pru said. "She has an innate sense of style and understands what is in fashion. She's done a brilliant job of this exhibition and it's thanks largely to her ability to curate it that a success is assured."

"She's a hard-nosed bitch."

"Pshaw! She's as talented in her way as you are in yours. It's a pity you don't get on. She could be the making of you. She knows the right people."

Ron bit back his ire. "I'll play the game, Pru, but for your sake."

"Silly boy. You'll play the game for your own sake. Mark my words, the reviews tomorrow will be raving about the ability of Roman. Look around you, dear. Has any other artist a more impressive body of work than yours? Zoe has done you proud. Tonight you stay close by her and let her do the talking. She'll sell you. You just be your own, natural, pleasant self."

"I'm not ready for this. I feel as if my spirit has been ground into dust under her organisation."

"Yes, you are pretty green, Ron, but she'll put the polish on your company manners. What you don't realise, and it's to your credit that you don't trade on it, is that there is a streak of earthy charm about you. Don't, whatever you do, camp it up and don't, for the life of you, let success go to your head."

He stood beside her, nervously waiting for the first arrivals.

Andrew was busy overseeing the catering arrangements. Margett's was also opening that night but Ron had been too self-absorbed to concern himself in the details of the restaurant. He knew the contract to run it had been let, and it was not until he saw Kostas crossing the yard with a tray of bread rolls, that he realised his past was about to catch up with him.

"Who's leased the premises?" he asked. "I'm sorry, Pru. If I've been told, I've forgotten."

"I'm sure Andrew mentioned it. It's the Populis Group. Brothers who emigrated after there was trouble with the military junta in Greece. You know the brother who runs the Delphi."

"Where I used to work? Not old Aristotle?"

"No. He's taken his brother, Constantine, into partnership. His nephew Kostas has been promoted to help him run it. Not Greek cuisine, Ron. That wouldn't go down well here. They'll do Mediterranean with a leaning towards Italian."

"I'll get fat."

"Huh! You'll not be able to afford their prices."

Ron grinned. "Kostas will keep me fed, I bet you. We're old mates."

Pru made her eyes cross and looked at him with a leer. "You won't dare to get fat. Whoever heard of a chubby artist? You'll not be able to wear those sexy pants if you're a blubber ball. Come on, help me down the stairs to join the party."

Margett's was packed. Even Ron, who was no fan of television, recognised many of its stars, famous sportsmen and women, a few politicians and civic dignitaries. He got to know more, for Zoe led him from table to table, making introductions. Most took little notice of him, for they were intent on the antipasto, the marinaras and the parmigiana. But when Zoe pointed out that the charcoal drawings on the walls had been done by Roman, and this was

Roman, they smiled at him and offered congratulations.

His shy response won their approval.

"Just wait until you see the gallery," Zoe said. "Then you'll really want to talk to him."

She parked Ron at a table full of art critics and left him to their mercies. Talking technical matters and chatting about the art scene was within his comfort zone, so he relaxed.

Then there were speeches. Andrew Darcy welcomed the guests and introduced Constantine Populis, who went bright red and stumbled over his opening words. He was not comfortable in the language of his adopted country.

"My partner is better at this than I am," he said, gesturing to a late arrival. "Ladies and gentlemen, I give you Aristotle Populis."

The bull snorted and pawed the earth-red carpet, tossed his horns and bellowed a greeting. Then he pranced from table to table, all smiles and unctuous handshakes, pats on the back and charm for the ladies. He waved to the doorway, where a stout figure, arms full of long white boxes, was staggering into the room. It was Mana Agnella, who opened the cartons to reveal dozens of long-stemmed roses. Aristotle circulated again, giving a rose to each lady and a large bouquet to Prudence.

"This will be a true partnership," he said. "Con and I will feed your bodies and Prudence Darcy will ensure you feast your eyes."

Ron looked at his detested former employer and felt nauseous. He glanced at Zoe, who stood glowering near the stairs to the gallery. She was glaring at Aristotle with the cold, green, stone-like stare of a basilisk. Zoe Xenos, the unflappable, was clearly upset.

"Are you feeling ill?" Ron went to her side, disturbed by her distress. He took two glasses from the bar and begged a bottle of wine from Andrew Darcy. "Come on, Zoe. Come upstairs and have a drink to compose yourself while this lot finish their desserts."

They sat on the bottom steps of the stairs leading to the attic. "I didn't know he'd be here," she said, after some minutes of silent wrath. "I thought Con was running Margett's. I should have known Con didn't have the balls to stand up to his brother."

"You know Aristotle?"

She gave him a look of such anguish that he felt as though he had been punched in the gut. "Know him? I should think I do. He's my father!"

"Oh!" There was nothing else to say, although Ron's curiosity was turning over at a million miles an hour. "I used to work for him."

"Poor you!"

"But your name is Xenos."

"Xenopopulis. Too much of a mouthful. I took one half, he took the other when we were naturalised. I've never forgiven him for what he did to my mother, the dirty pig."

All the tumblers lined up and the fruit machine rang jackpot. Kostas and his hairy cousin, the smart-arsed little prude who'd gone to Paris to be finished...Aristotle's wife who'd run off to Greece to become a nun...Aunt Clemmie...Zoe's mother. He wondered if she knew about Aristotle's affair with Mercedes.

"My father is a filthy, lecherous swine who'll lay any woman he can get his hands on," she said bitterly. "He even raped Mercedes. That's why she wouldn't come tonight, in case he was here. I thought he might drift in but not that he'd be the star turn!"

Ron let out his breath. So Zoe knew, but rape? It hadn't looked like rape to him. He remembered the pleasure on Mercedes' face as she squealed when Aristotle tried to drive through her to the wall at her back. And he recalled the fleeting expression of satisfaction on her face when she had seen him through the window. Mercedes had enjoyed being watched in full rut.

Mercedes liked older men.

He patted Zoe's knee. "Don't show him you care," he said. "Go up to my bathroom and put on new make-up. You're not Daddy's little girl. You're Zoe Xenos, your own person, in control, successful, going places. Your challenge is in the future, not in the past."

"Thanks, Ron. I needed a pep talk."

To his surprise she threw her arms round his neck and gave him a great hug. She was totally composed by the time the party drifted up the stairs to the exhibition. Pru, the centre of attention, beckoned to him and suggested he sit on the foot-stool beside her. She squeezed his shoulder. "Is Zoe all right?"

He nodded. "I'll tell you later."

If the mark of a good exhibition is sales, the number of red dots on paintings resembled confetti. Zoe was kept busy, although Andrew dealt with the business of cheques and receipts. It was Pru who talked portraits to would-be sitters who spent time discussing such matters with Roman. Ron played the role to perfection, rising from his patron's side to escort potential clients to the Roman room, talking about what they wanted from him and when they were available to pose.

"A camera can capture your physical appearance," he said. "But the brush can free your soul!" It was, he thought, a rather sick-making statement, but Zoe had coached him.

"It'll work," she said. "Most of these celebrities haven't got a heart, let alone a soul, but they'd like to think they have a depth of character that you alone can see."

When they were convinced, and he could tell that from the smiles of confidence they gave him, Zoe took over and made formal bookings.

"You're going to be busy," she said. "That's two newsreaders, one mayor, the captain of the State football team and Jayde Astor, the actress. I'm negotiating with a University chancellor. a couple of Captains of Industry and the Minister for Arts."

"Hell's teeth," Ron protested. "When will I have time for classes?"

She laughed. "You won't. Don't you realise, Ron, there's nothing more they can teach you? You've gone beyond your lecturers. Later you can study in Europe with better men than ever wielded a brush in this country."

"You're talking about Roman, Zoe. Not about Ron Turner. Roman has set his style, made his mark. Roman, I agree, looks like becoming a success, but Ron Turner still has a whole world to explore. I want to paint more landscapes, great Impressionist studies of the Outback, the people who live there. I want to do more pen work, more pastels, more figure studies..."

"More of your dirty little pin-ups? Who do you think will pose for those?"

He leered at her. "You think I'll find a shortage of artist's models? There's plenty of girls will take their clothes off for me!"

"Yes, prostitutes, I expect. You'll have to pay them!"

"We'll see. I've had a few offers tonight already!"

"You are disgusting, Ron. I keep telling you to think with your brain, not your dick!"

"I don't, Zoe. My brain thinks about what it needs, my dick's got it's own agenda!"

"Why, you foul-minded little turd," she snapped. "I'm going!"

"Not stopping for the after-show party?"

"No way. Apart from the fact that you are deliberately trying to wind me up, look who's just walked in? Kostas and my father. I'm off!"

Pru, looking exhausted, was almost asleep in her chair. Andrew put her feet on the stool and steered Aristotle into the other rooms.

Aristotle poked Ron in the chest. "I know you. You're the kitchen-pig. You're the one who fancied that waitress!"

"Mercedes. Yes."

"Was that her name? Tasty bit of crumpet, wasn't she? Where's she these days?"

"Shacked up with your daughter. She's gone off men."

"What? Don't you believe it, Ron, Roman, whatever you call yourself these days. She's a scrubber by nature. You did the right thing when you dumped her butt in the sink."

"So you haven't forgotten."

"Boy, I've had more women than you've had do-it-yourself jobs. And I tell you, that bird's a scrubber. Do you know how much she touched me up for? Two big ones. I could have had a fortnight in a brothel for the money."

"So? Maybe your daughter is paying for her services."

"Zoe? She'd have to be! She's so bloody ugly even I don't fancy her!"

***

The aftermath of the party was a sombre affair. Pru and Andrew turned up mid-morning and started to gather up the glasses and emptied the ashtrays. Ron was dragooned into pushing a vacuum cleaner over the carpet. Pru levelled the paintings and sighed with satisfaction at the number which had sold.

Mike arrived with his arms full of Sunday papers and suggested they retreat to the attic to read the reviews and to enjoy a coffee. The reviews had been written before the launch, after a special preview for the press. Mike, who had been unable to attend the main event, as he had been on duty in Emergency, had been to the special showing and now gazed with satisfaction at the series of pen and wash drawings of Cootimurra characters which he had reserved at the preview.

Ron had done the basic studies at shearing time and developed them at college. There were the gun-shearers and their cook, the wool-classer and the mechanic who kept the machines going. There was a study of the dogs and the auctioneer, who'd happened to drop by to see how things were. Central to the set was a portrait of Ron's father, lean and laconic, brittled by the hard life, and a study of his mother, pouring tea for the thirsty workers. O'Malley, the sheep-truck driver, was there, leaning on a fence with a fag on his lower lip.

"You should develop these into oil paintings," Mike said.

"I will one day," Ron replied. "But God knows when I'll find the time. Roman is going to have his butt hanging out."

Pru, warming her hands on the coffee mug, looked at him with concern. "Do them next week," she suggested. "Go up to Ephemeral and spend a couple of weeks painting. I want you out of here."

Dismay must have been written all over Ron's face, so she laughed. "I don't mean for good, silly. I've been looking around the attics and Zoe is quite right. She said they were in no fit state to invite important clients into. So you chuff off to the hills and do your own thing and she and I will get the builders in. Take Mike with you. It will stop him nagging me about my health."

"Can you get a break? Or are registrars not allowed holidays?"

"I can jiggle the roster so I can have a few days to take you there and another couple of days the next week, but that's all. I'd like that. Thanks, Mrs Darcy."

"Oh, don't thank me," she said, waving a laconic arm. "After the end of this exhibition I'll need new stock, for the walls are going to be rather bare. Andrew's going to Sydney to scout for some new talent while I get the whip behind the horses in my own stable."

Ron grinned. "I've never been called a horse before. Horse's arse, yes."

"I'd guess you're a fine buck stallion," said Andrew. "You'd better do as the boss suggests or she'll geld you!"

"I'll need a stack of materials and I haven't got the money for them."

Pru shook her head in exasperation. "Ron, dear, you're rolling in it. Do you know the value of the paintings of yours Andrew sold last night? And the advances Zoe took for commissions?" She named a figure.

Ron whistled. "And I thought Mistress Golightly was a good bet."

"Humph. I don't gamble. I only put my faith in winners and I knew you were one from the moment I saw your work."

"Yes, ma'am. No, ma'am. Three bags full, ma'am."

* * *

Balance is essential in any composition. After his productive break, Ron stepped into a studio which was light and bright, living quarters neatly partitioned out of sight, and all furnishings replaced with modern substitutes. He told Pru he was delighted.

He was less effusive with Zoe, who seemed to expect gratitude. Ron found it increasingly difficult to deal with her. One portion of his mind was filled with seething resentment, another with pity. When he submitted to her dictates he felt unmanned. When he protested at the way she tried to run his life, she sneered at him and called him childish. On the business and artistic level they rubbed along fairly well but she could not resist frequent digs about his masculinity, phrasing them in a way which made him cringe with embarrassment and a growing feeling of inadequacy. But, having put up with weeks of her crowing, for that was what it amounted to, about Mercedes preferring her love to his lust, he became aware that Zoe was deeply unhappy.

Kostas, ambling up the stairs one night with a dish of fegato alla Milanese, and a bottle of chianti, knew the reason. Zoe's cousin had been chuckling about developments for days.

"Mercedes has buggered off," he said. "She's gone back to Indonesia. That General her mum's been shacked up with has found Mercedes a job on television. She's going to read the news in English. Won't matter about the big tum as it won't be seen 'cos it's below the desk."

"Big tum?"

"She's still pregnant. Didn't you know?"

Ron went cold. "Zoe said she'd miscarried."

"Zoe is a liar. Haven't you discovered that? You don't want to trust her, Ron. She's a liar and a cheat. Been that way since she was a kid. Biggest whoppers you can imagine and, if they are whoppers that can get someone else into trouble, she gloats."

"The hell she does! She told Mercedes she would pay for an abortion."

"From what my dear cousin said, and it was hard to understand because she was blubbing all over Mana Agnella, Mercedes was too far gone to get rid of the kid."

"Mike warned me she was cutting it fine, but I couldn't raise the money."

Kostas goggled at him. "You don't mean it really is your sprog?

I thought Mercedes was pulling my leg."

"Kostas, she says it's mine and the dates fit. What am I supposed to do? Call her a liar? I thought it was why you dumped her on me."

"I thought you'd have taken her to a clinic to get rid of it weeks ago. Now here's a turn up for the books. But you can't believe what Zoe says where Mercedes is concerned. She and Zoe have been thick as thieves since they were at convent school. Funny the way some women are about one another. Beats me. So Zoe told you another fairy-story? Well, congratulations, mate. You're going to be a daddy!"

10

Olympian green; sometimes called Bremen green, is a copper carbonate which occurs in quantity in Madagascar as the mineral malachite, which takes its name from the Greek malache, or mallow, a leaf-green colour. It was used in early Egyptian paintings and was most popular in the 15th and 16th centuries. The traditional ore was ground from the natural mineral, related to blue azurite, but is now made by chemical reaction of copper sulphate and sodium carbonate.

A woman scorned. Poor Zoe. She'd seemed so certain that she had secured Mercedes' affection and there was no doubt she felt all the angst of rejected love. She no longer crowed to Ron about his prowess or lack of it. He sometimes caught her gazing at him, almost in bewilderment, as if she were adrift and had no compass to point her to landfall.

The bounce, the drive, the zest were gone. Pru, who had relied on her young assistant's strength, was nonplussed. "What's happened?" she asked. "Whatever is wrong with Zoe?"

Ron simply shook his head. It was not his place to enlighten Pru. If Zoe wanted to confide in the older woman it should be her choice to do so, not his. She might be the arch-manipulator, but he had no intentions of meddling. Anyway, after his evening of revelations by Kostas, he no longer knew what to believe from Zoe. He was so ambivalent about her truthfulness that he was quite willing to accept the entire Indonesian story might be a pack of lies. As the miscarriage scenario had, maybe, been false, so might the advanced pregnancy. In fact, he argued, the entire conception might have been a fantasy, more of a misconception than a matter of a foetus in a womb.

Mike, when this view was put to him, stamped reality firmly onto Ron's wavering grip. "Twaddle. Of course she was pregnant. I examined her."

"Did you? When?"

Mike went bright red. "One night, when you were out working."

"And did you?"

"Of course I did! Who had any choice when Mercedes was intent on seduction?"

"Good for you, was she?"

Mike bowed his head. "The living best," he muttered. "I envied you."

"Some mate you are!"

"You know how it is. Sometimes one can't help oneself."

"Oh, stop blathering and fetch us a beer. Forget the bloody woman. Write her off to experience."

Mike opened the new refrigerator and pulled two cans from a six-pack. "Got it nicely set up now, haven't you? All mod cons."

"Air-conditioning and all. But I had a hell of a row with Zoe over the floor-covering. Covering the wooden boards with beige linoleum was not a good idea, even if it means I can drop paint everywhere."

"Makes sense to me."

"Dammit, Mike, the light reflects off the floor and puts lights under the brows where there should be shadows. It's hellish difficult to work with." He sat down in the chair used by his models and invited the registrar to judge the effect.

"I see what you mean. What can you do about it?"

Ron chuckled. "She's going to kill me, but she's not coming in for the next two days. I've got a big can of fence paint and I'm going to cover the lino with Mission Brown!"

"Talking of missionaries, did you hear the one about the evangelist, the Mormon and the Franciscan missionaries who were captured by cannibals. They put the evangelist in the pot and added salt, they put the Mormon in the pot and added vegetables, then they untied the Franciscan and threw him into the stew, but he shot right out again. Go on, ask me why."

"Why?"

"He was a friar not a boiler!"

Ron groaned. "Lousy joke. Stay put while I set up the easel. I've a new commission starting on Monday and I want to get a rough idea of the pose."

The easel was a large, professional affair, fitted with cranks and levers, able to take much larger canvases than Ron had previously worked on. "Zoe's ordered enough stretched canvas to keep me going for months. She doesn't know I prefer to do my own and that I like a finer linen than she's bought."

"Ungrateful brat!"

"I am that, and when it comes to ordering paints and she's got me box after box of colours I never use, I get very tetchy. Look at this. A dozen yukky greens. What's the use of buying Olympian when I prefer terre verte?"

"Suggest you squeeze it all out on your Mission Brown floor and invite her to roll in it. Then you can strip her off, tumble her across a canvas and be an ultra-modern artist!"

"Call it Olympia Opus One?"

"Or Zoe Descending?"

The final clamp in place, Ron inched the easel towards the

southward facing windows and glanced at the light on Mike's face. "That's close enough. I wanted to be sure I wasn't going to have to hang off the window-sill to get a proper perspective. This place is too small, really. I need a studio like the one at Ephemeral for these big canvases."

"It's too far out. Your subjects would never drive that far to be painted."

Ron looked at him seriously and, before Mike's eyes, the mantle of Roman fell on his shoulders. It was compounded of a new confidence, a certainty about his ability and his destiny that had previously been lacking. "They will, Mike. One day they'll travel half way around the world to be painted by me."

"And pigs might, too! Come on, before your boots get too tight, and show me the rest of this gin palace."

It had not occurred to Ron that the quarters he had occupied in the attic were only half the available roof space, although he knew both Margett's and the gallery to be double fronted. Pru had knocked through the wall to give access to the full width of the building. The area which had served as a kitchen and bedroom had been gutted. It was now a proper kitchen-dining room, opening onto the roof garden. Where Uncle Alf's bed had once stood was a small sitting room where clients could wait for their appointments or conduct business if so required.

The new additions included a spacious lounge area and a large bedroom which had dormer windows overlooking the port. This bedroom had been decorated in olive green and brown, highlighted with touches of lime and orange. The modern divan was covered in tiger stripes and there were prints of wild animals on the walls.

"Zoe's decor?" said Mike. "Does she think you're King of the Jungle, or what?"

"Definitely or what. I think it's her sarcastic comment on my lecherous ways."

"You Tarzan, she Jane?"

"Me Tarzan, she chimpanzee. Come to think of it, I'd rather screw the chimp than Zoe, though there's not much difference."

"The chimp didn't have plastic boobs. Trust me. I'm going to be a plastic surgeon. I notice these things."

Ron, recalling the feel of those hard pointed bosoms beneath his hands, sighed. "Why do women do such things?"

"I expect she was flat as a pancake, before. Two fried eggs, that sort of deal."

"But why go to extremes?"

"Mistake, probably. She'll be sorry. Those implants don't last. The silica leaks out and she'll end up having to have more surgery."

"Bit of a mess, isn't it. By the way, has Pru's lump got worse?"

"Andrew says not that he can see, but she's gone coy on him. Will only take her clothes off when the light's out."

"What! Pru? Pru's not like that. She used to strip off in front of the whole life-study class."

"Well, she ain't doing it no more! So he thinks there's something she's hiding. Bruising, maybe, or another tumour."

"You think she guesses what's wrong?"

"Who can tell? That lady was wise when the Pharoahs were around. She's an old, old soul, if you believe in reincarnation."

"Ah, the mystic Orient. They do things weirdly in Asia, Mercedes told me. They look at things in a completely different way."

"Yeah! Followers of Islam wrap their women in black robes so no one can see them. Mind, saves your pride if you happen to have been forced to marry a dog."

"They eat dogs, don't they?"

"How would I know? Ask Pru. She spent a lot of time with Tamberlaine on the islands. It just beats me that Mercedes would leave a liberated, civilised country for one where most women are second class citizens."

"Mercedes would never stand for that. She'd insist on star billing, wouldn't she?"

"Who knows what she's been promised. Who knows who she's been promised to. Her mother may have fixed her up with marriage to a rich old man."

"She wouldn't care." Ron told him about the night of Uncle Alf's death. "She doesn't have hang ups; that's the trouble. If she had a few more, she wouldn't hurt so many people."

"She didn't hurt your uncle, did she?"

"No. She said he went with a smile on his face."

"Oh, bugger all this philosophy. Come on, Ron. Get your glad rags on and let's go on a pub crawl!"

***

Zoe was horrified by the brown floor and called Ron an ungrateful rat.

"Stop this right there," he shouted. "You're so damned know-all and you're so damned ignorant. You stand here, at the easel, and I'll sit there and explain. Use your eyes, not your big mouth, Zoe."

He watched her face closely as he spoke of shadow and reflections, of highlights and the importance of dark tones in bringing out the structure of bone and the expressions caused by minute tensions of muscles in the face. She went from dragon-fire to dead-ash as she regarded him thoughtfully.

"I'm sorry."

"Don't apologise. You can't be expected to understand what's never been made clear to you before."

"Do you think me very silly?"

"Not silly. But you have some damned odd ideas in that noddle of yours."

"Yes, I have. I thought Mercedes loved me."

"You shouldn't have let yourself be influenced by her."

Zoe shrugged. "I always have been. She used to tell me stuff at school. She used to tell me what her father did to her. She wasn't ashamed of it."

"She doesn't know the meaning of that word."

"I don't suppose she does. She liked it, because it gave her power over her father. I started to wonder why my father didn't treat me the same way. Aristotle had his way with every woman he could. He didn't care that I might be home for the holidays. He was quite indiscreet about it. I heard him carrying on and wondered why he didn't do to me what gave other girls pleasure. I felt cheated."

"Oh, Zoe. That wasn't a good way to be."

"I took all my clothes off and went into his room one night. I tried to get into bed with him. He laughed himself sick and told me to piss off before he spanked me."

"Oh."

"Yes, oh! And then he told Uncle Con what I'd done and Uncle Con told Mana Agnella and I wanted to die."

"Cruel!"

"That's when Mercedes started to show me what it was like,

how good it could be. It was always good with her."

"I'm sorry I couldn't help you."

Her eyes were full of tears and misery. "You could, Ron. Could you try again? Teach me what a woman really feels like with a man? I mean, slowly, gently, without another person looking on, interfering?"

"That's a big ask, Zoe. I hurt you before."

"Mercedes said it doesn't feel like that, after the first time."

It was a woman like a frightened child that Ron caressed that afternoon. He did no more than accustom her to his touch, sensitising her skin, stimulating her nerve endings until she relaxed beneath his kindly hands.

"Why am I doing this?" Ron asked himself what on earth had possessed him to be there, with a woman who bugged him, running his fingers through her great bush of hair and over her thrusting, silicone implants.

And a little devil said, "You're doing this to spite Mercedes, to make Zoe recognise that you are a better lover than her little playmate. You are doing this because it will give you power over Zoe, at a time when she wants to gain power over you."

Then Ron, knowing that Zoe was open to his suggestions and eager to go further, smacked her bottom and told her to get dressed. "We'll have another lesson tomorrow," he said. He was damned if he'd take another woman without a condom. Never again! Life was complicated enough as it was.

Ron took his time over the education of Zoe. It was weeks before he'd gentled her into actively pursuing him. And when he finally submitted to her pleas, he was kind to her. She walked with a new spring in her step and a smile on her lips. Her eyes were soft and her voice muted.

Andrew Darcy waved a finger at him and warned him against playing games with young women. "She's got a temper on her, that one. She's a woman that should have danger signs tattooed on her forehead. Don't cross her!"

"I won't. I'm just trying to make her happy."

Mike was blunter. "I'd as soon go to bed with a tiger-snake," he said. "You are protecting yourself, I hope? Got your Johnnies handy?"

"Don't need them. She's gone on the pill."

"Even the pill isn't one hundred per cent."

"What am I supposed to do? Knock it back when she's all over me?"

"You're a damned fool. You want a nice bit of slap and tickle, ask me. I know a couple of girls who are really friendly. Women that know what's what and won't take advantage."

"Liberated women? Bra burners and all that stuff?"

"Don't mock, Ron. They play the game the same way men do. Zoe comes from a different tradition. The Greeks settle things the hard way."

When summer had whimpered and cowered away, leaving a slick of sweat behind it, Zoe bought an electric blanket. By the time winter arrived, like a frisky puppy, ready to shake pond water over everyone, Zoe had half her wardrobe in Ron's closet and a green nightdress under the pillow. When the first cold fronts crossed the coast she gave up her flat and moved in, arguing that driving home in the dark on wet roads was dangerous.

Pru said nothing, because Pru didn't know. She had become accustomed to leaving the operation of the gallery in Zoe's hands and had joined Andrew on a visit to her proteges in Tasmania and Queensland.

Aristotle knew nothing because Zoe avoided him and Kostas was playing dumb. He was, however, voluble when he found Ron alone.

"How's hairy butt? She's got a ring through your nose, I see."

"Mind yours."

"It is mine. How come she's down at Margett's every night, ordering my father around, telling him Aristotle doesn't know what he's doing? And my Pa, being soft in the head, is telling his brother what Zoe's said, just as if he'd thought things through for himself. They're arguing all the time. I swear she's winding Pa up just to cause trouble."

"I hadn't noticed her interest in the restaurant."

"Told Pa Mr Darcy asked her to make sure it was up to standard! What the eff would she know about catering? She can't even toast bread."

"She told me she did a Cordon Bleu course in Paris."

"Yeah, and I warned you she was a liar, didn't I?"

"What would be the point of her saying that if it wasn't true?"

"She doesn't need a point, Ron. She does it because she likes deceiving people. She can't bloody help herself!"

Ron's fists bunched. He had an urge to snot Kostas on the nose. The young chef glanced warily at him and backed off, his hands in front of his face as if guarding against a blow.

"Sucker! That's what you are! Does she go down on you? Is that it, eh? She goes down on everyone else. Including me! Says old Aristotle taught her how to do it!"

"I don't believe you! She said her father rejected her!"

"Pig's bum, Ron. Her father'd stuff a budgie if there was nothing else handy."

Ron stared wide-eyed at Kostas. The suggestion was ludicrous. "Stuff a budgie?" He started to giggle.

"Yeah. You know what Aristotle says in the Delphi kitchen? You can beat an egg but you can't beat root! Get it?"

"Beetroot?"

"Yeah. Come on, Ron, me old mate. Get a grip on things."

Ron did not know what to believe. Only in his painting was his life secure. There he knew just what he was doing. Under his steady hands oils traced the shape of men and women, images come alive in his studies of the flesh. He knew how to manipulate under-painting to give warmth to the tones of cheeks and lips, how to fleck brightness into the eyes, how to make shadows things of mystery, not areas devoid of interest. He could make one tiny stroke and create the illusion of a smile seen in one light, yet the pout of discontent in another. A portrait by Roman was, like the Mona Lisa, never static. The eyes followed the viewer around the room, the lips trembled on an unspoken word.

His portrait of Pru Darcy was tipped for the Archibald Prize, Australia's premier art event. He was astonished and furiously angry when he learned that it had been withdrawn from the prestigious contest at the last moment.

"But why, Zoe? Why?"

"The timing is bad. I didn't want you to leave me."

"Leave you? Why would I have done that?"

"You'd have gone to the Eastern States and made your name over there. I'd have lost control."

Ron had never known such fury. He raged like a mad thing for more than an hour. By then Zoe was ready for bed. She was alluring in her silk gown, which shimmered dark green around her feet. She was sitting on the side of the divan, filing her nails.

"Anyway, I need you here," she said calmly. "We're going to get married instead."

"Married?" Ron thundered the word as if he were trying to blast her out through the tiles. "Why the hell should I marry you?"

"Because I'm expecting a baby."

"You can't be. You're on the pill!"

"I lied," she said with complacency. "I wanted what Mercedes had. I wanted you to do to me everything that you did to my darling Mercy. I wanted to know what it felt like to be her."

"Get rid of it!"

"No. I won't. She had your baby; I want mine."

"Get this into your thick skull, Zoe. I'm not going to marry you!"

She smiled like a cat with a lizard in its claws. "You will. If you don't I'll get my father to break your fingers."

"Ah, yes. Zoe, who gives head!"

"You've been gossiping with Kostas. You shouldn't believe what my cousin tells you."

"And who am I supposed to believe? The effing milkman? The Boy Scouts? The Fifth Military Districts Band?"

"I don't expect you to believe anyone. Word are cheap. Big hammers on knuckles are more effective. You see, my father'll do anything I ask him."

"Except sleep with you when you ask him?"

"I really do dislike the habit you have of remembering things I've told you." Zoe looked at him serenely. "Of course, I have an alternative suggestion, Ron. Marry me and I'll pay for you to spend three years in Paris and London. You can study in Milan and

Florence. You can have a Roman holiday! I don't need you, you know. Daddy'll look after me."

11

Emerald green; aceto-copper arsenate, is one of the most deadly pigments on the artist's palette. It was first manufactured commercially in Schweinfurt, Germany, in 1814, and is also known as Paris or Veronese green. It turns black when exposed to sulphur but can be isolated between layers of varnish. However, the natural pigment, used in Roman murals, remains stable.

If ever Ron had seriously thought of marriage, it was of himself walking down the aisle of some venerable church with a bride, in white lace, hanging off his arm. He had thought of happy faces of friends and relatives, the fun of the reception, the anticipation of a honeymoon with a shy yet eager girl.

He had not expected to sign the register in a pokey little office after a flat, dull, civil ceremony with only Kostas and Mike as witnesses. He had not expected to leave his friends in the back room of a pub while he was marched to a lawyer's office and presented with numerous documents to sign. Nor had he anticipated being locked out of his own home on his wedding night.

"That's it, then," said Zoe. "Bugger off!"

"What do you mean, bugger off?"

"I'm not having you poking me any more, causing me to miscarry like you did to Mercedes!"

Ron's jaw dropped. "But she didn't! She had the baby. You told me she had the baby. You told me the story about the miscarriage was a lie."

"Did I? Too bad. Anyway, it's your own fault. You've been doing dirty drawings again!"

"What? What on earth are you talking about?"

"I went through your sketch books. They're full of pictures of naked men and women. I won't have it. I told you I wouldn't have it!"

"You're barmy. Those are studies of the people whose portraits I'm doing. It's the way I always work. From the study of the flesh to the finished artwork. It's a matter of bones and muscles, nothing lewd about it."

"Well, you're not doing it in my home."

"Your home?"

"Yes. You've just assigned the lease to me. Didn't you read what you were signing?"

Ron, thunderstruck, shook his head.

"Tough. You can come in every day to finish the commissions in hand, then you'll have to find another studio. I need the floor space to expand the gallery."

"Does Pru know about this?"

Zoe looked a little shamefaced. "Not exactly, but she gave me a free hand to do what was necessary while she was away."

"And this...this was necessary? What about my work? What about you acting as my agent and promoting the name of Roman?"

She lit a cheroot and blew smoke in his face. "I'll still do that, Ron. You've signed over all Australian rights to me, and those of work I generate. And you were very generous with the commission you'll pay."

"Was I?"

"Yes, you were. That just leaves the matter of money. Do you want a lump sum or shall I pay you a monthly allowance?"

"I've got my own money."

"No, you haven't. It's held in trust for you by the gallery. I'll say what you get and when."

"You promised me three years in Europe."

"So I did. And I'll give you that money when you sign over all rights to the child. I don't want you having access to the baby. You'll ruin him."

"Him?"

"Yes. I had the tests. It's a boy."

Her self-satisfied smirk irritated Ron so much that he longed to smack her face but he saw the poisonous green lights in her eyes and reckoned she'd have him for assault if he so much as lifted a finger to her.

"I don't like this. I don't like it at all."

"And I didn't like having you paw me. I didn't like having to pretend to enjoy you bouncing around on me!"

"You loved it! You were begging for it!"

She sneered. "I pretended you were Mercedes. I shut my eyes and pretended."

There were tears of anger and frustration in Ron's eyes but he could not spill them, not there, on the street, outside the lawyer's office. "You, Zoe Xenos, are barking mad!"

"I, Zoe Turner, know exactly what I am doing. It's not my fault that you're a gullible prick, Ron Turner. You've served your purpose." She turned her back on him and started to walk off.

"But the portraits. I've got appointments!"

"Keep them. I'll not be around when you're there. And don't think you have access to the whole flat. I've had locks put on the doors from the studio."

The gloomy expressions on the faces of Kostas and Mike grew darker when Ron entered the bar.

"No party?" asked Mike, who was well away after sharing two jugs of lager on an empty stomach.

"More like an effing funeral. I think marrying Zoe was the stupidest thing I've ever done."

"And didn't we tell you so?"

"She's thrown me out."

"What? Already?"

"Divorce her," said Mike. "You haven't consu...consumm...damn it, shagged her yet."

"She's in the pudding club. What difference if I shagged her four months ago or today?"

Kostas looked blearily at his empty glass and held it out for Ron to fill. "She didn't tell Aristotle she was marrying you. She gave me fifty bucks to keep my mouth shut."

"What difference does that make? She's stitched me up tighter than a Christmas turkey."

"There'll be a reason," Kostas muttered. "There's always a reason even if we can't guess what it is. My li'l cousin is deep. Deep and nasty."

"Like the bottom of a cesspool," Mike added. "You wanna stay at my place?"

"Thanks," said Ron. "Some honeymoon!"

***

"You've not hung the Cootimurra pictures." Ron looked round the small flat where Mike hung his hat when off duty and felt disappointed.

"Not much point. My term as surgical registrar at the Royal finishes next month and I'm off to London. I've been offered twelve months training in cosmetic reconstruction at one of the big teaching hospitals and I'm taking it."

"Tits and bums?"

"No, correcting facial deformities. Cleft palates, hare lips, tumours on the skull, making new faces for those injured in car crashes, people disfigured by burns or by cancers. There's a huge need for specialists in Third World countries."

"You'll not get rich that way."

"What's rich? Money's not rich. Rich is the quality of the life experience. Ron, I can think of no greater reward than helping some poor kid who's been an outcast from the community because they look inhuman. Give them something like normal features again and they can assimilate. That's joy, to see the sort of smile they give. I know. We've had one or two cases over here, flown in by Rotary or other charities to see if we can help. My God, it's worthwhile work."

"Strange that I'm being pushed towards the beautiful and the famous and you're yearning to serve the poor and ugly."

"What's so strange? You're not me, I'm not you. I appreciate what you do; in time you'll understand where I'm coming from. Anyway, if you're rolling in it one day, you can sponsor a couple of kids to come to me for help."

"That's a promise."

"When do you start your travels?"

"In a few more weeks. I'm meeting Pru and Andrew at the opening of the Archibald Prize exhibition. They're ready to murder Zoe for withdrawing Portrait of Prudence Darcy. Pru's parking it with a friend in Sydney and is determined to put it up for the Doug Moran National Portrait Prize."

"Library of New South Wales?"

"That's the one. Biggest prize in Australia. One hundred thousand smackeroos!"

"That would buy a few beers."

"And I wouldn't have to cut Zoe in. It was painted on commission from Pru long before I got tied into this agent's agreement. In fact, I never asked a cent for it. It was thanks for the studio, thanks for the help, thanks for believing in me."

"Have you told them how Zoe's stitched you up?"

"No way! I've not even told them I married her. Pru will have a fit and I thought I owed it to them to break the bad news myself."

"Has Zoe coughed up the money for your study tour?"

"Yes. She bought the tickets and gave me a great wad of traveller's cheques. I'll get by."

"Do you want me to take the Vargas studies to London and place them with an agent?"

"Would you?"

"Sure. I've good contacts there. And if you sell them overseas, you'll foil Zoe. Your contract only gave her agent's fees for your Australian sales."

"My contract only gave her rights to works painted as Roman. If I sign myself Old Mother Hubbard she can't touch me."

"Big mistake on her part."

"Huge oversight. You see, Mike, if I can get established in Paris or London, I see no damn reason whatever that I should come back to Australia."

"Can you get a permanent visa?"

"Yes, thanks to Uncle Alf. I didn't know until he told me that my mother's family came from Cornwall. I qualify for a British passport."

Mike's shoulders started shaking and, presently, he gave way to his amusement and rocked with laughter. "Oh, you little beauty! She'll spit feathers!"

"She can lay a square egg for all I care!"

"Hoo, hooo, hoooo!" Mike held his sides, which were aching. "And have you got all your gear out of the attics?"

"Just about. I finished the commissions in the studios at college and Kostas helped me move the big canvases and easels up to Ephemeral last week. Kostas was pretty impressed. He said it was just the place for a dirty weekend."

"No dolly-birds. You told him, no dolly-birds."

"Yup. He was disappointed but he's agreed to go up once a month to keep the grass trimmed and the pool cleaned. I think he's planning to plant a crop of marijuana in the bushes."

"Smart move, as long as no one catches him."

"It's more likely to die because he'll forget to water it. Or the local kangaroos will go loco after nibbling it."

"You going up there again before you leave? Can I come too?"

"You're welcome. I need to fill my spirit with whatever it is in the air at Ephemeral. It's as Tamberlaine said. It's a recharge for your creative batteries. Pru should spend more time there."

"Maybe she will. Andrew said he's trying to wind down his business investments so they can retire and go off on a world cruise."

"It would do her more good to come home to the hills."

"Of course it would, but there's a huge problem with that."

"What?"

"Andrew Darcy has a phobia about heights! He says Ephemeral

makes him feel sick."

***

"I'm sure Zoe's not in," Kostas whispered. "Her car's not in the yard. "I've backed my van up to the side under the roof garden. I'll pick the lock of the studio and we can lift all the unsold Romans off the walls."

"Burglar alarms?"

"Connected to the restaurant. I've turned them off at the main power board. Now, go carefully here, Ron. We don't want you ending up among the pots and pans again."

They tip-toed through the kitchens and dining rooms to the main stairs. Kostas, a man of many skills and few moral restrictions, saw nothing wrong in taking back property which belonged to Ron. He had been incensed to learn that Zoe, once the commissioned paintings were finished, had changed all the locks to both studio and attics.

"Aunty Clemnystra should have put arsenic in her baby bottle," Kostas mused. "Or maybe she did. Maybe that's what makes her such a poisonous female."

They carried the framed works to the foyer of Margett's and stacked them inside the door, ready for loading. The attic lock gave way to Kostas' picks. Moving like mice they carried all the sketches and unframed canvases to the roof garden and wrapped the bundle in an old dustsheet which Ron kept handy to cover the floor during varnishing, as this tended to be a messy business. Kostas untied the clothes-line from the rails and used it to lower the precious haul to the ground.

"I can't get into the other half of the attics," he said. "She's got a Yale lock on the door."

"Damn. I particularly wanted to get Uncle Alf's war medals and his old Rolex watch. And there's some personal photos I'd like to have had."

"Where are they?"

"In the bedside cabinet, I think."

"There's a dormer window half open." Kostas was leaning over the roof, looking past the street-facing facade to the far end. "If I crawl along the roof above the gutters I think I can get in."

"Let me do it. It's dangerous."

"Done this sort of thing before? No, I thought not. Leave cat-burgling to the experts, will you?"

Heart in mouth, Ron watched his friend inch his way across the steeply-pitched roof, corrugated-iron giving way to tiles at mid point. He saw Kostas raise his head slowly above the level of the window and peer in. Then to his dismay, the young Greek retraced his path.

"No go," he gasped. "She's home, in bed. There's only a dim light in there, but it was enough to see she wasn't alone."

"Not alone?"

"No way. Uncle Aristotle was giving her the old one-two!"

***

The police were called in when Zoe found the studio ransacked. She, naturally, named Ron as the chief suspect.

"Search me," said Ron. "I'm as upset by this as she is. After all, it was my work which was stolen, not hers."

"You're the only one who'd gain from it," she screeched.

Ron looked sadly at the police sergeant. "Not so. All I have to do is paint some more. There's nothing catalogued that I can't reproduce."

"Your sketch books. The books full of dirty pictures. You could blackmail people with those."

"They're nude studies of people who asked me to paint them," said Ron, the voice of reason. "I couldn't use them for blackmail, as my so-called wife suggests, because the sitters know all about them and agreed to the drawings being made."

Had Zoe been the chimp she so resembled, she would have jumped up and down and bared her teeth. As it was she turned spite-filled green eyes on the sergeant and suggested he get a search warrant for the Darcy place in the hills. "He'll have taken the loot there," she bawled.

"You don't need a warrant, Sergeant. I'll take you there myself and you can hunt the place from top to bottom. I'm sure Mrs Darcy wouldn't mind."

"I'm coming too," Zoe snapped.

"You are damn well not! It's the one place on earth that you, Zoe Xenopopulis, will never set foot." He turned to the police officers. "I don't know whether this is prejudicial to my case, but I say it straight, I'd strangle that poisonous cow if she turned up at Ephemeral."

"And I," said the sergeant, as they left, "wouldn't blame you for doing so!"

Ron sat on the balcony sipping a cold lemon drink as the police peered into every cupboard, every nook and almost every cranny, including the space under the eaves. They did not find the wine cellar in the cave. Ron had made sure the bushes which concealed it had not a twig out of place.

He gazed out across the tree-tops and, like Pru, wondered what it would be like to fly. Only another day and he would know. He had already secured a window seat for he was fascinated by the thought of seeing the old brown bones of Australia from above. It was a new dimension of landscape which had been used to effect by others, such as Robert Juniper.

Juniper's 'In a Landscape' and 'Four Vignettes of Summer' had captivated Ron's mind, the expressive use of oils, acrylics and gold leaf in the famous artist's work having come as a revelation to him.

"Juniper won the Doug Moran Prize for portraiture but he's most famous for landscape," he mused. "Why must I stick to the one genre? Well, I can't, and I won't. So there."

***

That evening Kostas arrived with the loot in the back of his old jalopy. His passenger, Mike, carried a crate of beer across the bridge. "Party, party!" he crowed. "Kostas has got a pot of spag bol in the van. I'll dump this in the kitchen then give you a hand with the victims of crime!"

"You'll never guess where Mike hid this lot," panted Kostas, his arms full of boxes of paint. "We stacked them on a gurney, covered the lot with a sheet, and pushed the goodies into the mortuary. Scary, that place."

"Scary? From one who plays peeping Tom at bedroom windows?"

"Yeah, That was scary, too. I didn't know Uncle Aristotle was hung like a bull."

It was hard work, carrying paintings and books down three flights of stairs. Mike, chortling, came up for the last time with two dusty bottles of Grange Hermitage.

"Look at the vintage, man! Tamberlaine himself must have laid these down."

"Beer first," said Kostas. "You can't wet your whistle on wine."

The sun set redly, fading to an emerald green streak on the horizon in the last of the light.

"What makes Zoe tick, Mike? How can she hate her old man

and yet let him use her?"

"Sado-masochism? You always hate the one you love, as the song has it."

"Big words. The answer's simple," said Kostas. "She's nuts."

"She's nuts as far as sex goes, but she's smart in other ways."

Kostas yawned. "Yeah, smart enough to sucker you into marriage so she could get her hands on her grandmother's money. Oh, didn't I tell you?"

"I'll paint your balls red if you don't 'fess up. Tell me what?"

"Pa was talking to Mana Agnella this morning. She's spewing. They thought Grandma Sappho would leave her money to Aunt Clemnystra and it would come to the Xenopopulis line as part of her dowry and divorce settlement. Aunt Clemmie has really ditched her old man, this time, and told Grandma Sappho what her son-in-law had done. So the old cow bypassed Aristotle and left her estate to Zoe, on condition that she married before she could inherit. It's like winning the lottery."

"Holy pink potatoes! Zoe strikes gold. Then why the scene with Aristotle? You think he was trying to screw money out of her?"

"No way. I reckon he was punishing her. Big time rape of double-crossing bitch. You know Andrew Darcy's been trying to sell his business? Uncle Aristotle's been negotiating to buy the premises, restaurant, gallery and the apartment. Turns out the first thing Zoe did with her grandmother's money was make a counter-offer. The deal went through yesterday! She's pinched the goodies from under her father's nose!"

"Yeah," Mike said. "That would have been enough to annoy him, just a tad."

Ron laughed. "Yeah, for once in her life she's screwed him, not the other way round!"

PART TWO

Baroque - Rococo

12

Ultramarine blue: from the Latin, beyond the sea. Its use dates back to the 6th century in the Middle East, where it was ground from the natural semi-precious rock, Lapis Lazuli, making it the most expensive pigment in the world. The cool, deep blue was extensively used for illuminated manuscripts in Medieval times and, in painting, was reserved for the robes of Christ and the Virgin Mary. It became known as a sign of purity. However, in 1828 a synthetic pigment came on the market after a hotly contested competition to find a cheap substitute. It is manufactured from kaolin, soda ash, coal, charcoal, silica and sulphur, fired in a closed furnace, the residue being finely ground and washed to remove impurities.

The cold, dark blue of the Great Australian Bight unfolded below the wing of the aircraft. Ron, who had been enchanted by the flight across wheat-growing country, studded with salt lakes of pastel hues, like pearls scattered across the earth, had gasped at the clarity of the turquoise water on the shores of the Recherche Archipelago. Back over South Australia the patchwork of huge paddocks filled the eye to the horizon. Soon there were the dark greens of forests, slashed by ravines where light pooled in deep blue shadows, the hazy, eucalyptus smoke-green of the Blue Mountains. The grey and golden scars of rocks too steep for vegetation were abstractions known from observation of other landscapes.

It was the ocean and the seas that were a revelation. He realised that, to do them justice, he needed to review his palette. Bred in the hinterland, he had made few studies of the ocean, despite many trips on Andrew Darcy's yacht. On the Dreamdrift II he'd begun to appreciate the visual qualities of towering waves and calm backwaters, the effect of sunlight and moonlight on an ever-shifting surface and the way static objects on the shores looked at themselves in the mirrors of reflection.

Roman might see travel as the gateway to global opportunity. Ron Turner decided it made a wide, wet world of difference. "I must learn to master this new vision," he muttered. "I shall spend time painting seascapes and marine life. I shall think of the sea as another beauty whose image I must record."

Then, as the aircraft banked hard on the approach to Sydney, he saw the silver gleam of the Harbour and fastened his seat belt.

***

"You could have won the Archibald," said Pru. "It's as good as anything else that's been selected." She looked carefully at a Brett Whiteley and said, "I don't like it."

"Over the top." Andrew squinted at the startling portrait. "I prefer the Judy Cassab. What do you think, Ron?"

"Only that I've a great deal to learn. No, Pru, don't shake your head at me. I'm not suffering a crisis of confidence. It's simply that I've never before seen so many portraits together, especially of well-known personalities, and I'm amazed at the range of techniques."

"There's nothing wrong with your own!"

"Kind of you. But the possibilities! Pru, Andrew, can't you see how exciting this is for me? It's as if I've been blind and have had bandages taken off my eyes."

"That's why you're going to Europe, isn't it? To look, to learn?"

"I'm not running away from Zoe, if that's what you mean. I'd stay and confront her only I don't like her or hate her enough to bother fighting a war."

Pru sighed and sat down on a bench in the middle of the main gallery. "I'm sorry I let you in for all this trouble," she said. "I feel responsible, falling ill before the launch, letting her take the reins. I knew her father. I should have guessed what she'd be like."

Andrew, who had been carefully scrutinising a heavy impasto of a famous broadcaster, joined the discussion. "I wouldn't have sold Margett's to anyone from the Xenopopulis family if I'd known. But I left it in the hands of an agent."

"You understand, Ron, we had no intention to leave you without a studio. I intended you should have a long-term lease."

He grinned. "I got by. I'd have moved to Ephemeral if I'd been stuck in town for a longer period, but it seemed a good idea to make the break and travel. Perhaps it's for the best. At least Zoe's financing this trip. You said I should study overseas and I've been forced into doing so."

"You can rest easy on one point." Andrew took off his horn-rimmed glasses and put them in their case in his pocket. "We're revoking her power to touch the money held in trust for you. She'll be getting a lawyer's letter this week."

"You like poking sticks in wasps' nests?" Ron sounded dubious.

"My dear young man, your Zoe's a very small fish. She should be careful before she tries to swim with the sharks."

"And you're a shark?"

"Yes. Go on, say it. What big teeth you've got, Mr Darcy. All the better to gobble you up!"

"Wrong story, or am I missing something?"

"You are. When Pru ordered the renovations of the attic the builders found the roof timbers were riddled with white ants...there was termite damage everywhere. It wasn't Zoe's business and she was off choosing curtains and things. She was so desperate to beat her father to the sale she skipped having a surveyor's report. Tough. It will cost her a fortune to fix it."

Pru leaned over and pinched her husband's bottom. "Time to go home, darling. I'm worn out with walking round the exhibition. Call us a taxi, Ron, there's a dear."

It was bucketing down outside though it had been sunny earlier. Ron, huddled into a plastic mackintosh but unable to stop drips trickling down his neck, joined a queue. He glanced round as he reached the hot spot and waved to the Darcys.

"The weather in Sydney can be the pits," Pru said, gazing miserably at the rain-slicked streets. "Come up to our suite, Ron. There's something we need to talk to you about."

She kicked off her damp shoes and curled up on a settee. "We've cancelled our cruise. I've had a lump in my breast for ages but was told it was nothing to worry about. But the family doctor is an idiot."

"Mike was worried about you."

"I know. He wanted me to take tests but I wouldn't."

"You're an obstinate woman," Andrew said, pouring drinks for everyone. "You don't deserve your gin and tonic."

"No, I don't, but I don't deserve breast cancer either. I'm having them both off and then a long course of chemotherapy. We'll stay in Sydney. We'll fly over to Europe later in the year when I've recovered. Paris next springtime, not this. Yes? You'll meet us there?"

"I don't know where I'll be in the New Year. Zoe only bought me a ticket as far as Athens."

"Cheapskate! Beware of Greeks bearing gifts. Isn't that what they say, Andrew?"

"Probably, but unless Ron's hidden Zoe in his suitcase, it's not applicable."

Ron looked puzzled.

"The Trojan Horse," said Pru. "You must have heard of the Trojan Horse?"

Ron grinned in sudden understanding. "I thought you were talking about the runners in last year's Melbourne Cup."

"Idiot!"

"But it's all right. I'll do the Aegean first, then you know the widow Con wants Kostas to marry...Helene Pappas? I'm going to stay with her in Macedonia for the summer. They've got the immigration papers through but she's got cold feet. I've promised to talk her round."

"I don't like the thought of you wandering off on your own. Do you speak Greek?"

"I've got a phrase book. Look, don't mother hen me, Pru. You can get in touch with me through Mike at the London hospital. He'll always know where I am. He's booked straight through to UK, bar a couple of stopovers. He's taking the pin-ups with him."

"I'll drop him a line with a few likely contacts. Since Alberto Vargas died there's been no one to fill that niche market. You could strike lucky. Paint some more like that."

"Don't pressure him, Andrew. When we join you in Paris I'll find you some models. I've been asked to attend a reunion at the Paris Opera Ballet and I'm sure I can persuade the corps de ballet to pose for you."

"What, all at once?"

The gurgle of laughter was all Ron needed to hear. Despite the shocking news of her condition...which he had been half-expecting...it was clear her spirits were high.

"We won't be able to see you off at the airport," she said. "I've a tiresome date with a surgeon. But we've bought you a bon voyage gift. You'll have no time to paint and sketch everything you want to, so take photographs, hundreds of them. It's a point and shoot Pentax but there's a close-up lens for portraits. Point and click, point and click. And there's a dozen films to get you going."

Ron gave her a huge hug and shook Andrew's hand. "Paris in springtime, then. It's a promise."

***

The poets were right to describe the Aegean as a wine-dark sea, thought Ron, washing the acrylics off his palette in the shallows at the edge of the pebble-strewn beach. The cool, blue liquid stained the clear sea-water while the remains of the reds and yellows he'd used for painting the fishing boats swirled off into the depths.

The light was gone. His portable easel, which unfolded like a book to be propped on his legs or on a rock or a chair, whatever came in handy, was tucked into the canvas back-back he used on days when the muse took charge. The finished painting was almost dry and he knew it was one of his best studies of the Greek coastline. It was one he would wrap and post to Mike, ready for a solo exhibition just before Christmas.

"That's when people are shopping for presents and a touch of Mediterranean sunshine will be popular," he'd said, when they talked on the phone as soon as Ron had mastered the peculiarities of the Greek communications network. More net than work, Ron maintained.

The paintings which did not meet his high standards were laid out on the beach beside him as he started a new study. Most sold to passing tourists, who would watch, fascinated, for long periods. Ron did not ask high prices, except from fat pigs.

There were too many fat pigs this season, the fishermen told him. They came down from the northern countries, looking for good time boys. Greeks, since classical times, had a reputation for homosexuality. The Spartan ideal of love was man to man or, come to that, woman to woman. But that, they said was a question of the heart. What the fat pigs were after were boys too young to know the difference and ones too poor to have any alternative. This season the predators were casting their lures too wide and were propositioning young men of good families and strict morals. There had been incidents where young girls had also been approached.

The fishermen were wary of Ron at first, especially when he asked permission to paint some of the children. They stood guard while he did so, spitting melon seeds in the sand or whittling away at wood to make floats for nets. They repaired lobster pots with one eye on the cane and another on the artist. Now he was accepted as one of them and was quite likely to be asked to mind the children while the wives went to the market.

"Carry your bag, Ron?" said Alexandar, Helene's son, in halting English. He was only ten-years-old, a cheery urchin with the luck of the devil when it came to fishing. He held up a net of gleaming silver herring. "You come eat with us."

"I'll bring wine."

"And cola drink? Good-oh?"

"She'll be apples, mate!"

Ron wondered if Kostas knew about Alexandar. Helene was still grieving for her husband and found Ron's presence a comfort, for he chopped wood and dug in the garden, but made no unwanted suggestions. He would not do that to Kostas. He had won the bride-to-be's confidence and Alexandar was fired up at the thought of life in a new country. Ron was, the villagers agreed, a gentleman, even if he was an Australian. He disliked the fat pigs as much as they did.

It was Ron, in the end, who provoked the incident which brought the police down on them. A fat pig exposed himself to Alexandar one evening and offered him a handful of foreign currency. Alexandar spat on the man and ran for Ron, who jumped to his feet and threw turps up the pig's snout. The honking and hollering attracted attention. The crew of the Argos pulled their boat onto the shingle and converged on the foreigner, who was staggering around trying to clear his eyes. Suddenly there was a knife in the pig's hand and the fishermen growled in anger. The blades they used for gutting fish were razor sharp. Who did what to whom in the ensuing fracas was anyone's guess. But it was the fat pig who was taken away in a ramshackle ambulance to have his wounds stitched. The local doctor patched up everyone else. By the time the law arrived everyone in the village had been struck dumb.

"Me know nothing either," said Ron. "Efaristo poli!"

Helene kissed his cheek but packed his bags. "Better go before the fat pig comes back with more animals. Tell Kostas I will come one day. Not this year. Maybe next."

By August Ron had worked his way around the coast, passed from family to family, from friend to friend, as if he were a prized possession. Indeed, his drawings of the children were highly valued, though it was his paintings of the old men and the young peasant girls which attracted most admiration. He shook his head when his models asked to buy the results.

"For exhibition in London," he explained, and got someone to translate. The word went out. The watchers would look and nod and mutter, "Ah, good one. For London!"

He painted the harvesters in the fields and the women with baskets of grapes. He took photographs of men mending nets and girls spinning wool from a spindle as they walked behind the herds of sheep being driven along the road. He had images of ancient monuments and a mind filled with the mythology of the Greek Gods.

He rode a donkey part way up Mount Olympus and took a bus to Delphi. There, at the site of the Oracle, which had prophesied the fate of men and deity alike, he asked why she had not spoken to him while he toiled over the dishes at the restaurant which bore her name.

"You could have warned me about Zoe," he murmured.

And a voice in his head replied, "Kostas warned you but you did not listen."

***

When the leaves on the grape vines which covered the trellis over the back yard at the taverna, one of those at which he'd been staying since leaving the Pappas home, turned red and brown, Ron felt the tug of a newer civilisation. Not a better one, he thought. Just a newer one. Having landed at Athens with strong prejudices against the Greeks, and a particular dislike of dolmades, he had found a way of life which had changed little in centuries. Greece had survived despite the ravages of the Second World War, despite political chaos, despite the attempts by Turkey to reclaim land it had once ruled with the restrictive rod of Islam and the harsher rules of Greek Orthodoxy, in spite of the intrusive, culturally-eroding tide of tourism. Not only had Greece produced heroes and men of science, philosophers and artists, but she had retained much of their wisdom. It was as wine-dark and warm as the Aegean Sea.

Winds blowing from the north sent the fat pigs home to beer and sausages. The beaches were deserted and, at last, he could wander around the Acropolis without being jostled by crowds. He hitched a lift to Corinth, heading for the port from which ferries ran to Italy. The ferries were crowded with refugees from the wars raging between ethnic groups in the former Yugoslavia. He saw their need and changed his mind.

"I'm scrapping the plan for a Roman holiday," he told Andrew, during his regular weekly phone call. "I never liked the idea in the first place. Summer's over. It would be miserable in winter."

"Good. Pru and I would like to do the Italian experience with you next year. She's feeling much better, especially now she's found a wig she likes."

Ron chuckled. "Bright red?"

"No. She's gone blonde and curly. Says the treatment makes her feel light-headed so she may as well look like an airhead. Are you short of money, Ron?"

"No. I've hardly touched my travellers' cheques. My paintings are paying my way. I've sent dozens back to Mike."

"Then why are you set on this solo exhibition? Pru thinks you should hold off until she gets there. She wants to curate it properly."

"Mike will go ape. He says the spare bedroom is nearly full of my gear, though he's given the acrylics of Mercedes to the man you suggested."

"Then tell him to put your work in a lock-up. Get Pickfords to store them for you. Why don't you head south around the Mediterranean over winter and see Turkey, Israel, Egypt, North Africa? At least that will keep the chill out of your bones."

"Sound thinking. I ought to head north to Macedonia again, anyway. I ought to see Helene and Alexandar Pappas again. I've been putting off a trip to Thessalonika. It's what you might call a marital obligation. I ought to visit my mother-in-law. Maybe she can help me understand Zoe."

The Attic idyll ended when Ron took a bus into the mountains and walked the rocky footpaths to the nunnery where Clemnystra

Xenopopulis had taken refuge.

It was not a closed order, Kostas had said. Aunt Clemnystra, who was now known as Sister Clement, after a pontiff of that name, would be pleased to see him, said the sacristan. She directed him to a courtyard where, on a bench beneath a venerable olive tree, sat a small woman, her head covered with a dark blue shawl.

"So! You're my Zoe's husband, are you? More fool you!"

He was taken aback and said nothing. He simply sighed and sat on the grass beside his mother-in-law.

She asked after the health of Constantine and Kostas. She did not mention her husband or Mana Agnella. She asked after numerous acquaintances from her time in Australia and told him the reasons she did not like working at the Delphi. She held up hands twisted with arthritis.

"Why are you here?" she asked, drawing her skirts together as if ready to rise.

"I thought you should know that Zoe's going to have a baby next month. You'll be a grandmother."

She laughed scornfully. "Is that what she told you? Did no one warn you that Zoe tells lies? Zoe can't have children. And do you know why?"

Ron, stunned, shook his head.

"Because my husband abused her and made her pregnant. Because she told no one until she was too far gone for a legal abortion, but Mana Agnella insisted and did the job herself. She butchered Zoe. The shame of it! She had to have an operation or she'd have died from infection. That, Ron Turner, is why I left Australia. And that, Ron Turner, is why you are a damn fool if you think Zoe is carrying your seed!"

The long silence vibrated in the air. But, stifling his bitterness, Ron spoke gently to Sister Clement. "You weren't much of a mother, were you? Why didn't you protect your daughter? You must have known what Aristotle was like. You must have suspected what was going on."

"I never wanted a daughter. I wanted a son. I didn't want to marry Aristotle. I was in love with Constantine, his brother."

"The father of Kostas?"

"The very same, but the family arranged things otherwise. Aristotle was the first born and I was the one who had a big dowry."

"But why did you not love your baby? You must have felt love for Zoe when she was born."

"Why should I? She was a breech birth. She put me through hell being born just as her father put me through hell conceiving her. I never encouraged him again. I might have submitted, but never willingly. I put up with his women. Rather them than me, I thought."

"And was it that way with Zoe, too? Rather her than you?"

She turned on him a look of shame and chagrin combined. "At least it was in the family," she hissed. "I didn't have to put up with the fear of his tarts sneaking in the back door or worrying the neighbours might discover he'd been out all night, carousing."

"Is that why you emigrated? So people wouldn't find out?"

"He hadn't started with Zoe then, not properly. But I could tell how it would be."

"Poor Zoe."

Her eyes burned with malice. "Poor Zoe, poor Zoe! She loved it. She loved humiliating me! And I bet she loved humiliating you!"

"Yes, but I'm not humble," he replied. "I feel used, as used as a sheet of toilet tissue, if you must know, but I'm flushing that down the S-bend of experience. It's you who is still suffering. Is that why you've come here? To escape the past? To do penance?"

"But I haven't escaped the past, have I? You've brought it all back to me. Why did you come here, Ron Turner, Zoe's plaything?"

His smile was ambiguous. "Oh, for much the same reason as you came back to Greece. I'm running away from your daughter and your bloody husband!"

13

*Egyptian blue; one of the earliest man-made pigments, a
calcium copper silicate, appearing in Egyptian
hieroglyphics and tomb paintings from 3100 BC. It was
also used in Mesopotamia and in Roman times, from
which it draws its other name, Pompeian blue, being found
in frescos painted before the ancient city was buried under
volcanic ash in 79 AD. This blue, used mainly for royal
robes, is a lightfast, stable and non-toxic pigment It is
made by mixing calcium carbonate with copper
compounds or malachite and heating them at high
temperature with a silica flux for up to one hundred hours.*

"Step into the shoes of old Alberto, my son," yelled Mike, on a
bad connection to Cairo. "Andrew's contact has sold the Vargas
lookalikes. PanAsia Airway's In Flight Magazine snapped them up
and are planning to print them in a calendar for next Christmas.
And he's also lined up a contract with Immortelle, the French
Perfumiers, who want you to paint a series of Parisienne beauties
for their new range of Chique toiletries. What should I do?"

"Sign up. It's why I gave you power of attorney, isn't it? To act
on my behalf while I'm away? Take your cut, pay the commission
and book us a table at the Ritz when I get to London."

"PanAsia wants another series for '87. They want one of a girl
from each of the countries to which they fly. Miss Thai, Miss
Cambodia, Miss Japan and so forth."

"Do they want me to go there?"

"They're offering you a Platinum Pass flight card...go
anywhere, any time. But they say they can bring air hostesses to
your studio in London if that's more convenient."

"You didn't tell them my studio was a tent in the desert, did you?"

"Is it? When you rang last you were still raving about the Pyramids and blue-painted Pharoahs."

"Now I'm going off with blue-painted Tuaregs. riding camels across the Sahara. I'll ring you from the next oasis! Though they've probably not heard of the telephone in Libya."

"Don't believe it. You bet old Colonel Quaddafi's on the phone to the bloody terrorists every day. And the Yanks will be blowing in his ear shouting pack it in or we'll paste you."

"Bastard. I'd thought about flying from Athens to Cairo when I first arrived. Glad I didn't. I wouldn't have fancied being hijacked and seeing Beirut to Algiers four times."

"Watch yourself, Ron. They don't like Americans in that part of the world."

"But I'm Australian."

"Yes, but they don't know the difference. You've been in Israel recently. You'll be suspect. You still painting?"

"Tried it but even oils dry out too fast. Strictly a camera job. Travelling light. Having trouble getting the women to pose. I'll be all right with the Tuaregs. Their women don't wear the veil, but the series from Jerusalem is the last you'll get for some time. Hard to draw when you're lurching around on the back of a dromedary. How's your love life?"

"Like yours, I guess. Parched. Did you know that ninety-nine per cent of men who've tried Camel prefer women?"

"Bugger that!"

"That's what they thought."

Ron, to whom Mike's stale jokes were a constant trial, passed messages to the Darcys. "Tell Pru I'm thinking of her and remind her we've got a date."

"Bunches of them, I bet. Don't forget they're diuretic."

"Yeah. When you gotta go, you gotta go! Cheers." He hung up. He wasn't going to admit to Mike that he was in a club with a dubious reputation and a nice line in dancing girls. Ron was not carrying a case of celibacy in his travel baggage. He was, he said, studying the flesh in all its variation, from the slender, brown Tunisian houris to the dark-skinned beauties of Ethiopia. He was being educated far beyond the imagination of even Mercedes. But he never forgot his first encounter with the female of the species.

***

In early December he sloshed into the lobby of Mike's Knightsbridge apartment like a drowned rat, wearing filthy jeans and wet sandshoes. He had a hand-woven blanket over his shoulders and a French Foreign Legion kepi on his head. He paid off the taxi-driver who was unloading rucksacks and travel bags, while he grappled with a cumbersome pile of canvases.

"Where the hell have you dropped in from?" Mike said. "I thought you were in Spain for the rest of the year."

"But the rain in Spain doesn't fall mainly on the plain. It tips it down on me."

"It's no drier in London."

"But you won't expect me to eat onions, will you? And I never want to see another paella in my life."

"Fish and chips?"

"Fine. Now help me get this gear up those stairs. You planning on raising mountain goats, or something?" He staggered off with an armful of paintings.

"Not your usual stuff." Mike glanced at a few which had broken free of their wrappings.

"No. I'm in love."

"Who with this time?" They clattered down the stairs together and grabbed a couple of bags apiece.

Ron flopped into a chair and threw Mike a goatskin of red wine which he unearthed from the largest bag. "Not who. What. Atlanta. I thought I'd had my fill of the sea after Greece, but then I came across the Straits of Gibraltar and met the wild waters of the Atlantic. I worked my way round the coast to Cadiz and the Algarve. The power of it, Mike. The sheer power of wind and wave! You think I've caught the atmosphere?"

He took the canvases from their wrappings and propped them up around the walls. Mike was awed by the great swirling impressions of the ocean at its vicious moments, the rollers crashing against jagged rocks and the foam flying high in the storm-dark skies. There were the uninhibited strokes and thick impasto of Van Gogh at the height of his career.

But Mike scowled. "They're funking magnificent, but what are you going to do with them, Ron? You're turning into a dabbler. You send me magical paintings from Greece, you paint brilliant studies of Palestine and the people, you stay in Morocco long enough produce a series of Vargas-type studies which I've sold to Cosmos International. I liked the four bull-fighting studies and the flamenco group. They're in the Roman genre. Then you breeze in here with bloody seascapes and expect me to go ooh, aah. Why the hell weren't you here working on the PanAsia commission?"

"I was finding myself."

"Crap. You were pissed or high on hashish."

"Both, I expect. Why?"

"Listen, man. Don't give me any of your arty-farty airy-fairy bulldust. It's no different for you than it is for me and others like me. You've got a talent for painting. I've got a talent for doctoring. When I qualified I could have gone on to become a general practitioner, or a psychiatrist, or a brain surgeon. I could have trained as a consultant in cardiology, anaesthetics, paediatrics, stomach disorders or I could have decided to spend my life sticking my finger up men's bums. That's a proctologist. Looks after your prostate. But I had to make a choice. I chose reconstructive surgery and I'm getting good at it."

"And I'm not good at what I do?"

"Yes, you damn well are, but you can't do everything. You can be good in a lot of different genres, but you need to become excellent in a few of them. And, as for finding yourself, I can give you directions. It's between your legs. Keep on wanking it, Ron, because that's all you'll amount to if you don't learn discipline."

"I could do seascapes as Norma. I don't have to compromise Ron or Roman."

"And you can paint flowers as Moron, or kitten plates as Return. What you've got is like a multiple personality disorder. See a shrink or get a grip on things." Mike got up and slammed his bedroom door. He came out in a heavy duffle coat and a scarf swathed round his neck.

"It's not that I'm not glad to see you, mate, but I'm on duty. I've just rung in and there's a burns case coming in from a fire in Hammersmith."

"There's a burns case right here," Ron muttered. "You dealt me a scorcher, my friend."

***

The Thames flowed, grey and oily, past the wharf near Chelsea, where Ron had found a studio on the top level of a converted warehouse. He'd been assured there was plenty of good north light from panels set into the pitch of the roof and that the view from the picture windows could be masked by sliding screens if it proved a distraction or let in unwanted sunbeams.

The agents had not warned him that even a heavy frost could obscure the skylights nor that it could make it impossible to move ice-fast rollers. The large room was as cold as a morgue. Even the golden linseed oil was sludgy in its bottles. He'd arrived that morning to find the squirrel hair brushes, vital for the PanAsia acrylics, frozen stiff in the jar of rinsing water.

The tap above the sink was frozen but Ron had left a full kettle on the gas stove. He tried to light it, without success. Even the bottled gas was too cold to flow. Cursing, he opened the vacuum flask of hot water he'd brought from Mike's kitchen. He poured it slowly over the gas bottle until a soft hiss indicted success. The stove worked. The kettle boiled. He took it outside to the fire escape and let it trickle down the unlagged main water-pipe. The last cupful went on the inside tap which, stiffly but surely, allowed an icy stream to pour into the now empty kettle.

Only then was Ron able to boil enough for a cup of instant coffee. He went round the paraffin oil stoves, making sure the wicks were properly trimmed, hoping they would warm the room enough for his morning model to risk taking off her clothes.

The young Thai hostess was a new recruit. She was not yet acclimatised to European weather. There was no joy in painting a girl whose skin was all goosebumps and whose cold discomfort showed on her face. There had been no such problem with the Japanese beauty, who had posed behind an ornate parasol. Ron had suggested the accessory for, although her face was quite exquisite, her breasts were those of a young boy. He could have enhanced the curves, not revealing them completely, but by suggesting they were nicely rounded.

"Why don't you do that?" she'd asked.

"For the same reason you haven't had cosmetic surgery. I like things natural and you are very lovely as you are."

She smiled, the slow, charming smile of the geisha, all promise and no delivery. "They get bigger if they are excited," she murmured.

"I'll bet," muttered Ron, who had a deadline to meet. "I'll bet you're as pointed as Mt Fuji when your boyfriend's around. Does he like to ski on you?"

She blushed but lost her shyness and allowed Ron to pose her figure to the best, but discreet, advantage. Her only complaint was that his hands were cold.

Miss Thai was a more difficult proposition. She was quite heavy-chested. The plan was to paint her wearing the charming garlands of orchids that were made to welcome travellers but, no matter how he positioned them, they kept slipping into her cleavage and revealing her interesting bits. The hint of a nipple might be acceptable to PanAsia, but not the full bud. Exasperated, Ron had bought an dozen stalks of silk orchids which she could carry in her arms, thus preserving her modesty.

I'll have to get my Norma me to paint the blooming flowers, he thought. I can only afford a couple of real ones.

He had been so struck by the truth of Mike's critique that, when transferring his work to the studio from his tiny bedroom and the lock-up unit, he had stacked the various genres together. Romans stood against Romans, the Return seascapes, the pretty girl Rons after Vargas, the Norma floral studies, the landscapes and the studies of streets old before Christ, were grouped roughly. He recalled that, in Australia, were hidden the assorted pen and washes, pencil drawings, and impressions of the Outback which had not sold in the early weeks of the exhibition. Put them together and, he knew, an expert eye would judge them for what they were...a facile display of talent.

Only in the serious portraits of men and women at work and at play did he feel an honesty pulsating from the canvas. The fishermen of Greece and the spinners, weavers and housewives of the villages of Asia Minor had been joined by the old Rabbi at the Wailing Wall. A Sabra, an Israeli woman-soldier, proud in her uniform, on guard at the Gaza Strip, was flanked by a rare study of Yasser Arafat and another of a Lebanese refugee, anger etched in his eyes. There were paintings of camel-drivers from Cairo and rug-makers in Turkey, of men at the dyeing vats near Carthage, pulling lengths of deep blue material from the open air tubs of colour which, from adjacent roofs, looked like a giant palette of primary hues.

He'd painted boys with sheep. a young girl selling canaries in the souk, women laughing at the wells as they drew water, hesitant at allowing him to see their faces. It was rare for their men to approve this unveiling but some were poor and infidel money meant more at the moment than the dictates of the Koran. The houris had no such qualms, for they knew they were already damned.

Ron, who greatly admired Robert Inkpen's studies of Australian Battlers, knew the collection was at least as good. The bull-fighters and gypsy dancers did not look out of place in such company, nor did the peasant boy with the Spanish donkey, playing Sancho Panchez to an ancient Don Quixote with his arms filled with a basket of tomatoes.

"Very impressive," said a voice from the doorway. "No, don't hide them, Ron. I want to see what you've been doing in the past six months."

Zoe, dressed in chinchilla fur with a matching hat, peered at him with an intense gaze. She looked different. It took him a minute to realise she was wearing coloured contact lenses, lenses which reflected sapphire lights instead of the green-flecked hazel he was used to seeing.

"Invite me in, then. Or are you going to slam the door in my face?"

"I didn't expect you."

"Why not? I'm still your agent."

"Only for Australian sales."

"And for works commissioned through me. Read the fine print. Have you any commissions as Roman?"

"Not yet. I'm not known."

"Of course you're not. Careless of Mrs Darcy to let you loose on your own. How is she?"

"Recovering."

"I can find you work."

"I've got work. My model is due soon."

Zoe stepped in front of the easel and looked at the part-finished portrait. "Quite charming. Rather theatrical and stylised. I liked the Mercedes paintings better, but then I liked Mercedes. The tart's not coming, by the way. I met her outside and sent her home."

"Dammit! She flies out tomorrow and her schedule won't see her back in London for two weeks."

"Tough. Anyway, it's too cold in here to expect sitters to pose in the nude for your dirty daubs."

"They sell for squillions."

"So that's the price you put on your soul, Ron Turner? Squillions? Where are the Mercedes paintings?"

"Andrew Darcy found a buyer for them." Ron was not about to reveal to her the PanAsia deal.

"You said they weren't for sale. So where's my commission,

then."

"They were painted at Pru Darcy's place with materials paid for by her and finished weeks before you tricked me into signing that agency agreement."

"I should expect no better from a thief, I suppose," she said, calmly. "Why did you think you needed to steal your own work?"

"Oh, I don't know. It seemed like a good idea."

"I expect Cousin Kostas put you up to it. And was it Kostas who suggested you visit my mother?"

"You've been to Greece?"

"Round and about. Buying works by Ron. I like your sketches of the children. I bought dozens."

"They were thank you presents to the parents for their hospitality. They wouldn't sell them."

"I gave them photocopies. They didn't cost much."

"Why did you want them? You don't like children."

"Because I can't have any? Illogical, dear husband. Let's just call it an investment in you, shall we?"

"Hypocrite!"

"I couldn't buy the picture of Alexandar. Helene wouldn't sell. I hear you painted her. Where's the portrait?"

"I sent it to Kostas. It was a birthday present."

She stood and walked across to the stacked paintings. She said nothing as she went through them. Her lip curled as she passed judgement. "Do you cook the same way that you paint, Ron? Throw everything in the one pot and hope it will taste good together?"

"What's wrong with that?"

"They make pig swill the same way."

"Oh, thanks very much."

"Now about these commissions. The Pan Hellenics have seen some of your work. They want a portrait of Andreas Papandreou for their headquarters."

"Never heard of him."

"He's the Premier of Greece. He's in London next week for a conference. He's a friend of my father's. These are the times he's available. He'll come here but tidy the place up a bit, Ron."

There is a type of chameleon which sits on a wall, waiting for prey to come within reach of its extendable tongue. Ron felt as if he were a fat grub about to become dinner for a scaly predator.

Zoe ignored his obvious reluctance. "I've lined up Nana Mouskouri and Melina Mercouri. That's the Greek connection, for now."

"I'm too busy."

"Twaddle, Ron. The big project will start in the spring. I'm talking to Bob about Art Aid. There's no reason artists can't raise money for starving Africans if musicians and sports stars can do it."

Ron protested. "Charity can't fill the mouths of everyone who's hungry. What's needed is a charity for the children who've been orphaned by AIDS."

"Yes. I like that. Focussed. Bob would buy that. You'll start off with his portrait and then charge quarter of a million to charity for every other celebrity you paint. You'll only take your costs out of the money but the publicity will be huge. There'll be other artists involved but I want Roman to be the leading artist. After all, it was your idea, wasn't it?"

"No, it bloody well wasn't."

"You didn't hear me very well, did you? I said, 'It was your idea.' Oh, dear. You'll have to be coached. You really do need someone to organise your life."

"You're not staying, are you? What about Margett's Restaurant and the Gallery?"

"Oh, tush! I should have told you. I sold at a profit to Uncle Constantine!"

The sensation of a quicksand sucking at his legs came over Ron. "You're going to live in London?"

"Oh, no. It would cramp my style. I'm going to Paris. Remember the Sinatra song, *I love Paris in the Springtime*? It's close enough for me to keep an eye on you, beloved, and it's where I'll find civilised company."

"The Darcys will be there in April."

"What fun. I'll enjoy crossing swords with them. I don't like cheats and they sold me that place without telling me about the white ants."

"And I don't like cheats who trick me into marrying them."

She turned the flat blue gaze on him and smiled. "Them? Plural? Who else has been twisting you around, Ron? I thought you were my own special victim!"

14

Prussian blue; despite the inclusion of a cyanide molecule in this pigment, it is not toxic. The colour was first manufactured in 1704 in Berlin by a fairly simple process in which a solution of potassium ferricyanide is mixed with iron chloride. The resulting precipitate is then washed and the residue ground with oil to make the first of the modern blues. It is very dark, has good permanence and is still used extensively.

"It's like being in the bloody army. Do this, do that, be here, go there. Who the hell does Zoe think she is? Hitler? Zeig Heil, Zoe. Jawohl, Zoe. Ve haf vays of making you vork?"

Mike told him to shut up. "You're getting hellish boring, Ron. If you ask me, which you won't, Zoe's doing you good. At least you've stopped tinkering around. You've nearly finished the new PanAsia series. Do they like it?"

"Yes. Have I shown you the proofs of the calendar? I thought they'd use it last Christmas. I didn't realise there was such a long lead-in from agreement to publication. But they are going to feature Mercedes on the cover of the June issue, with an order form for the calendar so companies can buy in bulk for their customers, as Pirelli do."

"The tyre people? Hey, there's a huge demand for those. Like hen's teeth in every men's clubroom."

"PanAsia reckon theirs will be every bit as popular. They want to put me on a five-year contract. Zoe hasn't twigged. You'll carry on investing the fees for me?"

"Sure. How's the Papandreou job going?"

Ron laughed. "Fine now, but you should have seen the look on his face when I told him to strip off. Zoe nearly had a fit...she baby-sits the celebrities...so I threw her out because she was the cause of the embarrassment. We got on swimmingly after that. He's a great man. He's quite a guy. Did you know he took a law degree at Harvard and served in the US Navy?"

"Hell, Ron, I didn't know who he was until you told me."

"He wants to mount an exhibition of my Greek paintings in Athens next summer. I gave him a painting of boats at Corfu."

"You gave him one?"

"Yeah. It's an investment in the future. He wants me there in August to paint his wife. Not a formal portrait...on the beach or in the gardens, like the studies I made of the ordinary Greeks. And he wants charcoal sketches of his children."

"Nice. Talking of children, how's yours?"

Ron looked blank. "Mine?

"Yes, yours."

"I told you. That was a Zoe nonsense."

Mike raised his eyebrows. "Not hers. The baby you had with Mercedes. Out of nappies by now. Walking, I expect. Don't you have any interest in the kid?"

"Christ, Mike, I never even thought about it. After Zoe told me Mercedes had miscarried I blanked that episode from my mind."

"That's a pretty irresponsible attitude, isn't it?"

Ron's cheeks burning, he rested his head in his hands and felt ashamed. "What should I do?"

"Ask Zoe. I expect she keeps in touch with her buddy."

"Zoe wouldn't necessarily tell me the truth."

"Then write to her mother. Mrs General Ihza Dinegoro, or

whatever he's called. Write care of the Indonesian Government. That'll find her."

"I don't want my life complicated by Mercedes again."

"Says you! At least she's easy on the eye, unlike Zoe." Mike carried the breakfast things through to the small kitchen while Ron put the milk and marmalade in the refrigerator. He caught the drying-up cloth Mike threw at him and did his share of the chores.

"You are coming to the hospital with me today, aren't you? I really need your help with this young Bangladeshi woman. She's got this terrible growth on her cheekbone and it's distorted the whole of her face. But she's scared stiff of having the operation."

"And you want me to draw her as she'd look after it was done?"

"Could you do that?"

"I think so. It's as you taught me, look at the bones, look at the muscles on top of the bones, then add the flesh and the skin tones. You tell me what you intend to cut away and rejoin and I'll do my best."

The London Institute of Plastic Surgery was an annexe of one of the great teaching hospitals, and was an ultra modern building set in spacious grounds.

"The Germans very considerately dropped a five-hundred-pounder on the Victorian mansion that was here before. It didn't get built on earlier because there was a dispute about the estate. The old lady left the property to a charity for retired gentlewomen, but the last of them sold the land to LIPS and lived it up on the Riviera until her death last year."

"LIPS?"

"Acronym. Someone wanted to call it the London University Medical Plastic Surgery but they felt LUMPS was inappropriate, even though getting rid of them is part of what we do."

"You crease me, Mike."

"Well, hang on to your sense of humour while you're on the wards. You'll see things that'll turn your stomach."

Masked and gowned, Ron followed his friend on his rounds. He felt physically sick in the burns treatment room, where nurses were changing the dressings on skin grafts. He wanted to cry in sympathy when he heard the agony of those whose charred, dead skin was being scrubbed away. In the cranio-surgical theatre's observation gallery, he watched a surgeon, with delicate precision, lift a pedicle of skin and muscle, still attached to a patient's abdomen, and shape it into a nose. The centre of the Venezuelan child's face was a yawning gap where a tropical bug had eaten away the flesh.

"He'll never be lovely but he'll be able to breathe properly and live some sort of a life," said Mike. "We'll replace the top jaw later with a section of rib. Then it's over to the dental prosthetists to make him dentures. Long job, Ron, but then, they often are."

"Wouldn't it be kinder to..."

"Just let them die? How would you feel if you were deformed? Looks aren't everything, Ron. You spend too much time chasing the ideal of beauty."

"Not true. You know I love painting faces with character. Old people, warts and all."

"Never seen one study of an ugly subject."

"No. Golda Meier's dead and Zoe won't pose for me!"

The tour ended at the ward where the girl Mike called May was resting, on her side, staring through the window. She had pulled the blankets up to her chin and only part of the left profile could be seen. Her hair was glossy and shone with dark blue tints, the skin was clear and the brown cheeks were flushed like the bloom on a peach. Long lashes fringed one dark eye and the visible corner of her mouth was soft and gentle.

When May sat up, Ron suppressed a gasp of horror. The tumour on her cheek was huge. It had pushed her right eye to one side and had distorted the nose, which lay twisted to one side, the nostrils closed by the pressure. Skin from the jaw had been forced into a jowl below her face, and her teeth had grown crooked and rotten on that side.

She was one quarter beauty and three quarters monster. A great bubble of pity choked Ron's throat and he was unable to do more than offer her a tentative smile. Mike took her hand and spoke reassuringly. An elderly nun, who had accompanied May to Britain, translated and relayed the reply in a soft Irish brogue.

"She is eager for the man with magic in his fingers to show her what she will look like one day," the Sister said. "Tell me how you want her to sit and Dr Carney and I will leave you alone."

"Tell me first what you mean to do, Mike. I wouldn't want to raise false hopes in her."

"The tumour should lift off in one piece. We're pretty sure it's a hard, solid mass of bone-like growth and it may come clean off the cheekbone. We're not sure how much damage there is to the underlying structure but we're assuming the eye will drift back into its normal position once the obstruction is gone. How much sight she'll have left we don't know. It depends if the optic nerve has been pinched too much and whether nerves and blood vessels below the tumour are involved."

"That's a lot of ifs."

"Sorry. We think we'll have to rebuild the bridge of the nose. We can add cartilage by working from the inside of the nostril so there'll be no scars there, but I don't think we can avoid some disfigurement of the cheek. If there's enough slack in the skin over the tumour we may be able to hide the facial scar in the hairline. That's how we'll work. We'll peel the right side of her face back from the side, take out the unnatural matter and then close across it. No rejection of foreign tissue that way. It will be all her own bits and pieces which complete the jigsaw."

Ron did his best. He projected the unmarked features onto the ruined face and used his imagination to guess how May might look. He was careful not to gloss over what might remain as imperfections. He was no more capable of falsehood in this art than he had been over enhancing the cup size of the Japanese air hostess.

He put the final shading on the picture as Mike and the Sister re-entered the room. He passed the sketch to them and the Sister gave it to May. The young woman said nothing. A large tear gathered in her left eye and ran down her cheek. She whispered to the nun.

"She is sad because she will not be beautiful," the Sister said.

Ron gulped. "Tell her she will be beautiful inside because she has suffered. Tell her to be good and happy, because happiness will make her even more lovely."

May listened, then gave Ron a shy smile, a smile which was terrible to see.

"When you are better, I will come and bring your red roses, because you will be a new person," he said. "And red is a happy colour."

May started to cry, and buried her face in the nun's shoulder.

"What did I say to upset her?"

The old nun looked at him sadly. "Red is the colour brides wear in her country. You reminded her that no one will ever want to marry her."

"Then maybe she will become a Bride of Christ. That's what your order calls you, isn't it?'

"Yes, I wear Christ's ring," the nun replied. "But it is not an option I could suggest to May. You see, she's a Muslim. We are a nursing Order, not an evangelical one. We do not seek to convert the beliefs of our patients."

Mike thanked him and asked Ron if he would prepared to do such work again.

"Not until you prove me right," he replied. "Make sure you do a good job on May. Why May, by the way? It's not a Bangladeshi name."

"They're all May, cases like that," Mike sighed. "They're Maybe we can and Maybe we can't."

"But never Maybe we shouldn't try?"

"Got it in one."

"Don't you ever fail?"

Mike shuddered. "Yes. Of course we do. Burns victims are a nightmare. There's such a shock to the system that the body starts shutting down. Deep burns, right through the skin and down to the flesh, can't simply be covered by grafts. The body starts oozing fluids, starts swelling, and this puts stress on the kidneys and the heart. Even when we've made good progress with grafts and artificial skin, infection can set in, like lightning. One minute we've got them safe; the next they're on the critical list. We lose a lot of cases."

"Why do you do it, Mike? Why this, above all else?"

"Coffee?" Mike shoved coins in a vending machine and led Ron into a small garden courtyard which, though cold, was sheltered from the wind.

He let a cigarette, a rare indulgence, for he, like other doctors, condemned a habit he was constantly trying to break. "There's not much love in the world," Mike said, fumbling for words. "There's plenty of what passes for love. Kissy-kissy, wife and family stuff. Caring for partners, thinking more about someone else's welfare than their own, facing up to duty and responsibility. There are more good people than bad ones, Ron. Battlers, trying to make a go of life. Most of them don't know all the fancy stuff about relationships. They just muddle through, loving one another as best they can, just as their parents did and their grandparents before them."

"What are you getting at, Mike?"

"Seems to me you've never had much of that sort of love in your life, Ron Turner. It makes it hard to explain what I'm thinking about."

Ron ran his fingers through his hair. "I have known love," he protested. "Uncle Alf loved me. And I think Pru does. Maybe Andrew, too. And you. You've been a brother to me, more than my own kith and kin."

"You've noticed? What I put up with from you!" Mike sighed again. "To me true love only starts at that level. I'm not going all religious or anything, Ron, but there's a higher level of love. There's a need in the world to put humanity before self. To find fulfilment in service, to give rather than to receive. First do no harm; that's the doctor's first principle. My philosophy goes further. If you can do good, you have a duty to do so. Does that make sense?"

"Sounds religious to me. 'Pick up your nets and follow me.'?"

"That's a big ask. Don't think I haven't considered becoming a medical missionary. I have, but there's one major problem with that."

"There is?"

"Yes. I'm an atheist!"

***

The query to the Indonesian Government, made through its Embassy, was quickly answered. Ron's letter was returned, unopened, inside a heavily embossed envelope, to which was attached a memo from a diplomat, pointing out that as the General's wife had succumbed to malaria, personal correspondence was not being forwarded.

Bet they didn't know where to send it, Ron mused. Heaven or Hell, or whatever Muslims have instead! He thought twice about writing to Mercedes through the television network, then thought three times and forgot the matter.

It was no wonder. Art Aid was stretching his endurance to the limit. Roman had, as predicted by Zoe, become a celebrity himself, the media having been taken by his lean good looks, his high ability and his modest bearing in the light of their searching questions. There had been magazine articles about the talented young Australian and his endeavours to help the poor. He had been interviewed by Michael Parkinson, no less, and articles on him and his portraits had been published in major newspapers. There had even been a story in Paris Match, for Zoe's influence was pervasive.

Although he made little profit from the scheme, it paid for rental of the studio, his living expenses and enough to keep the bank manager happy. However, the Art Aid charity was raking it in as the rich and famous clamoured for his services. Three sittings was all Roman allowed. The first was to set the pose and to do the quickly-executed nude study, the second brought the portrait to life with draperies to the body and flesh to the face. By the time of the final session all that remained to be done was to deepen or lessen shadows to emphasis expression, and to add highlights to hair, lips and eyes.

Roman's technique did not desert him. All the years of rapidly-done sketches had melded eye and hand so that he was able to work with surprising speed, gaining a fluidity of brush-stroke that was much admired. There was a freshness and spontaneity to his commissions that appealed to the less traditional market for portraits. There were still men and women of power and political influence who demanded his services, even a Bishop and a Cardinal...their Art Aid contributions paid for by concerned parishioners, but it was among the younger stars of film and stage, music and sport, that his work proved most popular.

"They are a market no one else has mined," Zoe said with satisfaction, relaxing against the Victorian day-bed on which some of his subjects posed. "Are you sure you can't manage another commission next week?"

"No way." Ron wiped his brushes and looked critically at the second stage of the McCarthy canvas. "I'm meeting the Darcys in Paris next week."

"Damn. I've got Ivana Trump lined up."

"She'll have to wait. Look, Zoe. If it helps, I'll go to New York at the end of the year and paint for six weeks solid. You line up twelve commissions for Art Aid and charge them double the fee paid over here."

"If I do, you'll do the chat show thing? You'll go to Gala Dinners? You'll let film crews watch you work?"

"Not during the first session. You know those are always private."

The tip of the cheroot glowed as she drew deeply of its fragrance. "I have never understood your interest in seeing life in the raw. Is it sexual?"

"No, it's damn well not!" Ron hesitated. "Well, at least, not most of the time."

"Paint me," said Zoe. "I'll pay you."

Ron goggled at her. "You know my conditions."

"Yes. Paint me. Now."

She shrugged off the chinchilla furs and threw them across the arm of the chaise longue. She was naked under the heavy coat. She leaned back against the support and draped one arm over the ornately-carved end-piece. Her olive skin was thrown into contrast by the grey fur.

"I've had my boobs remodelled," she said, cupping them. "You like them better?"

"Much better. Zoe, what is all this about?"

"I think it's called exerting my conjugal rights," she purred. "It's been a long time, dear husband. I'm frustrated."

"This is not a good idea."

"Yes, it is. You're the only man who's ever bothered to help me enjoy intercourse." Her hand stroked her dark fur and she opened her thighs to explore further.

"Please," she said, in a little girl's voice. "Please, Ron, help me."

A glimmer of amusement lit his eyes. "You wanted to be painted!"

"Yes. Yes. With your hands!"

Pheromones have a lot to answer for. He could smell her need, could remember her taste on his lips and, despite reservations and anger at her behaviour, his body responded. Damn it, he thought. If I don't join in, the bitch will come without me!

**

He painted Zoe the next morning, with the furs draped from her shoulders, the swell of her breasts showing in the cleavage above hands that held the chinchilla together loosely. He painted a woman with lips red from kissing, with breasts partly exposed, with eyes heavy-lidded and the dark blue lenses hiding her inner thoughts. Her hair was tousled as if she had risen from a bed, as indeed she had.

No one, seeing the finished work, could mistake what was on the mind of Zoe Xenos, Zoe Turner, Zoe Xenopopulis. Jolie laide she might be, but she was all woman, all very satisfied and satiated woman. She had been laid, and well laid. And when she saw the results of the second sitting, she asked to be laid all over again.

15

Cobalt blue: this was first used in colouring glass, in which process it was known as smalt. It can be made in the laboratory by homogenising cobalt and aluminium chloride which are heated together for a short period. The modern pigment dates from 1804, when the French Government ordered improvements to artists' colours. It was then manufactured by heating cobalt arsenate and cobalt phosphate in a furnace and grinding the residue with a high percentage of oil to avoid the yellowing effect of mixing with linseed. It remains popular, especially for painting skies.

"It's only an April shower," said Pru, shaking her umbrella and standing it to drip in the hallway of the Darcys' suite in the Hotel Meurice, near the Louvre. "I don't know why I always expect the sun to shine in Paris, for it's no better and no worse than any other damn city I know."

"You're just cross because they didn't have the frock you liked in your size." Ron grinned. He'd spent the morning escorting Pru to every salon she fancied on the Rue de Rivoli. Andrew Darcy had gone to the Bourse to meet business acquaintances.

"Frock? Frock, Ron? One doesn't come to Paris to buy frocks. One comes to buy gowns."

"I thought we came for the Culture."

"In Paris, dear boy, Fashion is Culture. Tomorrow you may take me to the Musee d'Orsay and we'll look at the Renoirs. You've seen Les Parapluies at the National Gallery in London?"

"Yes. Interesting. Did you notice how he changed his style and his palette in that picture? He painted most of it in cobalt blue and finished it off with the new French ultramarine."

"No, I did not notice that. Do you like his nudes?"

"Mmm. Pearly, luminous skin. You feel you could pinch the bums of his models. I wish I could paint that well."

Pru bit back the comment that he could, he did. She did not want her protégé to become self-conscious about his work. From what she had heard in the art world, those in the know were already whispering about Roman, the Australian who'd started Art Aid. He had, in the short time since she'd been separated from him, taken giant steps. She longed to see his work but knew Andrew would not countenance a move to London until she had recovered from the flight from Sydney. Although it had been done in short legs and in first-class comfort, she was far from well.

"You've been here a week already. What have you seen?"

"I've concentrated on the Impressionists. Manet, Sisley, Van Gogh, Monet, Pissaro. It's damned annoying to find most of their best works are in art galleries and museums all over the world. I saved the Renoirs for you. I wanted to look at them in your company."

"Good. And I'll give you a crash course in ballet through Ingres and Degas. And my favourite old rascal, Toulouse Lautrec. You know Andrew's negotiating a series of your Vargas-style studies of the Opera dancers? Cosmopolitan, no less."

"Great. Pru, why the insistence that I keep Roman and Ron separate? I feel a merging coming on. My portraits are getting more like those early acrylics of Mercedes, not the pin-up poses, but the way the flesh glows."

"Don't ask me. I'm not the boss any more. Zoe's the one in control, isn't she? She's the one moulding your career."

"Moulding? My God, Pru, I feel more as if she's got my balls in a vice."

"You are, I presume, keeping your relationship on a business footing?"

Ron went red.

"You don't mean she's got her hooks into you again! Ron, you're a damn fool. You can't cohabit with her and expect to get a divorce on the basis of separation."

"Do I want a divorce?"

"You darn well ought to want one. You ought to be thinking wife and children."

"I've already got a child."

"And much good it's doing you. You don't know where it is or even if it's a son or daughter. Surely Zoe keeps in touch with Mercedes? Lesbians don't lose touch with their lovers. They're a damn sight more constant with their relationships than heteros."

"It's a closed topic between us. She walks out if I raise the matter."

"Bah! I'll bet you any money that they still meet. I'll bet you Zoe will chill you out for a year or so and lead you round like a pet dog with a collar. And when the year of celibacy is up, and you might start thinking lawyers and divorce, she'll come on heat again and have you wagging your tail like it had never seen pussy before."

"Go on, put the boot in. Hit me where it hurts!"

Pru looked at him, aghast, and burst into tears. She hadn't meant to be so ruthless, so blunt. She ached for the man she loved as if he were her son. She felt sick and miserable and powerless to help him.

***

"Why are you living in the Latin Quarter? You could have stayed at my apartment in Montmartre." Zoe was disgusted to find Ron had booked into Maxim's. He said it was a great little hotel and close to 'Parisien Life'. That was how the travel agent had put it. Now here he was, sitting at a pavement cafe on the Left Bank, trying to believe he was really there, not looking at the scene through the eyes of Monet. Zoe was looking with distaste at his frothing expresso. She was sipping a short black.

"It's comfortable and the rates are reasonable," said Ron. "I didn't want to impose on you."

He tried to avoid her gaze for he was taken off balance by the change in her. The blue lenses had gone and the hazel eyes were framed by John Lennon granny glasses. She had streaks of blonde in her hair, which had been cut very short in jagged spikes. She looked like a punk.

"We're married. Where's the imposition?" She was in as prickly a mood as the hedgehog hairstyle suggested.

He looked at her bleakly. How could he tell her that mating, for it was not love-making, was a draining experience when she was the recipient of his prowess. It was not that she was unskilled, unwilling, uneager. It was that she gave him a sexual hangover as severe as any aftermath of alcoholic excess. Mercedes had always left him longing for more; Zoe cloyed. Desire sat in the pit of his stomach like cold porridge.

"Or you could have stayed at Hotel Meurice with the Darcys. Didn't they invite you to join them?" The snide was coming out, big time. Zoe had refused to meet Pru and Andrew. They were, she said, part of a past she was trying to forget. Ron thought she was an ungrateful cow. It had been Pru who had set her on the ladder to success as an art curator. Zoe Xenos had memory shorter than her hair.

"Lord, Zoe, what fun would I have in a classy joint like that? It's full of antique furniture and even older guests. Hell, the women have got better bow legs than the furniture. No, Zoe. I've got dates lined up with a bunch of air hostesses from PanAsia. I want to be near the action."

"I'll bet." She made a grimace of distaste. "This coffee is disgusting." She pushed back her chair as she got up. "I had a letter from Mercedes last week. Why did you try to get in touch with her mother?"

"I wanted to know about the child."

"Liana? Oh, Liana's all right."

"You've seen her?"

"Of course. I went to Darwin for the birth. It nearly killed her. I held Mercy's hand. She screamed a lot."

Ooof! The news was like a punch to the solar plexus. "Where's the baby now?"

"Who knows? Mercedes gave her to her cousin."

"Gave her to her cousin? You can't simply give children away."

"Why not? The cousin's infertile and wanted a baby. Mercy had one going spare. No problem."

"I'd like to see her."

"The child? Or Mercy? Forget it, arsehole. You're not laying a finger on Mercy, never again!"

"Are you afraid I'd rather sleep with her? After all, your Daddy likes her more than you!"

Zoe screamed and swung her handbag at his face. It was, Ron discovered, very hard to cool a situation when a hysterical woman is making a scene in a French cafe, where everyone is gabbling in a foreign language and one hasn't got the foggiest idea what is being said. He was aware that several dozen accusing eyes were staring at him and that the patron was about to hand him the bill.

"Merci, monsieur. How they say, please do not come here again?"

Zoe, a self-righteous look on her face, watched as he walked away amid a muttering of what he took to be 'poor girl' Paris version.

He grinned as he turned to wave farewell, giving her the good old Australian gesture.

To his surprise, Zoe merely laughed. Then up went her hand, fore and little finger extended, the Greek sign for a man who couldn't keep his woman. Her meaning was quite clear...she was the cuckoo who had pushed him out of Mercedes' nest. Zoe had made a cuckold of him.

***

"That Xenos woman is making a fool of you," said Andrew Darcy. "How much money are you making out of the Art Aid programme?"

"I clear about three hundred pounds a time. That's six a week, plus what I pick up from PanAsia and Immortelle. I'm comfortable."

"You're stupid. You'd earn thousands on straight commissions."

"It's for a good cause. The publicity has been magic. I could never have got known so quickly without it."

Pru nodded. "That's true enough, and I can't criticise the results. After all, it's similar to Tamberlaine's pet project, but on a bigger scale."

"The trouble is, I can't stay in Paris any longer. I've got two pop stars beating at my doors and an appointment with the Sunday Times next week."

"You'll come back?"

"Sure, when the Paris Opera Ballet gets back from New York. I'm supposed to go to Greece in June, but Zoe says it's iffy-butty because of some scandal over the Bank of Crete."

"Would you paint Nureyev if I could line him up? Not as an Art Aid commission, but as a private deal. He's an old friend."

"For you?"

"Yes. I'd pay for it."

"You wouldn't, you know. I'd paint him because he's got an interesting face, but I'd do it for love. You do know I love you, Mrs Darcy? In the best sense of the word."

She watered up and gathered him into her arms. "I wish you were my boy, Ron. You're very dear to Andrew and I, and I know Tamberlaine would have loved you as much as our own sons."

"You'll make my mascara run," he said, covering his emotion with a sniff and a wry smile. "Come on, Mom Darcy, before I race you off from under Andrew's nose. Lunch at Maxim's."

***

It was hard to settle into life in Chelsea after a brief visit to France, for the sights and sounds of the Left Bank and the feast of masterpieces in the Paris Galleries and on the streets of Montmartre had saturated his mind. A dreadful sense of urgency possessed him, as if there was never going to be enough time in his life-span to accomplish all to which he aspired. He knew the feeling had also gripped Renoir, who had painted with a brush strapped to his arm when rheumatics crippled his fingers, who had taken up sculpture in his latter years, directing a student's hands to fashion the three-dimensional forms he saw in his mind. And there'd been Monet, half-blinded by cataracts, who'd carried on, even when the gardens at Giverny wore a mask of red over the lush green, a colour shift caused by his visual impairment.

Ron never lost his obsessive desire for Mercedes, though his artistic drive pushed physical need into a dusty corner of his mind. But no other breasts felt quite like hers against the palms of his hands, and no other woman gripped him with such tenacity.

But now the cherry blossom dusted the lawns of Kensington Gardens like snow and the daffodils danced in window boxes of Edwardian terraces. Rose-bay willow-herb and purple loosestrife struggled through the rubble around the warehouse and swallows built nests under the eaves. He'd finished the studies of Miss Gardenia and Miss Rose for Immortelle and had sent off the last of the PanAsia girls, a Gaugin-type from a Polynesian island.

His appointment book was full. Zoe had stayed for a week and had filled all available time with Art Aid sitters. He shook the stiffness out of his shoulders and opened the door to the fire escape. It was a pleasant place to sit on a warm day, coffee mug in hand, a toke between his fingers, letting dreams crowd out worries as he gazed over the Thames, now sparkling cobalt in the reflection from a late-May sky.

He clattered back up the iron stairs and, flexing his fingers, looked at the nude study of the Jamaican-born athletics star who was his latest model. Hers was a lithe figure of chocolate-brown perfection, of perfect muscles and zinging health. It would, he felt, be a shame to clothe such beauty. He wondered how she would react if he said this was the canvas he wanted to complete, not the one they had discussed, with her in the track and field singlet she ran in.

He'd painted her coming out of the starting-blocks, poised on fingertips, her face brightly fixed on the finishing-line ahead, willing herself to run like a gazelle.

"No way," she said, when he put the idea to her. "Look, even in the singlet my tits stick out. Let's keep it decent, shall we?"

"But you're so darned exciting," Ron replied, his fingers itching to tweak her.

"Thanks, but I'm in training. Call me next winter and you can take me out for dinner."

"You don't mind me lusting for you?"

She had a smile to die for. "I'd be upset if you weren't," she laughed. "I'm used to it, man!"

He tipped a brush with red to touch up a logo on her singlet. "Are your sponsors paying for Art Aid?" he asked. "You don't earn that much, do you?"

"I get by. I work as a personal trainer at a gymnasium. I give a mean workout."

"And I do great push-ups."

"Perhaps. Anyway, Ron, I don't get to keep this painting. It'll hang in the foyer of the sponsor's building."

"Will it?"

She gasped. "Man, don't you even know how your own scheme works? How many individuals can afford the fees? It's business that pays for most of your scheme."

Ron chewed the end of a brush and felt stupid. "How's that?"

"Look, if a company writes a cheque for Oxfam or Save The Children Fund, they get two lines in the newspapers and a thank you letter. That's it. Through Art Aid they get something they can put on show, with a nice plaque on the frame which tells everyone who looks at the painting that they are cool dudes who care. It's a ripper idea."

"Zoe's never discussed the way it works. I leave business to her. I just paint until my fingers drop off."

The athlete took his hand in hers and bit the ball of his thumb. "Save a few fingers until winter, then. You can paint me in chocolate sauce."

Hell, it was a long time until winter, he reflected later in the week, scowling at the study of the fat society dame who'd refused to remove her jewellery and whose plump, be-ringed fingers never left her chest, covering the interesting bits and distorting their fullness. Ron hadn't even bothered finishing the preliminary sketch. He'd suggested she bring her fat Pekinese puppy to the next sitting and be painted with Ming Ping in her arms, thus hiding a multitude of post-dietary excess. She oozed bonhomie. She breathed out gin fumes. Ming Ping farted.

He had promised two years of his life to Art Aid. That was about one hundred studies, an output Zoe called stunning and Ron found exhausting. It was, she said, a project which had the appeal of a limited edition of prints or porcelain. Places were limited. Hurry, hurry, book now. Do good, play mother and father to children who have lost their parents to the scourge of AIDS or who had contracted it at birth and were living lives as short as they were unhappy. There was seductive warmth in her exhortations but no matching kindness in Zoe's eyes. Ron reckoned they still rang up three oranges and paid out only for the jokers.

Now she was in New York, lining up bookings for his two-month stint in the Big Apple. She'd booked a suite in the World Trade Centre for his use as a studio. It was, she said, a landmark of international significance and one which could be useful in publicity. Ron refused point blank. He hated skyscrapers. Ephemeral was as high as he wanted to be off the ground. He wanted a small pad in Greenwich Village and a room in an old brownstone hotel. He did not want to work in the world of steel girders and concrete slabs, or live in a plush hotel with hot and cold running room service.

"But your image!" Zoe wailed. "Reputation is all about image."

"In your dreams, dearest wife. In your dreams. My reputation is in my fingers, not in your imagination."

Soured by the telephone call, as he so often was in his dealings with Zoe, Ron ran a thin imprimatura of terre verte across two new canvases and tacked fine linen on three more stretchers. He hammed in the wooden wedges to tighten the fabric, hit his thumb with the hammer and threw it into a corner. "Damnation!"

He ran down to the ground floor, unlocked his new racing bike from the recess under the stairs, and rode through the back streets to the Embankment. It took half an hour to get to LIPS, and another ten minutes to locate Dr Mike Carney.

"How's May?"

"Good. The tumour came away along a plane between it and the bone and we put the new cartilage in the nose. She's very bruised and feeling sick as a dog, but she'll be glad to see you."

"Magic Man!" cried May. "I getting better."

"She's becoming a real chatterbox," said the nun, who sat placidly knitting by her side. "She's learning English quite fast. She's a good girl."

"When I better, Sister is going to show me to knit."

Ron looked at her hands, which were attached to drips and with stents bandaged into veins through which drugs could be fed and blood samples taken. He was never sure which was for what. There was a device for measuring blood oxygen clipped to one slender brown finger and a bag of urine from a catheter swung at the side of the bed.

"You can knit me a scarf." he said. "A long striped scarf to keep me warm in winter."

"Yellow and green for Australia. I know." May smiled, though only the corner of her mouth could be seen. "Doctor Mike tells me you make pictures. You live with him?"

"He's a friend. It's his flat but he lets me sleep in a small room."

"How big?"

"Big enough for a bed and a place to hang my clothes."

"Oh, but that is so huge! You have all that space to yourself? I sleep with all my brothers and sisters. Rashid, Wazim, Fatima, Petula, Suzie Q..."

"Suzie Q? Petula?"

"They sing songs. They are sooo cool!"

The Sister chuckled. "Pop music invades everywhere, even into Bangladesh!"

"Was her family affected by the floods last year?"

Sister put her finger to her lips and wrote something on a scrap of paper. She passed it across the bed. 'All drowned, but we haven't told her.'

Ron's heart turned over. He knew already that tens of thousands of people had died in the catastrophic storms which had swept in from the Bay of Bengal. Almost three-quarters of the country had been inundated. May, who had been in hospital in London for months, having preparatory tests, had escaped the tragedy. But would it be more of a tragedy to be left an orphan?

He looked at the Sister, passing her his response, a scrawled, "What will become of her?"

The nun sighed. "The Red Crescent fills the same role as the Red Cross. Maybe they can help. Or the Thatcher government may grant her a permanent residency on compassionate grounds."

May looked from one to the other, not understanding the gravity in their voices. "What is this you are saying"

Ron took her thin, brown hand and kissed it. "I asked Sister what you were going to do when Doctor Mike had finished making you beautiful."

May laughed. "I shall marry. Will you marry me, Magic Man?"

Ron shook his head. "I'm sorry, May. I have a wife already."

She squeezed his hand hard. "That's no trouble. I can become your second wife. Allah will allow this."

Wondering what Zoe would say if he brought another woman home, Ron started laughing. "I don't think so, May. I don't think Mrs Turner would agree."

"Then I shall ask Doctor Mike."

"I wouldn't. He has smelly feet."

She slapped his wrist. "No. Not so."

"Last week his socks walked out of the bedroom by themselves and got in the bath with me. Phew! They didn't like the pong either."

"Magic Man, you are a...what is the word, Sister?...a fibber. If he had a wife like me she would look after him properly!"

"If he had a wife like you, she'd have to wear a clothes peg on her nose!"

The Sister chuckled. "You are a terrible tease, Mr Turner. You're confusing the poor girl."

16

Indigo: used by the Romans and the ancient Greeks, this colour is derived from Isastis tinctoria and other plants of the woad family. It is fermented in vats until the dye is extracted and is then dried and fixed in a medium for oils or water-colours. It takes its name from the Greek indicon, of India, for that is where Marco Polo saw it being extracted on a large scale. In modern times it is manufactured from o-nitrobenzaldehyde with acetone. It is a very dark blue but fades rapidly unless stabilised under varnish.

"I'm going to Athens," said Zoe. "Mercedes wants me to try to get Hugo out of prison."

"Hugo?"

"Her brother. The fat slob."

"But why? Wasn't he convicted of drug smuggling?"

"He said the opium was for medical purposes, ordered by a pharmaceutical company in Amsterdam."

"That one's got bells on it."

"The judge reckoned the same thing, but Mercedes said General Dinegoro has found papers showing the shipment was in order. He should know. After all, it was grown on his wife's land."

"That would be land she inherited from Mercedes' father after he was shot?"

Zoe looked doubtful. "I suppose so."

"She said the family grew coffee."

"Modern times, Ron."

"Zoe! You don't condone heroin, I hope."

She shrugged. "I've tried it."

"What haven't you tried? I've heard about your carrying-ons in Paris. Who was it last month? That South African model?"

"She's beautiful."

"She's probably got AIDS. Half the Blacks have got AIDS from their swinging partners. You stay well away from me!"

"I have not got effing AIDS, Ron. Have you?"

"No, I have not. I practice Safe Sex."

"I hear you've been doing some swinging yourself. Haven't you been painting that he-she pop star?"

"Yes. So what?"

"I bet he tried it on when you did the first sitting."

Ron blushed. "Well, he did, but I turned him down."

"He says you didn't. He says you are a passionate lover."

"Kee-rist!" Ron threw his palette against the wall. It hung there, glued by the great dollops of paint he had just squeezed onto it.

Zoe took a tissue from her bag and gently teased it free. "This studio's leased, dear thing. Do leave it in a decent condition."

"Why should I leave it?"

"You're going to Greece in June, aren't you? Then through Italy with the Darcys? When you come back you'll only have another month before you start thinking about New York. Is it worthwhile renewing the lease for such a short time?"

"This place suits me."

"It's not fashionable and it's not convenient. You're known now. You should have a classy studio in Knightsbridge or

Kensington."

"Bollocks!"

"Have you still got any after freezing them off last winter?"

To his surprise, her dry comment made him laugh. "Oh, Zoe. You kill me! But where would I store the Art Aid pictures which are finished?"

"When you're in Europe I'll start getting them framed. The charity plans a half-way exhibition in late November. We'll hire a large gallery and charge the public admission to raise more money."

"Yeah! Repeat after me, it's all in a good cause."

"Well, it is. By the way, Mercedes said you could have these photos. The family had duplicates made."

"Photos of Mercedes?"

"No. I'm keeping those. You were asking about Liana. No, I don't want to see them. I've seen all I want of that squawking infant...all covered in blood and white crap. No thank you, Roman. You can have a sentimental time all by yourself."

They were not good snapshots. They were taken on old black and white film. Most were out of focus, and had obviously been taken over a long period, for some were of a small baby and others of a toddler, trying to walk, pushing a toy cart, playing with a ball. There was nothing to distinguish where the child lived or under what conditions. It was just another little girl in a world filled with them. She did not look much like Mercedes.

He took them home and showed them to Mike. "Not much of an image to hang a reality on, is it?"

"What sort of a hook do you want, Ron? You were quite prepared to have the kid aborted. Do you seriously mean you want to be involved? Claim parentage or something?"

"No. I couldn't very well do that, could I? Though I was prepared to marry Mercedes and raise the child."

"I don't think that was the kind of message you were sending out at the time. I didn't hear that coming through loud and clear. Maybe Mercedes didn't, either. What was obvious, then and now, was she didn't want a baby getting in the way of her career. This isn't your child, Ron. Liana was fostered out to a family that wanted her and, presumably, is being brought up with love and care. Don't stick your nose in. You could wreck the kid's life."

"How so?"

"Well, suppose she was like May, living in a Muslim family. Finding out her birth father was an Infidel could really upset the foster parents."

"But finding out he was an Australian could give her rights to be brought up in a better society."

"Poppycock! She was born in Darwin, wasn't she? Anyway, what's so good about Western civilisation? You think there's something second class about living in Indonesia?"

"Poverty, health care, education...why are all the Indonesians with wealth buying up property in Australia and sending their kids to school over there?"

"Because the economy is booming. It's one of the Asia Tigers...growing and snarling and making huge strides in gross national product."

"At the cost of Australian jobs! Good old Australian companies are moving manufacturing offshore to get lower unit costs of production. It sucks!"

Mike raised his eyebrows. "Where do you get this stuff?"

"Andrew and Pru flew over last night. Andrew was in a funny mood. He was ranting on about it most of the evening. They want you to join them for dinner tomorrow night. Can do?"

Mike beamed. "A pleasure. I'm off-duty for two days."

"Then come art-seeing with us. National Gallery at 10am, dinner at the Dorchester at 7pm. Either or both?"

"Both. Are you going to visit May today? We're taking the bandages off her bad eye."

"How's she looking?"

"Terrific, but what have you been saying to her?"

"Oh. Only joking with her. Pulling her leg."

"I don't think she understands Aussie humour. She seems to think I'll die of terminal footrot if she doesn't marry me!"

***

"Tomorrow afternoon we're coming to your studio, Ron," said Pru, wiping her lips daintily after forking up the cream-filled eclairs. "I just adore croque-en-bouche and you needn't scowl at me, Mike. I've lost so much weight I need to fatten myself up a little."

"It's your funeral," he said gloomily, and then looked as if he wished he'd chosen his words more tactfully. "I'm sorry. I'm just tired. I've had a disappointment."

Andrew patted his hand. "We heard. Ron told us. The young Bangladeshi can't see. Is that it?"

"Yes. The eye looks all right but May says everything is still a blur. Just a haze of white light."

"Give it time, Mike. Perhaps it will come good in the weeks ahead."

"I hope so, but we're running out of options. There's not much more we can do to improve her face, except fix her teeth."

"Then what?"

"We still haven't heard about a visa for her. If there's no joy from Thatcher's mob, she'll have to go back to her own country."

"And that worries you?"

"Yes. I'm fond of May."

Pru ordered coffee while Andrew suggested brandy all round. "I like the way Frank Tamberlaine operated," he said. "Tackling problems where they were, not taking people to distant places to fix things. You fly a kid half way round the world into a foreign environment, when the need is in their own country. If we spent more on better equipment for hospitals overseas, your sort of work could be done close to home."

Mike shrugged. "It'd never work. Every country is crying out for more of the budget to be spent on health because we're upping the stakes all the time. Every advance in technology means a greater demand for services for our own people. How could you justify, for example, a cranio-surgical unit like LIPS in Bangladesh when we haven't even got a proper facility in Australia?"

"The sort of work you do gets done there, all the same."

"Yes, but here we're doing the research, finding new and better ways to operate, testing new materials in clinical trials. And to do the research we need patients with severe deformities. I'm sorry, Andrew. You've got to believe that the techniques we develop eventually filter down to Third World countries."

"Maybe the Tamberlaine Foundation could set up a clinic to use the skills of people like you."

Ron was intrigued. "You mean we should have done Art Aid for the Tamberlaine project?"

Pru shook her head. "No. It's the right cause for the times, Ron. When you get back to base in Australia I'll twist your arm to carry on with Tam's work. We look after a different sort of orphan...if that's what you call them. Andrew, take me back to the hotel. I feel dead beat."

Pru was looking quite refreshed the next day, even if she found the stairs a little daunting. Ron, to his dismay, felt nervous. Pru and Andrew were the two people in the world he needed to impress, if that was the right word. It wasn't. He knew that theirs was the critical judgment he valued, even beyond that of Mike, whose discerning eye and pithy comments had, in many ways, shaped what he did. Zoe, who could judge to a nicety what the market wanted, and how to put him in the forefront of public opinion, counted for nothing in the true appreciation of his worth. Pru did.

He left them to go through the stacked canvases, despite their suggestion he talk them through the various subjects. Instead he went out to the fire escape with a cup of coffee and watched the gulls wheeling over the river. He was so nervous he reached for a cigarette. He had flicked three butts towards the Thames before Pru joined him on the iron steps. Andrew followed her, so that they were stacked up on the narrow rungs like acrobats on a high-wire, feet under one another's armpits.

"You can light me one of those," said Pru. "It's utterly forbidden but I feel like it."

"Verdict?" asked Ron, passing a lit Benson and Hedges over his shoulder.

There was a long silence. Then, "Zoe's ruining you," she said, quietly.

"That bad?"

"Oh, not that bad. It's just that she's prostituting your ability. Selling you to the highest bidder...that sort of thing. Don't get me wrong. There are many successful courtesans. They can charge the earth for their services, but expecting you to paint two portraits a week smacks of Wham, Bang, Thank You, Ma'am!"

"Are they so bad?"

"No, strangely enough, they're good. Your reputation is built on them and it's justified, but you'll not go down in the history books as a painter of note."

"Andrew? Is she right?"

"In some ways. You've flooded the market, dear boy. Zoe's product orientated. Wants goods to sell. She doesn't take on board the importance of scarcity."

"You mean less is more?"

"More or less, if you'll pardon the pun."

"Then what do I do about it?"

Pru coughed and blew smoke in his ear. "What did you most enjoy painting? Be honest."

Ron thought hard. "I enjoy the Art Aid work...meeting interesting people. I love doing the Vargas pin-ups, but to be frank, the time spent in Greece and North Africa was magic."

"I thought so. Now, the day after tomorrow Andrew's going to hire a car and we'll go across the Channel to Holland. I want you to look at some Dutch paintings."

"Rembrandts?"

"No, my boy, you'll never be a Rembrandt. Too much dark, too much play on highlights. No, we think you should look at Vermeers."

"Why?"

"Portraits done in settings. Where the subject is part of their environment, where what they are doing is as important as how they appear."

"Zoe'll be angry."

"Zoe's in Greece, isn't she? Chasing after that no-good brother of Mercedes? Using her Xenopopulis connections to get him out of the hoosegow? Then why worry about her?"

"She's booked Martina for a sitting. It was hard enough fitting her portrait into her fixture list without me delaying things."

Andrew laughed. "You wouldn't like painting her. She's got the same tastes as Zoe."

"At least I'd feel safe. I really hate the ones who try to lay me."

Pru chuckled. "Oh, so many are there? Getting picky in your old age."

"No. Just damned tired of fighting them off!"

"Hooo! Hear that, Andrew? Cocky little sparrow, isn't he?"

Ron looked over his shoulder at her and grinned. "Only teasing! But I know now how some pop stars get with their groupies. Makes you sick!"

Andrew eased his bum back onto the platform outside the door and suggested they went in and sat on comfortable seats. "This 'Here we sit like birds in the wilderness' lark is getting to my joints," he protested. "Ron, don't you get piles from parking your butt on these iron steps?"

"Not me. I'm fit as a fiddle."

"Then you'd better get Mike to find you a doctor who'll certify that you've got repetitive strain injury. We've got to find a way of slowing down the number of paintings Zoe books."

"I wouldn't want to abandon Art Aid."

"No. But you must have more time to create a masterpiece or two every year. You must have time to become what you were meant to be."

"And what's that?"

"Why," said Pru, "Only great. That's all I've ever expected of you, Ron Turner. That you'll be the very best you can be."

***

Three weeks later a thick, embossed parchment envelope was hand-delivered to the studio. It bore the seal of the Indonesian Embassy. Ron, who expected to find information about Liana inside it, was staggered to withdraw a gilt-edged invitation to a diplomatic reception. Mr Ron Turner and Dr Mike Carney were requested to turn out, in formal evening dress, with medals, to meet General and Mrs Ihza Dinegoro.

"I thought Mercedes had lost her mother," Mike said, wrinkling his brow. "What a lark. Shall we go?"

"I must have misunderstood the earlier letter. Perhaps she was just ill at the time. But, yes. Let's strut our stuff. You never know, Mike. You might get invited to be a surgical consultant in Jakarta."

"And you might get asked to paint this General."

"Or his wife. Mercedes said her mother is a stunning woman."

Mike looked at his old dinner suit and decided to hire a smarter version. Ron's had been tailor-made only a year ago, when Zoe decided he'd need one for image-making occasions. They splashed out on a taxi to the Embassy and joined the long line of penguin lookalikes and their penguinesses, waiting with Indonesian nationals to meet the Ambassador and the Guests of Honour.

Ron was glad to have Mike's company, for he was uneasily aware that people were looking at him and passing remarks one to the other.

"Are my flies undone?" he hissed.

"No. You've obviously arrived." Mike smirked. "They know you're Roman. Oh, isn't it fun to be in the company of a real, live Celebrity!"

"You'll keep," Ron growled, shuffling forward along the red carpet. "Hey, Mike. Look at these women. Did you ever see a better collection of drop-dead gorgeous?"

"Look behind you. There's a flaw in the collection."

Expecting to see a large tubby lady, Ron turned his head, trying to disguise his curiosity. With all the confidence of her kind, Zoe was walking past the other guests, saying, "Pardon me. I must join my husband."

With smiles and bowing of heads, she was waved forward, like a blowfish coming in on the tide. She was holding the hand of a young man dressed in a white dinner suit.

"There you are, Roman," she said, quite loudly. "Nice to see you Mike. Meet Hugo."

"Mercedes' brother?"

"Yes. Isn't he delicious?"

Hugo smiled greasily. Prison life had obviously suited his physique, if not his sanity, for he was no longer a fat slob. Ron thought he might still be a slob, but the man was now painfully thin. He looked nothing like his sister. He had a long, pointed chin and a yellow-brown complexion, as if he were jaundiced. His irises were startlingly blue, the only sign of his Dutch ancestry. There were hollows in his cheeks and around his eyes were dark shadows of indigo, as if they had been bruised. His expression was not an indicator of a happy nature. He was, Mike whispered, high as a kite on something.

Zoe, incongruously dressed in pink by Versace, was high as a kite on smug. To those who know the joy of self-satisfaction, smug is more enjoyable than cocaine. Zoe was flying.

"You were successful in Greece, I see." Ron shook Hugo's hand, surprised at the limp grip which was the response.

Hugo giggled. "Pretty boy," he said to Zoe. "Can I borrow him?"

"He doesn't play your sort of games," Zoe said, in an exasperated tone. "I'm afraid prison ruined him, Mike. He's got a fixation on young men."

"No cure for that. I expect he's got worms as well."

"What are you going to do now? Are you going back to Australia?"

"I am, as they say, persona non grata." Hugo spoke carefully, as if his mouth wouldn't shape the words he wanted. "I am going back to Jakarta to run the family business."

"I gather you're in pharmaceuticals," Mike drawled.

Hugo tittered. "Dear boy, I can't even say it, let alone spell it. Do you mean drugs?"

Zoe stamped hard on Hugo's foot with the heel of her bejewelled evening sandals. She hissed at him to behave himself or he'd be back inside...and this time it wouldn't be a civilised prison in Athens, but a cell in Indonesia.

"Now I expect he'll sulk all night. I can't think why Mercedes wanted him released. She'd have been better off letting him rot."

Hugo retaliated by grasping Zoe's hand and bending back one finger in an agonising come-along grip. She yelped and tears sprang to her eyes.

Mike, who knew a few tricks of his own, jabbed a finger into a nerve centre on Hugo's back. Hugo glared and turned to strike Mike, who chopped one hand into another with the cool aplomb of one who knows judo.

"Learned the moves when I was an intern on a psychiatric ward," he explained to Ron. "You need to defend yourself against violent clients."

The line of guests had divided around the tense tableau and

were moving onwards to the reception hall, from whence came the sounds of a gamelan orchestra.

"Damn you, Hugo! Don't make a scene before the night's even started. Come on!" Zoe linked her arm in Ron's and pushed her way through to their original place, caring not an iota if she were rude.

Apologising, Mike followed, dragging Hugo with him. The room was lit by glittering chandeliers and crowded with people, many in national dress. There was a strong contingent of military men among them, imposing in mess dress and medals. British Defence Forces were also present. The penguins were outnumbered.

"I should have worn my Father Christmas outfit," Mike murmured. "I feel rather under-dressed."

An ornately-uniformed flunky took their invitations and passed them to the Master of Ceremonies, whose face and size resembled a large Buddha.

"Mr Roman Turner and Mrs Zoe Turner," he intoned. "Dr Michael Carney and Mr Hugo Vandermeer."

The Ambassador shook their hands and begged to introduce the principal guests. "May I have the pleasure of introducing General Ihza Dinegoro and Mrs Dinegoro," he said.

Ron shook the hand of the imposing senior officer and looked beyond him to the beauty who was the mother of Mercedes.

"I believe you met my new wife when she was living in Australia," said the General. "Weren't you at Art College together?"

It was Mercedes herself. Ron, trying to loosen the muscles in his jaw that had clamped tightly, took refuge in cliché. "Ships that pass in the night, I expect!"

17

*Azurite: a copper carbonate, takes its name from lazhward,
the Persian word for blue. In Ancient Egypt it was ground
from the natural mineral, but in the 19th century it was
made synthetically by dissolving copper in nitric acid. The
precipitate was separated from the liquor and dried with
quicklime, which turns greenish deposits into a beautiful
blue, which is cheap and permanent.*

Silk robes the colour of a summer sky shimmered around the
slim form of Mercedes. Ron guessed the full length gown was
strapless, but her shoulders and arms were concealed by a jacket
of an even deeper azure. A gauze scarf was draped around her
neck, with one end over her hair in the way of modest Islamic
women.

He smiled ruefully for, in repose, she looked like a statue of the
Virgin Mary. There were sapphires in her pierced ears and a heavy
necklace of blue gems around her neck. They sparkled, but there
was no such light in her eyes. They looked dull and glazed,
although a tiny dormouse of fear peeped out from time to time.

"Ron," she said softly. "It's good to see you." She turned to
embrace Zoe and, over her friend's shoulder clearly mouthed the
words, "I must see you!"

He nodded and stepped back, getting a good view of the angry
confrontation between the General and Hugo.

"I told you to go straight back to Indonesia," said Ihza
Dinegoro. "What are you doing here, Vandermeer?"

"Came to see my sister."

"Stay away from her, you hear? You're to have no contact with her, understand?"

"Says who?"

"Have you lost your wits, you silly damn fool? Have you forgotten who I am and what I can do to you?"

"Yeah! Kiss my arse goodbye, like you did to mother. As you did to my father. You're like a fucking enema, Ihza. The ultimate purge. Treat everyone like shit!"

The General turned his back on the young man and raised a quiet finger to an aide camp. "Escort Mr Vandermeer from the premises," he said. "And do it quietly."

"Not before I've kissed my little sister!" Hugo lurched past him and embraced Mercedes, pressing something into her hand.

"No, you don't," Ihza snapped, taking the packet from the hand of his new bride. "You're not going to act as her supplier!"

The Ambassador, who had been striving to ignore the slight impasse behind him, tugged at the General's sleeve. "Not now, Ihza. I know you want to murder the little sod, but not here, not now."

He turned to Mike. "Now, Dr Carney, I'd like you to meet the Minister for Health who's over here for a conference. Rashid here will take you to him. Mrs Turner, I hear you are the agent for this excellent young artist. There is great interest in Indonesia in Roman's work. Would you consider a six-month contract to paint members of Cabinet?"

Zoe's eyes glittered. "Not this year. Roman's not really free until 1988. We must bring Art Aid to a conclusion."

"Ah, yes. Such a worthy project. My wife is very eager to play her part. Could you accommodate another contributor?"

He took Zoe under his wing and gently guided her to a small group of diplomatic wives. Ron, unsure what to expect, noted that the Islamic restriction on alcohol was not being enforced and took a glass of wine from a salver being offered him. The receiving line was over. Late arrivals went unannounced. People were circulating. He started to drift around the room and, finding a series of open doors to the gardens, sought the cool night air.

There were sounds of a muted quarrel in a pagoda-like summer house. He recognised the voice of Mercedes, pleading, begging.

"Please, Ihza, please. Let me have Hugo's present."

"No. Oh no you don't. I'll break you of this if it's the last thing I do. You're not going to go the same way as your mother!"

"You're cruel. You made me as I am and now you use it to control me!"

"I did and I will. I didn't drag you out of the gutter for you to disgrace me. Toe the line, Mercedes, or I'll divorce you. No home, no job, no money. What would you do?"

"I'd survive," she hissed. "I'd work in one of your bloody brothels. See if you'd like that, Ihza! I could make you a laughing stock."

"Ah, Mercedes, sweet little Mercedes. Your head is full of clouds. You're my whore, and no one else's. Do you think I would allow you to disgrace me?"

"Don't Ihza, don't. You're hurting me!"

"It would be so easy to arrange a little accident, Mercedes. Now be a good girl. Kiss me better. Come on, wrap your lips around your favourite plaything. And don't bite!"

Ron, peering into the darkness, watched the blue-gowned woman fall to her knees and lower her head. He could bear it no longer. He turned quickly and made his way back to the reception rooms and found Zoe.

"Did you know Mercedes had married that bastard?"

"Of course," said Zoe. "She owes him everything. He wouldn't help Hugo unless she agreed."

"He's old enough to be her father!"

"She understands older men. But she doesn't love him, if that's what you think. She still loves me. She's mine."

"I thought you were married to me."

"Try citing her in a divorce action and get laughed out of court, Ron. Grow up, will you?"

"Then why?"

"Stupid boy. Isn't it obvious?" Zoe glared at him and pushed past to greet some acquaintances. Ron looked around and saw Mike, who caught his eye. Mike tapped at the face of his watch and jerked his thumb in the direction of the exit.

"Time to go, old buddy. I'm on duty at 6am."

"I'm right behind you, Mike. This night has been a shocker."

"Lord, yes. We should have stayed home and watched the television."

They thanked the Ambassador and said formal farewells to the General.

"I will come to your studio tomorrow," said Ihza Dinegoro. "I will make your apologies to my wife."

Mercedes, who had seemingly recovered her composure, was engaged in an animated discussion with Zoe, who merely waved a languid hand at them. As they made their way to the far side of the room and the corridor to the outside, normal world, a man tapped Ron on the shoulder. It was the managing director of PanAsia.

"Roman," he said. "I hoped I'd find you here. We have a major problem on our hands. A crisis, even."

Mike looked pointedly at his watch. "We have to go. We really have to go."

The PanAsia man nodded in acknowledgment. "I'll come to your studio tomorrow. Yes?"

"Zoe's right," Ron sighed, as they hailed a taxi. "It is time I moved. Half of London seems to know where I work."

"And it's time you got a flat of your own, too. You're cramping my style."

"You want me to move out?"

Mike's face was rather red. "Yes. I think you'll have to. You see, I've asked May to marry me."

"You've what?"

"It's the only way to stop them sending her back to Bangladesh."

"But you don't love her!"

"Don't I?"

Ron hesitated. "Well, I suppose you do, in a fashion. But her face. It's still not right."

"I'm used to it. It's not perfect, but then, who is? She's brave and she's good and she has a fabulous sense of humour, now she's learned to speak more fluently. I think she's really very intelligent."

"She can't be. She likes Petula Clark."

"So what's to hate? Anyway, she'll make sure my socks get washed. I didn't realise you found them so offensive."

"It was a joke, Mike. You haven't got smelly feet, honestly."

"Good. But I notice you still have a problem with perspiration.

Didn't I see you break out in a sweat when you saw Mercedes?"

"God, yes. I got an instant stiffy. I wanted to stick my tongue down her throat and nail her to the carpet."

"That, my dear fellow, would have made a most entertaining floor show!"

***

The Embassy Rolls was already parked outside the studio when Ron arrived on his bike. The chauffeur opened the door and stood to attention as the General unfolded his long legs from the interior. The General was in full dress uniform, not mess dress, but the ceremonial uniform, complete with swags of gold and a chest hung with full-sized medals, rather than the miniatures worn at functions.

"Where do I pose?" he said, after scanning the studio.

"Pose?"

"Yes. I am here to pose, am I not?"

"Are you?"

"Of course. It was arranged with your wife."

"I have another engagement for Art Aid this morning."

"She has postponed it. She has rearranged your schedule to leave the week clear for my portrait."

"But she can't. I fly to Greece next week."

"She has rearranged that, too. Have you a problem, Roman? This is not an Art Aid commission. This is a real one. I have already paid her."

The hell you have, Ron thought. It was just like Zoe to turn his life upside down without consulting him.

"You know my conditions?"

"The strip session? I'm not ashamed of my body, young man. I keep fit. But I want the pose like so." He drew his sword and leaned on it, in a manner typical of Van Dyck portraits of cavaliers. "Full length, naturally."

Ron sighed and pulled a suitable stretched canvas from the shelves. "If you'd given me warning I could have had the imprimatura done already," he said. "That's the first glaze to cover the white. I'll have to work fast in terre verte. While you undress I'll just give the canvas a quick rubbing with dull ochres to give an all-over tone."

The General was right. He did strip to advantage. There was no paunch, no belly-fat at all. He was muscled and lean. Ron had already noted there was not a grey hair on his head, though he was probably older than Mercedes' father. He was a handsome man, with a more pronounced nose than usual in Asiatics, and rather large ears. His body was hairier than expected, tight whorls of springy hair around his chest continuing in an unbroken pelt to his groin. He was impressively hung.

Ihza Dinegoro was amused by Ron's scrutiny. "I have some Portuguese in my ancestry," he said. "My father said the sailor who came with Vasco Da Gama was a bull-fighter. My mother said he was probably the bull!"

Ron laughed. Why, the man was proud of himself. He loaded the palette and set the position, chalking the feet to ensure the General returned to the same angle after a break. One hand on the hilt of the sword, the other on the hip. The chin held high, the expression haughty, the lips stern. Power personified.

The preliminary work went smoothly. Ron had no intention of completing the nude study. This was one he would happily over-paint. He didn't like the man; he resented the commission. He was fascinated by Ihza's masculinity, his common sense obscured by images of Mercedes whimpering beneath that gross intrusion.

"Have you known your wife long?" he asked, in casual conversation.

The General smiled. "Oh, yes. I knew her father. He introduced me to her when she was a mere child. You might say I have known her intimately since she was ten or eleven."

"You were married to her mother, I believe."

"Yes. A fine-looking woman, but stupid. Mercedes is intelligent. She is well respected at the television station. She is popular with viewers. Her interviews for current affairs programmes are always interesting. And, of course, her diction is superb."

"No Aussie accent?"

"No. Very BBC. I gather the nuns knocked that out of the girls when they were at boarding school. Elocution lessons and deportment. Mercedes, you know, had ambitions to become an actress."

"What stopped her?"

"She had a baby. We don't tolerate single mothers in Indonesia. She had to work for a living. The child's fostered with a new family. Very devout."

"Is that the girl they call Liana? My wife knows yours quite well. They write every week." Ron discovered that speaking half-truths was as tacky as used chewing-gum on the carpet.

To his surprise the General smiled. "Well, there'll be no trouble with this Liana, not like there was with Mercedes and her mother. The adoptive parents are very traditional. They'll circumcise the child before puberty. That will stop her chasing men."

Ron, who had not heard of the practice, decided to ask Mike. "Is that some sort of Islamic thing?"

The General leered. "It takes the pleasure out of intercourse for a woman. Your hairy-legged feminists would be horrified, I expect, but a circumcised woman is tighter for a man. And there's nothing in the Koran to indicate that women are supposed to enjoy sex. They are here to serve the needs of men."

"Then why did you want Mercedes?"

"My dear young man, my wife has been trained to give pleasure, not to lie there passively. She has, I find, a grip like a torque-wrench and the ability to work a man without moving a limb."

Ron was interested to note that even thinking about his new wife had excited the General. "I think you can get dressed now," he said. "I've seen enough." And wondered how Ihza was going to fasten his flies over that one.

"My wife will sit for you on Wednesday," the General said, as he prepared to leave. "She will, naturally, be chaperoned. By your wife, I understand."

"By Zoe? Oh, Good Lord!"

"Don't you like your wife, Mr Turner? No, I can see you don't. But she is an excellent businesswoman. You should convert to Islam. Then you could take another to warm your loins at night."

"I think I'll settle for a hot water bottle," Ron quipped. "I haven't your stamina, sir!"

"Few men have, and you, after all, are just a youth. You should eat goatweed. It would make a man out of you!"

Ron chuckled as he cleaned up. If goatweed would make him a man, he guaranteed Zoe would make the General a fool. He could guess what Mercedes and Zoe would be doing in Ihza's absence. It wasn't playing billiards.

He went outside to empty his teapot over the fire escape and had made a fresh brew by the time the PanAsia manager arrived.

"So what's the problem?" Ron poured the tea and added milk

and sugar. "You liked the Beauties of Asia series?"

"They're brilliant, but we're going to have to advance the schedule and run them on the 1986 calendar instead of next year's. Thank goodness we only did a small test printing of the Mercedes paintings. We had no idea she would marry Ihza Dinegoro. We simply daren't risk offending him by putting his wife's body on display. It would grossly offend the Islamic majority."

"Mercedes isn't a Muslim. She went to a Roman Catholic school."

"Marry one, become one. Luckily the cover painting for PanAsia In Flight is very tame. We can get away with that, and we've done an interview with her for an inside story about her life. The General has approved it. But we had to reprint the advertisement for the calendar. The cost has been horrendous. You should have told us who she was. It was only by chance that we realised she was the newsreader."

"Does that make a difference? She agreed to pose. There was nothing underhand about it."

"Roman, it would destroy her reputation utterly. And then Ihza Dinegoro would revoke all our operating licences. We rely on our Indonesian airports. Inter-island flights are the mainstay of our business."

"Has she seen the calendar?"

"I'm afraid so. Her lawyers served writs on PanAsia two days ago to stop publication."

"But Ihza doesn't know?"

"He's the last person Mercedes would tell. I gather, from what she said, that her past wouldn't bear too close a scrutiny. You need not go so red, Roman. It's obvious from the poses that you knew her intimately."

"I suppose I'd better give you back your money."

PanAsia waved a dismissive arm. "No. You just owe us another series. We thought Island Life would be rather good. Use your Platinum Pass and go to the Moluccas, Sumatra, Lombok, Bali, Irian Jaya, Aceh, Ambon. A free hand."

"But I'm booked out for next year."

"I'm sure you'll find the time. I'd hate to sue you for breach of contract when there are four years left to run."

Ruefully, Ron reflected on his promise to Pru to make time for one or two serious works each year. That was a promise made to be broken. And Art Aid would have to settle for less output as well.

"What about the originals?"

The PanAsia man sighed. "I never want to see them again," he moaned. "I've shredded all I could find. If any more turn up I'll have them couriered to your home address. I thought you'd find it awkward to have them on the premises with the General coming and going for his sittings. That is Ihza Dinegoro, isn't it?" He stared at the nude on the easel. "It's right what they say, then. He is a big man."

***

"Has May been circumcised, Mike?"

"No. She's all intact. Why?"

"Don't all Islamic people do it?"

"Of course not. It's barbaric. Only the real freaky fundamentalists still practice genital mutilation."

"What, exactly, do they do?"

"It varies. They cut off the clitoris and maybe the labia...that's the soft skin inside the folds, and then they sew the sides together, just leaving a small hole for urine and other fluids to seep out."

"And a small hole for men to sneak in."

"Sure. It must be painful for intercourse and agonising if they get pregnant. The whole shebang rips open. Bleeding, infection, the works. If we realise when they come into hospital we can do an episiotomy to stop tearing, but most of these woman have their babies at home. We get them after the damage is done. I bet thousands die from the effects during circumcision and in childbirth in Third World countries. It's revolting."

"The General thinks it's a good idea. He said they may do it to Liana when she's older."

"Poor kid, but it's one of those weird customs like binding the feet in China. They thought it very civilised a century ago. But it isn't only in Third World countries that genital mutilation takes place. Some mullahs in London order it and I expect there are communities in Australia where the old ways are still followed."

"Gross." Ron was seriously upset by the thought of the child being deliberately maimed, but could see no way of stopping the act. "Has a parcel arrived for me?" He was eager to change the subject.

"On your bed. You're supposed to be clearing out your things, not adding more."

"Just checking. I'm slipping out to the Post Office to send it to Kostas. Pickfords are picking up the studio nudes and crating them to ship to Australia. Zoe's having everything else framed while she finds new premises for me. I'll be out of your hair by the end of the month. But it's a damned nuisance having to stay an extra week. I'll have to go straight to the Papandreou commission without spending time with Helene and Alexandar first. I was looking forward to that. I felt I deserved a break. Alexandar and I go fishing."

"I remember when...those were the days, Ron. I'm off. Night duty."

The phone rang. Ron answered it.

"Meet me at your studio. Please. In half an hour." Mercedes. She rang off before he could reply.

There were no lights on his bicycle. He put on running shoes and jogged all the way. It started raining and he was soaked by the time he reached the warehouse. He dripped up the stairs and unlocked the door.

The switch inside was rarely used. With dismay he discovered the bulb had blown. He felt his way across to the big spotlight he used with a reflector to bounce effects onto the faces of some subjects. He tilted it so it fell on the study of the General yet gave muted light to the rest of the room.

There was a pile of unused towelling rags in the corner. He stripped off and rubbed himself down, then reached for a clean painting smock which Zoe insisted he wear for publicity shots. The light made a big mirror of the wall of windows. He caught sight of himself and laughed. His legs were long and hairy, looking as if they did not belong with the rest of him, like the stick drawings kindergarten children make, with a rough triangle for the body and limbs coming off at odd angles.

Mercedes laughed as he opened the door to her. Mercedes put her arms under his smock and hugged him closely. Mercedes stroked him and lifted her blue gown to press her flesh against his. He carried her to the chaise longue and took off her clothes in the shadows. And she was all his once more. All the sweetness of her, the rippling excitement of her, the taste of honeyed lips and the sensation of pearly teeth on his skin. No other woman he had known was so enchanting and none had drawn from him the deep pulsating surge of total satisfaction.

"Oh, Ron," she sighed, clasping him inside her so that he was ready again. "I do love you so much."

"And I love you eternally," he gasped, striving for control, then losing it. He brought her, crying out with animal intensity, to a quivering, spasming climax and knew himself drained.

"I've never had another lover like you," she sighed. "You're still as wholesome as a nut, though much more skilled. If only..."

"If only what?"

"Oh, if only I were a different, nicer person, Ron. I tried to corrupt you, you know."

"Why?"

"I was jealous of your innocence, maybe. Mine was stolen. Oh, I don't know what I thought. I punish myself through my other...liaisons...is that how I say it?"

"I ache for you, often."

"Then you will let me have the originals of the PanAsia calendar," she murmured, kissing him sweetly. "You will, won't you?"

"I don't have them," Ron said, surprise in his voice. "They're on their way to Australia."

"They can't be. PanAsia told Zoe they only delivered them to you this afternoon."

"Her Majesty's Mail has them. I sent them Air Mail. Express Delivery. They could be on an aircraft by now."

"Dammit! I wanted them for Zoe. Zoe's always wanted them."

"You didn't want them as a present for your new husband?"

"Ihza? Ihza'd kill me if he saw them. Ihza'd kill you if he knew you'd painted them. Ihza is not a nice person, Ron Turner." She stepped into the bright illumination of the spotlight in front of the General's portrait. "Ihza Dinegoro is possibly the wickedest man I have ever met. Look how he uses me."

Her skin was a pastiche of bruises in various stages of blue and yellow. There were weals across her back and buttocks. There was a livid burn on her breast. And all along her inner arm were the marks of heroin injections.

"He owns me, body and soul," she said sadly. "And he is a very jealous man."

18

Cerulean blue: first made commercially in 1860 by George Rowney, though known earlier in the 19th century. The cobalt stannate takes its name from the Latin, caeruleum, meaning sky or the heavens. The French know it as bleu celeste, celestial blue. It is made from salts of tin and copper, which are mixed with calcium sulphate and heated. It is very permanent and stable but does not have the intensity of cobalt blue.

The skies are wide and an unearthly blue in northern Greece before the midday sun bleaches them to shimmering paleness.

"Maybe I should stay here and marry you, instead of letting Kostas have you," said Ron, his head resting on Helene's stomach.

She laughed and dropped another wild strawberry into his mouth. "Maybe you should. Why don't you?"

"What? Join the Lotus Eaters and enjoy an endless summer? It's been wonderful, Helene. You know how much I've enjoyed staying with you and Alexandar."

"Yes, you have been a good friend to us. He misses his father. My husband was too young to die, in such a pointless, cruel way."

"Mmm. War is terrible. And lusting after land is the worst reason for it."

"Worse than lusting after another woman? My namesake...Helen of Troy?"

"The face that would launch a thousand ships? My wife's face would sink a fleet of bulldozers."

"Zoe's not that bad."

"I forget you're all distantly related, you and Kostas. Was your first marriage arranged by a matchmaker, too?"

"It was, but we came to love most dearly."

"You'll love Kostas as well. He's a good man. Very funny. Very hard-working. And you'll like Australia."

Helene looked seriously at him and smoothed his brow. "Why don't you love me?" she asked. "I'd come to your bed willingly. Not last year, perhaps, but now I am ready. I have put aside my sorrow."

Ron rolled on his side and leaned over her, fighting the urge to kiss soft pink lips and to light the fires in her eyes. "Because I don't deserve you," he said. "Because I've seen enough deceit and treachery in my life not to visit it on any of my friends. What sort of a man would I be, Helene, to spoil your chance of happiness with Kostas?"

"I could be happy with you. Alexandar too."

"Here, yes. Beneath the vines, listening to the bees humming in the flowers, watching the hens scratch in the dust, smelling the sea and wondering what Alexandar has caught for supper? Yes, I could be happy with this, but I don't live in this reality, Helene. You'd hate my world. I do love you. Really, deeply, truly." His finger traced the edges of her lips. "If you need me, you only have to ask. I'll come running. But ruin you is something I couldn't do."

"You're afraid of Zoe, that's it!"

"And your Uncle Aristotle. She says he'll smash my hands if I play around." He stretched out his fingers, itching to place them around her full bosoms, just to see what they felt like. They looked womanly. Helene was all woman. He knew a twisting envy of Kostas. It had been a summer for feasting his eyes, but not by a single gesture had he let slip his desire for this Greek beauty. And yet she knew his heart.

She had, by her peace and her dignity, by soft words and sensible talk, soothed the agony of his last encounter with Mercedes. He had painted the General with red fury in his eyes and bitter hatred in his hands. He longed to put the artist's fingers around that thick, proud neck and squeeze the rope-like arteries until the blood stopped running to that cruel mind. For Mercedes' sake he had played the civilised man, for in truth, Ihza Dinegoro could have countered physical attack with as much ease as swatting a fly.

He had suffered the torture of painting his first love, refusing her offer to again pose nude before him, for hers was a body he knew so well that, even were he to live until ninety, he could have painted it from memory. He did not need to see the bruises fade, nor was he eager for evidence of fresh abuse. Zoe, who had obviously been looking forward to his discomfiture, made her displeasure with him quite clear. They had been damning, damnable sessions, during which his wife's tongue had lashed him with leathers dipped in caustic. Mercedes, withdrawn and drowsy, looked at him in speculation, as if she could not quite remember what lust was, but knew she ought to feel some emotion. It was as if their last encounter had been wiped from her mind.

It had been a relief to finish his other bookings and to catch the plane to Athens. It had been soothing to paint family portraits, free of constraint, in the company of pleasant, ordinary people, who neither abused their position nor his vulnerability. The following weeks had lulled him from misery into contentment and he rued the ending of the idyll.

"Is everything you need in your case?" he asked Alexandar, who came from the beach heavy-footed, dragging his toes through the sand, his fishing rod scraping the ground behind him. "I'll put your rod in the roof before we go to the airport," he promised. "It'll be safe until you come back for holidays."

"It makes me sad to leave here," the boy said. "Are you sure I'll like Kostas, and Rome, and Australia?"

"You don't have to go to Australia if you don't get on with Kostas. You've got a month in Italy before you make a firm decision."

"Why couldn't he come here?"

"You know why. He doesn't want to be a soldier."

"Is he afraid?"

"Your father was his best friend. Of course he's afraid. Your mother's afraid, too. You should cuddle up to her in bed tonight to make her feel safe and loved."

"Should I? That's for babies."

"Yes. You should. Even when you have a beard, you will still be her baby. It is like that for women."

Having neatly disposed of the opportunity to give way to temptation, Ron went to his lonely bed. He dreamed of floating over clouds in a pure, blue sky, where butterflies named Helene emerged from pupae to spread fragile and beautiful wings.

Kostas met them in Rome. He had acquired, on the way to the airport, a huge bunch of balloons. He tied them to the handle of the baggage trolley and told Alexandar he could let them go in the grounds of the hotel where Pru and Andrew were already staying. His wide grin and fluent Greek captivated the boy. It made Helene, whose command of English was still imperfect, relax and become quite a chatterbox herself. They were, Ron guessed, catching up on family gossip. He was left holding the balloons with his arm outside the window of the hire car, while Kostas drove with quick and confident speed through the chaos that was the capital of Italy.

With utter delight Ron realised that instantaneous bonds had formed. He felt relief that he had done nothing to spoil Helene's memories of himself, and that he had behaved honourably to his friend. He left them enjoying the sight of red and yellow balloons soaring into the heavens above the spires and roofs of the ancient city, and sought the more peaceful company of the Darcys, who were sitting on the terrace.

The art-lovers had a large folder of information about what galleries were open when and where, how to get there, what to see, whose work was great and whose imitative.

"Hey, is this a crash course, or what? I'll never cover all this ground."

"No, you won't. And nor will we. Andrew and I are going to point you in the right direction while we take siestas. We've decided we're too old to rush around in the heat."

Andrew chuckled. "We'll simply garner your impressions when you get back each day. We've hired a car and chauffeur. We'll come with you to Florence and Milan, but we'll return to Paris by train when you go back to London."

"I'm not going back until I see Kostas off on the plane with Helene and Alexandar. If it doesn't work out, I've promised to take them back to Greece."

"Tush. Of course it will work out," Pru said. "These matchmakers know a thing or two."

Botticelli, Utrillo, Titian, Michelangelo, the great Leonardo, Pierra Della Francesca, Giotto di Bondone, Caravaggio, Tintoretto...names, paintings and histories reeled before Ron's eyes as he was rushed from example to example, town to town, from church to gallery, from hotel to hotel.

"Enough!" he said in Venice. "I'm stuffed."

"Thank goodness. Andrew, I never thought we'd wear the rascal out. Go back to Rome, and rejoin your friends. Andrew and I are going to spend a few more days sitting in gondolas with bottles of wine, appreciating the history. Take the car, take the driver, take your time."

Kostas and Co had gone missing. They were, according to the message at reception, spending a few days at the beach. Ron was at liberty to visit the Forum, the Colosseum, the Trevi Fountain, Vatican City and to study more closely the works of Raphael. From the great tradition of Renaissance art he drew little knowledge, for almost every technique had been surpassed and new pigments had taken over from earlier times.

What he drew from the Roman experience was the understanding that it was not enough to impress ones contemporaries, or to be financially successful. What Pru had been leading him to was recognition that his work must stand the test of time.

If, in the Roman Empire, every road led to Rome, it was equally true that every stroke of Ron's brush had, in total, to point in the direction of immortality. It was a sobering thought.

Realising that he was probably a bit of a prat, up himself, suffering from an inflated ego and delusions of grandeur, Ron got blind, rotten drunk. It did not help to see the happiness of the new Populis family.

"My father'll be mad at us for not waiting," Kostas said. "But we wanted to sleep together and Helene wouldn't without a ring on her finger. It's a good thing you made us get all the documents together just in case. It was a breeze when we knew how to set about it."

"You're right, Ron," said Alexandar. "I like him. He's funny."

"You were right, Ron," said Helene. "I love him already."

You were right, Ron. You weren't good enough for her. Ron had a large dose of the glums as they waved from the gate of the Departure Lounge. He wished he were going with them, to stay at

Ephemeral, which Pru had offered for as long as Kostas and family wished to use it.

"If I could lie on the floor of the studio there, and look out of the window at that vast triangle of sky blue poised above the trees, I could pretend I was a bird. I would like to be a bird, free to ride the waves of the wind, free to soar to the heavens, free to sit among the high branches and sing as the sun arises," he thought.

"You're nuts," said Mike, who met him at Gatwick and proudly presented the new Mrs Carney.

"Not nuts. Is a very nice dream," said May. "I know about these things. You stay with us this time. Your flat not quite ready yet. Wet paint."

"Wet paint?"

"Yes. It brown when Zoe say hokay. I buy more paint. I paint it red. Happy colour."

Mike burst into laughter at the expression on Ron's face. "Don't worry, mate. It is 'hokay'. May only painted the woodwork."

***

It was inevitable that Zoe would find out about his commercial art and try to cut a slice of the action.

"I'm sorry, Ron. After I'd paid PanAsia's expenses for scrapping that disgusting calendar, you were pretty broke, so you'll have to put up with the old studio. The flat's in Kensington, not far from Mike's. It's furnished but you'll need other things. You can eat Greek at Sav's, tandoori at the Regent or grab a pie from Auntie's."

Ron stared at her in amazement. "I'd squared things with PanAsia. I just have to do another series."

"My way is better. You stay out of Indonesia."

"Why? So I don't find out about you and Mercedes? Are you two at it again?"

Zoe glared. "She's in rehab. She's still in London. The General approves of me trying to wean her off drugs."

Ron bit his lip. "You always wanted to experience what she had. You sure you've not been getting some rough from old Ihza?"

"Pig," said Zoe. "Where are the Mercedes paintings?"

"Where you'll not find them. Now explain to me why I'm nearly broke."

"The frames cost a fortune."

"Wonderful. Now I've got all my money tied up in square bits of wood. Zoe, when are you going to sell some of my work?"

"I'm saving it for New York."

"I'll send some of them to Pru, in Paris. She'll shift them."

"I'm your agent, not Pru."

"You are my agent in Australia and for commissions you find for Roman. You are not my agent for other work in Europe. You are the agent for Art Aid, and a bum deal you cut for me on those. I know now what the other Art Aid artists are taking and you underpriced my take by thousands."

"Silly boy, then. Find your own commissions."

May, who had taken cover in the kitchen, peeped round the door jamb. "Is she gone, Magic Man? She is not a nice woman. She is like a tiger, grrrr! Big teeth, claws, rip your heart out!"

Ron laughed. "Make tea, Mrs Carney, if you please."

"Yes. Dr Carney come home soon. I make curry."

Mike picked up the ringing phone as he came through the front door. "It's Pru, Ron. She's in a hell of a state. Told me to watch the news."

"I fix cuppa," said May.

Ron listened to Pru with one eye on the BBC. There had been a series of terrorist attacks in Paris.

"Andrew was hurt. Ron, Ron, what do I do? He's just lying there, in the hospital, but they say he is not urgent. He's been hit by shrapnel in the head. There are many more serious."

"Keep calm. I'm on the next flight to Paris."

"You are not," Mike snapped, snatching the phone from his hand. "Listen, Pru. It says on the news more than a hundred people have been injured and many killed. The Paris hospitals will be in crisis. Have you got private health cover?"

"Yes, and I can pay cash. Andrew's got millions."

"Right. Then give me the number of the hospital. I'll talk to them. If it's possible to move Andrew we'll hire an air ambulance and fly him back to London. If it's shrapnel I'll deal with it myself, at LIPS. Just stay by the phone."

Ron watched the news follow-up in anguish. May bustled around, gathering what seemed like a mountain of household goods.

"You go to your new flat. I come, make up beds. Get meal ready. Pru stay with you, close to her husband. Good thing you sent Mike that Greek money. I buy beautiful things, you'll see."

Mike nodded approval. "Take a taxi. I'll stay to take phone messages and call in favours. You'll have to put up with the paint smell. You're used to it, I guess."

It was past midnight before Mike came to collect May. Andrew was sedated and in intensive care. Pru was spending the night in a room kept specially for the relatives of critical patients.

Mike, who said he was dog-tired, wanted to go home. "I can't do a thing until the swelling's reduced," he sighed. "And the radiologist's gone off duty. Go to bed."

Only Mike slept well that night.

***

It was more than a week before Mike had any idea if the operation on Andrew had been successful. The bomb had been filled with scrap metal such as nails and other iron waste. The Darcys had been on the far side of the street, yet the blast had sent them reeling. Pru had shouted at Andrew to get up and take cover, but it was only when she tried to lift his head that she had realised his blood was on her hands.

There was an ugly depressed wound on his temple and fragments of skull-bone had been driven into the brain. The nail had spun as it penetrated and had passed close to the optic nerve.

"It's out, but what it's destroyed on the way through won't be known until he comes round," Mike said to Pru and Ron. "He may be blind."

May, who had kept Pru company for days, shook her head. "We must hope," she said earnestly. "My eye that not see good is coming hokay. I can see the television."

Pru kissed the new Mrs Carney and gave her a hug. "You're kind, May. You don't know how much I rely on you."

"That's fine. Mike and Ron good to me when I sick."

Ron, who had become used to having Pru underfoot, taking her depression in his stride, was hard at work. New portraits stood against the walls, waiting to be varnished before going to the framers.

He had changed his routine to accommodate the intense pressure. The nude studies went by the board. He bought a Polaroid camera and recorded his subjects with that. It saved almost a day's painting time.

On Pru's advice he bought the sort of display stands used in art galleries and hung a selection of his work on those. By now he knew the market and set realistic prices on his seascapes and paintings of the people of the Mediterranean. This brought in a steady stream of hard cash. He set some aside to cover the cost of framing and found himself a tax accountant.

He had strong words with PanAsia about Zoe. "She is not my agent for your work," he said. "Pay her nothing, take nothing from her. Is it true you want me to cancel the Island Life series?"

"Of course not," the managing director said. "We're relying on it for 1988. When can you do them?"

"Late October, early November, maybe, and into the New Year," Ron replied, looking at his diary. "That will give you a full year for production. You plan the itinerary and get visas and so forth. All I want to think about is my work but, as you gather, I can't rely on Zoe. In fact, I simply don't trust her."

Day by day progress with Andrew was minuscule. He remained in a coma for weeks. Then slowly, his fingers began to move, picking at the sheets. Pru squeezed his hand and he returned the pressure. They removed the ventilator and he began to breathe on his own, though raggedly, so they kept him on oxygen. He opened his eyes and responded to light shone in them. But that was all. It was not encouraging.

Kostas, who rang frequently to say he and the family were loving life at Ephemeral, added to Ron's concerns. It was winter in those distant hills and an unusually wet one.

"There's water seeping through the wine cellar," Kostas said. "I've had to get bricks and prop up the paintings on those, but it smells hellish musty in there. And I don't know where I'll stack the next batch you send me."

"We'll have to go to plan B, as we discussed in Rome. Buy an insulated sea-tainer...the sort of container they use to ship frozen goods. Get your mate with the bulldozer to come in from the road on the far side of the creek and cut out an area large enough to put it on."

"Right. Then I lay drainage pipes on the platform and cover them with ballast. Yes?"

"That's it. Get a crane and drop the container on the foundations, backfill with more ballast and then doze all the earth back on top of it so it's buried. Put the topsoil back last, together with as many shrubs as you can find. Throw down morning-glory seeds. By spring you shouldn't be able to see it."

"You got planning permission from the council?"

"Bugger that," Ron snapped. "This is supposed to be a secret store. If you seek council approval half of Australia will hear about it. No, there's hardly any traffic on the back road and, if you choose a long weekend for the work, you should be in and out without anyone noticing it."

"Right. I'll tell Alexandar not to talk about it at school."

"Good. Better if he doesn't know about it at all. Send him off for soccer coaching. If he asks, tell him it's a new septic tank. Just one thing, Kostas, old buddy. Make sure the door doesn't get buried as well!"

"I'm daft, but not that daft. I've my eye on some bushes which I can plant in front of it with bridal creeper. If anyone asks, I'll put it out that we're doing the fire-breaks early."

"Fine. Then start moving the gear out of the cave. Take it round in the car so you don't leave a beaten track through the bush from the house. That would be a dead giveaway."

"Can do. And now for the good news."

"I could do with some."

"Helene's pregnant."

"Holy gemoli. You were quick off the mark. Congratu-bloody-lations!"

***

Shortly before the New York trip Mike asked Ron for another before-and-after sketch of a child from Nigeria who had fallen face first in a fire. Ron was engrossed in the work when the door opened and the chief executive of LIPS brought a visitor into the ward.

Ron got to his feet in a hurry when he saw who it was. A cool, slim hand was offered him and he bowed over it.

"You're the artist they call Roman," she said. "I've heard about your work for AIDS children. It's one of my favourite charities. Would you consider painting my portrait?"

Would he? Wow! Would he ever. He smiled at one of the loveliest women in the world, standing there with her sweet lips curved enticingly, her skin flawless under the casually-styled blonde hair. He was startled by the depth of colour in her eyes, a clear, celestial blue.

"I'd be honoured," he said, his words half-strangled by surprise. "But I'm booked solidly until the New Year."

"Then I shall see you after Christmas," she purred, her husky voice light and pretty. "I will look forward to it." She turned at the door. "I'd prefer you told no one, Roman. I want the painting to be a surprise for my husband."

"Discretion is my middle name," he promised.

She gave a gurgle of laughter. "No, it's not. I've heard your middle name is sexy!"

PART THREE

Chiaroscuro

19

*Violet; The only artist's pigment in the modern purple
range is made from cobalt chloride or cobalt arsenate. A
solution of cobalt chloride is mixed with a similar quantity
of hydrogen phosphate. This creates a precipitate of dark
purple which is filtered and dried. A preparation made with
arsenate gives a light violet which is highly toxic. Both
forms are very permanent and have been in use since
1859.*

A winter of discontent marred Ron's excursion to New York,
largely because Zoe was constantly under foot. Other than
privately chivvying him, bullying him and trying to undermine his
confidence, she was an enthusiastic publicity machine. Ron might
be reticent about his work, but Zoe laid it on with a trowel. His
modesty did him no harm, especially in contrast with his garrulous
wife, who insisted on appearing with him on chat-shows, and who
dominated the interviews. She was, he realised, as intent on
promoting the name of Xenos as that of Roman. She had retained
the World Trade Centre space he had rejected as a studio and
opened her own gallery there.

Zoe networked. Ron made friends. He liked the life of
Greenwich Village. He liked meeting ordinary people. He enjoyed
the company of real stars, artistes who had lived in the world of
greasepaint and recording studio, who'd danced on the stages of
vaudeville theatre and on the sprung boards of the American
Ballet Theater. They liked him. They liked his work. They approved
of the aims of Art Aid. He was invited to stay in the USA, even
offered a position at a university as a Professor of Art. What he
had never realised was that the cameras liked him. His rangy,
country-boy looks were photogenic.

"You could be another Mel Gibson," said a studio executive. "But you're better looking. You interested in movies, Roman?"

Ron laughed and shook his head. "This is what I do best," he said firmly. "I'll make my pictures, you make yours."

Consequently the solo exhibition was a sell-out. Ron, having been sternly lectured by his accountant, insisted on detailed records of transactions. Zoe deducted twenty per cent commission and split the cost of the lease. She debited the hire of the studio and his hotel rooms from the total but it was still a sizeable sum which was banked to cushion Ron against lean times in the year ahead.

On his return to London he realised he would have to work even harder than expected, for he now had few completed paintings. He would have to go through his sketch books and the slides of his travels to bring his stock up to workable proportions.

"I'm going to put a bed in the studio," he told Pru. "I'm working late and I hate to disturb you when I come in."

"I don't even notice most of the time." Pru's spirits were very low. She remained almost totally focussed on Andrew's recovery. "He's sitting up, now, but he's lost the swallowing reflex. They still feed him by tube."

"Can he see?"

Pru shrugged. "Who knows. He can't talk so he can't tell us. He can hear things. He likes listening to the cricket."

"But there's no cricket at the moment."

"A friend at the BBC borrowed some tapes for me. Andrew doesn't seem to care if it's India versus Pakistan in 1978 or New Zealand versus England last season. He just nods and smiles and rolls his eyes when a wicket falls."

"Miserable for you."

"Not really. May's taught me how to knit. The nun showed her. I knit for the children at the Tamberlaine Foundation. Did you know May was expecting?"

"Marvellous. I'll buy her some flowers."

"Mike's agreed to join Tamberlaine when he finishes at LIPS. We'll set up a clinic for him in Indonesia where he can do simple surgery. The nuns are good nurses. They'll send patients in from the Missions but Mike and May will bring really serious cases back to LIPS. I'm teaching her island language so she can translate. She's learning Bahasa quickly. You must learn, too."

"Then teach me. It will be useful when I work for PanAsia."

"I will. I like keeping busy. It takes my mind off my worries."

He took her hand. "Has it been very bad?"

Pru burst into tears and howled all over him. "It's been horrible," she sobbed. "And I don't see an end to it. Oh, dear. I'm sorry. Have you got a handkerchief?" She blew her nose loudly. "There, that's better. Thank you, Ron. I needed a blubber with someone I trust."

"Count on me."

"I know, but I'm not much help to you, am I?" She looked ready to water up again.

"I'm a big boy now. You can't play Mum to me for ever." He patted her shoulder and walked out of the flat before she could have another wallow in unhappiness.

Grey skies and wet streets palled. He found a slide of boats on the beach at Kavalla, in northern Greece, and conjured himself back to summer. He found another slide of Alexandar, intent on scaling a fish he had just caught. 'Boy with Boats' took shape in his mind and he took a canvas from the rack.

He'd found a place in his mind which transported him to the

worlds he wanted to paint. There, as advised by Pru, figures and landscape would be complementary. The rough sketch was executed quickly. Only when he was certain the composition and the tone structure was balanced, did he select the colours he would use. This was not to be one of his quick impressions. This was to be the painting Pru said was within his capability. This was to be mastery of the technique and magician of the pigments. This was a painting to which would be added that elusive dimension...heart.

He worked on the beach scene at night, after the Art Aid portraits palled. He did not like artificial light but there was little alternative in Britain at that time of year. He took a break and went to his much-loved look-out on the fire escape, watching the tug-boats on the river, the men walking their dogs on the footpath alongside the sluggish water.

He admired the grace of the woman in the track suit who was jogging past the lamps on the pavement, heedless of the puddles, splashing with enjoyment, her pale gold hair spangled by rain. There was a tall, athletic-looking man behind her, adjusting his pace to hers. She looked up to the warehouse, smiled and waved. Ron waved back but thought nothing of it.

He put the kettle on for coffee and picked up his brushes. The painting was at a critical stage. The groundwork had been done but the fine detail remained. He was working on the sea... the wine-dark sea...flecking tiny violet lights onto the water, but carefully, so that the tone value of the background did not jump forward and dominate the central figure. The knock on the studio door made him jump and leave more paint than he wished. He cursed and threw down his rigger brush, ready with a curt "What do you want at this time of night?" for a would-be brush seller or Holy Joe.

"May I visit?" she said. "I'm sorry to be so late but I had to settle the boys for the night."

Ron was speechless. He held the door wide and waved her through.

She ran her fingers through her hair. "I don't suppose you've got a towel? It's only damp but I hate it when it gets limp and flops in my eyes." She sat on the chaise longue and gave her head a vigorous rub. Then she looked around the room with bright, alert eyes.

"Mmm. Love the smell of turpentine," she said. "Now, about my portrait. I thought we'd better decide where and when."

"Yes, ma'am."

"Oh, Lord, Roman, don't you start that stuffy business. Use my name."

"If you use mine. I'm Ron."

She smiled. "Fine. Then do you have a cup of coffee for a girl, Ron Turner? No, don't stop what you were doing. I'll make it."

"It's only instant."

She gurgled with amusement. "That's about my level of cooking. Where are the mugs?" She clattered around, finding and fixing, while Ron, with a strange feeling of unreality, gently removed the cobalt violet error from the Aegean. She set down his coffee at his feet and kicked a milk crate into position behind his left side. She sat on it and looked intently at what he was doing.

"I like this very much," she said. "Where is it?"

"Kavalla. Near Thessalonika."

"You know the boy?"

"I'm his guardian if anything happens to his mother. He's my fishing buddy."

"Yes, I can see the affection in the way he looks at you. And the way you've painted him. He looks happy, absorbed in what he's doing, but alive. I wish I felt like that."

Eyebrows raised, Ron glanced round at her. "Don't you?" He cleaned the brush and covered his palette with plastic wrap. Then he sat down on the floor at her feet and looked carefully at his visitor.

"I feel half-dead," she murmured. "I sometimes wonder what it's all about. If it wasn't for the boys I'd be lost."

"But you always seem so full of spirit, so energised, so caring."

"I try to be. Oh, how I try to be. Do you understand despair? Do you understand what it is to be used?"

"Yes, very well," Ron replied. "I have a domineering wife."

"And I have a husband who is in love with another woman. Why do you smile? What's funny about that?"

"I was just thinking that our cases are similar. My wife is in love with another woman as well!"

She gave a delighted giggle. "Oh. I see. My husband's uncle had the same problem with his wife. She was a notorious Les. What do you do for love?"

"Not a lot. Take it where I find it."

"Me too. When can you paint me, then? I'm going to be difficult, I know. I've lots of official engagements."

"Is it easier for you at night? My days are booked solid."

"Fine by me. I don't want anyone to know about this painting. I want it to be a surprise for You-Know-Who."

"It's for your husband...him?" Ron was quite bewildered. It was not what he expected from a rejected wife.

"Yes. I want you to paint me in a way that will remind him what he's missing. You see, Ron, I do love him. He's incredible. I want my eyes to follow him around the room and my expression to show my affection. Can you do that?"

"We can work on it."

She glanced at the Art Aid portraits. "I want something more impressive than these. They're good, but they're not as good as you can do, are they? The beach boy is a different quality."

"Perceptive, aren't you?"

"My husband thinks I'm an airhead."

"Foolish. You're young, that's all. Was he ever young?"

"God, no! Nannied to the hilt, bowing to Mummy, scared stiff of Daddy. Taught to be brave and keep a stiff upper lip in that rough school and then trained to be a hero in the Forces. No, he was never young in the way I want our sons to be young. But he's funny and charming and quite, quite delightful company. It's simply that I don't see enough of him at those times. He's off with his mistress. Says the people expect him to keep a mistress. Says everyone in his position has and he's got no precedent for following middle-class morals."

Ron frowned. "His grandfather wasn't like that. He was straight as a die. Devoted to his wife."

"Yes, he was. I'm surprised his grandmother doesn't remind him of that. She dotes on him."

"As we say in Australia, they're a weird mob, your rellies."

The bell-like laughter came again. "Are your rellies weird?"

Ron gave a shout of amusement. "You'd not believe the folk at Cootimurra." He gave her a quick word sketch of life in the Outback, of the odd ways of his brother, of his mother's idea of a treat...eating a bar of Violet Crumble while doing the ironing...of his father's insistence on reading old newspapers in the dunny, of the brothers who'd died.

She laughed until she cried and Ron, his ribs aching at retelling incidents of which he had never before seen the funny side, gasped, "And the folk at Cootimurra would never believe this, either. Me sitting at your feet, telling tales about them. Do you know it's nearly midnight?"

"Oh sh..sh..sh..sh..sugar! My bodyguard will be fuming." She pressed a bleeper and paged him. "Ready now." She got up and stretched her legs, then walked to the window wall and admired the view. "Hopkins will take a while to get here. He does some serious running when I'm otherwise engaged. How do I contact you?"

"I've got a silent number," Ron said, scribbling on a piece of paper. "Ring first to make sure I haven't got company."

"You know what it means to be discreet, I see."

"Hell, yes. I don't want Zoe finding out about you. She'd embarrass you."

"Would she? How?"

"She wouldn't blow a trumpet on my behalf. She'd hire the entire brass band."

"Oh. Like that is she? Then we'll have to be super careful."

"We're safe for now. She's gone back to New York to hang another exhibition at Xenos, her gallery in the Twin Towers. She been scouting new talent because she's concentrating on foreign artists who aren't known in the USA. That's her 'motif', from the name, Xenos, meaning strange, exotic. I, according to her, am as strange as they come, which is why I sell well in the States."

"Is Boy on the Beach destined for America?"

"No. It's for the Royal Academy."

They stood at the window, quietly talking until the bodyguard came into sight. The visitor smiled at Ron and kissed his cheek. "I enjoyed our talk," she said. "I'll be in touch."

With that she was gone. Ron rubbed his cheek and watched until he saw her jogging away, breathing deeply and smelling the subtle perfume she had left on the air. Then he pressed his fingers to his lips and wondered if he had been living in a dream.

***

It was ten days before she called. "I'm free on Saturday. The boys are watching polo with their father. I want to take you for a picnic. I'll be waiting for you round the corner at 10." She hung up.

Ron felt irritated. He had no way of telling her he was otherwise engaged but, as he wasn't, he simply did as suggested. She wore a headscarf and sunglasses. If she hadn't waved at him he would not have recognised her.

"Where are we going?"

"To my home. To my father's place. I want to show you the background I want for my portrait. Now be a darling, Ron, and don't talk. I need to concentrate when I drive."

She pushed in a cassette and a medley of the latest Top Twenty boomed around the interior. She took up the beat with her body, mouthing the lyrics, moving her shoulders in rhythm, pulsing the accelerator in time with the drums. Ron detested driving with her. She was fast, she was frisky and she was decidedly risky. He'd have put ten dollars on her at the races, but would never have chosen her for a milk round.

By noon they were turning into the gates of the ancestral residence. The imposing pile, her family's home for five hundred years, was not her destination. She swung off the carriageway onto what looked like a farm track and followed it past a lake to woodlands.

"Bring the hamper, picture man," she said, after parking under a weeping-willow tree, out of sight of the track. "It's soft under foot but the grass isn't that wet. I'll bring a rug."

Their picnic place was in a quiet valley where in spring, she said, the woods were filled with violets and, a little later, bluebells. "That's how I want to be shown. Sitting on that fallen log, with the countryside behind me, and my arms full of spring flowers."

"A sylph? A spirit of the air? Shall call you sylph? Or a wood nymph? Yes, I'll call you Nymph."

"I am not a nymphomaniac!"

"I didn't imply that."

"It's stuffy. I like Woody better. Have you met Woody Allen?"

Her mind was like quicksilver, rolling from one subject to another with deceptive speed. It was almost as if she were nervous. She had nothing to fear from him, surely?

Ron smiled, cheekily. "Woody it shall be. That's how I feel when I look at you."

She gurgled with amusement. "Have you got a stiffy?"

She spread the rug and curled herself on it, suggesting Ron sit next to her. "I've heard how you work," she said, shyly. "That you demand every subject should pose in the nude. I thought we'd get it over with today."

Ron shook his head. "No, Woody. There's no need. It's too cold."

"Rubbish." She pulled her jumper over her head and unfastened her skirt. She leaned back against the log and looked at him seriously. "Will I pass? Am I too thin? My husband says I'm scrawny. He says women should have something to grab hold of."

So she was nervous, not of Ron's presence, but with fear that she might not meet his approval.

"You are one of the most beautiful women I have ever seen," he said with some truth. She was a wild rose compared to the exotic Mercedes, but he knew which was the most tempting.

"You don't mind the stretch marks?"

"They're like the silver veins on a dragonfly wing. Those give the wings strength. There is nothing to be ashamed of in the signs of motherhood."

Her laugh was a benison. "Thank you. Such a pretty thought. We should make love now, Ron, because I always feel sleepy after lunch."

There was nothing of the shrinking violet about Woody. She gave herself with generosity and received the worship of his body with gratitude.

***

Spring came and the violets peeped shyly from beneath the ferns in the glade and, in due course the cuckoo called from the valley and the bluebells were a wash of cerulean between the ancient trees. There were purple orchids in damp places and anemones danced in the wind, lifting their mauve overskirts to reveal the fluted white petticoats below.

They came to the glade several times, to refresh the vision, she said. But she came to his bed and he to hers many nights and on stolen afternoons. She had a need and he filled her with delight and a new confidence in herself.

"Am I better than your first love?" she asked.

"Mercedes?" She had been shown the only remaining copy of the Mercedes calendar and had posed for similar sketches. While his hands were busy with pencil and charcoal, he had told her everything. "She has muscles that can play a man as if he were a clarinet," he chuckled, describing her internal prowess.

"I could learn to do that, too. It's only another sort of pelvic exercise. But if she's so good, why waste her talents on Zoe?"

"Beats me, Woody," sighed Ron. "But you don't need to do all that fancy stuff. Mercedes drains a man. You replenish me. You make me feel stronger, happier, greatly blessed."

"And you make me feel cherished. I've never felt cherished before. I feel as if you've gathered me under your wing to protect me from the storm."

Ron loved her tenderly but was conscious, as he had been from the start, that theirs was a fragile affair. It was as if such moments were dewdrops on a dawn spider's web, sparkling in the sun, yet able to be broken by the slightest breeze. He knew a storm would blow their happiness into tatters.

20

*Carmine; this deep red pigment is obtained by crushing
small insects, such as cochineal, native to the New World,
or kermes, used to make scarlet cloth in Arabia and
Mediterranean Europe since ancient times. The insects are
boiled for a long period and the liquid drawn off. The
residue, thick and heavy, is dried and blended with
medium. Although both forms have intense colours, they
are not permanent and fade in sunlight.*

Woody's portrait was magnificent. It did for her beauty what
Pietro Annigoni had done for the Queen at the same age. It made
it timeless. Behind her the landscape captured the spirit of all
England, and she was part of it. Blue sky could be seen beneath
the fresh greenery of spring. She wore a simple dress of white
cotton edged with broderie anglaise, and her feet were bare. Her
neck was long and graceful and her head was poised as if she had
turned from contemplation of the beauties of nature to greet a
loved one.

Ron, who had at first thought the bluebells would look well,
had rejected the obvious for the symbolism of the wild rose. He
painted a briar-rose bush behind her. She held a deep pink bud
and a full-blown blossom loosely between her fingers, as if she
had just picked them ready to put in a man's buttonhole. There
was welcome in her eyes and her lips held the promise of a kiss.

"Thank you, thank you, my darling," she cried, her arms around
Ron's neck. "Now, take the photographs so I can show my
husband the surprise."

She stormed into the studio two days later, black-browed and
wicked. "He says I look common! He doesn't want it hanging in his

private rooms and he doesn't want it at our country home, either. Oh, damn him, Ron. And damn that dog of a woman."

He ached for her and her lousy marriage. She was like a kid at Christmas, who'd been promised a nice present and had opened the wrapping to find it had been used, and was broken and shop-soiled.

"I'm hurting, Ron. I'm hurting. What shall I do?"

There was no kissing her better, not this time. Imps of anger were dancing in her eyes.

"It's too bad it's too late for the Summer Exhibition at the Royal Academy," she said. "It would have been even more acclaimed than your Greek boy, and Alexandar wowed the critics. I know. I'll send it to Sothebys. They can auction it and you shall have the proceeds for Art Aid."

"If you do that, Zoe will benefit. Give the proceeds to Pru's Tamberlaine Foundation instead."

Pru, who was persuaded to come and see the finished work, and to meet its sitter, sat down all of a heap and burst into tears.

"Don't you like it, Mrs Darcy?" said Woody, kneeling beside Ron's patron.

"It's brilliant. It's what I always knew he was capable of doing, but it will ruin him, and it will probably ruin you, too."

"Why on earth should it? You're the only one who knows about our relationship."

"Twaddle," snapped Pru. "You may have intended this as a token of love for your husband, but it's perfectly clear it's the artist you've been bonking!"

Ron knelt facing Woody and touched her cheek. "I didn't mean to make it obvious."

"But it's true, isn't it. That's who I was longing to take in my arms. Ron, I mustn't see you again. I must try to undo some of the damage I've done."

"Can you mend my heart?"

"No, but I can draw off the bloodhounds."

"And how can you do that?"

She gave a delicious giggle. "Easy. I'll just take another lover and let the paparazzi find out about it!"

"Oh, nice one," said Pru, suppressing urges torn between wanting to pat their heads and say, "Bless You My Children," and a great desire to knock their skulls together.

***

The trouble with putting your heel on a living organism is that the crunch is followed by the bleeding. Deep red, viscous, sticky blood. The organism, doubtless, suffers intense pain as it dies, leaving only the stains of its life to get smeared around.

It is much the same with the end of an affair. Like carmine, it fades with time, but the fibres retain the memory of what it once had been. Not permanent; not able to withstand light. Ron ached with the loss. He stood at the studio window and ached.

Running in the rain, running in the rain. The dark runner approached and swung away from the river's edge and out of sight. Ron sighed. It wasn't Woody. He had not seen her again. There had been no phone call, no letter, not a whisper, but the gossip columnists had been busy.

Men. She'd been seen here and there with men other than her husband. She'd been playing up, out all night, doing the town. Rattle, rattle, rattle. Hiss, hiss, hiss. Media speak with forked tongue. Society writers dip their pens in poison. Woody's mates reveal all about the rotten deal she's had. Friends of the husband throw mud at her. She's bad and she's mad and she's sick.

He was startled by the quiet knock.

The burly bodyguard pushed past him. "Put the light out. I want to make sure no one's watching."

"You're the last person I expected to see, Hopkins."

"And I doubt you'll see me again. Come away from the window. They may have a sensitive microphone trained on it."

"You're paranoid!"

"It's my job to be paranoid. That's what Special Security Policing's all about. You're not bugged. I swept this place while you were at your flat. And I swept the flat while you were here."

"Why? It's over."

"Mr Turner, I have been watching your back for months. I have tailed you on your country excursions; I have hidden close at hand and made sure you were not being followed. I have stood guard while you were otherwise engaged. You are in more danger now than you have ever been."

"I told you. It's over."

"How can it be? The portrait exists. He knows who painted it. He has friends who protect his interests. The artwork is in the vaults of Sothebys and will not be auctioned until next year, but the whispers have started. He has the photograph of it. There may be copies. Did you make sure the photographer didn't take duplicates?"

"Hell, no. I just used a one-hour service."

The man sighed. "You should have used Polaroid. Could I have a cup of tea? And can we sit down somewhere, out of the line of the window?"

"You want me to make tea in the dark?"

"Put the bedside light on."

"Only if you've checked it for bugs!"

"This isn't funny, Mr Turner. Your friend wants me to make sure there is nothing here that could incriminate either of you."

"Oh, sugar, as Woody would say. Sit on the end of the bed!" Ron brewed the tea and pulled the milk crate over to the divan. "What is all this about?"

"You've been very careful, very discreet, but Woody, as you call her, wants to know what you've done with the sketch books. And all the Polaroids."

"Tell her not to worry. They're not here."

"His men will search the premises of anywhere you live and anyone with whom you are friends. They'll even get access to the bank."

"Even to safety deposit boxes? I think not."

"Safety of the Realm and all that jazz?"

"Tell her they're not even in this country!"

"Why were you so eager to conceal them, Mr Turner? Are they incriminating?"

Ron went dark red. "Yes, they bloody well are, but I haven't hidden them from your Great Panjandrum. I got them out of my hair because my effing wife is arriving any day!"

"But you don't cohabit."

"We don't co-anything."

"Why don't you divorce? I'm just curious. Are you afraid she'll want half your estate?"

Ron laughed harshly. "My estate? I'm not wealthy. I get by. I did well in New York last year, but taxes chewed up a lot of that. I had to pay provisional tax on the lot in advance because the bastards now expect me to earn the same this year."

"You earned money in Greece."

"How the hell do you know that? Dammit man, I repatriated most of it to Australia, declared it and paid tax on it there. If you want to talk money, don't talk to me. Talk to Zoe. She handles the business. She's the moneybags in this partnership, if you can call it that."

The man looked at him kindly. "Got you over a barrel, has she?"

"Yes, and if she finds out about Woody, she'll knacker me!"

"Ah, well. I've passed the message. Woody said to tell you not to believe all you read in the papers. She sent her love."

"Likewise. Are you going?"

"Yes, Mr Turner. And if you want my advice, you'll go off on your PanAsia assignment as soon as possible."

"I don't want to leave Mrs Darcy while her husband is so ill."

"Don't worry. I'll keep an eye on her. Tell her to expect a visit from Mark Hopkins and that I'm a friend."

***

Boy on the Beach had brought Zoe running from the Big Apple. "You let that go for five thousand pounds? Have you any idea what a Roman is worth these days?"

"No idea. I don't see much of the proceeds, wifey, dear."

"I'm entitled to my dues."

"Not if you're not acting as agent. And the taxman will get most of this sale. Anyway, what harm has it done? I got great critical reviews for it."

"By luck. Don't forget, it's my promotion which made your name."

"That's odd, Zoe. The critics seem to think it's my talent that counts."

"Damn you, Ron. I hope your work's on target before you fly off to do those disgusting PanAsia paintings."

"Spot on, even if I have to work until midnight. I'll not let Art Aid down. But I'm not hurrying back. The Indonesian Ambassador and General Ihza have got me the commission he promised. All the Cabinet."

"You're chasing Mercedes again!"

"Zoe, it may be hard for you to believe, but I rarely think of Mercedes these days."

"You've still got the hots for her. I know. Mess with her and I'll fix you."

"You really are a silly bitch," he sighed. "Take what you want for Xenos and get out of my hair."

Zoe riffled through the recent canvases and set a dozen aside. "I'll send the shipping agents for them tomorrow," she snapped.

"If you don't, it'll be too late. I fly out on Tuesday."

Tuesday. It seemed to race towards him. Time only for dinner with May and Mike, to admire the new baby, cradled in the arms of Pru, who was playing the doting grandmother. Time only to visit Andrew, nodding and grinning vacantly in his chair in the nursing home, with the deep Yorkshire voice of the cricket commentator talking about maiden overs and silly-mid-ons and bowling statistics.

Time only to pick up his tickets and itinerary from PanAsia.

He took a glass of whiskey with the managing director, who was giving him detailed instructions on the sort of scene the airline wanted.

"We've done market research on Beauties of Asia. The girls are all very lovely, but we found they were offensive to followers of

Islam. As the population of Indonesia is sixty per cent Muslim, you'll understand that we should modify our approach. We want women in national costume, doing things, like winnowing rice, picking coffee, making batik. More like your wonderful painting of Boy on a Beach. Can you do this?"

It would, Ron realised, be a relief. He was moving on, away from the Vargas style, drawn to the Vermeer concept, as Pru had suggested. They had a long discussion on the matter. Almost as an afterthought, Ron asked, "Did you ever find any more of those calendars of Mercedes Dinegoro?"

The man looked at him with alarm. "Only a couple. Didn't you get them?"

"You promised to courier them to me. What did you do with them?"

"I'm so sorry, Mr Turner. I gave them to your wife."

Ron felt the heel on his flesh again. Zoe's heel. His blood ran cold with apprehension.

***

The Spice Islands lived up to their name. There was the smell of star anise, of cumin and coriander, of pepper and all-spice, of nutmeg and cinnamon, and over it all, the fragrance of frangipani blossoms. In the markets were piles of shredded coconut and mounds of red coffee beans, heaped among the fresh vegetables and gleaming, niffy fish.

Ron saw no signs of the other crop General Ihza allowed to be grown on the former Vandermeer land. Opium poppies, which needed dry, high land, were, he now knew, as illegal as in Australia. It was, he realised, typical of the corruption endemic in certain quarters, that one who was in theory an upholder of the law was also undermining it. It was the two faces Indonesia showed to the world, the coffee on the side of the volcanic peaks facing the rain, hidden poppies on the dry ashes in their shadow.

Elsewhere the hillsides were stepped into rice paddies, the green tiers rising in narrow terraces along which water flowed. Ron painted a woman planting rice, her face reflected in the still mirror of the flooded land. He came down from the heights of Kalimantan with a portrait of an old woman holding a baby orangutan. In Iryan Jaya he captured the concentration of a bride weaving a head-dress for her husband from the feathers of birds of paradise.

He practised Bahasa wherever he went and was understood, for it was taught in schools, but found the dialects spoken in Java, Sumatra and Ambon distinctly different. Although one of the largest countries in Asia, the variety of cultures, religions and ethnic backgrounds was staggering. The Hindus did not mix with the Muslims, the Buddhists were something else again, mainly Chinese traders. In communities off the beaten track, the beliefs of the natives were animalistic and pagan. There were seven million Christians on the islands and in parts they were loathed. In places they were slaughtered. There were few Dutch left. They had not left in peace but in savage resentment. It was not a society in which European, American or Australian values counted for much.

However, he could not escape images of Mercedes. Western values might have no currency, but the investment dollar did. PanAsia booked him in new, tourist hotels affiliated to the airline, and wherever he stayed, there was television. He became a compulsive viewer of her English news bulletins, not from fascination with her face or her seductive, cultured voice, but with the need to stay rooted to his own background. He was an alien in Indonesia, feeling as if he were floating in luxury on the top of a forest-fringed lagoon, within which crocodiles might lurk. It was reassuring to him to hear of events in New York, the Philippines, in Lebanon and the Persian Gulf. It was like putting down a foot and finding firm sand at the bottom of the lake, instead of fathomless depths. It was a twisting wrench to see Woody opening charity events, for the Indonesians shared the world's interest in the English beauty. But the news remained dominated by the aftermath of the collapse of the Wall Street stock market. Ron wondered how his wife had fared. He reflected, not for the first time, that it was a good thing to be too poverty stricken to chase funny money.

Whatever Zoe had done to rehabilitate Mercedes, it had obviously succeeded, for his first love was very much in control and, now, very much the professional. It was with some surprise, therefore, that PanAsia informed him she was to be his final subject. They flew him to Surabaya, and on to the Tugu Monument, at Malang. Mercedes, they said, would pose by the lily-ponds, the ancient monument in the background, with her arms full of water-lily blossoms.

Ron came to the session reluctantly. Mercedes was just as wary. She was unsmiling.

"This wasn't my idea," she said.

"Nor mine. It's going to be hard to paint you naturally with old Ihza sitting in the car over there, chewing on his fat cigars."

Mischief fired up in her eyes for a brief moment. "Ron, you don't expect me to pose au naturelle in a bloody duck pond, do you?"

He grinned and ran his fingers through his sun-streaked hair. "Not unless you cover yourself with insect repellent. This place is plague-ridden. The mozzies could fly off with you!"

"Chicken. Come on, how shall I sit?"

It must have become apparent to the General that there was no sexual chemistry simmering between them for, on the second day, he merely delivered his wife and made the excuse that there was work to do on their property. He wanted to ensure the beans were being properly roasted.

"Pig's bum," said Mercedes, when he had gone. "I expect he wants to tumble Hugo. Shocked, Ron? My beloved husband has found himself a new lover."

"Puke!"

"No, it's just that it's an experience he hasn't tried before. Ihza says I have become boring and if it's good enough for me to meet Zoe from time to time, he can't see why I should object."

"Do you?"

"Well, of course I do. Hugo haunts the brothels. Venereal disease is an issue. But what can I say when my own brother is the one who buys in the kids for Ihza's tourist traps?"

"How can you be so calm about that? Don't you hate to see children corrupted?"

"You know my past, Ron. How do you think I feel?"

"Honest to God, Mercedes, I haven't got a clue."

"No. I don't suppose you have."

Her expression was strange, a faraway haunting look, of the child outside the sweetshop window, hungry for something she could never have; in her case, he felt it might be innocence. He painted her like that, calm and wistful. Like all the Island Life paintings, it held all the magic of his new ability. He was determined that these should go to the 1988 Academy Exhibition, although the rights to reproduction were already sold.

When rain interrupted his work, Mercedes, who had driven herself to the assignment, suggested he might like to visit a village. It was a pretty place, beside the sea. She led him down a muddy path to a small house, where a woman, wearing the headcloth of a Muslim, was preparing vegetables. A child sat at her feet, playing with a basket full of shells.

"My cousin," said Mercedes, who started a rapid conversation in the local patois. She ignored the child, whose face was shadowed by a cloth. "Talk to her. She goes to school and learns Bahasa."

Ron decided to try. "Selemat Pagi," he said to the little girl. "Good morning. Siapa nama anda? What is your name?"

The child looked up at him with pale grey eyes, like the clouds when the cyclones stream in from the Timor Sea. "Nama saya Liana," she said, pulling off the headscarf which covered her fine, blonde hair. "Senang berkenalan dengan anda."

"She says it is nice to meet you," said Mercedes. "Spitting image of you, isn't she?"

Liana's foster mother looked from the child to Ron and let out a scream of fury. She ran at Mercedes, beating her on the head and chest. She turned angrily on the child and slapped her face. Ron had lost track of the conversation, but he knew the woman was calling Liana 'dirty'. The child ran, crying, into the house.

"We should go," Mercedes said. "She's very angry."

"But why?"

"She says I cheated her...and I did. Liana was born with black hair but it came out. She doesn't like having a child who looks like a Dutch baby. People say she slept with an Infidel and, as they are Santri, very strict Muslims, the child is regarded as a disgrace. Her husband knows Liana is fostered so he hasn't divorced her, but it's been touch and go. The mullahs are at him all the time."

"But why turn on you now, today?"

"Because of you. I told her the fair hair came from my father's side of the family. Now she accuses me of being a wanton and bringing my dirty lover to their house."

"Why did you do so? I was delighted to meet Liana but whatever possessed you to stir the pot? Devilry?"

"I was curious. I thought you were alike but I wanted to see you side by side."

"Can I send money to her mother? Make life easier for them?"

"I make an allowance. They do all right. They'd be insulted to take money from you. If they need extra the husband, Putu, goes and works in tourist resorts here or on other islands. He says he spits in the Infidels' food before he serves it."

"Christ, Mercedes, what a life you've pushed the poor little mite into. She's an outcast in her own family!"

"Not really. Her skin's the right colour and she's been brought up as a good little Muslim. She'll be fine."

Ron frowned. He could hear his daughter sobbing and his heart turned over.

21

Madder and Madder Lake; Two pigments extracted from the root of rubia tinctorum plant, the former having a purple component and being known, from Medieval paintings, to lose colour. However, when the process of laking the dye, by adding alum, was invented in the early 19th century, the strong reds and purples gained remarkable resistance to sunlight. They are popular as a glaze and their use continues until the present day, although a synthetic pigment, which lacks purpurin, has largely ousted them from the palette.

"Come home at once," Pru cabled. "Zoe's on the warpath!"

Ron rang England immediately he got back to Surabaya. "What's up? What's the panic?"

"Zoe's heard about the Woody painting on the art grapevine and has flown in looking for trouble."

"Sothebys won't talk to her about it. They're as tight-lipped as a Swiss bank."

"No, but You-Know-Who's friends are sniffing around like dogs looking for a bitch on heat. It's in their interests to discredit your girlfriend, for want of a better name."

"It'll blow over."

"No, it won't. Zoe's playing the wronged wife card. She got Mercedes off heroin, but, if you ask me, she's got a cocaine addiction. She'll be wearing a bone through her nose if she doesn't pack that in."

"Oh, it would suit her. Very savage, our Zoe."

"And madder than a cat with a poker up its bum since she found out you'd been seeing Mercedes."

"Damn it, Pru, I haven't even kissed her!"

"She reckons you'd get round to your old ways, sooner or later. How much longer must you stay?"

Ron explained the complications of discovering Liana. "I've got all these damned portraits to do for the Government," he sighed. "And I want to try to bring Liana home. She is, after all, an Australian. Born there and to an Australian mother."

"Have you any idea how difficult that would be? How much trouble you'd cause the kid? It would be a journalist's scoop and you and Mercedes would be pilloried."

"And General Ihza would go berserk. Yes, I know. I don't know what to do."

"Simple. Postpone the commissions. Get back here and gag Zoe. Worry about the child later. Let me make inquiries through the Tamberlaine Foundation about the problems it could involve."

Ron shut his eyes in bitter confusion. "Yes, Mum. All right, Mum. I'll be home in time for the dog's breakfast! But Zoe will have to wait. There are things I must do and places I must go."

"What is more important?"

"Kostas and Helene. Alexandar and my new god daughter. And Ephemeral."

"Oh," said Pru, letting out her breath. "Oh, of course. That really is important."

***

PanAsia didn't care; their work was complete. General Ihza was nonchalant about the whole matter, although he stressed it was an honour to be allowed to paint portraits in a country dominated by a religion which did not approve of the depiction of living things.

"However, I am not devout," he said with a smile like sour cream. "And you have not given me offense. You have shown respect to my wife. I shall explain. You may return."

"And who do you think you are?" thought Ron, who'd had it on good authority that the General's power was waning; that younger, gung-ho men without questionable business interests were striving to oust the Suharto government. It was not crocodiles which lurked under the rippling surface of Indonesia's currents, but political activists. And behind them, coiled like dark snakes, were the religious fanatics.

He caught a flight to Denpasar and from there to Australia. The flight passed, near as damn it, over the bare red earth of Cootimurra. Ron felt tears prickling. He was coming home to people he loved. Alexandar had grown a couple of inches and was, he was proud to announce, a keen soccer player. "I've been selected for trials for the State Under-13s. If I get in, I get to play in Darwin. Good, isn't it."

Kostas hugged Ron and shook his head at his stepson. "Don't count on it. I don't know if we can afford the fare."

Helene, with the heavy baby in her arms, frowned as she kissed Ron. "It costs so much for Kostas to drive to Margett's every day and his father's not making much money out of the restaurant. We can't stay at Ephemeral much longer, Ron. It's been a nightmare since she grew out of the playpen and started crawling. We've had to put safety gates across the window to the balcony. What will we do when she starts walking and climbing? I'll be terrified."

"I'm not scared of heights," Alexandar said. "I can shimmy down the poles like nobody's business!"

Ron, recalling with a lurch of the guts how high off the ground was the balcony, shuddered. "We'll sort something out," he promised, getting into the slightly newer van that seemed a part of Kostas. "I'll shout Alexandar his trip to the Territory. And maybe Pru would let you rent her place on the coast. She shows no signs of planning to move Andrew back to Australia. And, in the meantime, gimme. It's time I cuddled Roma. It was nice of you to call her after me."

"We didn't," said Kostas, blushing. "She's called after where she was conceived!"

***

From the mezzanine bedroom Ron could look straight out over the tops of the eucalypt trees to the blue summer skies of his homeland. It was going to be another scorcher. He went quietly down the stairs so as not to wake Kostas and Helene, stepped over the wooden railings they had fitted across the entrance to the balcony, and peered over the edge. He could see which pole Alexandar favoured, for it was worn shiny with use. Plucking up courage, he swung his hips over the side of the deck and wrapped his legs around it. He gingerly transferred weight to his hands and started the descent, gaining confidence as he neared the bottom and finishing with a fast slide to ground level.

The pool was clear and tempting. He plunged in and swam briskly for ten minutes. Alexandar emerged from the house with two mugs of coffee. "I thought you'd want this," the boy said. "Sleep well?"

"I always do in this place. It's like being on a cloud."

"It's great, but it's out of the world, if you know what I mean."

"You mean it's inconvenient."

"Yes. It's a long way for mother to drive me to soccer and I have to ride my bike a couple of kilometres to catch the school bus. Kostas is seriously fed up."

"That's a pity."

"Yes, it is, because Mum and he are made for one another. I'm pretty happy about Australia, but the rellies! Well, have you met Mana Agnella? And Uncle Aristotle?"

"Not my favourite people."

"I like Grandfather Constantine; he's OK but you should hear him quarrelling with Uncle Aristotle. They're mad at one another. They keep threatening to sue their pants off. What does that mean, Ron?"

"Who'd know? Your mother's calling. If you don't hurry you'll miss the school bus."

The area around the house had been kept tidy but, beyond the lawn, Kostas had let the plants of Ephemeral grow wild. Fire-breaks were in, and fairly recently by the look of it. Ron found a pair of rubber boots in the garden shed and put them on, hoping there were no redback spiders in their depths. He strolled along the fence line, avoiding long grass and thick shrubbery in favour of the slashed area, for he wanted to leave no mark of his passing on the dew-damp slopes.

There was no sign of the shipping container. It was completely hidden by green shrubs and tangles of vines. He moved a curtain of morning-glory to one side and unlocked the door. There was, as Kostas had told him, a torch beside the door-jamb, a large powerful flashlight. The air in the hidey-hole was cool and fresh. There was no sign of damp or the musty smell of dry rot or fungus.

This was his graveyard. Here lay the bodies he had committed to canvas. The studies were unmistakable likenesses. No one saw the nudes. They were his private filing system, his defence against boredom, his inner rebellion against the type of art into which his wife's avarice had steered him. He was weak. He knew he was no match for her vitriol, for her dominating personality, for her power over his financial affairs. He had tried to revolt but, she kept reminding him, his father-in-law's men still had hammers and there were few artists who did well when their knuckle joints had been crushed.

He had refused to paint a conventional portrait of his one-time tormentor to hang in the boardroom of the family company. The private version was another matter. He had painted Aristotle as a rampant bull, hooves crushing a hundred broken hands. Zoe, painted in anger, with eyes like cash-registers, was stacked beside her father. There were many nudes of Mercedes, painted when she had lived with him. Ron unwrapped the waterproof covering from the series for PanAsia and riffled through the sketch books wrapped with them.

He undid the strings around the portfolio which contained the studies of Woody. She had inspired him where Mercedes had exploited him. He ached for Woody and the torment she was going through. He broke his heart that she was obliged to play wanton for his sake. He hoped her new lovers would be kind to her, for she deserved devotion. He had wanted no other woman since. It was his tragedy that he had loved the unattainable, and hers that she had loved the impossible.

He spent a long time looking at his fairy-tale love, reliving every stolen moment. Then he set everything to rights, locked the door and went slowly back to the world of the living, and not of the captives of his wayward talent.

***

Zoe was venomous.

"Lost lots of money when Wall Street crashed, or have you just got PMT?" Ron said, tiredly. PanAsia had routed him back via the Philippines, for a quick photographic session with local hostesses who were not as reticent as the Indonesians. He had ended up in the middle of riots by supporters of Ferdinand Marcos. Armed street-fighting was not his idea of a Pacific paradise. "Zoe, I've had a hell of a flight and I'm not best amused."

She threw a photocopy of the portrait of Woody onto the table. It was a bad reproduction but it was clear who the subject was. "How stupid can you get?" Zoe screamed. "How much did she pay you for that, or was a shag enough?"

Ron fetched her a furious right-hander to the jaw. His palm tingled from the force of it and his fingers left marks of deep madder on her skin. There was a trickle of blood from her mouth.

"If the Establishment doesn't ruin you, Ron Turner, I will," she said, spitting red at him. "I'm calling my lawyer."

"And who will you cite, Zoe? I'll swear haven't slept with you for two years and there's no citing people for adultery these days."

"I can murder your reputation in the press. And hers!"

"That's blackmail. And I could name you as a Lesbian, or have you outed yourself yet?"

"You'd destroy Mercedes? Well, if you do, I'll send the calendar to General Ihza and he will destroy your daughter."

"Leave Liana out of this."

"No. Why should I? Don't you realise, you damned fool, that if her mother is publicly named whore, the girl is disgraced as well? I think the phrase is 'Gotcha', Ron Turner. Gotcha by the short and curlies!"

***

Ron looked miserably at his feet. Pru had demanded a full account of his excursion and an even more detailed story about Ephemeral and the Populis family. She had nodded sympathetically about the concerns of Kostas and Helene and, as

Ron expected, made the offer of the other home without prompting.

"Maybe I could go back to Australia if Kostas and his wife would help me with Andrew," she mused. "But I won't run out on you until after the Art Aid launch, the Summer Exhibition and the Sothebys auction. No way. You need someone to watch your back. And now that Mike and May are on their way to run the Tamberlaine Clinic, you'd be all alone."

"Boo hoo," he said with a smile, knowing it to be true and feeling relieved she hadn't forced him to ask for support. "You shall be my lady with the Umbrella, Les Parapluies. You shall protect me from the storm."

It was hovering ominously despite the form of a dashing soldier whose name was linked to Woody's and was made the target of the Press Barons. The thunder started rolling when he realised the London studio had been searched, though he had changed the locks when Zoe rode back into town. Lightning flashed when Kostas reported that Ephemeral had been ransacked.

"They didn't find a thing, though," he said, his voice crackling past a bad international connection. "But it's spooked Helene properly. We'll move to the Darcy place next week."

"Good. You can safely leave the gardens alone. The mushrooms are doing fine." Ron was conscious that his phone could be tapped. "Did Alexandar make the team?"

"Sure did. He's playing away this week. By the way, would you ask Pru if we could borrow the Dreamdrift II? She needs her bottom scraped and then the boy and I would like to try fishing from her."

The hiss of high wind in the palm trees could not have been louder than the sibilant tongues of the gossip columnists and, as the opening of the Art Aid show approached, their false sentiments clattered louder than their false teeth...all plastic grins and dentures. Anticipation approached the fever of Oscar season, the American Academy Awards. In fact, a much-loved and much married film star, a great supporter of AIDS charities, had agreed to open it.

Ron, arriving for the pre-ceremony drinks, with Pru on his arm, was dazzled by the flashlights and the interest, the pushing, tasteless interest, of the media mouths. "Is it true you slept with..." The names went past in a blur, running from David Bowie, who he'd never met, to Julie Andrews, who he had on one occasion, past Marilyn Monroe who had been dead long before he came to fame. "No," said Ron, but he had had a serious affair with Donald Duck. He felt the sharp nastiness of Zoe in their tongues, he felt the blood-lust in their eyes and their mercilessness hearts. And he saw Zoe, in the background, smirking and nodding approval.

One night, one night was all he had to contend with, while Woody had to live with it, day in, night out. There were pretty speeches and a sweet lady talking about the wonderful way Business and Celebrities had come together to help those in need. The scheme had, she said, raised forty million dollars, and its instigator, Roman, had single-handedly painted more than a hundred paintings over two years. This alone had brought in more than twenty-eight million pounds. The total sum was enormous. It was gross enough to bring guests to their feet, cheering approbation, while Ron and his fellow artists blushed and bowed.

A well-known supporter of the Realm, and a BBC journalist of popular and sentimental wit, took the microphone. The man was unsteady on his feet. "And now I call upon Roman, as Ron Norman Turner is popularly known, to say a few words."

Ron, white-faced and miserable, was pushed forward by hands which propelled him, rather like the gait of a millipede, to the dais. Pru, in his wake, told him to stay calm and keep it simple. The broadcaster drew Ron to his side and said, "I've been asked to put a simple question to you, Roman. I calculate you raised more than twenty-eight million pounds. How come the Art Aid Trust has only received only part of that money?"

Ron, aghast, saw the malice in the man's eyes and, without thinking, smashed him in the nose.

"So you do bleed red, not yellow," Ron roared. "Now, just what are you implying?"

And a piercing voice from the back of the room yelled. "I bet he's spent it on his Royal Tart!"

***

Ron's position was irretrievable. Surrounded by lawyers and tax accountants, Ron was able to prove himself innocent of any wrong-doing. The Fraud Squad lost interest in him, but the media put the worst possible interpretation on his outburst. You do not snot popular figures in front of television cameras and the paparazzi and expect no one to notice the red stuff flying around. You do not make suggestions of criminal activity in front of news-hounds and expect the public to believe your denials. You do not get good press when you are hauled in front of a magistrate for assault, fined eight hundred pounds and put on a bond to keep the peace.

You are not exactly surprised when you hear, via a tall burly man who runs in the night, that Sothebys have cancelled the auction and are planning to sell to a private buyer. Nor do you open the door in the morning expecting a stream of clients to offer commissions.

"We've got the proof we need to charge your wife with fraud," said the senior CID man. "Thing is, she's done a bunk. She was ripping off the charity by deducting twenty per cent commission, not on what the artists got, but on what Art Aid received. There was eight million from her fiddle of your fees and a hell of a lot more taking it across everyone involved. How much did you say you received in the past two years?"

"Fifteen thousand pounds a year, and from that I had to meet costs," said Ron ruefully. "I'm ruined, aren't I?"

"Unless we find her and bring her to trial, sir, I rather think you are. You see, sir, it isn't just your reputation which is washed up. It's his. You know, the big honcho. He doesn't mind being cuckolded by his wife, he just doesn't like the world laughing at him."

"Are we talking about the same thing?" asked Ron, bewildered.

"Oh, I think we are," said the CID man. "After all, the BBC man who set you up is one of the inner circle, a very close personal friend of You-Know-Who!"

Pru, her eyes red rimmed and her pose that of a doll from which the sawdust stuffing has leaked, sniffed loudly.

"Well, it was fun while it lasted," she said flatly. "Ron, I really think it's time we all went back to Australia."

22

Alizarin crimson: the synthetic form of Madder was patented in Germany in 1868. It is chemically identical with the natural product but, because it lacks the rapidly fading purpurin, has improved lasting qualities. Painters complained it was less brilliant than madder and that it did not cover so well. However, it became popular because of its ease of handling. In the laboratory, sodium carbonate and aluminium sulphate solutions are mixed and precipitated with aluminium hydroxide, then blended with castor oil.

Nothing gets accomplished overnight. There were paintings to be crated, items of furniture to be sold and household goods to be packed. The removalists did much of the work while Pru and Ron attended to matters such as surrender of leases and business which could not wait. To Ron's dismay he found Zoe had stripped the bank accounts and had left him with bills for the Xenos Galleries in London and New York. He was forced to fly the Atlantic to discuss the problems with Zoe's other artists and found a buyer for the lease of the World Trade Centre property.

Pru performed the same service at the Paris end. It was Darcy money which had to foot the bills and Pru was, he guessed, worried about financial matters. Andrew was a stock market player. Their investments had been hit badly in the October '87 nosedive in the States. Caring for him in a private nursing home was proving exorbitant. Kostas had welcomed her suggestion that he become valet to Andrew during the day. Arranging flights for an invalid had taxed her patience.

While Ron was in New York, Pru sought an appointment with

Woody. "It's all very well Sothebys bowing to pressure and refusing to auction that effing painting," she said bluntly. "But lover-boy is broke and the Tamberlaine Foundation needs the money you promised from the sale. I don't give a damn if You-Know-Who doesn't like it. Send the portrait to America and auction it there."

There came a giggle of delight. "Oh, yes. I've got good friends there. They don't give a toss about my husband. But tell me, is Ron coping? It's horrid what they've done to him."

"Bluntly, it's not easy what you're doing to him either. Don't you realise how it hurts him to see you throwing yourself at these other men? You're not pretending to be in love with them, are you?"

She shook her head. "They all want a piece of me, that's all. They all say they care but, when it comes down to it, they'll all sensationalise our relationships and make money out of the experience. Ron's the only one who cared enough to protect me."

"And you unintentionally destroyed him."

"Yes, I did. I'm so sorry. Could I see him before he returns to Australia?"

"Is that wise?"

"Oh, utterly crazy. But I'll make sure I'm not followed."

Ron grinned at the inappropriateness of that promise when, from the window of the bare studio, he saw her running along the riverside path. There were a dozen paparazzi on her tail, jogging with difficulty under the burden of cameras, lenses and tripods. followed by television crews and sweating journalists, notebooks and tape recorders in their hands. She did not even glance his way but ran on into the night, like a fox with the hounds scenting her trail.

Twenty minutes later she knocked and almost fell through the door, laughing and panting with exertion. "Hopkins and I ran through the door of a maternity hospital and out through the kitchens," she chuckled. "We left the mob being confronted by an angry matron and security guards."

She looked round the bare space in dismay. "Not many comforts," she said, with a smile, putting her arms around his neck and kissing him.

"I saved the milk crate for you."

"Silly! You can't make love on a milk crate!"

But they did, and locked face to face they were as one. And if Ron had square crimson marks on his bottom for a week after, it mattered not a jot.

"Not forever, Ron. Not goodbye forever, please."

"You only have to ask. The only forever is that I am yours." He wiped a tear from her cheek. "Goodbye, my wild rose. I do love you."

***

The milk crate took centre stage in the Ephemeral studio. No one asked why it had been shipped over with the rest of Ron's things or why he had painted it in reds and violet. Alexandar got into trouble when he borrowed it to use as a wicket while playing cricket during a weekend visit. Roma put her doll in it and pushed it round the studio floor until her godfather took it away and put it on the far side of the gates barring the balcony, out of the child's reach.

It became Pru's favourite seat, for she often squatted on it, watching as he finished the Philippines paintings for PanAsia. They had threatened to cancel his contract at the height of the scandal but had renewed interest when English Rose sold in America for an unprecedented amount.

Ron was not without work. He flew to Indonesia once a month, for one politician at a time was all he could stand. He spent more time painting the children, the ones the Tamberlaine Foundation bought to save them from life in the brothels. Others were victims of the fat pigs who came to the islands in increasing numbers since the child pornography trade in the Philippines had come under international censure.

With the money from English Rose, shelters had also been set up in Thailand and Manila, and the nuns were hard at work rehabilitating the damaged and frightened children, some not even in their teens. The irony of the Tamberlaine situation did not escape Ron, who felt Pru's first husband, Frank, had his tongue hard in his cheek when he'd started painting the waifs and selling their pictures to the men who lusted after them.

"Pru, the pigs take the pictures back home and wank in front of them," he protested.

"Better than letting them rape the poor little mites," she replied. "And the money we rip off the sex tourists is just so much less they have to spend on corruption."

"I hear the brothel owners aren't happy about what we're doing."

"Yeah! It sticks in their gullets that the nuns get to care for the children. But I haven't seen the local mullahs setting up workshops to train them or educate them for other work, let alone put food in their mouths. All they teach is the effing Koran. Day in, day out, chanting verses and having their heads filled with thoughts of jihad. I'll given them Holy War. What Tamberlaine is doing is the only sort of Holy War worth fighting...saving lives, not taking them."

"I'm glad Mike's got May with him. The fact that she follows Islam takes the heat off their clinic."

"For now, but there's a funny mood in west Sumatra and Aceh. Westerners are not welcome, even if they do as much good as Doctor Mike. It's not just in Indonesia. The Iraqis have been poisoning the Kurds, the Iranians are in the hands of the fundamentalists who organised the Paris bombs which injured Andrew, the Lockerbie air disaster's been sheeted home to militant Libyan fanatics. And now there's more trouble in the Gulf. Did you know Mike's been called up to operate a casualty unit in the front line?"

"In Kuwait?"

"The very same. God knows what the mullahs will say if they find out he's been fighting with the Infidels."

"Will May close the clinic? It won't be safe for her and little Farah, will it?"

"I'll move her down to Tamberlaine in Surabaya. I'm going there next month. It may be the last chance I get, while Kostas and Helene are able to look after Andrew."

"How is he? Has his sight improved?"

Pru let out an exasperated breath. "Yes, but some damn silly therapist has introduced him to tennis. Cricket was bad enough. Now he sits and watches tapes of Wimbledon with his head going left right, left right, ping pong, until it drives me mad!"

Pru always avoided talking about the news of Woody in the papers, the sensational books and revelations of her affairs. And Ron never mentioned the letters he received from her. They were not deep and meaningful. They glossed over the speculation. She wrote mainly about her sons, light-hearted notes, posted from strange places, such as suburban post boxes.

Ron could not write back. In some ways he wished she did not bother, as all the brief scrawls did was to reawaken his longing for her delicate touch. He read the books and despised the writers.

He felt sick at the way her life and marriage was drifting onto the rocks.

His marriage was over. He had obtained a divorce from Zoe in absentia. God knows where she was. He had suspicions at first that Mercedes might be sheltering her, but he saw General Ihza's wife frequently and she denied complicity. Mercedes had become ultra-conventional. She was no longer cowed by Ihza, but was her own woman. If she had lovers, they were taken with discretion. She made no overtures to him and that was a relief. She knew he was still in love with his princess. There was a tacit understanding that they now shared only an interest in Liana, but that was sporadic, as neither were welcomed in the Santri community.

"Liana does not acknowledge me," Mercedes said sadly. "And she detests you!"

But Ron still went to the village, whenever he was in east Java. He was ignored, but he sat and talked to Liana for hours, about life in Australia and reassured the child of his regard for her and his wish to care for her.

He might have been a stone for all the notice she took.

Then one year she was gone. The entire family had vanished and no one would say what had happened to them.

***

In 1993 Andrew died peacefully in his sleep. His passing exacerbated the red hot row that was burning in the Populis family. Constantine was locked in legal action against Aristotle. He had accused his brother of having been party to the deceit about the condition of the premises he'd bought from Zoe. Aristotle, arguing that Zoe had bought Margett's from under his nose, in fact, while he was negotiating the purchase with Andrew, was incensed, largely because the major witness in his defence was now deceased. While Andrew was alive there had always been the chance he might recover his wits and be able to testify.

Mana Agnella raised hell with both of them. Kostas was caught in the middle and got a earful from his father and his uncle. He was sick of it. Now freed of responsibility for the invalid, and too old to be caught for National Service in his place of birth, he told Constantine he could no longer work at Margett's because he was taking his family to Greece for a holiday.

"We'll stay at Helene's place," he said to Ron. "You said it was a smashing spot, Kavalla. And Alexandar can go fishing with his old friends. The beach will be safe for Roma, he says."

Ron looked at Helene with concern. "What sort of state will the cottage be in after being empty so long?"

"There's a caretaker. Uncle Aristotle found a widow lady to keep it clean. She lives in the little bedroom on the side of the house where you used to stay. She'll not be in our way."

"I wish I could come too."

"Why don't you? You can share Alexandar's room and Roma can sleep with us."

"Why don't you, indeed?" Pru echoed. "I'm going to stay with May while she has her second baby. Andrew, bless his dear heart, has left us at a good moment."

Pru had been calm about her bereavement. As she said, Andrew had died, in all ways that mattered, in June of 1986. The terrorist bomb had destroyed his humanity.

They stayed with the Xenopopulis family in Thessalonika for a week. They took Alexandar to see Roman and Byzantine monuments in the city which was named after the sister of his namesake, Alexander the Great. Kostas and his stepson toured the port and Helene took Roma to meet friends.

Ron, fascinated by the mixture of Hellenic, Turkish and Jewish faces in this cosmopolitan city, once centre of the Ottoman Empire, took photographs which he would later develop as paintings. He visited the great Mosque and the even older churches, but he was glad when Helene and Alexandar took Roma on the bus to the village in which she had lived with Petros. Kostas, who had business in Athens, was to travel with Ron, who had a courtesy call to pay on the newly re-elected Andreas Papandreou.

Ron had much to talk about with the man he counted as an old friend. Papandreou, who had lost office four years previously, and had been embroiled on the periphery of a banking scandal over $210 million dollars, was sympathetic about the financial mess created by Zoe. He had known the family from before the Second World War.

Any Xenopopulis was, he said, about as trustworthy as a weasel, and Aristotle was as hard as they came. "Liars, one and all. But they look after their own. You were a fool to marry Zoe. Clemnystra did the right thing getting out. Constantine was decent enough but Ari? What a nasty piece of work."

"You think Zoe hid the loot in the bank you were talking about?"

"It wouldn't surprise me."

Ron did not repeat this conversation to Kostas, who rang Helene to say they would arrive the next day. Helene assured him the caretaker, who was usually dressed all in black, with the veil of a True Believer, stayed out of their way. Neighbours had told her the widow was a quiet woman who kept to herself. Distant cousins of the Xenopopulis family brought her supplies but, for all intents and purposes, she remained a stranger in their midst.

"But it's a funny thing," Helene said, at the bus stop. "There's something about her that seems familiar. Must be a family likeness."

"The hell it is," said Ron, catching sight of the enigmatic figure as they approached Helene's home. "That's Kostas' hairy cousin Zoe and my missing ex-wife."

Kostas peered into the distance. "Blood oath, mate. You're right. What do we do?"

"Call the police," said Ron. "Helene, come back. Don't go to the house."

"I must," she protested. "Alexandar's on his own with Roma. I must go to them." She broke free of Ron's restraining arm and ran.

There was no safety margin in waiting for re-enforcements. Zoe, trapped in the kitchen, had a carving knife to Helene's throat. Kostas and Ron stood motionless in the doorway, afraid of what Zoe might do if provoked.

Roma, looking from her mother to the dark figure of the fugitive, set up a loud wail and ran to cling to Helene's skirts. Zoe, distracted, tried to push the child away. Seeing her drop her guard, Alexandar, with all the skill of one who was in the State Soccer side, kicked the knife from her hand.

As the cliché goes, it was all over bar the shouting by the time the police arrived. Zoe was still screaming when they took her away.

She had not stopped hollering weeks later. The nightmare had only just begun when Ron landed in London.

***

Against all advice from Pru, Kostas and Helene, Ron felt he had little alternative than to return to talk to the Fraud Squad and his lawyers. Even Mike, chuffed at the safe delivery of a son, Felix, was not able to change his mind.

"You're walking into a bigger jungle than I live in," Mike warned. "You realise that Aristotle's got to be up to his neck in arranging to hide her. I wonder how she enjoyed living the simple life."

"Not at all, I gather. She was all for going to Brazil but her father's banking connections advised her to stay near to hand. Aristotle, it seems, has some funny deals going down. No wonder they sent her to get Hugo Vandermeer out of prison."

"You mean old man Populis is into drug running?"

"Yeah. Turns out he's got connections to the Turkish growers. Zoe wasn't wearing the Islamic veil for nothing. The old lady who left her all the money on condition she marry wasn't Greek but the relict of a Turkish landowner. Kostas says he's mortified to think his mate Petros was killed by the mob he turns out to be related to. And you can imagine how sick that's made Helene feel."

"It's not surprising, Ron. Northern Greece was part of the Turkish Empire for centuries."

"So? It was trampled all over by the bloody Crusaders, sacked by the Saracens, flooded by Jews and desecrated by Germans. What's new?"

"You are. You're getting sharp. You're pulling your head out of the clouds and watching where you put your feet."

"I need to. Zoe's hell bent on cutting the ground out from under them. They've bailed her until the trial and she's talking to the media."

"What's she got to say that would interest them?"

There was a long silence. "If you can get Pru to stop burping Felix, ask her to tell you. She knows what happened. Get her to explain. Frankly, Mike, I'm too choked to talk about it."

Being back in London was the last place on earth Ron would have chosen. While he was not going to allow Zoe to tells lies to the Press or to further blacken his name, the timing was atrocious. His presence coincided with a furore about the Royals, their affairs and their strange conversations on telephones.

He was able to afford only a tiny studio apartment in Battersea, of all places, with enough room for a single bed, and a gas ring for cooking. He couldn't even stretch to a television set and read the newspapers in the local library. He'd grown a beard and let his hair get long enough again for a pony tail. He was, he saw ruefully, in the cracked bathroom mirror he shared with other tenants, going grey at the temples.

He did not want to flag his whereabouts to PanAsia, which was pressing him to spend several months in Japan and China, where it had just opened a new service. He did not want the Establishment to get interested in him again, because he knew Woody needed him and anonymity remained his only protection. He had no desire for her in a physical way for he had become less and less interested in things of the flesh. Had Mike examined his friend, he would probably have diagnosed acute depression. Ron ate little, drank more than was wise and developed a bad reliance on nicotine.

He could still paint. He attempted nothing of major significance. He painted touristy pictures of people and places in the sunshine which were snapped up on grey days by visitors to street markets and on the Portobello Road. He made enough to get by, for drawing on his bank accounts would alert security snoops to his closeness to the source of the media frenzy. The only good thing about the crisis was that it drew attention from the Art Aid scandal.

He met Woody in dark and secretive places, and listened to her unburdening her mind. She had been, she said, stupid, so stupid. "Maybe I really am an airhead," she sighed. "I'm buggered, aren't I?"

"Up the creek without a paddle, as we say in Australia," he replied. "Done a proper perish."

"At least I don't go round boasting about floating around in a toilet bowl and being flushed round the bend like You-Know-Who."

Ron laughed and gave her a hug. Her sense of the ridiculous was her salvation. All the doubts and fears which haunted her were driven off by this imp of fun. And driving all, was the powerful instinct of the mother.

Strange that Ron, who had lacked mothering and who had not experienced the force in the either Zoe or Mercedes, was so drawn by Woody's sincerity about her role. To abandon her sons was not on her agenda. She would give up everything rather than their custody. The Establishment had her over a barrel. She was forced into a meagre settlement.

"Do you realise that English Rose fetched twice that amount at auction?" she protested. "It's a disgrace."

"I'll paint you again and you can keep the proceeds."

She laughed. "After all the trouble I've caused you? And when could I sneak away for sittings?"

"You don't need to. I only have to close my eyes and you're there."

The ripple of laughter moved him more than tears. "Goodbye, Ron. It's a lovely thought, but how can you paint with your eyes shut?"

***

Ron kept his eyes tightly shut during the trial of Zoe Xenos. He did not want to see the hate in his former wife's eyes. He gave evidence but reluctantly. The Royal divorce drove the media wild and Zoe's case was relegated to later pages. However, although

Art Aid was vindicated and Ron's name cleared, few knew of it. Zoe had been sentenced harshly, as much for her violence against Helene as for fraud. She would not be released until the turn of the Millennium. She glared at the judge, in his robes of crimson, as blood red as the damnation in the eyes of the jury. But she admitted no guilt and gave no clue to the location of the missing millions.

23

Red lead; a lead oxide used from antiquity. It has excellent covering power but is unstable. It is ground from minium, a mineral found near the River Minius in Northern Spain. In synthetic manufacture, letharge is heated in air, or molten lead is oxidised. In German it is known as Bleimennige. It is a very toxic pigment but widely used as an anti-oxidant.

Ron took Wood Violets to the framers himself, as soon as it was dry enough to take a couple of coats of varnish. The pose was quite different to English Rose, with the figure kneeling among the wild flowers, picking them to add to posies in a basket at her side. Through the trees could be seen her ancestral home. Her face bore a wistful, dreamy expression. Her dress was the colour of her eyes and the sun kissed highlights into her hair.

Ron liked it better than the first portrait and knew it to be equally masterful. It had been difficult to paint, for the second-hand easel, which was all he could afford, was too small for the large canvas. It had been bought ready-stretched, for he had none of the tools for a do-it-yourself job. He had bought the best quality he could get, but the outlay was alarming. So he had to carry the sheet-wrapped canvas by bus and by foot, knowing the frame and the shipping costs would leave his pockets empty. He'd said nothing to Woody about the gift. The New York auction house would handle the sale and had been instructed to remit the proceeds directly to her.

He was relieved, when he called at the small gallery on the Portobello Road, to find four of his Greek seascapes had been sold. He could eat again. He could pay the rent. He could afford to travel to the gaol where Zoe was imprisoned.

He did not want to see her, but felt it his duty to do so before he left London. She was not pleased to see him. She had shrunk into herself. The drab uniform of prisoners made her olive skin look dirty. Her hair was dull, as if she had not rinsed the soap from it, and her eyes were empty. Zoe, who had been proud of her long finger-nails, had bitten them and had chewed on the quick.

"You look a mess, Ron. Come to gloat, have you?"

"No. To see if there was anything you needed."

"Freedom?"

"The experts claim prisoners are inside by their own choice."

"I'm in here because of treachery. I suppose Hugo told you where to find me."

"Hugo?"

"Hugo Vandermeer, Mercedes' brother. My father's dealer. Oh, don't look so shocked. You must have known my father's cronies were criminals."

Ron shook his head. He rattled its pixels until he brought up images of Aristotle at the Delphi, cards in hand, carafe of wine at his elbow and a fat cigar in his mouth, laughing with other dark-browed men in the back room. Yes, yes, surely that one, the one with the long hair, he'd been in the news...was always in the news...the big fish that the police could hook but never land.

"Your father into brothels too?"

Zoe sneered. "Only on the supply side. The madams order the girls; Hugo smuggles them in. It's a profitable sideline. You don't think he got rich on the restaurant trade, do you?"

"Why wasn't the money you inherited enough for you, Zoe? Why did you rip off Art Aid?"

Her face twisted in bitterness. "Because it wasn't enough for Mercedes. She wouldn't stay with me because I couldn't afford her extravagant tastes."

"In drugs? You got her off them and then started yourself. Why? Why did you do that?"

"Because it still wasn't enough for her. She wouldn't leave Ihza, even after he beat her and abused her. I'd have given her the world. What did she want that I couldn't give her?"

Ron choked back the simple reply...a man's part...and sighed.

"She's not like you, Zoe. Mercedes is bisexual. You hate being with men. You'll do it, but you hate yourself for doing it. She loves it. She loves it every which way."

"Yeah! Even with Hugo. She tried to talk me into a threesome. Cobblers to that, I said."

Zoe started chewing her nails again. It seemed to demand all her concentration for she met all other questions with a blank look and a renewed nibble. Ron felt sick. He pushed back his chair and signalled that he wished to be let out of the prisoner contact room.

As he was about to depart, the chewing stopped. "I sent the calendar to General Ihza," she said, her voice full of venom. "And copies to the Indonesian press. See how Mercedes likes that! That'll teach her to prefer her brother to me! That'll pay Hugo back for his double-cross!

Ron did not have the heart to tell her it was Hugo who now enjoyed the General's favours and that Mercedes had been sidelined. He did not have the streak of cruelty in him that would be needed to reveal it was Aristotle who had encouraged the visit to Kavalla, knowing that Kostas would immediately recognise his cousin. He did not understand the complicated and perverted relationship between Zoe and her father, but he guessed Aristotle knew where the money was banked. It was highly probable, he predicted, that the account would be empty by the time Zoe was released from custody.

***

China and Japan were colder than London. Ron's bones ached. His fingers were numb and his testicles shrank tightly to his body as if burrowing into a warmer place. When he passed water he half-expected the burning stream to turn into an icicle before it hit the hole in the ground. He ached for a warmer place than the basic hotels of Manchuria and Tibet and, when he was again in luxury accommodation, spent much time sitting on the bidet in the Tokyo resort, bathing his bum with warm water.

He sent the slides of his proposed work to PanAsia and used his Platinum Pass to fly to Jakarta. After a short flight to east Java he was met by May and driven to the Tamberlaine Clinic. Pru, who was spending less time than ever in Australia, was minding the children. Mike was in clinic. There were no nuns on the premises. May had advised Pru to keep the good Sisters at the orphanages and training centres, but to employ proper nurses to assist Mike.

"Many people who need help will not come here if they think it is a Jesus Christ place. They would rather die than offend Allah."

"They don't mind Mike?"

"Oh, no. I have told them Mike doesn't believe in anything but is on earth to serve. He goes to the mosque from respect and keeps our Holy days, but I wear the hijab. They know I am Muslim and I have won enough respect for both of us!" May's eyes crinkled. Ron chuckled to himself. She wore the nikab full-face veil in public from no sense of religious fervour, but because she was still embarrassed by the scars on her cheek. They were almost invisible, yet she loathed them.

"How's Pru?"

"Worried." Traffic was heavy on the outskirts of the airport.

There was a jam of bemos and a scuffle of bicycles. "Mr Darcy made some very bad investments before he was injured and she's lost a great deal of money. He went heavily into insurance and the insurance company went broke. And he got caught in some dreadful property deals. She's putting his house on the market."

"Not Ephemeral?" Ron's gut churned.

"No," said May. "That's the Tamberlaine estate. The Darcy house is where Kostas and Helene live."

"Where will they go?"

"It's easier now Alexandar is away at medical school. Kostas asked his father if they can rent the rooms above the restaurant."

"My attic? It's riddled with white ants."

"Mike says it's been fixed. Kostas has turned the little waiting room into a bedroom for Roma and they're pretty happy. Helene helps in the kitchens. They're making good money."

"And where will Pru stay when she goes back to Australia?"

May changed gears and steered around a pair of water buffalo. "Didn't she tell you? She's moving back to the hills. She's going to look after you."

"That's fine."

"She says you'll be cross. Last time she went home she moved your things downstairs. She says you can't have the mezza-thing any more because she's the one who needs to live in the sky. I don't know what that means but she was quite insistent on it."

Ron grinned. Of course May wouldn't understand the layout of Ephemeral. "It's high time you and Mike brought the children to Australia," he said. "You should meet his family."

"Not until I finish weaning Felix," said May. "And we'd better hurry because he'll be screaming for a feed by now."

"You're not looking well," said Mike, the next morning. "When did you last have a check up?"

"Years ago. Why?"

"Come to the surgery with me. I'll give you a thorough examination. Anything wrong?"

Ron laughed and said nothing that abstinence wouldn't fix. "I've been drinking too much. It's playing hell with the waterworks."

Mike took blood samples and sent them to be processed in his laboratory. He tested Ron's blood pressure and blood sugar levels. He had a simple electrocardiograph machine, thanks to English Rose, and wired Ron to it with sticky pads on sensitive points. He looked at the print-out then handed him over to a nurse for an X-ray. On return Ron found his friend examining the plates and the ECG print out.

"Strip and lie on the examination table," he ordered. "I want to palpate your abdomen. How long have your balls been swollen like that?"

"Ouch," said Ron. "I hadn't noticed. But they're sore."

"Roll over. You're going to hate this, mate, but I'm going to stick my finger up your arse!"

It was, Ron thought, the most intrusive sensation he had ever experienced. Hell, to think Hugo called that sort of thing a pleasure.

Mike looked at him grimly. "You should see a proctologist when you get back to civilisation. I think you've got trouble down under."

"What do you call trouble?"

"I'm no expert, Ron. See a specialist. Your prostate gland is dodgy."

"So is your effing finger!"

Mike gave an apologetic smile. "Take me seriously, Ron. You should get this checked out."

"I will. I promise."

***

Some promises get filed away in the 'another time' drawer.

Ron was commissioned to paint the daughter of former president Sukarno. It was, Mike said, a feather in his cap, for she was a person of great political influence. "But don't let on to General Ihza," he said. "She's not exactly on the same side as the Suharto regime."

He met Mercedes in the capital after the initial sitting. "You didn't ask her to pose nude, did you?"

"No. May said it was culturally inappropriate."

"Good. Because I worked hard to land you that job. I interviewed her for television. Ihza would have a fit."

"I'll be careful. But I like her ideas on democracy."

"I expect you do, but she's not got the majority behind her. Even her own party are iffy-butty. How was Zoe when you left England?"

Ron paused while a waiter brought coffee to their table. "Miserable. Unwell. What did you expect?"

"Not much different. Zoe's crazy. A real drama queen. What on earth possessed you to give her the calendar?"

"I didn't. She wheedled a copy out of PanAsia."

"You heard what she did with it?"

"She told me what she'd done."

"You could have warned me, but it didn't make much difference. I'd already filed for divorce against Ihza."

"You're divorcing him? That's almost unheard of in Muslim society!"

"Since when was I Muslim?"

"But why? What grounds?"

"Ron, do you really think I'd put up with my husband taking my brother to bed every night?"

"Zoe said you and your brother were like that, as well."

"Well, Zoe lies. You know that. Zoe is very unstable. I couldn't take her sick mind any more."

"She says you promised to live with her permanently if she stole that money."

"There! What did I tell you? That shows how twisted she is. And I suppose she blames Hugo for sicking the police onto her?"

"She said he's her father's playboy."

Mercedes laughed. "Darling, there's one thing you should know about Aristotle. I know you hate him, but he is one hundred per cent testosterone, one hundred per cent heterosexual. If it hasn't got skirts, he's not interested."

"You know him better than I thought."

Mercedes went pink. "I've met him from time to time."

Ron hastily decided to change the subject. "What about your work? Won't the General make trouble for you?"

"It won't worry me. I've been offered a contract with a commercial television network in Australia. I'll be the main anchor for Spotlight on Asia. I'll be doing Jana Wendt's sort of interviews as well, travelling all over to news hot-spots."

"Congratulations. Out of Darwin?"

"No, from Sydney. Better flight connections."

"You'll do well. Maybe our paths will cross."

"Bound to," she said. "PanAsia's sponsoring the programme. And talking of PanAsia, have you still got the originals of the calendar studies?"

"Yes, why?"

"The television station wants to buy them. They don't have the hang-ups that Indonesians have and they sure ain't sensitive about baring the flesh!"

Ron weighed the pros and cons. What was the point in keeping them? He no longer wished to look at them. He was cash-strapped until the commissioned portrait was paid for, and Pru was in dire financial trouble. It would tide them over until he finished the Japan-China series back at Ephemeral.

"Right. Give me a contact to talk to when I get back Down Under. I'll dicker and deal."

"I hope you get a better bargain than you got last time you said that."

"Dicker and deal? When was that?"

"The night I got you to break Zoe in."

Ron went bright red. Red lead, dead lead, mislead! "I try to forget that episode."

She smiled like a cream-tongued cat. "I like to remember it. Do you want to sleep with me again, for old times sake?"

Balls aching, as they did after long periods of abstinence, Ron shook his head. "I don't think that would be wise."

"And when did wisdom ever have anything to do with you and I?" she said, stroking his hand. "If you do, I'll tell you about Liana."

***

Alexandar came home for a brief visit at Christmas, before joining Mike at Tamberlaine for the vacation. He had developed a huge admiration for Dr Carney and was determined to follow in his footsteps.

"I'm going to apply to do my registrar training at LIPS," he said. "I'll do my intern year at the Royal and try for a place at a cosmetic reconstruction research clinic in the States. Then Mike can pull strings for me. At least, that's the plan, Ron. I hope Aunty Pru will back me up."

How easily the mantle of aunt had slipped onto Pru's shoulders, thought Ron, watching her play with Roma in the swimming pool. And how easily they had become used to living with one another. She never bothered him with trivialities. His painting was not affected by her comings and goings. She cooked delicious meals, kept the place tidy and pottered in the garden. She was all things that a man needed in a mother.

She had taken over the role of agent and ensured a steady stream of work came his way. His name was so well known by now that his subjects came to him. As Mike had predicted twelve years earlier, Ephemeral was no longer back of beyond. Suburbia was reaching out to the hills and the roads had been improved. There was now a four-lane highway within a ten-minute drive of the studio.

Much of her time was taken up with administration of the Tamberlaine Foundation. Thanks to English Rose there were now rescue centres in the Philippines, Bangkok and Phuket. There were others in Bali and on Lombok. She was on Government committees looking at ways of fighting child pornography and international paedophilia. She was hated in many quarters for her aggressive defence of innocence and her vitriolic pursuit of the guilty.

She was pure poison in the nose of General Ihza Dinegoro and his fellow sleaze-buckets. But she seemed invulnerable as, with fading strength, she had cut back her visits to the islands. It was Ron who still made the journeys and Ron whose paintings still funded the purchase of waifs and strays. It was Ron who could be hurt, and Hugo who thought of a way of doing so. But Ihza shook his head. The country was going through a financial crisis which was shaking the whole Asian region. It was no time to create adverse publicity when so much hung on the continued popularity of the islands for tourists.

"Wait," the old General said. "Wait until the rupiah is strong again. Wait until the people are so hungry they will do anything for the money we'll offer them. Be patient, my pretty one, and trust your master."

***

Free will is a concept the philosophers have trouble getting a handle on. May's beliefs in karma and destiny were easier to live with, thought Mike, watching Ron as he nursed young Farah. Alexandar was on duty at the clinic. The trainee doctor was able to deal with cuts and bruises that were all that might be expected during the evening. It was a rare chance for him to spend some time relaxing with his family.

He looked fondly at May, who was feeding mushed up rice to Felix. Her belly was already beginning to show signs of another Carney. She had taken off her headscarf, for she was with family, and her hair swung in a glossy swathe across her cheek. He glanced from her to Farah, who was so like her Bangladeshi mother. He noticed Ron's finger stroking the child's cheek and the expression of alarm on his face.

"What's up?" asked Mike, quietly.

"How's your French?" said Ron.

"I get by."

Ron fumbled for the words. "Cherchez sous la plan. Farah est comme May. My fingers feel what my eyes cannot see."

Mike went white. "You're sure?"

"Positive."

"Go to your room and play with your dolls while Uncle Ron and I go out to water the garden." Mike kissed Farah on the cheek, his lips brushing her face. Outside the door he turned and beat his fists against the wall. "How come I didn't see it?"

Ron sighed. "I thought it was my imagination. I noticed the shadow ages ago but now there's a slight change in the curve of the bone. But I thought, kids face change all the time, my mind's playing tricks."

"I can't believe I missed it."

"No. You're the one who told me always to look below the surface...sous la plan. First the bone, then the flesh, and only then the skin. The growth is definitely on the bone."

"But very small."

"Almost imperceptible, but it's there, Mike. I'm sorry. She's developing the same deformity her mother had."

"That settles it. The University Department of Medicine attached to LIPS has offered me a chair in reconstructive surgery. We're going back to London. I was thinking it over. We like it here at Tamberlaine. We do good work. But family comes first."

"Pru won't argue with that. Does it mean closing the clinic?"

"I've an old mate from Army days who's bored stiff running a practice in the wheatbelt. He'd come like a shot. And, after all, there's no hurry. It may be years before Farah's tumour is ripe enough to operate."

"Ripe?"

"Yes. We'd want to be sure there was a plane between her bone and the bottom of the growth. But I'll have it off long before it does the harm it did to May."

"She survived. Farah will be the same."

"But Ron, you don't understand. I should have taken precautions. It's a genetic defect. Felix and the new baby may also be affected."

24

Realgar; a naturally occurring mineral, known by the Arabians as rahj ah ghar, the powder of the mine, occurs near hot springs and volcanic deposits, and in some limestones and dolomites. The pigment, a red arsenic sulphide, is formed by heating the mineral with sulphur to form a purer residue of orange red pigment. This is blended, with great difficulty, with an oil medium. It is highly dangerous and cannot be synthesised in the laboratory.

Mercedes pushed Ron away.

"It's been a long time. I want to know you properly again," he said, panting, easing her back onto the couch in the Ephemeral studio.

"I don't think so." She tucked him back and zipped him up, nipping his skin as she did so. "My new husband is a perceptive man. He wants a portrait which he can show his friends, not one which makes me look like a mistress."

"Dammit, woman, you were his mistress off and on for years."

"And now I am his wife and respectable. Paint me that way or not at all."

"I could paint you from memory, as I've known you, lusting."

"I can act lust very well."

"You weren't acting, in Jakarta."

"I got carried away, just as you are now. I was feeling deprived."

"I shouldn't have taken this commission."

"Probably not, but I knew I'd force Mrs Darcy's hand. She knows you worry about Liana."

"You broke a promise to tell me where she was."

"She was in no danger...not then."

"And she is now?"

"Everyone is. I'm glad to be out of Indonesia. I'm sorry the fanatics burnt the Tamberlaine Clinic."

"It's crazy. There was millions of dollars worth of equipment in it. It was for their own good. Why did they do that?"

"The machines were made in America, Ron. Or were donated by the Red Cross. Fundamentalist nutters think in very simple terms. With Allah or against Allah. Full stop. At least no one was hurt."

"No, but Pru's had to go up there and sort things out. She's not well enough to tackle the mess. And the locals we'd trained to assist have run off."

Mercedes fastened the last button on her hot orange dress and picked up her Gucci handbag. "Until next week," she murmured. "You'll finish by then? We're off to the Seychelles for a holiday. Thank God my husband's retired from business and can move to Sydney. I really don't want to commute every weekend to make it with you."

He turned his back on her and merely grunted. His hands reached for his brushes and were already busy mixing the right tone for her flesh. Golden-brown she was in summer, only the paler skin under her g-string and the minuscule bra of her bikini betraying her mixed racial heritage. Once she'd been all golden and toast hot. He added a touch of burnt sienna to the palette and stroked colour onto the canvas with a lightness as intimate as the finger of a caress.

This nude study was one he could not resist, even though it was what he called an 'Opus Noir', because the sitter brought out his blackest moods. What Mercedes had done recently had driven him mad with anger and jealousy. His lust for her was renewed despite and because of his hatred of the man to whom she had given herself.

So he painted in fury in a bid to destroy memories of that cold studio in Chelsea, overlooking the river. Mercedes had put on weight in the past year. Her breasts were heavier than when she'd posed for him by the lily-pond at Tugu, in Malang. They were heavier than when he'd fondled them in Jakarta. Her new husband was a lusty man. She had been well-used and recently. There were bruises on her hips where hands had grasped her and the indentations of finger-marks on her buttocks, where she had been lifted and slammed repeated onto her conqueror.

"Why the hell did you marry Aristotle?" Ron had hollered at her in disgust when she first broke the news.

"Because he's rolling in money and he's like a rampant bull. He's lost nothing with age. And he doesn't care about my other little habit."

"You're on heroin again?"

"Ecstasy, darling. I couldn't go on camera with puncture marks, could I?"

"What did he think of the calendar?"

"Chuffed as hell, Ron. He made hundreds of copies and sent them to his friends and business colleagues with a memo, saying, "Look at the bird I landed!"

"Does Zoe know about you?"

"Who cares? Ari's disinherited her and left his money to me." Her words were defiant but there'd been apology in her eyes. "Why should it worry you, Ron? I know you're over me. I know who's the real keeper of your heart."

"That's finished. You know that was an impossible affair."

She shrugged. "I like father-figures. You've never understood, have you? I loved my father! You're old in your ways, Ron, but you're still in your thirties. Too young by half."

"You're weird. Aristotle revolts me, but if you work him hard enough you should be set up for life. He'll drop dead with a heart attack and you can get yourself a whole football team of toyboys - or geriatrics, if that's really your preference."

After her departure Ron had dragged a dry fan-shaped brush, loaded with realgar, across the dark fur of her groin. It made the bush appear to burn, just as her juices set a man on fire.

"Bitch! Whore!" His face ran with tears of wanting. He looked to the other easel, to the formal painting he had recently desecrated. He cleaned the smears he had made on it in temper and picked up the one of the loved and despised naked flesh. He carried it down to the wine cellar in the cliff behind the house. He did not want casual callers to see it, and he refused to store it next to the new studies of his other obsession.

Even Pru did not know of their existence. He was glad of her month-long absence. The letter from Woody had been full of joy. He had not heard from her since her exuberant thanks for the money from the sale of Wood Violets.

"I'm about to be married again. Dearest Ron, please would you do a series of paintings of me like the calendar you did of Mercedes? I'd like to give them to my darling as a wedding present. Send me photos when you've finished so I can show them to him when we go to Paris to celebrate our engagement."

He'd smiled at her assumption he'd do anything she asked, without thought of the time it might take, without offering payment. She had not considered he might ache at the thought of her exposing herself to another man in the same way she had posed for him, after hours of mutual passion. But that was Woody. She commanded. He obeyed. He'd sent the photos to Mark Hopkins. He'd wrapped the studies ready for posting and had taken them to the lock-up.

When he reached studio level again he dragged the milk crate to the balcony, and sat on it, drinking a beer. There were storm clouds on the horizon. It was his last night before Pru's return. He wondered what she had found out about Liana.

* * *

"There's no mystery about it; not really," said Pru, sinking exhausted onto a chair at the kitchen table. "Ah, that smells good. What is it?"

"Steak and kidney stew with dumplings. Just what you need on a cold August night. My mother used to make it. Your tea, ma'am!"

"Well, thank you, kind sir. No, there was no mystery and why Mercedes had to make one, I don't know. I like your portrait of her, by the way. Is it finished?"

"I just need to rework a little of the background. I want to bring out the red and gold in the tapestry behind her. It's a Turkish rug Aristotle inherited from his grandfather, apparently. We're trying to avoid batik. I had to paint the first background out. It was too Bali for Mercedes' taste. Come on, Pru. You can goggle at it later. Give me the news."

"Oh, it was just part of the Government's policy to homogenise the islands. They moved whole communities from Java to Kalimantan, and other folk from one island to the Moluccas. It's not been popular. Created more trouble than you'd believe. No, old Ihza was told to move Muslims east and Hindus west, so he did."

"What, not everyone in the village?"

"Lock, stock and blooming barrel. They went to Jembrana Regency, near the Bali Straits. Settled down between Gilmanuk and Negara on the south coast. Rice-growing country, but Liana's foster mother hated it so they upped and went to Nusa Menjanga...that's on the north side of the island, overlooking the Java Sea. They grow tea on the mountains so they felt more at home. Putu, that's the father, said he didn't like having to work in Kuta. It offended him to see the women in bikinis."

"Cripes! He'd rather pick tea?"

"No, the mullahs got him a job in the Taman National Park. He sells water to the backpackers."

"How did you learn so much? Every time I went near the family they went apeshit and wouldn't talk to me."

"Easy. I took young Doctor Alexandar with me. Mike and May are helping to set up a new clinic in Bangli before they leave, so she drove us, all neatly dressed in her hijab, and me in a kaftan and a headscarf. Alexandar talked to Putu and told him his grandfather was a Muslim, as indeed he was, and showed him photos of his great grandmother, all decked out in the abaya and veil."

"Alexandar's never met his great grandmother."

"Of course he hasn't. They were snaps he took of Zoe playing the caretaker at Kavalla."

"You met Liana?"

"She's pretty. But she won't do well in their new village, of course. The mother says she'll have a hard time marrying her off."

"She's in her teens. Pru, did you get a chance to ask. Has she been cut up?"

"No. May started talking about it. Said they didn't enforce it in

Bangladesh and reminded them Liana was an Australian by birth and the Darwin Police would prosecute if they touched her. That started Liana yelling that she wanted to be made a real woman and her mother yelling she wasn't wasting good rupiah on having her done when no man would want to bed her anyway, because she looks like a Dutchwoman!"

Ron laughed. "How did you solve that?"

"Alexandar bought her!"

"The hell he did! You didn't let him tie himself down like that!"

Pru chuckled. "It's fine. He only put down a deposit. He told the father Liana was too young to marry and he'd come back and pick her up when she was eighteen. And he's paying them to look after her until then."

"Straight up?"

"Yup. And Liana was very pleased with herself. First in her class to get betrothed. Putu said it would be all right with the mullahs because Alexandar was half Turkish and halfway to being a good Muslim. He said Liana would have to teach him the way of Allah and gave his blessing!"

"Well, that's a relief. How's Alexandar feel about it?"

"He's quite taken with her. They were chatting away like mad when we left. He said he'd come back on the bus to catch his flight from Denpasar."

Pru went to bed early, but he heard her get up in the night and spend time in the bathroom, vomiting. He drew water for her and made her a cup of tea.

"Get the tablets from my bag," she moaned. "The analgesics are in the green packet."

Ron did so and looked at her in grave concern. Her face was grey with pain and she was sweating. He remembered the prescription from a long, long time ago.

"The cancer's back, isn't it?" he said. "Why didn't you say anything?"

Pru grimaced. "Because I wanted to make sure Tamberlaine was in order. Mike took X-rays, Ron. He put dye in my body to locate the tumour but it's everywhere. It's only a matter of time."

Ron held her in his arms and rocked her in gentle sympathy. "Then let's make the time count for something," he whispered.

***

August 30 drove all other concerns from their minds. Ron and Pru sat pinned to the television as the awful truth broke on the world. The car crash in a Paris subway brought a young woman's dreams to an end, left her two sons motherless, and turned an entire nation into mourners. The sense of grief which swept through Ron was unbearable. Pru tired of it.

"I've rung Alexandar," she said. "He'll pick you up at ten. You're to spend the day on Dreamdrift II, fishing. I want you out of my hair while I spring-clean this place from top to bottom."

"Spring-cleaning? In your state of health?"

"Spring-cleaning is very good therapy. Anyway, Ron, I want to put my affairs in order. I want to turn out my drawers."

"Good grief!" he said, trying to force a joke past stiff lips. "And will you burn your bra as well?"

"Silly man," she muttered. "You know what I mean."

The phone rang in the middle of the night. Ron, sleep befuddled, answered in on the fifth ring. "Whosat?"

"You know who," said a deep, familiar voice. "No names, no pack drill. They've found the photographs. In her handbag."

Ron was suddenly as awake as if he'd been dumped in a bath

of ice. "Damn!"

"They'll be looking for the originals. There's the biggest cover-up going on that you can imagine."

"They'll not find them here." Ron wasn't too sure about that, but he could think of no safer hideaway.

"Good. But they'll look. Count on it."

"I will. And, mate, I'm sorry."

"So am I. The paintings are brilliant. Tasteful but pure magic. Why the hell did she have to fall for a bleeding Muslim?"

"You mean what I think you mean?"

"Who knows. But I reckon she signed her own bleeding death warrant." Hopkins slammed the phone down, leaving Ron shivering in the cold of a dark winter's morning.

It was irrational to feel such fear. Whatever, nothing would happen for days. It would take time for the Establishment to send out the bloodhounds. He'd not let it spoil his day on the water with Alexandar. He needed the peace of the slow, steep swell of the Indian Ocean.

The front came in from the sea at noon. They battled rough seas back to harbour but it was mid-afternoon before they tied up at the mooring and staggered across to the beat-up old car Alexandar drove when on vacation.

They saw the smoke and heard the fire engines before they got to the hills. They could not get into the road to Ephemeral. It was taped off by the police.

Ron, in panic, directed Alexandar to the side roads on the far side of the valley. They got out and stood on the verge above the buried container. The slopes below Ephemeral were ablaze. And, as they watched, too horror-stricken to say a word, the poles supporting the house collapsed and brought the entire structure down in a blazing, red and orange fire across the front lawn.

"Pru!" Ron's agonised cry rang across the valley and, with his young friend on his heels, he charged through the scrub along the fire-break, towards the brigade men who were desperately trying to dowse the flames.

There was a red blanket covering a body on the lawn.

"There was nothing we could do," said the fire officer. "It was going like a furnace when we got here. She threw something out from the balcony but her clothes were ablaze when she jumped. She came sailing out into space with her arms spread wide, like a bleeding firebird."

He shuddered and gestured toward the swimming pool. "That's what she chucked overboard. We fished it out of the water. It might be worth salvaging."

The face of Mercedes looked up at Ron, her flesh darkened by smoke and the corner of the canvas, with the Turkish rug, scorched by fire.

"This was no accident," said Ron. "This was arson."

And he guessed who was responsible. The fire had been the one certain way of destroying anything on the premises. Those who had set it had no more compunction than the French agents who had blown up the Rainbow Warrior in New Zealand, in 1985. He blamed himself for ignoring the warning he'd been given, for underestimating the speed with which the nameless men would act. He felt responsible for Pru's death.

And yet, knowing what her future would have been, as cancer ravaged her body, he wondered if this was, in some way, a merciful release.

She had died, flying, like the Firebird, a role she had danced in her youth. And he hoped the music of Stravinsky had drowned her terror as she kissed the air and let her spirit soar.

He remained grim-faced and taciturn through the hours of questioning. He voiced his suspicions to no one. Ephemeral had gone and his mother figure had died. He would have his revenge for them, and for the English Rose.

He sat in Alexandar's car later, drinking a cup of coffee brought by a torch-wielding neighbour, who had clearly been crying.

"We saw you here, Ron. We're so sorry. Mrs Darcy was a wonderful woman."

Alexandar made the right noises and they sat on, watching the firemen hose down the still-smoking timbers. They kept an uncomfortable vigil through the night. Only at dawn did Ron tell his companion what he suspected.

"They'll get away with it," Alexandar exploded. "They'll get away with murder."

"Yes, but they didn't get what they were looking for. The originals are more or less under our feet."

"I never knew. Kostas never said a word."

"Funny, you were the one person I thought might have found the secret store-room. You found the cave when you were a boy."

"I wasn't into nature at that age. I was always off, playing soccer."

"Who'd have thought I'd be grateful to a soccer ball. But they won't get away with it, old son. Do you know anyone with a top-of-the-range computer?"

"Of course. Scanner, printer, the works. At the University Department of Medicine. And in the Medical Library. What are you going to do?"

"Buy a digital camera. And then we're going to spread images of the originals all over the World Wide Web. How do you fancy a quick trip to New York? They'll spot me, but you could carry the paintings to the auction house that handled the other American sales. We'll sell the bloody things and raise the money to make Pru's memorial a living one."

PART FOUR

Impasto

25

Red ochre; this anhydrous iron oxide is a natural earth used since prehistoric times. Significant deposits are found at Minas Gerais, in Brazil, and on Cyprus, in the Aegean Sea. However, in Australia, the site known to Aboriginal artists and traded across the continent, is at Wilgie Mia, in Western Australia. This brilliant red-brown pigment is used extensively in indigenous painting. It has retained its popularity on the palette of the modern artist, offering a safe, permanent colour which dries rapidly and has excellent covering power.

Little had changed in the attic above Margett's, where Ron was staying. Alexandar had insisted he would be welcomed by Kostas and Helene,

"Where else would you go?" Alexandar asked. "You can have my bed while I'm in New York. Kostas enclosed the roof garden and it's a bit draughty, but it suits me fine. When I get back I'll sleep in a swag on the floor. It's what I'm used to at the Tamberlaine Clinic."

Ron, who was by then moving like a zombie, so choked with grief that he was barely articulate, simply nodded. "You'll be back for the funeral."

"Yes. And then you and I will take the Dreamdrift and sail to the islands. You know where she'd want her ashes scattered."

"In the middle of the Timor Sea? Where Tamberlaine and her sons were drowned?"

"I think so. She loved Andrew, but not for eternity, if you know what I mean."

Mercedes came to the funeral with Aristotle. She agreed to collect her portrait, now restored, after the wake in Margett's Restaurant.

"Do you remember..." she began, after she'd followed Ron up the stairs.

"Of course I remember. Love you; hate you; I never forget you, Mercedes."

"I'm glad," she said quietly and, sitting on a settee, held out her arms to embrace him. Only then did the tears come. Great shuddering sobs of anguish, drawn from the very depths of his being. It took some time to compose himself.

Kostas came up to see if he was all right. "The mourners are leaving," he said. "Uncle Aristotle wants to come up and talk to you. And the Darcy lawyer says he must spend some time going through Pru's will."

Aristotle's hair had gone white. He had lost his bullishness in a fleshy padding of contentment. Mercedes had tamed the man. He looked at the portrait and said he was delighted, but his voice was heavy with pent up emotion.

"It's a good job I didn't let Zoe persuade me to break your fingers," he said, stiffly, trying to force a smile. "I've got more bad news for you, I'm afraid. Zoe went berserk when she learned I'd married Mercedes. She took what she did to Helene a step further and knifed a prison officer. It looks as if she'll be inside for life, unless she's certified insane. They're talking about sending her to Highpoint Prison, in Suffolk, with Myra Hindley."

"Christ, I'm sorry," said Ron, flatly. He felt so numb that he could not respond adequately to the man's obvious distress.

"It's about the money."

Ron looked up in disbelief. "What money?"

"The money she ripped off you and Art Aid. I know why she stole it."

"I told him," Mercedes sighed. "It was better he knew. We messed her up properly, he and I. You shouldn't have married her, Ron. She was a mental nightmare. A mess."

"She meant well. She made my name."

"And then she destroyed it. She was sick, even then."

"She thought you loved her."

Mercedes spread her hands in a gesture of bewilderment. "Love? What do I know of love? I 'love' Ari. What does that mean? He protects me."

Aristotle looked acutely embarrassed by her candour. He coughed to draw attention back to himself. "The money. I know where it is. What do I do with it?"

"Hell, I don't know. Art Aid is all wound up. Give it to the Pru Darcy Memorial Trust."

"Not to the Tamberlaine Foundation?"

"That's doing nicely with the money from English Rose. And the proceeds from Wood Violets was returned to me. The princess said Tamberlaine needed it more than she did."

"Are you still hurting?" Mercedes asked. "I told you before, I guessed about the two of you."

"You never really talked about it."

"What was there to say? Tough luck?" She got up and took her husband's arm. "We must say goodbye to Constantine and family."

"We've settled our differences," Aristotle explained. "I'm a reformed character."

"Just as well, because you'll not like what Pru's memorial will be."

Mercedes raised an eyebrow.

"It'll be dedicated to her fight against child abuse!"

***

Dr Mike Carney was made executor of Pru's estate and chairman of the Tamberlaine Foundation.

"It should have been you, Ron," he said awkwardly, glaring at the lawyer.

The man ran his hand across his bald head and shrugged. "Mrs Darcy said Mr Turner's useless with money. She says he has no business sense. Is that right, Mr Turner?"

He grinned sheepishly. "I bet she also said I'm easily side-tracked and if I had too much in the bank I'd stop painting."

"She didn't have much personal money, anyway, young man. She'd given almost everything from Andrew Darcy's estate to Tamberlaine shortly after he died. She's left money for Dr Alexandar to finish his education and gifted money to Kostas and Helene for looking after her for so many years. Mike couldn't benefit as executor but May and the children are provided for. As for you, Mr Turner, she bequeathed you a life-time use of Ephemeral and a basic income, just enough to make sure dear Roman doesn't starve, as she put it, in her humorous fashion."

"Ephemeral? Dear God, that's ironic. All her dreams burnt to ashes."

The lawyer looked sternly at him. "It will be rebuilt. It was insured. Andrew Darcy saw to that. And the plans were lodged with me when I took over the affairs of the Foundation. Oh, yes. We will rebuild, but I think in steel and concrete, this time. Not in timber."

Before Alexandar and Ron set sail for Indonesia, Kostas

suggested they took Mike and his family to see the place where Pru had died. "This may sound crazy, Ron, but I want to make sure the fire-breaks have been cleared."

"And I want to reach out and listen to Pru's voice," May said, catching her breath on a sob. "She'll still be there, Ron. Until you take her to her resting place, she'll still be there."

Forensics had finished investigations and the insurers had agreed the debris could be cleared. The site bore only the marks of the bulldozers, great scars of red ochre on the hillside.

"Ephemeral," said Mike, solemnly. "It grows, it flowers, it dies."

"And then Allah sends the spring rains and it lives again," said May. "Allah is merciful."

***

Ron spent several years on the islands, buying children. The riots of 1998, the student demonstrations which followed the re-election of President Suharto, and the political turmoil of the Habibie years, were of little interest to him. They were a gross inconvenience to General Ihza Dinegoro, who looked at the growing power of National Awakening with dismay. It did not suit his agenda to have a deeply committed Islamic party in a position to influence decisions by the People's Consultative Assembly, the Indonesian parliament.

The plunge of the value of the rupiah in 1997 had increased poverty and made it easier for Hugo to obtain children for the child pornography trade. Brothels were a lucrative source of income at tourist destinations, but too often, these days, Hugo found his targets had been snaffled before he could follow leads. The fat pigs were going home with paintings instead of dirty pictures and leaving behind less trauma and disease. It was economic disaster for those who depended on filth for a living. There was a whisper in the underworld. "Fix Tamberlaine."

They tried to torch the Bangli Clinic but Mike had ordered security guards be hired and large dogs with big teeth let loose in the compound at night. They tried to make trouble at the orphanages, but the nuns had organised watchmen and had drilled the children into an informal militia, skilled in martial arts. They tried poisoning the water supplies but the nuns suspected after the first signs of sickness and used bottled water. They cut off supplies. Alternatives were found. They tried dropping pamphlets condemning the Infidels who were subverting the Faith of the Chosen. Pru's network held firm. Islamic child protection agencies sank religious differences and came out in support of Tamberlaine.

General Ihza, fat and sluggish with advancing years and creeping general paralysis of venereal excess, took a personal interest in the matter. He blamed Mercedes for making him an object of contempt by citing his affair with Hugo as grounds for divorce. He blamed Ron for encouraging her. Ron was Tamberlaine, in his eyes. Hugo followed his instructions and visited the families of those who had sold children to Ron and obtained signed statements confirming the purchase.

Not every Tamberlaine rescue was a success. Some children, disliking the hard work, discipline and the plain fare of the shelters, had gone back to a trade to which they had already been accustomed. They were happy to concoct stories of personal abuse by the tall Australian artist. They were well coached by Hugo, who suggested perversions of which few had any direct knowledge.

Armed with a thick dossier, General Dinegoro presented a case to a friend in the judiciary, a friend with an appetite for prepubescents, and argued that Ron Norman Turner was corrupting Indonesian children.

There was no trial, no lawyers, no chance to protest. One day Ron was sketching in Bandung, the next he was in a prison cell with five others who equally protested innocence. A Suharto crony froze all Tamberlaine bank accounts. Public Health inspectors condemned sewerage systems. Union leaders claimed the workshops were exploitative and used slave labour. Visiting teachers were posted to distant islands. Nuns had their visas withdrawn and were quietly deported. Fundamentalists were offered the vacant premises as training colleges for Islamic law.

The children? Ah, the children. They grew old, very quickly.

Some were exported; some were put in the militia; some were sold as slaves to rich paedophiles. Some turned a dozen tricks a night. Those who were diseased were left near the rubbish tips and in the back alleys of shanty towns.

Ron was left to rot in conditions of total squalor. He felt the itch of lice and scabies on his skin, the pain of the rattan on his back, the degradation of abuse by rapists and the hollow sickness of starvation. And he didn't know why he was there, or what was going on in the outside world. And the outside world did not know where he was.

Then the misleading statements obtained by Hugo started arriving on the desks of sensation-loving news editors. They were shocking allegations. Ron was pilloried. There was little coming out of Indonesian in the way of interesting news, for the new Islamic leader, who was more used to communications with Allah than with politicians, was wallowing in the murky waters in the wake of the Suharto regime and Habibie's reforms. Opponents tried to mire him with similar accusations of corruption.

The man in the street grows weary of politics, even of endemic graft. Juicy revelations never cloy. 'Porn fighter's double life' made headlines. And, because of who he was, and because the Establishment had cause to hate him, he was featured in all the British tits and bums rags, and front-paged in Australia.

Mike, who had been struggling to cope with the collapse of the

Tamberlaine Foundation in Indonesia, went crazy. He rang Mercedes.

"He used to be your friend, your lover," he yelled, down the crackling line, after a week trying to find her. "Do something!"

"What the hell do you expect me to do from East Timor?" she shouted. "There's a bloody massacre going on here!"

"Don't you get the papers there?"

"Who's got the time? I've been up the mountains with the Fretilin Freedom Fighters. I've been inside the barracks with the bloody militia, and I mean bloody! What's wrong with you?"

"You must have heard about the trouble with Tamberlaine?"

"It'll blow over when Ihza gets his finger out of his arse!"

"Ron's been missing for more than six months."

"Bull shit. Hugo told me he's in New York."

"He's been killed or he's in prison. Do something! The press is crucifying him. They say he's a paedophile."

"Ron? Don't be such a sicko, Mike. You know he hates the fat pigs."

"Yeah, but it's the fat pigs that are doing all the grunting."

"I'll call you," screamed Mercedes. "The Timorese Militia have opened fire on this building."

It was two days before she rang back. She was quiet, chastened, apologetic. She was in Darwin, covering the departure of Australian troops as peace-keepers in East Timor.

"I lost the plot for a month or so there," she said. "I've been reading the files. You're probably right. But there's not much I can do. As far as the new President is concerned I'm an Infidel whore. I'd probably get stoned to death by fundamentalists if I set foot in Jakarta."

"Try Megawati! She's related, for God's sake."

"You try Megawati. I can't do a damn thing until the United Nations settles things down in Dili. But I know what you can do. Get the Art Aid celebrities on the case!"

***

May must have written hundreds of letters begging for help. "Petition the Indonesian Government on Roman's behalf," she asked. "You know he is not a child pornographer. You know he has given the best part of his life fighting to save children, not to exploit them. Please, please write." Many replied, promising action. Others, who still believed he was party to Zoe's fraud, replied in disparaging tone. Some wrote stinkers. The tabloids used it as a chance to rake up speculation about his Affair. They used a capital letter. It was a welcome diversion, in some quarters, from tattle about Mediterranean cruises with Woody's arch-rival. The United States, which didn't have much of a clue about East Timor, but had a lust for scandal, still preferred the English Rose to the huntin', shootin' and fishin' substitute, even if the latter was in New York.

How many really wrote, Mike wondered, but even if they had, it did no good. Diplomatic inquiries met a brick wall. Alexandar fumed. He'd been staying with May and Mike during the year working as registrar at LIPS, and had assisted in removing the growth from Farah's cheek. His admiration for Mike Carney was enormous, but his hero in all things was still Ron Turner.

"If I went home and took the Dreamdrift across the Timor Sea, would the Tamberlaine Foundation fund me? You're the one holding the purse strings, Mike."

"What sort of funds are you talking about?"

"Buying information. If he's in prison, bribing guards. Paying officials to turn a blind eye...getting me out of gaol if I throttle

Hugo!"

"Hugo? Mercedes' brother?"

"Yeah. It's always been the same. If old Ihza farts, it's Hugo who makes the smell."

"Open cheque book," said Mike. "First, Tamberlaine can't stand this bad publicity, second, Pru wouldn't want us to do nothing and three...which should have been first..."

"Yes. Ron's innocent. Right, you pay for my flight through internet banking and I'll get my bag packed."

"Just like that?" said May. "Aren't you going to call Helene and Kostas?"

"No way. Why worry them? My mother would have pink kittens if she knew I was going to play James Bond."

***

"Have you come for me, Dr Pappas?" said Liana, doubtfully. "My mother says you only paid a little money and I can't marry without the full bride price. She's talking to that nasty man from Surabaya."

"You're still too young," said Alexandar. "When you're eighteen, yes? I'll give your foster mother some money on account. Would that help?"

She nodded.

"But I'll come to see you as often as I can. Tell your family I need your birth certificate."

"I haven't got one. General Ihza's wife kept it and my mother won't ask her for it because she is a filthy Infidel whore."

"Oh, dear. Forget I spoke. Where's your father?"

Putu was reluctant to talk. He was busy filling 'Spring Water' bottles from a green-scummed tank behind the information hut in the Taman National Park. It took a large bundle of rupiah to get the good gossip. It took even more to find a contact. Alexandar sailed across the Bali Straits to Java and hitched a lift in a bemo to Surabaya. He hired a car. He made the link. He drove to the grim prison and waited in the street behind it.

A scruffy guard tapped on the window and held out his hand. He opened the envelope Alexandar passed him and riffled through the high denomination notes. Ten minutes later, during which time the young doctor thought he'd kissed the cash goodbye, an emaciated figure was dragged to the car and bundled into the back seat. Not a word was spoken. Alexandar looked carefully to make sure he had the right man. Ron was barely recognisable.

The Dreamdrift sailed before dawn. By the time they reached home port Ron had been deloused, wormed and treated with the heaviest dose of antibiotics Dr Pappas could feed into his veins through a drip. The patient had been semi-conscious for several days. The weather was rough. Ron threw up most of the food Alexandar got into his mouth. Only south of Exmouth did the storm abate and Ron stagger to his feet to have his first pee without a catheter. And by that time Alexandar knew there was more wrong with Ron than prison life.

Alexandar sailed to the moorings single-handed and went below to help Ron to the deck. It was choppy and not an easy step from the boat to the jetty.

"Give you a hand?" said the man on the shore. Alexandar squinted into the light of the rising sun. It was a police officer. Behind him stood three others and a paddy wagon.

"Federal Police," said one. "We'll take Mr Turner into custody now, if you don't mind."

"What for?" Alexandar was horrified. "What the hell for?"

"He's the one that's the child porn pedlar, isn't he? New laws, Dr Pappas. You can't mess with kids overseas and get away with it back home. Now, if you please."

Ron moved like a zombie while Alexandar hurled abuse at the police. "Get me a lawyer," Ron urged. "I'm innocent."

"That's for the court to decide, Mr Turner. You're arrested and will be held on remand. Bail? Not a dicky-bird's chance. In the van, mate. You mustn't keep the other prisoners waiting. You can get breakfast at the prison farm."

Thirty minutes later the van drew up in the prison yard and the old lags, hardened criminals with a deeply ingrained hatred of rock spiders, their term for child-molesters, got out and strolled nonchalantly away. Ron, with his trousers around his ankles, lay on the floor of the van, groaning in agony. When the escorts tried to roll him over, he screamed. He had been screaming since the other convicts had held him down and twisted the wire into a tourniquet. They had been deaf to his noise, heedless of his protests.

"We've got kids at home," said the biggest brute. "You deserve this."

The Federal Police looked at one another in alarm and rang for an ambulance. Alexandar was waiting at the hospital when it arrived. He had been arguing the toss at Police Headquarters ever since Ron had been taken away. He had been there with Ron's lawyer when the news came through.

"How is he?"

The ambulance man shook his head. "Not good, Doctor. They've knackered him good and proper."

Alexandar struggled for words, watching as Ron, under sedation, was prepared for theatre. "If it's any consolation, it's only hastened the inevitable," he said. "He's got cancer of the prostate gland."

The lawyer looked grim and flared up at a worried-looking police inspector. "It's a disgrace," he said. "My client has done nothing, absolutely nothing to be ashamed of. He's been framed by corrupt men and you have not one piece of evidence on which to press charges. What Dr Pappas says about my client's medical condition makes no difference to the degree of police culpability." He turned to Alexandar and spoke quietly. "Does Mr Turner know he's got the Big C?"

"He was warned years ago. But he ignored it. Thought it would go away. Like most men. Waited until it was too late. He might pull through. Depends if it's metastasised."

"Hell," said the lawyer, his face deep red with emotion, like the wattles of a turkey-gobbler. "It's a pity that crooked General didn't just shoot him."

"Might have been kinder," Alexandar muttered, and went home to pour out his misery to his mother and to beg a stiff drink from Kostas.

How was he to tell them that Ron had been castrated?

26

Zinc white; metallic zinc was originally imported from the East Indies, now Indonesia, but in the 18th century economic deposits were found in Europe. By 1794 zinc oxide as a paint had been patented in England. Although originally a water colour, sold as Chinese white from 1834 because it resembled the colour of porcelain, it was a French colourist who devised a way of blending it with poppy oil. It is slow drying and the cleanest and coldest of the whites, taking tints well and having no adverse chemical reactions. However, used alone, it has a tendency to crack.

There was white above him, white covered his body and white wavered on either side. Ron did not know where he was when he came out of the anaesthetic. Slowly the vision steadied and he realised he was in a hospital bed. Helene drew back the curtains and smiled at him uncertainly.

"What do I say?"

"Hello, Ron. Nice to see you." His voice was scratchy from the tube which had been down his throat. "Got a kiss for me?"

"Alexandar's coming. He's stopped for a word with the policeman who's sitting outside the ward, looking very bored."

"I'm not going anywhere."

"No. You're not. That's what he's trying to tell them. They're wasting taxpayers' money."

"How bad is it?"

Helene turned her head away. She was trying not to cry.

"Oh. That bad."

Alexandar shooed his mother from the room. "Too early to tell, Ron. They got all the glandular material and took most of the lymph nodes. It's not in your waterworks or in your bowels, from what we can see. They've inserted a neat little zapper...a sort of chemical time-bomb which will knock out any regrowth near the prostate. You'll have chemo and radio-therapy. If the oncologists are still not sure, they'll attack stray cancer cells with T-cell antibodies to which they've linked radio-isotopes. It's a new, 'hunt a killer' procedure."

"What do you do about the ones that get away?"

"Slow them down. Make them sicker than you are."

"Sounds delightful. I'm finished, aren't I?"

"You've got plenty to live for."

"What, as a fat eunuch? Will my voice change? Will I grow tits? Have you removed my joystick?"

"Rubbish, rubbish, rubbish and yes, but you may never get a response from it again. On the other hand, many men regain function. Synthetic hormones help. You'll be sterile, of course."

"So all I've got is a dribbler."

Alexandar looked sadly at him. "It may come to that, yes. Some patients remain incontinent. We can make it less embarrassing with a drip-bag down your trousers."

Ron turned his face away. He was surrounded by white, but within him was a great black hole of misery. Hope had sustained him in the vile conditions of the prison cell but here, in sterile, painless, drugged-to-the-eyeballs safety, he lost the will to live, although he escaped the curse of AIDS.

Kostas, who was usually so cheerful in the face of adversity, could find little to say to his friend. Others talked too much. Even

Mike was a pain, trying to interest him in how the rebuilding of Ephemeral was progressing, talking about the way the Tamberlaine Foundation was rebuilding, thanks to a goodwill campaign spearheaded, would he believe, by Mercedes?

"She did an hour-long documentary for Spotlight on Asia last month. She took the cameras into the flesh pots of Phnom Penh and Bangkok, she filmed the AIDS hospices and talked to the child sex-workers. She named prominent citizens who run porn as a side line to legitimate business interests. She named General Ihza Dinegoro."

"Taking a risk, wasn't she?"

"Not at all," said Mike, with a wry smile. "Ihza was so eager to give himself an alibi for the time of your arrest that he got himself attached to the Militia in East Timor. He disappeared during the massacres. Now that it's coming out about the atrocities committed by some of the Indonesian Army, he's been made the scapegoat. Mercedes reckons he's at the bottom of a deep pit somewhere, and that the Freedom Fighters put him there."

"I'm not crying." But he was, deep inside. He was crying like a newborn baby, not because he didn't know what the future held, but because his instinct was for self-pity. Hence he despised pity in others.

If he had drawn a picture of his psyche, it would have been very small, very withered, and crouched in a foetal position. As the world worried about Y2K bugs and how to celebrate the new Millennium, Ron knew an urge to return to his roots. When the Director of Public Prosecutions finally admitted they had no grounds to pursue charges against him and would, in fact, pay compensation for his injuries, Ron started planning his escape.

Escape? Escape from friends who cared about him? "Why would I do that?" he asked himself. " Because I don't want them to watch me die. Death is a personal and private matter. I want to creep away like a sick dog and lie down under the house and lick my wounds. Not my physical wounds, because I've never been an arse-licker, but my battered, shattered, splattered self-esteem. I am but a smear of paint on the canvas of life. I need to rub myself out!"

Yes, indeed, it had come down to that. The urge to self-destruct was strong. And he had the means to do so. Arsenic, cadmium, cyanic acid, lead, mercury...yes, he would be happy to die with vermilion on his lips.

But no, not yet. Not until the pain got bad again. There were still things to do. He wrote orders and cheques and bought in the supplies he'd need, all to be delivered on or around the end of August. It was a symbolic anniversary for him. Kostas brought him ordinary clothes so that he could walk around the nursing home where he was recovering. He was slowly regaining strength. He was taken in a wheelchair to see the rebuilt Ephemeral, although he could explore no further than the big studio.

"The Arts Council is selecting Artists in Residence until you are well enough to return," said Mike, on another flying visit from LIPS.

Ron shook his head. Pru had flown like the firebird. He knew himself to be a black bird of ill omen, who would flop off the balcony and thud to earth with a 'caaaw' of futility.

He wondered if the nude of Mercedes was still hidden. He wondered if he could still enjoy studying flesh, even if he could do nothing in response.

Three days later he called a taxi and had himself driven to the stockyards. As arranged, O'Malley's truck was there, though the original sheep-shipper was long dead. Dixie, a Yamagee stockman with a wide grin and a taste for Country and Western music, gave him a leg up to the cab.

"Got your medicine, Mr Turner? I got mine!" Dixie waved a can of Emu lager around. "I got a coupla dozen in the Esky. See us through to Cootimurra all right. You want to lie down in the back, just ask. If we stop at Meeka, I'll sleep in me swag under the truck."

There was no one at the turn-off to meet him, only a large, faded For Sale sign, but Bert had left an old bicycle under the grevillea bush. Ron lowered himself gingerly onto the seat. It didn't hurt too much, for the incontinence pad formed a good cushion. He kicked off nervously and, wobbling in the white, dry sand and bumping across the cracked surface of the claypans, rode back to where he had begun his adult life. But he defined it in starker terms. The foetus was returning to the womb.

***

Bert greeted him with a grunt. "I'm off then. There's no stock left so don't worry if the effing windmills don't work, except the one for the house. You'll need that for the generator. The phone works. Your woman rang.

"My woman?"

"That Mercedes. Seemed to think you'd be here. Seems your mates have been in a proper panic about you. I said you were on yer way. Like a dog returning to its vomit, I said. And about the dog. Feed it or shoot it. I don't care which. My turn for the bright lights. You're welcome to bloody Cootimurra until the bank finds a buyer."

"Where will you go?"

Bert sniffed. "Booked myself on one of those sex tours of Thailand."

Ron swung a blow at his face but his brother caught his hand in a fist as large as a baseball glove and laughed at his weakness. "Gorn, Ron. You couldn't swat a fly! I was only winding you up.

Got job in the mines at Kalgoorlie. Your gear is stacked in the back room."

He pushed Ron aside, picked up his holdall and threw it into the back of his Commodore. He threw a bunch of keys at his brother. "The old ute still runs, mate. You're welcome to it. It's parked out back of the shed where Dad broke your nose."

He drove off in a cloud of white dust and silence settled on the weatherboard house, which leaned into the wind as if tired. An old blue-heeler looked at Ron with bleary eyes and sidled towards him. When Ron collapsed into a chair on the verandah, the dog came closer and, with a sigh, laid her head on Ron's boot.

The great singing silence of the Outback was a benison. It was punctuated by the creaking of the windmill, the buzzing of insects and the small twittering of hungry birds. The cicadas kept up an insistent chirrup and a sheet of loose galvanised iron flapped on the roof of the laundry. The coat of paint he'd given it eighteen years earlier had flaked off. Even the zinc coating had been scoured away by the elements. The entire roof was corroded until it looked as if it had been over-glazed with red ochre...ferric oxide...rust.

The back room, Bert's old bedroom, was a mess. The supplies were piled haphazardly in a corner and his brother had opened a few of the boxes. He'd had some of the tinned food and taken a bottle of brandy. He'd obviously been uninterested in the art supplies.

The room was unusable for sleeping. The part of the floor where the bed stood was rotten with termite damage. The white ants had started on one leg of the base and it had fallen through the boards. Hornets had built nests on the dirty mattress.

Bert had moved to the room in which his long-dead parents had conceived him. His brother had had a woman there but had not shared his parent's desire to procreate. There were several used condoms in a stinking pot under the bed. The sheets were soiled. Ron gagged on his way to the dunny.

He found clean but threadbare linen in the blanket-box his mother had always used to keep out the moths and other creepy-crawlies. It stank of naptha. He gathered handfuls of the crushed moth-balls and strewed them around the room, then brushed away the dust of neglect. He'd bought insect repellent. He set off a couple of cockroach bombs in the house and, with the dog at his heel, strolled slowly down to the dry creek bed behind the homestead.

He passed dead trees, their barks as white as porcelain, and the tell-tale signs of salt on the earth. He passed bleached bones of dead sheep and the empty-eyed skull of the house cow. There was nothing in the creek except the scratched holes in the sand where kangaroos had dug for the last of the water. Curious, Ron dug deeper. Even at arm's depth there was nothing. Even the wild life had done a perish, though, from the number of wedge-tailed eagles soaring above the paddocks, there was still carrion on which the vultures of the bush could feed.

On his return he opened the windows and let the hot, dry air sweep through the rooms. Things fell from the ceilings and lay, quivering in the throes of death. He covered his mouth with a handkerchief and fetched a tin of bully beef from the stores. He ate it with his pocket-knife and the remains of a bread roll bought on the road from the city. The chemical smell inside the house was still too strong. He drew water from the tap outside the laundry and fed the remains of his meal to Dog. He filled her bowl and she panted with gratitude.

He made up the bed at midnight and slept as if he were dead. It suited him. He didn't care if he never woke up. It was mid-afternoon when he finally surfaced and then it was only because Dog whined to be fed.

The hours crawled by and merged into days, weeks, a month, and Ron did as little as possible to sustain life. It was his own personal purgatory. He had come from hell; he anticipated another state of being, for Pru and Woody were still near enough to sense; Andrew too, and the ghosts of his parents and dead brothers still flickered in a corner of his mind. "I'm too young to kark it and my body's too old to live," he told Dog sadly. "Shit, I'm not yet forty!"

It was ironic that, having come to Cootimurra to die, the time of lethargy was helping his body to recover from the draining effects of the therapy he had undergone. He was not aware that his health was improving until, one day, he realised he had stopped dribbling down his leg. The pads he wore at night were dry. He looked at the large bottle of pain-killers and saw it was nearly empty. He found the keys to the ute and told Dog to hop in the back.

It was two hours drive to the country town where he had gone to school. He checked in with the local doctor and got his prescriptions renewed. He went to the bank and drew money. He bought fresh bread and milk, bones for Dog, and steaks for himself. He bought fresh vegetables and seeds to replant his mother's garden. He had the pharmacist fill three repeats of drugs and knew himself fixed for several months. Only on his way back to the homestead did he realise his actions were those of a man who was determined to live.

It was then that he started to paint the great, sweeping canvases of the Outback which were, in later years, to be toured all over Australia and to galleries beyond her shores. It was as if, weary of his own flesh and jaded by painting that of others, he went to the very bones of the earth and caught the spirit of the drifting sand, the tortured sandalwood and the red ochres of the soil into which the ancient rocks had crumbled. He knew how the needles of spinifex felt as they pushed new silver-green growth from their hedgehog pads of old straw-yellow stalks. He knew what the wind sang as it turned the bush grass into waves of shining vitality. And he gasped in awe as, after a brief spring rain, the flowers of the Outback carpeted the land. The Ephemerals bloomed but for a day, a day of glory, then were gone.

And later, when Dixie brought his family to Cootimurra for a 'bit of a bash' - Country and Western music, a barbecue and proper bush tucker, followed by a corroboree - Ron at last felt comfortable with other people around him. They were not part of his past; they had not shared his sorrows, his achievements, his dreams and his loss of manhood. But they offered him simple friendship and the sense of fun with which Aboriginal people are richly endowed when not sucked in by the stupidities of the white man's culture. They had a ball, and the children crowded around Ron as he drew them in charcoal. Such lovely children, loved and loving, mischief sparkling in their eyes, even if the bushflies pestered them for moisture.

Throughout that year Ron started to paint the Cootimurra neighbours, the Elders and the young women with babies in their arms, the chuckling grandmothers who showed him how they used to separate tin from sand with a yandi dish. He painted young bucks learning how to straighten sticks to make spears which they now used for fun, choosing a rifle for serious hunting. He learned to play the didgeridoo and loaned them tapes of Django Reinhardt and Edie Piaff. He chuckled to hear the children singing 'C'est merveilleux' in between snatches of the latest raps.

He did not listen to the radio; he neither wrote letters nor read them. He was incommunicado to all humanity except those who were native to the land and who seemed as much a part of it as the desert sands.

It therefore came as a shock when he returned from Faraway, where he had finished a study of the derelict Downs homestead, to find a modern car parked outside the front verandah of

Cootimurra. There was a figure asleep in the front seat, which had been laid back for comfort. Long, jean-clad legs and desert boots were hoicked onto the dashboard. There was a newspaper over the face to keep off the sun. He reached in through the open window and pressed the horn.

"Pig!" yelled Mercedes. "You're a bastard, Ron Turner!"

"Mercedes? Mercedes! Mer-bloody-cedes! What are you doing here?" And he hugged he and kissed her and spun her round as if she were a giggling girl.

"I've come to live with you."

"The hell you have!"

"Yes. I have. Ari died last year."

"I knew. Kostas told me when I was in hospital. So? You're a rich widow?"

"No way. Ari was a gambler. There wasn't much left. We talked it over. He left his estate in trust for Zoe, in case they ever let her out of prison."

"You're so skint you have to bludge off me? I don't believe it. What about your job?"

"After September 11, I pulled the pin. I couldn't stand all the Muslim crap and the extremists muttering jihad and my own daughter with posters of Osama Bin Laden on the wall of her room at college. College? Some college. Fundamentalist brain-washing academy, if you ask me."

"Mercedes, I don't know what the hell you're talking about."

"You don't? You haven't heard about the World Trade Centre? Ron, where the hell have you been?"

"Here. Only here."

"Well, your sweet little daughter, Liana, has been in

Afghanistan, would you believe! With the Islamic Youth Group, all fired up to join the Taliban to fight the Americans. I had a hell of a job getting her out of there. Alexandar and I had to force her on to the PanAsia flight. Well, it wasn't as bad as that. He gave her a shot of something. She's home, but she's spitting chips."

"You know, I feel like that red-neck politician from Queensland...Pauline what's-her-name?"

"Hanson? The red-headed fish and chip dame? The anti-Asian panic merchant? Why?"

"Please explain. That's what she always says when she doesn't understand something that's basically quite simple."

"There's nothing simple about the world these days."

It took hours and a dozen cold beers before Ron grasped the horror of terrorist events that had stunned Western society, before he got a handle on the United States, Britain and Australia, with other nations, fighting the fundamentalists in Afghanistan under a United Nations peace-keeping mandate.

"I buried myself alive when I came here, didn't I?"

"Sure did, Ron Turner. But I'm here now, and I have come to deliver the kiss of life!"

He was very quiet. Very still. "I can't relate like that, Mercedes. I'm not a man any longer. Don't taunt me."

She knelt beside him and gave him a hug. "You've never understood love, have you, Ron? I've always loved you but you've always seen me as only a sex-plaything. You've lusted after my flesh, but you've never realised I had a heart. If you'd loved me, way back then, I'd have stayed with you. If you'd truly wanted me I'd have kept the baby. If you'd not shown disgust at the way I'd been abused, as if it were somehow my fault, I'd never have taken Zoe as a lover."

"You said you wanted a career."

"I was hurt. I was proud. I was in the middle of a hormonal battleground. I liked sex then. It masked my deeper need."

"You married Ihza; you married Aristotle."

"And I've slept with many other men. And women, if it comes to that. There are times when I've hated you, but there've been more times when I've disgusted myself."

He tipped her chin upwards and gazed into her eyes. "I've nothing to offer you."

"Comfort? Company? Caring? The three big Cees? Could you settle for that?"

"Is it enough?"

"Yes. It will be enough."

And, with her spooned against his body that night, warm and fragrant, undemanding, sleeping like a child, he felt comforted, and cared for, and glad of her companionship.

Nothing changed that perception in the weeks ahead. She busied herself with domestic chores, watered the garden with the grey water from the laundry, groomed Dog, cooked meals and sang as she filled the passing hours.

One night, when his confidence had been restored and they had kissed deeply and with hunger, she said. "There are many ways of making love."

There were, and they were very sweet. And Ron's spirit soared. Like the Ephemerals, his manhood blossomed again.

27

Titanium white; the most brilliant white ever known, is named after the Greek, tito, the sun, and from the Latin, Titan. Titan was the giant who was brother to Kronos, god of time. The pigment is made from rutile, a mineral found in sands in Western Australia, and many other parts of the world, but was not developed as a paint until 1921, when it was mass-produced in America, at Niagara Falls, New York, and at Kronos Titan, in Norway. It is very stable and of unquestionable permanence.

The memorial to Pru Tamberlaine-Darcy shone white and glistening through the surrounding trees in the grounds of the London Institute for Plastic Surgery. The Church of the Children had been built on land donated by the University in exchange for the Tamberlaine Surgical Complex. The suite of operating theatres and laboratories contained the latest equipment for microsurgery, every technological advance which would make reconstruction of the most severe deformities possible.

The flood of donations which had followed the documentary made by Mercedes had ensured its completion to Professor Dr Mike Carney's exacting standards. With it, he said, anything was possible, even techniques tried on only cadavers in the past. Other land had been leased to bio-tech companies, where artificial skin, bone and cartilage could be grown and new products given clinical trials. It was part of these agreements that LIPS was to have access to cutting-edge products at cost.

The documentary had also done much to restore Roman's reputation, especially when it was learned that the sale of Wood Violets had funded the memorial. But it was the church which was the reason Ron had left Cootimurra and had been lured back into the civilised world. Mercedes had been insistent, as insistent as she had been that he marry her before they left Australia. So it was that, after a simple ceremony attended by Kostas and family, close friends and a select group of Dixie's people, Ron and Mercedes went through the departure gates for PanAsia's flight to London, showered in confetti. They travelled first class and beaming cabin crew brought them champagne and presented the bride with orchids. Other travellers smiled, but hung back on arrival as the honeymooners were greeted by a media barrage.

Ron knew the scope of the work he was about to undertake. Mike had sent plans of the church and the preparatory drawings, known as cartoons, had already been couriered to Tamberlaine headquarters. Art students, hired by the score, had completed the basic frescos on roof and walls. Ron was to over-paint these in his inimitable style, with his flawless use of colour and his unique ability to make flesh glow as if it were alive. Only Renoir had ever done it in a similar manner, but even he was out-mastered.

In the great dome above the octagonal church Christ gathered to him the children of the world, with the painted ribbon in royal purple bearing the text running along the horizon of the celestial blue sky, a looping ribbon which said, in gold leaf, "Suffer little children to come unto me, for theirs is the Kingdom of Heaven". Dixie had posed for it. There was the blood of Afghan cameleers in his veins but his Aboriginal identity robbed the portrait of any political significance. Ron, on his back on the scaffold, playing Michelangelo, smiled with contentment as he added the finishing touches to the hands of the children of every race under the sun, who were reaching out to the main man.

He had already finished the first six panels; Pru, wearing a loose veil over her hair, poured drinks a la Vermeer, for the Tamberlaine orphans; Mike, sunburned and bearded, dressed the wounds of Kuwaiti and Iraqi children injured in the Gulf War.

Helene, laughing, sewed a patch on the trousers of a little boy while watched by a dozen youngsters who crowded around her feet. There was Kostas, feeding hordes of starving mites with bowls of tomato-rich stew, and Alexandar, on the beach, a boy again, laughing as he threw fish to his playmates. There was May, dressed in her hijab, ("Bugger the Muslim haters", said Ron) leading a crowd of waifs towards a better life, out of a refugee camp to a waiting aircraft.

There was, half-completed, a sinking boat from which children begged for help, and the hollow cheeks and pot-bellies of east Africans on the point of starvation. He had painted a blonde-haired slip of a girl, in a flak jacket, arms around the little victims who had lost limbs to mines. He had only the highlights to put on the panel which showed Andrew Darcy, giving alms to the poor.

The last two panels, on either side of the door, were truly horrific. Dark clouds roiled, volcanoes erupted, houses collapsed, bombs exploded and in the chaos, as in an Heironymous Bosch painting, were the faces of the war-mongers, the terrorists, the fat pig sex-traders, the slavers and the ugly, complacent women with poodles who ate chocolates and didn't give a damn. It was a stunning indictment of all that was wrong with the world.

Above the altar, before which she increasingly knelt, was the face of Hope. Mercedes had posed for it reluctantly, as if she had sinned too much to deserve the honour. Hands raised in supplication and the expression of trust clear on her face, she was the woman in blue to whom all Catholics pray for intercession with the Holy Father.

There was no self-portrait of Roman, but his words were being etched into the bronze panels which would stand in the porch which shaded the great door.

Dust sheets covered the black marble floor. The seating would be set in circles around the still baptismal pool in the centre of the church, which would reflect the painting overhead. The fountain at one side was even now being cast, cupped hands in dark bronze, from which water would pour in a slow, musical trickle.

Near silence, said Mike, was essential in the Church of the Children. Many parents would come here to pray for their sons and daughters while he and others fought to save lives crippled by accidents, savagery, fire, war, or the cruelty of genetic malformation. Many would come to mourn. The architects had used the latest technology to inactivate mobile phones or other electronic gimmickry. The sound of water would be heard, a balm to the spirit, and the only music would be the faint, background recordings of the breeze rustling in the trees, distant birds singing and the waves lapping on the shores of faraway lands.

Mercedes, a woman with peace in her eyes, came often to watch him work. She brought him lunch and made sure he ate properly. She put flesh on his bones and even gained a little herself. She had made firm friends with May and her children and even spoke wistfully of her sadness at having passed over the experience of motherhood. "I was such a fool," she sighed.

"We could adopt," said Ron, knowing no agency would accept them, with his risky health profile. "We could try IVF, with donor sperm. You're young enough."

"I've still got my periods, if that's what you mean, but my biological clock is about to stop ticking."

"Try," said Ron, and she did. Mike, at May's instigation, donated the sperm. The first attempt failed. The second took and, in September, Mercedes went alone to the Chapel of Our Lady, in the nearby Roman Catholic church, and gave thanks. She had quietly joined the congregation on return from Cootimurra, for there was something about that great, wide, open country, which had re-awakened her belief in an Eternal Father.

"Give me the child and I will deliver the man," was how the

Jesuits had phrased it. Her years with the nuns at boarding school had not been forgotten. She had sinned, and been forgiven. She had prayed, and had been blessed.

She did not attend the dedication of the Church of the Children, for she had morning sickness. The Archbishop, who had been painted by Ron in the Art Aid series, conducted the service. Royalty and its sons were present, for the young men were eager to see the new portrait of their mother. There were celebrities and merchant bankers, diplomats and charity workers. Outside were hundreds of parents and children, of all nationalities, who had posed for Ron, who had advertised for subjects and who had picked them by lot, according to age and colour of their skin. They all wanted to see the final work, how they had fitted into the great collage of humanity which was the memorial to a special lady and her life's work.

"Are you feeling all right?" said Ron to Mercedes, when he got home after the pomp and congratulations were over.

"Mmm. Just a bit of a headache," she said. "Perhaps I need glasses."

Ron drew up a stool to sit by her side. "You'll never guess what You-Know-Who said to me. He looked at Woody's panel for a long time and said, 'Ahem. That was painted with love, wasn't it?' and I said, 'Yes, she was very lovable.' He said, 'Yes. Pity about that. I just couldn't see it at the time.'"

"Oh. Touchy," said Mercedes.

"Then he asked if I'd paint his wife-to-be and I refused. I said I was a one woman man."

"You liar!"

"He offered me megabucks, but I shook my head. I'm afraid I was rude."

"Why?"

"He said he was sorry about that and I said, 'Tough titties!'"

Mercedes shook with laughter. "Oh, Ron, I do love you!"

***

Two weeks later Alexandar called. "Trouble," he said. "Liana turned eighteen this week."

"I know. We sent her a birthday card and her mother chose a bracelet for her."

"And I turned up with her Australian passport and an engagement ring. She said she'd rather go into a brothel than marry an Americano."

"Holy cow! She's been got at. Mercedes said the mullahs had done a job on her."

"It's not that simple. Her mother says Hugo's going to buy her and the brothel business is no joke. He's promised them heaps of cash. She says Liana's bride price has gone up."

"How much?"

"A hundred thousand. It's exorbitant!"

"I don't have that sort of money. I hate blackmail but I'd give it to you if I had it."

"You do have it, Ron. It's sitting there in that bloody container at the end of the garden in Ephemeral. Sell the nudes!"

"Sell the nudes?"

"Yeah. What use are they? Your life has moved on. Use them to save Liana."

Ron snorted as a laugh fought against his indignation. "Where are you?"

"At the new Clinic in Bangli."

"I'll be in touch."

Ron, alternating among fear, anger and amusement, asked for the advice of Mercedes.

"You've never told me about your collection," she said, reproachfully. "Am I in it?"

"I expect so. I wouldn't sell any paintings of you."

"I should think not, but done the right way, others might buy their own. Are they good?"

"Some are terrible."

"Burn them. Write or phone your sitters, and say you are putting the collection on the open market and are offering them privately first. How many do you have?"

"A couple of hundred, I should think."

"Ask a thousand dollars each, US. Hugo can't seriously expect you to match his first price. Alexandar will have to dicker and deal."

"Are you coming with me?"

"No. The gynaecologist says I'm not to fly, not at this early stage."

"I hope he said you're well enough to give me a loving goodbye."

She smiled. "I might just manage that, my darling."

***

Kostas threw himself into the project with chortling delight. It was the first time he'd seen inside the sea-container, though he had been the one who'd put it in place. He carried out the portraits while Ron looked at them critically.

He did not always like what he saw, though they were uniformly good, if the eye could reach past the swollen paunches, the sagging breasts, the varicose veins on the legs, the matted hair veering down to the men's navels and the mojos, large or small, flaccid or erect, rendered as they had been seen. He'd been kinder to women, though just as truthful, welcoming only the sight of the young and nubile or the interest of the old and withered. If he had detested the client he had developed the nude study in a Dali-esque fashion.

He was fond of the portrait of a well-known feminist, who had been subtly distorted by acid dripping from her breasts onto men squirming in agony in her juices. She would, he guessed, pay thousands not to have the picture on public exhibition and, ironically, he knew just who would have delighted in buying it...a popular glossy magazine which specialised in tweaking the sensibilities of pompous and puffed-up people. But it smacked of blackmail.

"Trash pile," he said, throwing the canvas to one side. "Get rid of your Uncle Aristotle, too. And Zoe."

Kostas protested. "My father'd love the one of Ari. He'd put it in his office and laugh his socks off."

"It's your call. But Zoe goes. No, you're not having Kylie. She'll buy."

The parameter Ron set was that quoted to him by Mike, the doctor's creed. First, do no harm. He was done with hurting people. While he had not embraced the deep religious convictions which Mercedes now held, he felt himself responsible to a higher power, though how to define it more clearly was beyond him.

There was beauty in some of the nudes of older people, beauty which would stand the test of time, and these he saved. Even if they did not recall who they had been, for they could be dead or senile, their families would find no shame in the paintings.

As an afterthought, Ron walked up the hill to Ephemeral and scraped the dirt from the entrance to the storage area. Mercedes' nude looked just fine. He would, he thought, frame her and give it to her as a present when the baby was born.

But rude, crude, lewd, went on the reject stack. And so did bad. Ron had known off days, when he was uninspired and the work mediocre. The good was then stacked in alphabetical order, so they could be found easily for packing, and the rubbish loaded into the van Kostas had brought. There was a fire ban in place, or they would have lit a bonfire. Instead they drove to a commercial incinerator company and watched as the furnace flames devoured men and women of dubious artistic distinction.

In London Mike contacted the art students who'd worked on the memorial. Under the direction of Mercedes, who was armed with Ron's book of contacts, they started the ring-around. When the digital images started to come through on the net, they forwarded them to potential buyers. Most were willing to pay by credit card through the international money exchange network and, within three days, there was a hundred thousand in the bank. The rest was slower. Many buyers did not have the ready cash and, while eager to purchase, needed time to raise the money.

Armed with signed agreements to purchase, faxed to Margett's Restaurant, Ron brokered a deal with the bank. Constantine, chuckling, gave him a cheque for five thousand. The painting of Aristotle was, he said, worth every cent. The whole project was a winner. By Saturday Ron had passed the target and had enough extra cash to tell Alexandar to buy a house as a wedding present for himself and Liana.

"I'm on my way," he said. "You arrange a meeting. I want Hugo, Putu, Liana and a lawyer sitting around the same table."

***

The lightweight cotton jacket Ron selected for the confrontation was rather too formal for the time of year and the place they were going to, but it had one great advantage. It had button-down pockets. There was a banker's draft in one, a wad of American Express traveller's cheques in another, in US dollars, and a sheaf of high denomination rupiah in a third.

Alexandar asked him to carry Liana's passport in his top left hand pocket. He flicked it open and stared at the photograph. "That's not a proper passport photo."

"It was good enough for the Government," Alexandar said. "I took it from a snapshot she posed for last year, before she got involved in all this Youth Party crap. A mate who's gung-ho with a computer worked on it and pulled off the number of images we needed on the sort of quality paper the professionals use. Professor Carney signed that he'd known her for years and that it was a true likeness. Everything was cool."

"You're born to be a crook, Dr Pappas."

Ron slipped his jacket over his T-shirt and put his wallet in his back pocket. He asked reception at the beachfront hotel to put his passport and other valuables in the safe.

"I'm carrying a small fortune," he said. "If Hugo ambushes us in a dark alley, I want to be able to get home."

"If Hugo ambushes us, it'll be a body bag you'll need, not a passport."

"Scaremonger!" said Ron. "Let's go buy ourselves a woman! Paddy's Bar, here we come!"

28

Vermilion; an orange red of high permanence, used from ancient times in the form of crushed cinnabar, a natural mercuric sulphide mineral, ground and heated to give a bright red similar to that of primitive cochineal. This gives rise to the origin of its name, from the Latin, vermiculus, little worm. In modern times it is manufactured from a five to one compound of mercury and molten sulphur, creating a black form which is heated in earthenware pots to produce red crystals. These are used to make the pigment, which is poisonous.

The streets of Bali were crowded with holiday-makers heading for a night of partying. The narrow roads were dangerous, for vehicles and pedestrians jostled for position and tried to avoid the hawkers who solicited trade from their kerb-side barrows. Music blared from bars along the verges. It was noisy and sticky and Ron wondered why the hell he had agreed to meet in such an unsuitable spot.

He bellowed the question at Alexandar.

"Hugo says he's got a drug deal there tonight and he's flying back to Jakarta tomorrow. He said there or nowhere. And no bloody lawyer!"

Hugo had secured a table near the front of the drinking hole. Putu had his nose deep in a lemonade. Liana, looking uncomfortable without her headscarf, was sipping a fruit concoction. Her blonde hair shone like platinum under the lights of the mirror ball over the crowded dance floor. She wore traditional Balinese dress, a flowing skirt and a camisole top, over which was the long-sleeved lace jacket popular with her age group.

Alexandar caught his breath. "She's beautiful," he said, raising his voice to be heard over the music. "Her mother's golden tan and your hair is a magic mixture."

"Yeah! Nice blend of genes. Pity about the company!"

"You haggle. I want to dance." He pulled a reluctant Liana to her feet and steered her onto the dance floor. Ron watched as his young friend coaxed and cajoled until he was able to slide an arm round the girl's waist and pull her close into an embrace. Although Liana smiled at Alexandar, she kept glancing towards Putu as if frightened. And her eyes also flickered to a pair of swarthy men standing near the entrance.

Ron looked at them with interest. They might have been plain clothes police. They had that watchful air, as if noting who was present. They were quite clearly not there to enjoy themselves. On the other hand, he thought, with a frisson of distrust, they might be Hugo's men, thugs, ready to deal in the powders of death.

"They are made for one another," Hugo bawled, slamming a drink down in front of Ron. "You have the money?"

"Of course."

"One hundred thousand US."

"Over the top. Half that. Banker's draft."

"Seventy-five."

"Seventy."

"Travellers cheques?"

Putu shook his head. "Rupiah," he said hoarsely. His eyes bulged as Ron unfastened his pocket and started counting out the local money. He laid the banker's draft on the table and Hugo put his hand on it.

Putu shook his head and yelled angrily. Hugo sneered and shouted back.

"What are they saying?" Ron asked Alexandar, who had come to see what the fuss was about. Liana looked in dismay at her foster father and Ron.

"Putu says Hugo is cheating him," Liana translated from the rapid fire Bahasa. "He says the banker's draft is not real money. He wants all his share in rupiah. If he doesn't get it, he's taking me home. He's only ever expected a hundred thousand rupiah. He's just realised Hugo was bargaining in dollars."

"If this arsehole won't deal, you're not going home at all, Liana. You can start work at Hookerama tonight!" Hugo leered at her and grabbed her breast. Liana screamed as he pinched her nipple.

Alexandar put an arm-lock on Hugo. "Outside, you! I've a message for you, Mr Bleeding Vandermeer."

Ron did not intervene. He put the money back in his pockets and stared impassively at Putu, who threw up his hands in disgust and started haranguing his daughter. Putu grabbed her by the lapels of her jacket and shouted wildly at her. Liana fished in her bag for dark glasses, put them on and stared back at Putu with lenses that shone red-orange, effectively hiding her expression and serving as a clear indication of disinterest. It was as cheeky a gesture as any woman could make.

Ron couldn't stand any more of the tension. He spotted the sign for the toilets and went inside. In the safety of the cubicle he took off his jacket, removed his cotton T-shirt and put the shirt-like jacket back on again. It was cooler.

He bundled the damp knitted T-shirt in his hand, wiped his brow with it, and headed back into the bar. Putu and Liana were still at it, only now it was she who was screaming defiance.

In the street Alexandar fronted Hugo and delivered a sharp

head-butt to his nose. "Durrbrain!" he bellowed. "You're pulling a double-cross!"

Hugo snarled and wiped blood from his nose. Then the world blew apart in a flash of brilliant white light. Hugo collapsed against Alexandar, who, ears deafened by the explosion and the screaming, collapsed under the man's weight. He struggled to push Hugo away but Mercedes' brother coughed suddenly and vomited blood over Alexandar's chest. The hands of strangers pulled Hugo off and, struggling to his feet, Alexandar saw that a huge shard of metal had been driven into Hugo's back. He was quite dead.

An inferno was raging in the bar. People were running, screaming, crying, clothes ablaze. Fear drove Alexandar into the maelstrom, shouting for Ron, searching for Liana among the fallen timbers, the dismembered bodies, the choking smoke and the burning, burning flames.

A charred and burdened man dragged a body over the debris, over the embers, past the death and the injured, through broken glass and bundles of incandescent straw which was falling from the rafters.

"I've got her," Ron croaked, his hands under Liana's armpits. "Putu took the worst of it, but his body kept the flames off most of her. I put my T-shirt over my head to get to her, but I was too late to get her out before the roof caved in."

Alexandar looked at the girl in horror. Her face was a mass of burns, deep burns. She was unconscious. Ron's hands were charred almost to the bone.

"What the hell happened?" Ron shouted. "Are you injured?"

Alexandar looked down at his front, which was stained bright red with Hugo's blood.

"I'm all right. I think it was a bomb. No, bombs. They got the

Sari Club, too. Get your hands under water. Get medical help. Where's Liana's passport?"

"Still in my pocket."

"I need it."

Ron was crying with pain. "I'm sorry. I'm sorry. I can't undo the buttons." His hands, already swelling, fumbled helplessly at his clothes.

Alexandar drew a pocket knife from his trousers and opened it to a blade. He slit the sleeves of the constricting garment and eased it off Ron's body. "I'm taking the money," he shouted. "I'll need it more than you. Go back to the hotel and get help. I'll have to go to the hospital with Liana. Meet me there."

Ron nodded and pushed past tourists seeking desperately for friends, local families trying to find loved ones who had worked at the bar, and emergency workers striving to restore some sort of order to total chaos. The hotel looked like a war zone. Bodies were laid out on the marble floors and uninjured men and women, even children, were tearing sheets into bandages. Nurses and doctors, still in their resort clothes, had set up a triage line and were doing what they could to help those who were mortally wounded or capable of being stabilised until they could be brought to proper medical facilities.

And all through the balmy night, the sounds of fire engines and police vehicles fought with the piercing cries of agony and the groans of those who could not believe that terror had come to Paradise.

Ron looked at the pools of blood and the gore-filled wounds welling carmine and vermilion. He felt the scene swimming before his eyes and fell to the ground in a dead faint.

He floated in and out of consciousness in the hours ahead for, as soon as possible, he was taken to a make-shift evacuation centre at Denpasar Airport. There he was given drugs to numb the pain for the flight to Australia. He recalled little of the days ahead, until he came round in the burns unit at the Royal.

There were loose bandages enclosing his hands, which felt strangely as if they did not belong to him. The dressings were the size of boxer's gloves. He could not make them move as he wished. There were tubes in his veins and the dreaded catheter in his bladder. He groaned through swollen lips and cried out for water.

He was helped to drink from a beaker with a sealed top and a flexible straw. The nurse adjusted his drip and stuck a needle in his thigh. He sank back into oblivion, knowing only that he was safe, wherever he was, and being cared for.

Two days later the doctor in charge told him, with infinite sorrow in her voice, that they had been forced to amputate most of his right hand and that they were fighting to save the left. Gangrene had set in.

"Does my wife know?"

"She's been ringing several times a day, Mr Turner. She'd be here now but her doctor has forbidden her to fly. You're expecting a baby, aren't you?"

Ron nodded. "We were so happy," he whispered.

She smoothed his brow. "You'll be happy again," she promised. "The shrapnel wounds on your face and your body are relatively minor. You won't lose your good looks."

"I never was an oil painting," Ron sighed. "And I don't suppose I'll ever paint another."

***

"How's Liana?" he asked Kostas, when he was finally allowed a visitor. "Is she in this hospital?"

"No. Alexandar got her on a flight to Darwin. He stayed on to help at Denpasar. They were desperately short of trained medical staff. He said he could do nothing for her, anyway."

"But she's alive?"

"If you can call it that. It was only her face that took the blast. You said there was another body on top of her."

"Her foster father."

"His remains haven't been officially identified. Those that didn't get out or weren't dragged out were incinerated. Burnt to cinders. It's a bloody tragedy. So young, many of them. Many Australians. More than a hundred at the last count. The number's rising."

"Terrorists? Al Qaeda? Osama?"

"Dunno. Islamic extremists, whatever. There's a major manhunt on."

"I hope they get the bastards. At least I'm alive."

Kostas looked at him grimly. "But your hands!"

"Forget my hands. I can get along without all my fingers. As long as I've got two left to hold up to the Government. But how does Liana survive without a face?"

***

The news from Darwin was discouraging. Liana's face was badly swollen, her eyes closed by the fluid gathering in her tissues, her lips grossly enlarged. She had to be intubated, a tube fed down her neck to prevent the larynx from closing, making it impossible for her to breathe. Fluids were being dripped into her body to replace those seeping from damaged tissue. But she was young and fit, so although her system had to fight against toxins and shock, she did not suffer the general breakdown of circulation and kidneys which affected those who had been burned over a greater proportion of their bodies.

However, nothing could be considered in the way of grafts or reconstruction of tissue until the head looked less like a football. She was being kept under sedation. Alexandar, knowing what to expect, had returned to the Bali hospital as soon as she had been safely stretchered onto an RAAF Hercules. He would have had problems had he not been able to produce her new passport. After that she was given priority. He looked around the hangar where a temporary hospital had been set up. Volunteers worked alongside doctors who had flown in from Australia's Defence Forces. There was the sheen of sweat on their faces and a look of hopelessness in their eyes. He realised many emergency workers were as traumatised as the victims.

That, he finally admitted, also applied to himself. There was a scalp wound above his ear and blood was still oozing from the place where flying glass had sliced through his shirt to his shoulder blade. Back at the scene of the outrage he'd persuaded a fireman to hose him down. He guessed that his bloody appearance, from Hugo's death throes, would lessen the confidence of patients. He had no trouble finding an ambulance to take him to the hospital, for the injured were still being shuttled from the Sari Club. He was greeted with open arms by the staff, for there were few doctors present who were fluent in Bahasa and English, though many Indonesians had trained overseas. When the Tamberlaine Clinic's team arrived he heaved a sigh of relief.

At long last he felt able to join Liana. He had no compunction about using Ron's money, even if it was a little scorched round the edges, but he was given a free flight to Darwin. Among uninjured tourists who were being evacuated, he found as much anger about what had been done to the Balinese people as outrage about the death of their own.

He was at Liana's bedside day and night as the doctor's fought to replace charred skin with tissue which had been taken from her back or artificially cultured. Time after time he watched, with despair, as the tiny patches sloughed off.

"Is her condition more or less stable?" asked Mike Carney, when he rang London to ask for advice.

"A little less than more, but she's showing no signs of respiratory complications or of infection."

"Then try to get her here. There are brilliant surgeons in Australia, but they haven't got our resources. Keep her warm, keep up the fluids, feed her high protein drinks and hold her hand."

"I thought of doing that, but the major airlines won't take her."

"Call Ron. Get him to put the hard word on PanAsia. Get them to rig an isolation tent. Good publicity. And get him here as soon as possible, as well. The last thing he needs is more worry, but Mercedes is ill."

"She hasn't lost the baby, has she? What's wrong?"

"We're not sure, but she's getting blinding headaches. I want her to see a neurosurgeon."

***

"What do you mean, you can't fly?" Mike snapped. "You're not dying, are you?"

Ron hesitated. "It's not that. My hands are in a bad way, mate. I couldn't go to the toilet on my own!"

"Then pay for Kostas to travel with you! Come to think of it, bring Helene and Roma! They can take it in turns to hold your willy!"

"Well, thanks a lot!"

"You don't expect sympathy, do you? Just get here. Mercedes

needs you. Liana needs you, and if you don't do something, Alexandar will go to pieces."

"What can I do for Liana?"

"Ron, you and Mercedes are her next of kin. There are grave decisions to be made. You have to be part of them."

***

There was bitter cold in the mountains that winter; in the mountains where Allied Forces hunted the Taliban and the Al Qaeda network. It was icy in the caves and the hidden valleys where the fundamental nutters sought refuge in the villages of sympathisers, or slunk over the border to countries where others of like mind lurked under the skirts of democracy. The wind howled through the ruins of Kandahar, and through communities trying to rebuild their shattered nation. There were cold threats against Saddam Hussein and the Axis of Evil from the White House and the Pentagon, threats of war against the Iraqi dictator, which sent shivers down the spines of those living in the free world.

It was cold and grey in London, and Kostas put on the sheepskin Ugg boots he had brought from home. Helene had refused to pack them, so he had stowed them in his cabin bag when she wasn't looking. She had refused to travel with him because Roma had to finish the school year, and because she would not leave Constantine in the lurch until the Margett's Christmas rush was over. Only then would she come to Europe.

"You've forgotten how it is in winter," she said. "You will need woolly underpants. And gloves. Thick sweaters."

"I'll need a warm woman in my bed," he grumbled.

"I packed you a hot water bottle," she said consolingly. "You'll have to make do with that!"

There was no room for Kostas in the apartment where Ron and

Mercedes lived. Even had there been, he would have refused to stay there for, he said, they needed their privacy. Mercedes had found him a pleasant room in a family hotel nearby, and had been promised an adjacent apartment before his wife and daughter arrived. Kostas, having done his duty by Ron, and having been given a period of unexpected freedom, was intent on 'doing' London.

Ron and Mercedes were intent only on one another.

"Thank God you survived," she said, her head on his shoulder. "I nearly had a heart attack when I heard about the bombing. Mike sent May round when he heard and got one of the off-duty nurses to mind his children. We were glued to the television and crying and praying and...oh, Ron. I wanted to be with you so much."

"Mike says you've not been well."

"Only headaches, Ron. Only the worry. Stress related, I expect. But you, your poor hands!"

"They'll heal. I've still got arms to hold you!"

"But how will you paint?"

"My darling, darling girl. My mind is filled with the sights of that night. All I can see in my mind is a swirl of red anger. There's no vision that I want to put on canvas...not yet."

"It will pass. Ron, please believe it will pass. I wish you could find peace and faith that God is good and that there will be..."

He interrupted, bitterly. "What? A better world? That Allah is merciful? That Christ will redeem us? Sorry, Mercedes. When I was working at the Church of the Children I was learning to hope and believe. Now I cannot face the fact that no God, no Universal Deity, is worth a prayer. What sort of a God allows such carnage?"

"I do not know," she whispered. "I find it hard to come to

terms with it myself!"

* * *

Alexandar slept in a room at the Memorial Centre, in a suite which LIPS had not yet commissioned. Tamberlaine had put Dr Pappas on the staff, but Mike did not expect him to complete the research work which he had been allocated. It simply kept him busy while the burns unit team tried desperately to stop rejection of grafts. Liana, who had been kept in a coma, could now talk, but only in a hoarse whisper through a tracheostomy which could be capped. She had little to say, but was reassured by the sound of Alexandar's voice.

Although her eyes had been protected by sunglasses, they were bandaged. The team ran no risk that she might see the reflection of her face in a shiny surface, such as surgical instruments or on glassware. There were, of course, no mirrors, neither was she allowed television, in case there was news from Bali and her memories were stirred. She lay, day and night, in a frame which prevented her from moving her head or reaching it with her hands.

The room was made sterile and those entering were masked and gowned. No hint of infection was to be allowed inside and the air in the room was filtered.

Ron was not allowed to see her without similar precautions. He took one look and left the room. He leaned against the wall of the corridor, slid down it and put his head on his knees, in a bid to stop fainting.

"Dear God," he cried. "Dear, merciful God, help her."

29

*Van Dyck brown; also known as Cassel or Cologne earth;
this pigment contains ninety per cent humic materials,
derived from peat, earth or lignite. It has been in use from
the 16th century and continues to the present day. It is a
transparent dark brown made from natural materials
which are homogenised and mixed with an oil medium. It
is instability in the oils which have caused some problems
in portraits by Anthony Van Dyck, the Flemish master,
student of Rubens, who died when only 42.*

There was no strength in Ron's hands to paint full-size
canvases. Nor had he developed a technique for handling the
paints he was accustomed to using. But, like his idol, Renoir, who
had strapped brushes to his wrists when his hands became too
crippled to hold them, Ron knew he had to practise his art. He
sought advice from fellow artists and devised a way of continuing
to express his love of life.

Using tiny brushes, pigment mixed with water, honey and gum,
he had started painting miniatures. They were exquisite. He
needed no great space and could work in the apartment on a
small easel set up on the dining room table. Working from his
prodigious memory, he was re-creating the Art Aid portraits,
making a collection to leave to the National Portrait Gallery. For,
no sooner had the images of the Bali deaths faded from his vision,
than he became aware of his own mortality.

He had developed a grating cough and his sputum was flecked
with blood. He said nothing to Mercedes but dutifully took the
linctus she bought for him and sipped lemon and honey drinks.
"It's the foul weather," he said.

But he knew it wasn't. The pains in his body, which he had previously believed to be the aftermath of shrapnel wounds had, he realised, more sinister significance. He found a lump in his armpit. It needed no oncologist to tell him the prostate cancer had spread and returned with a vengeance. If the metastasis had been kept at bay, perhaps through the peace of Cootimurra and the devotion of his new, old love, the terror and debilitation of his injuries had weakened his immune system. He kept his fears from Mike.

It was important, his friend had said, to shield Mercedes from any further worry. The pregnancy was causing problems for, as he pointed out, Ron's wife was not a young woman, despite appearances. It was of no account that her skin was as soft as that of a young girl, that her hair was glossy with apparent health, or that her eyes sparkled with joy at the prospect of motherhood, the prospect she had spurned in her youth. She was not at a favourable age to give birth again and her system reacted to the changes in her body with spite. Her blood pressure soared to dangerous levels. The extremes to which fear had brought her over the Bali incident, and her continued concern for Liana, were enough for any woman to bear. Ron refused to add to the heavy load on her shoulders.

"How can I leave you so soon, my love," he thought. "Now, when all our misunderstandings are at an end and I have become the man I should always have been, how can I bear to see the misery in your face as I shuffle off the old mortal?" For Ron was, in all things, a realist. He found a doctor in a distant part of the city. Reassured that the man had no connections with Professor Mike Carney, he had himself checked out and went back on tablets to retard the invading cells. They made him nauseous but he hid it well. He was, he said, coming out in sympathy with morning sickness.

"Is the pot belly another way of sending me up?"

He laughed and blamed her cooking, though he was merely picking at food.

He spent hours sitting with Liana, talking about his youth and his adventures with his brothers, of people he had met and places he had been. And he talked of Mercedes and her wayward spirit, in no way running her down, but passing on such bitter-sweet incidents as that of the night that Uncle Alf passed away.

"I was so angry," he said. "It was years before I understood what she had done, given him the gift of herself."

Liana made a growling noise in her throat, her sign of dissent. How much she understood of his ramblings he did not know for her English was not perfect and his Bahasa was shaky. He got more growls than huffs of agreement. It took some time before she would even let him touch her, pulling her arm away when he tried to stroke her skin.

Only when Alexandar was present did she open up and try to speak more clearly, and then in a whisper only Dr Pappas could hear.

"She wants to know if she's blind," said Alexandar. "She wants to know why she is imprisoned. She fears she may be totally paralysed."

"Surely not. Mercedes said she had explained a little."

"But Liana doesn't like Mercedes. She's been told her mother is a whore since she was a baby. She won't change her views in a few weeks."

"And all her life I've been the wicked man who seduced a schoolgirl. Isn't that what she thinks?"

"No. Hugo told her you were the agent from Hookerama who wanted to buy her services. She still finds it hard to believe you're her father."

"After all these years?"

Alexandar looked at him gravely. "Ron, when I was at school, I asked the chaplain if she could prove there was a God. She showed me a box of matches. It was labelled matches. When she shook it, it sounded like matches. She said you don't have to open it to prove what's in the box. You can accept and that's called faith! In your case, your daughter's been told you are a bad man by her foster mother and the mullahs. And, as anyone who looks western is intrinsically evil, according to them, she's trying come to terms with a different reality, to open the box to see what you're like inside."

"A bit empty, actually. I rattle."

"I'm not surprised with the number of pills you're taking. Do you think Mike and I are fools?"

What was there to say? "You'll not even drop a hint to Mercedes."

"No. How long?"

"I'm going to hang in there until the baby's born. Scout's honour! I know Mike will look out for Mercedes. After all, he's more deeply involved than I am, in a way. And he and May are so potty about children that he'll just draw another under his wing."

***

"We should go and see Zoe before I get so big I won't be able to sit in a car," Mercedes said. "I don't suppose anyone has told her about your hands or Liana's condition. She is, after all, the girl's godmother."

"Is she? I had no idea."

"You knew she was at her birth?

"She told me. But why make her a godparent?"

"We were good little Catholic students together, remember?

Before we found out about sin and being sinned against. I used to write but she never replied."

"Are prisoners allowed to write letters? I wasn't given access to pen and paper."

"Good Lord, I don't suppose she even knows you were in prison. I bet she'll wet herself laughing!"

"Does she know I've married you? And that you're having a baby?"

"There, you're right. We must definitely see her. It will cheer her up no end to get good news!"

They were driven to Suffolk by a chauffeur, in a BMW. Highpoint was no-one's idea of a holiday home. It was, and looked, grim. And Zoe, thin and weathered, was as grey as the building.

Delighted was not the word to describe her reaction. Her face twisted as she looked from one to the other, her two former lovers. Her fingers clenched into talons and spittle dribbled from her mouth. She looked as if she had had a stroke which had palsied one side of her face.

"So, bitch, you had it all, didn't you? The looks, the money, the hottest body south of the tropics. You screwed my father and my husband and my whole bloody life. And you, Ron, Roman, bastard, I'm glad your hands are ruined, for you ruined me, didn't you? And you come here, all smiles, to talk baby talk? Go rot in hell, the pair of you!"

She lunged forward, as if to rake the face of Mercedes, but she was restrained and led away, screeching curses.

Mercedes, white-faced, was stunned and clearly in distress. "Hold my hand, Ron," she said. "Help me out of here, I can't see a thing for the tears."

"Case conference," said the neurosurgeon, Wolf Zeigowicz. "You were right to bring her to me when her sight started fading in and out, Professor Carney. The scans show an aneurism in her brain. It's a weakness in a blood vessel which, as you can see on this image, has caused it to balloon out. And if you look at the lateral of the same image, there's the indication of the blood leaking from it. That's what's causing the intermittent loss of sight and the migraines. She's lucky she's not had a major haemorrhage."

"Prognosis?"

"Grim. We could go in and inject a substance to form a gel which would close the weakness, but this particular vessel feeds major control centres. And we're not sure where its influence stops. She could lose memory, be permanently blinded, or be left paralysed. But if she's not operated on, with the rising blood pressure, she could suffer a cerebral trauma that could kill her."

"And she's pregnant."

"Yes. Pity about that. She'd lose the child, of course."

"Not if we can keep her stable for another month. The baby'd have a chance at six months. Slim, but a chance. We could do a Caesar, and take the new-born straight to our unit for ultra-premature babies...the unit where we try to correct foetal deformities before birth."

"The mother'd have to be admitted for the remainder of her term. She'd have to be monitored, night and day."

"We have the facilities. Have you seen the range of theatres we offer visiting specialists?"

"No, but I've a feeling you're going to show me, Professor Carney. And that you've a special interest in this case. Why?"

"It's an IVF conception. I was the sperm donor."

* * *

The arrival of Helene and Roma was a huge relief for everyone. Not only did Ron stop worrying about Kostas getting into scrapes, for he already done so, but showing Roma the sights became her father's main concern. It gave him a valid excuse not to visit the hospital, for only duty forced him to sit with Liana. Her appearance, he admitted, churned him up. Although her eyes were now open, her face was a patchwork of new pink grafts, granulated tissue and ridged and puckered skin. She could not wear the pressure mask which smoothed out healing tissue on the body, for her face was still too damaged and the slightest friction set up infections.

Helene had been kind, but after the first time, agreed that Roma should not have to go through the pretence that all was well. She farmed their daughter out to May, who was happier with every extra child she had under her roof. "She's a born mother hen," she said to Mike.

"Yeah, and clucky with it. She wants another three children. I think she's compensating for all the brothers and sisters who died in the floods in Bangladesh. Does Kostas mind taking a mob to the zoo?"

"Lordy, Mike, he's just a big kid himself. He'll have more fun than they will."

"Even in the snow?"

"He likes building snowmen. He's never had the chance before."

The arrangements freed Helene to spend most of her days with Mercedes, who was confined to bed in the ante-natal wing, wired up to machines that buzzed and hissed, and to alarm bells that would sound if there was any drop in blood oxygen levels or a significant rise in pressure.

"You know those spinning tea-cups they have at fairgrounds?" Mercedes said. "That's how Ron and I were when we had to break the bad news to one another. We felt as if we were spinning round and round in small circles while the whole wheel of life was going faster and faster and taking us with it. And now we've accepted the worst case scenario, it's brought with it a sort of peace. He knows he hasn't got long, and I'm realistic about my chances."

"How can you be so calm?" Helene, who knew what loss was like, could not understand how her friends could look death in the eye and smile at it, as if it were welcome, not an enemy.

"There's enough of the Asian in me to accept the notion of reincarnation, and enough of the Catholic to believe in a life hereafter. I look back at that young Mercedes and I wonder who she was. She doesn't seem as if she had anything to do with me; when I went to Cootimurra I went from feelings of guilt about the rotten things I'd done to him, about the way I'd thrown his love back in his face. I was doing a penance, making a sacrifice of my own life for him. Very drama queen, I suppose. Then, when I really fell in love with Ron, I felt I was reborn. And if the baby lives, I'll feel I have received an unexpected blessing."

"And you have Liana, too. You've made your peace with her."

Mercedes shivered. "Have I? I wronged her, Helene. I threw her life away for my own selfish reasons. I'd do anything to make it up to her."

"Love is all you can give her. Make sure she knows you love her."

"I do, and I will."

***

Ron was still functional. He could walk around the clinic,

though Kostas now pushed him to and from the apartment in a wheelchair. Helene cooked the evening meal and, when Ron was well enough, he joined them in the flat on the upper level. He spent the mornings in Mercedes' room, quietly talking to her while the latest miniature took shape. After lunch, when it was time for her to have her afternoon rest, he visited Liana.

He kept a special box of paints in her room, brushes which had been boiled and heavy quality watercolour paper which had been sterilised. He used water from the room itself and had his own beaker in which brushes could be washed. The honey and the gum of gouache were forbidden. Even the outside of the tubes of paint he used had been soaked in an antibacterial agent. He was scrubbed and gowned.

He was painting a series of natural history pictures for her, monochromes of birds and animals from the bush, tiny finches and the mighty wedge-tail eagle, kangaroos with their joeys and frilled-neck lizards basking in the sun. The illustrations fascinated and delighted the patient. It was so very peaceful an occupation. They were, Ron said, his wedding present to her and Alexandar.

"What are the people of Cootimurra like?" she asked. "Are they all black?"

"Oh, some of the Aboriginals on the coast have skins as rich brown as bitter chocolate," he said. "And there are other families where there is a sheen of dark blue about them. Thousands of years ago some people reckon the winds blew boats across the Indian Ocean from Africa, and the Somalis intermarried. They are a very handsome people, the east Africans."

"Mercedes...my mother...said some have blonde hair and fairer skins because the Dutch got ship-wrecked in Australia. Is that true?"

"As true as that your grandfather was a Dutchman. Your fair hair comes from him."

"That's sad. I thought you had given it to me."

He smiled and stroked her hand with his maimed and stubby fingers. He had only two middle digits on his left hand, the thumb and forefinger on his right. She ran her shapely hand across his and looked at the scarred skin.

"Is my face like that? Is that what burns look like when they heal?" There was anguish in her voice.

Ron could not bear to look at her. He had no reassurance for her. He took out a new tube of paint and started mixing it with water. She did not press him for an answer but there was misery in her eyes.

"I'll paint you the children of Cootimurra," he offered. "I'll paint you Dixie's daughters. Victoria and Geri. They're called after the Spice Girls."

"Yes. Please. I'd like to see that. What colour are you using?"

"Van Dyck brown. It's named after a Dutchman. He was a famous artist."

"You are famous too. They call you Roman. Mother told me. How is she?"

"Oh, bearing up. She sends her love."

The awkward moment passed. Liana watched as the faces of the dark brown imps came alive on the page. "That doesn't look like the paintings you did of my mother on that calendar," she whispered. "It's not so smooth, not so soft."

Ron blushed to think his daughter had seen the Vargas studies, which were provocative, to say the least. He covered his embarrassment with explanation. "The Cootimurra children are done using a wash technique. You saw how I did that. The calendar girls were finished with an air-brush."

"Show me how."

"I haven't got one here, but I can give you a rough idea how it works." He took a thick plastic straw from the glass at her bedside and bent it half way. He made a tiny nick at the angle of the tube and placed one end in a pool of paint. He held a new sheet of paper in front of the tiny hole and blew gently through the other end. The brown pigment was sucked up by the venturi effect and settled softly on the surface, in a smooth, even film.

"It's better with a proper air-brush," he said. "You can control it more easily." He blew again and started coughing. The paint flew wildly and splattered the page, instead of being released in a fine aerosol mist.

"Damn," he said, "Look at the mess I've made!"

The nurse who came to help clean up frowned at him and gave him a lecture about taking off his face-mask. "You know the rules," she said. "No germs allowed. If you've got a cold, don't visit."

Ron, thankful that he had not choked up a mess of blood, pinned the paintings to the cork board on the wall and said goodbye.

Mike called him in the morning, sounding furious. "What the hell were you painting with yesterday?"

"Brown paint. Van Dyck brown. Why?"

"What's it made from?"

"God knows," said Ron. "It was a new tube, honestly. Why?"

"The spray went onto Liana's face. It's set up an infection. Find out what was in the stuff, for God's sake. This is serious!"

Ron rang the makers of the pigment. The answer made him feel sick.

"It's good, natural material," the man said. "It's humic, made from peat and earth and brown coal. We just pulverise it into a homogenous form and mix it with a medium to make the colour run smoothly."

"You don't sterilise it?"

"No. Why ever should we? We've been selling it for four hundred years and no one has ever questioned the way we make it before."

Ron cringed. "I might just have well have thrown a bucket of manure in her face. I wonder what really killed Anthony Van Dyck?"

30

Flesh pink: Though sold widely by commercial pigment makers, flesh pink is used mainly by students. Professional portrait painters prefer to mix their own, usually choosing a zinc white to which red, gold and browns are added in proportions to suit the natural colour and racial characteristics of the subject. The slowness with which the paint dries enables subtle shadows and highlights to be blended in, allowing the bone structure and muscular development of the face to be clearly defined.

The seriousness of the situation did not immediately become clear to Ron, though Mercedes had been told of it by Alexandar, who was ripe for murder.

"Of all the halfwit things to have done! Just when we were making progress!"

"But you weren't, were you? Mike told me. She's no better than she was a month ago. And don't give me that crap about not caring how she looks; that you still love her and want to marry her. Alexandar, do you know what she's going to do the moment she sees her face in a mirror? She's going to try to kill herself."

He looked at her in torment. "Yes. I do know that." He swallowed hard. "But as things are, she may never do that. The cryptococcus is having things its own way. Nothing seems to stop it. Liana may not get the chance to make that sort of decision."

"Well, I've made mine. You know what I want you to do. "I've discussed it thoroughly with Mike. He's got approval from the ethics committee. But you're to have no part of it, Alexandar. You're too close to the issue. You look after Ron."

"I don't even want to speak to him!"

"That's not fair. He didn't cause Liana's infection deliberately. He's already withering inside from guilt. Now he's started blaming himself for my condition, saying I wouldn't be ill if he hadn't been so keen on us having a child. It was, after all, my idea, not his."

"I've seen the ultrasounds. The baby looks fine."

"Yes, such a big boy. Mike took one look at the scans and said, 'Well, he's a proper little man. He's got enough willy to get himself into a lot of trouble.' It made me giggle."

Alexandar laughed with restraint. He knew the foetus was as advanced as they could hope. It had been treated to ensure its lungs were not going to get sticky and collapse through immaturity. And the gynaecologist agreed with the Wolf Zeigowicz, the neurosurgeon, that the operation was essential and urgent. The aneurism was getting bigger and the pain in Mercedes head was causing her to slip in and out of consciousness.

"Ron's signed the consent forms?"

"Yes. We both have. Liana can't very well, can she. She won't know a thing until she wakes up."

"If she does."

Mercedes frowned. "You're a right little pessimist today, aren't you? Wish me luck for the morning, and then go to see your mother and Kostas. Take Roma to a good horror movie. You, Dr Pappas, are losing your sense of proportion. Now wheel in your fishing buddy. Ron and I have things we must say to one another. You see, I know this is going to be our last time together."

"I found a folk song you'd like," said Ron, pressing the buttons on a cassette recorder. "A duet. Dearest girl, it says everything I feel."

"Hold my hand, and take the kiss of parting. Hold my hand as you go so far away. All of me is grieving, because I know you're leaving, But I'll keep on believing that we'll meet again some day."

***

The undercurrent of excitement at LIPS and the Tamberlaine Centre was enough to sweep the unwary off their feet. But everyone knew what was being tried that morning. Two operating theatres were ready and the teams were well rehearsed in a procedure never before attempted with living flesh, although both in the United States and London experimental work had been done and reported in Lancet. Back in 2002 it had been predicted that the first operations were six months to a year away. But the present circumstances were unique and it had been agreed it would be a scientific crime to miss the opportunity. How often, after all, was donor tissue so compatible? Obviously it was not perfect, but what in life ever was?

They were on tenterhooks as Mercedes was wheeled into the birth suite. From there she would come to the theatre where the neurosurgeon was ready to remove the huge swelling from her brain. Much hung on whether he could or could not save her life. If he failed, Plan A would swing into action. If he succeeded, the B team would be stood down.

Only Mercedes knew for sure what the outcome would be. The baby was to be delivered by Caesarean, under an epidural anaesthetic...a numbing injection in the spine. She would be conscious throughout and able to see her son as he was lifted from her uterus. She anticipated intense joy.

She also knew the epidural would kill her.

She had told no doctor that Liana had been delivered under an epidural block. She'd checked in advance with the anaesthetist, who was now waiting in the birth suite. He told her what was to happen and what would be injected. It was the same anaesthetic as had been used in Darwin, nearly nineteen years earlier. She had suffered a violent allergic reaction to it, which grew in intensity as contractions forced Liana into the world. Only then had Mercedes gone into convulsions as her blood pressure soared.

It was Zoe who had held the baby while the medical staff fought for the life of Mercedes. Zoe had looked at the blood-smeared new-born with revulsion. It was Zoe who'd blamed the daughter for causing the near-death of her mother. It was Zoe and her acid tongue which had driven any chance of bonding from the mother-child relationship.

Ron, masked and gowned, held his wife's hand as the incision was made and the tiny boy brought into the world. "He's beautiful. I love you, Mercedes. You're magic! Pure magic!"

She smiled, then her eyes rolled and her spine arched in spasm. It was panic stations as machines to which she was connected went wild and alarms started ringing.

"We're losing her!" The anaesthetist yelled. "Get her to theatre. Put her under and take that damned monster out of her head!"

Ron, crying, was left in the birth suite, watching as the midwife washed the tiny boy, wrapped him in soft cloth, and placed him in the arms of his father.

"Only for a minute," she said. "He needs an incubator, but you can come with me to the neonatal wing and hold his hand. Even very tiny premmies like this need to be loved."

***

"She's gone, Dr Pappas," said the Sister. "They lost her even before the neurosurgeon finished clamping off the blood vessels feeding the aneurism. He's not even bothering to close."

"The other teams are ready?"

"About to start. Mr Zeigowicz suggests you join him in the observation gallery. He says he wouldn't miss this procedure for a million bucks."

It took hours to peel the face of Mercedes from her skull, carefully, so that the four arteries and veins were ready for reattachment. They took the fat along with the superficial tissue, and ensured nerve endings and muscles were retained.

Next door the burned horror of Liana's flesh was removed, and the infected material saved for scientific analysis. The bones gleamed as Mike worked to ensure no cryptococcal material remained, flooding the site with fungicide and bombarding it with antibiotics, but not those so strong they would in themselves cause harm. He proceeded with infinite care, for he hoped to ensure a clean bed for the donor material.

Liana was kept in what amounted to a state of suspended animation during the operation. It took more than ten hours. Not only did every vein and artery have to be reconnected with microscopic stitches, but Mike was determined to join major facial nerves which would restore feeling, and muscles which would bring expression.

"It's no good giving her an unanimated face," he'd told Alexandar. "We want her to be able to smile, don't we?"

"That would be good, but I hope that one day, she'll be able to kiss me," he'd replied. But at the moment he felt more like kissing Mike!

Professor Carney glanced up to the gallery when the final stitches were put in around the hairline and gave a thumbs up sign.

"Damned fine work," said Wolf Zeigowicz. "Does she look like her mother?"

"Not really. She's got her father's bone structure. It'll settle down into a face that's uniquely her own."

Alexandar watched anxiously while they got the patient's circulation going again. Under the golden brown of the face of Liana, crept a faint pink flush.

He grabbed the neurosurgeon and danced him around the gallery. "It's wonderful," he cried. "A blooming miracle. A miracle in the flesh!"

***

After the death of Mercedes, Ron felt as if he was on the platform of a railway station, waiting for a train to pull out to Far Away, knowing she would be there to greet him. Food tasted like station cardboard, water like over-stewed tea. But he didn't know what time the train would arrive and was jostled by the passing crowds as he watched them alight and climb aboard for scheduled services.

Crowds. Yes, there were jostling crowds of media monsters. The face switch was a world first and a sensational story. LIPS had recorded the operations through its medical illustration team and had released selected photographs to the press. A video documentary of the procedures, made to show to other reconstructive surgeons, found its way to the desks of television moguls. That the donor was a beautiful woman, a media personality in her own right, and the daughter had been injured in a terrorist bombing; this added interest.

It was several days before it clicked that Liana Vandermeer was the daughter of Roman. Paintings of Mercedes became much sought after. The framers, to whom the nude had been sent on arrival from Australia, invited the press to look at the gift which she had been promised after the birth of the baby.

Baby? What baby? Hadn't they heard she'd died in childbirth? Heartbreak material for the women's magazines. And was it true the father was Professor Carney, the man who had given the daughter the mother's face? Speculation and a whiff of shock and horror for the tits and bums. Questions on Ethics in the Establishment dailies, the broadsheets read on commuter trains by men with bowler hats and umbrellas.

They all wanted to talk to Liana but Mike refused to let anyone near her. Dr Alexandar Pappas was trundled out to meet the media and do the Public Relations thing. As Liana's fiance, he had enough credibility to hold their interest and, since he had been there during the Bali crisis, he was able to side-track them from tricky issues.

He ignored bait such as, "Is it true that Miss Vandermeer fought for the Taliban in Afghanistan?"

"Many Indonesians went to Afghanistan," he said. "Indonesia offered to send troops to the United Nations Peace-Keeping Force."

"Is it true that Liana is a Muslim? What does she think of Coalition plans to bomb Iraq?"

"I've no idea," said Alexandar. "You see, she can't speak yet. She's got to learn how to use the muscles in her new face."

"Does she mind having her mother's face?"

"I'll let you know when she finds out."

There was a strange silence. The man from Reuters raised a hand. "Do you mean she doesn't know what's been done to her?"

"She knows she has a new face. She hasn't realised who the donor was."

"And what does Roman think about this?"

Alexandar looked sternly at the woman, a noted Society writer who had done her share of dragging Ron through the mud in the past.

"Mr Turner is seriously ill. He collapsed after his wife died and is now in the hospice attached to the institute. He has not been well enough to visit his daughter, nor she to see him. She is, of course, in isolation."

"And when will Mercedes be buried?"

"Mrs Turner was a multiple donor. She has donated her kidneys, corneas, heart and lungs to the transplant service and her body to medical science. It was her express wish that her remains be cremated and buried with those of her husband at a later date."

Alexandar had had enough of the vultures. He turned his back on their harrying questions and went back into the research institute. He did not think it appropriate to pass on the final touch of the humour of Mercedes.

"They can have any bits of me you want, Alexandar, but don't try to transplant my genitals. They're all tuckered out!"

***

Storm clouds were gathering over Iraq even as Dr Pappas spoke. Forces from the United States, Britain and Australia were massed on the borders of Kuwait as diplomats from the United Nations and envoys from the Coalition tossed around options to avoid war and resolutions to authorise it.

And in quiet, secret rooms and hidden training camps, extremists fumed and plotted. The men who remembered that Liana had been trained by them were not Indonesian. They did not even speak her native language. But they knew their version of the Koran backwards. Most Muslims cried theirs was a religion of peace, but the fanatics thought otherwise. Its more sinister interpretations were graven in their twisted minds. They saw an opportunity to make a political statement every bit as telling as the attack on the Twin Towers. It was only a matter of time before they would implement it.

When Liana opened her eyes and saw the new doctor in her room she was not alarmed. Nor did she flinch when he came close and shone a light in her eyes. She was relaxed as he spoke quietly to her, drawing her under his hypnotic influence. When he was satisfied that he had imprinted her subconscious with what she must do, he bade her sleep.

"You will not remember me," he said.

She did not. She only remembered the cold desperation in her mind, feelings that pushed to one side her growing delight in Alexandar's love and her confidence in their future happiness.

When at last he brought a mirror to her room she was surprised. She was like her mother yet unlike her, for the cool grey eyes were alien in a face which had previously framed sparkling irises of pansy-dark brown. And the regrowth of hair on her shaved head was coming through baby-blonde and curly, hiding the marks of the tiny stitches which would soon be completely obscured.

"Is it me?" she whispered, stiff-lipped.

"It is you and you are lovely. Tell me, Liana, if I kiss you, can you feel it?" He'd washed his mouth with Listerine and swabbed his own lips.

She didn't like the antiseptic smell, but cooperated eagerly. "It was better last year, but perhaps my tongue will know yours," she murmured. And it did. She tried to lift the corners of her mouth in a smile, but he stilled them with light kisses.

"Give it time. It will come naturally in time," he promised.

"It is strange to think that you are really kissing my mother."

He burst out laughing. "No! No way! The body is always renewing itself. The skin sheds its surface cells and grows new ones. What I have been kissing is you...a new you!" It wasn't quite true, but he knew he had to reassure her.

"How is baby Alf?"

"Gaining weight. May is there every day, and Mike, whenever he can get away to the nursery. Alf looks like Mike. He has very blue eyes and is as bald as his father."

"I would like to cuddle my brother. Has my father seen him again?"

"Kostas or Helene wheels him over every day, but not for much longer, I fear. Ron is very, very ill."

"I would like to see him before he dies. How soon before I can come out of the isolation wing?"

Alexandar stroked her cheek. "I promise you will be able to be with Ron before he slips away. A promise. Cross my heart!"

There was little warning when the end came. Ron was in transit from the material world into the spiritual, but he had moments of lucidity. It was in one of those that Mike fetched Liana to his room, asking Kostas and Helene to leave them alone with Alexandar.

"May and I have already said our goodbyes," he murmured. "And May brought Alf's humidicrib here this morning. Ron was able to hold his son for a few minutes."

"He's at peace," said Alexandar, holding Liana's arm as she moved slowly to the side of her father's bed.

She leaned over and kissed his cheek.

His eyes opened and he looked at her in wonder. "You are so beautiful," he whispered. "You are as lovely as your mother. Be happy, Liana. Remember how much we both loved you, although we did not always know how to tell you, or how to show it."

And Liana took his poor, ruined hands in hers, hands which she knew had been burned while saving her from certain death, and kissed them. Then, copying her mother's farewell gesture to Uncle Alf, she lifted them under her blouse and laid them against her naked breasts.

Ron smiled in pleasure and closed his eyes, happiness and recognition of the simile hovering on his lips.

She stayed with Alexandar, holding her father's hand, until his breathing stopped. It was over. A life had been lived. She shed slow tears as the pink faded from his flesh, leaving the quiet, ashen hue of death.

31

Retrospective 2003

Black powder; otherwise known as cordite, a smokeless compound of nitroglycerin, guncotton and mineral jelly. It is lightfast and long-lasting. When mixed with acetone it gels into strands like brown twine. It requires a detonator to generate heat and activate the explosive, which then expands like a ball of gas, spreading its destructive impact over a huge area.

The Archbishop looked at the tightly packed congregation in the Church of the Children. Gathered there were celebrities and sponsors of Art Aid, the top executives of PanAsia, diplomats from Australia, the United States and Indonesia, high-ranking politicians from all countries, Royal patrons of children's charities, medical specialists who fought the scourge of HIV/AIDS and who pioneered reconstructive surgery at LIPS and elsewhere around the globe.

There were security police everywhere, for the presence of Woody's sons alone was enough to make the funeral a target. But it was Mike and May with their children, Kostas and Helene with Roma, who joined Alexandar and Liana in the front row of the pews which rose on tiers from the central aisle. And on the other side, the chief mourners were children who had posed for the great murals which decorated the walls and the domed roof of the memorial.

"We have just sung the hymn, 'Immortal, Invisible, God only Wise; In light inaccessible, hid from our eyes,' " said the Archbishop. "While God is may be inaccessible, Ron Turner was not. He brought light to the darkness and made visible man's inhumanity against his own kind. He loved little children and, unknown to many who reviled him and brought false witness against him, he went into the back streets of the cities of the world and rescued thousands from a life of degradation. He followed in the steps of Frank Tamberlaine, who founded the organisation to which Ron dedicated most of his life, inspired by his patron, Pru Darcy-Tamberlaine, who was, in every sense of the word, his mother figure.

"God, in his wisdom, gave a great gift to Ron Norman Turner, who, painting as Roman, used that gift in the service of others. He sought no honours, but was honoured. He was a humble man who drew love to him and who gave selfless devotion, devotion which at times lasted beyond the grave.

"At his request, and with the blessing of the estate and the church, his last resting place will be in a woodland glade where his two most famous paintings, English Rose and Wood Violets, were inspired. There he will be buried with the ashes of his first love, who came to him late in his short life, when his faith had been shattered, and restored in him the confidence to continue God's work.

"In the words inscribed on the tomb of Sir Christopher Wren, in St Pauls Cathedral, 'Si monumentun requiris, circumscribe.' If you require a monument, look around you. Roman made his own immortality in the past twenty years."

During the next hymn, Mike made his way nervously to the lectern, to deliver a personal eulogy. May knew he was unhappy, for he did not like the limelight and he knew his words would remind some of truths espoused by Ron which would raise eyebrows.

Liana felt hot and cold by turns. She was glad of the anonymity of the black skirt and blouse she had borrowed from May, her head covered by the hijab and her face veiled, for she was still humiliated by the bold stares of those curious about her new appearance.

She glanced around the congregation and saw the strange doctor. Memory flooded back. She knew he had been in her hospital room the night before, with another man who had glued the device to her breastbone. She remembered they had discussed what had been done in the funeral parlour in the early hours of the morning. She knew what she had to do, in the name of Allah, to earn her place in Paradise.

Her arms were full of flowers, pink roses for Woody, golden ones for Pru, orchids for Mercedes, and lilies for herself. She would lay the bouquet on the coffin and follow as the pall-bearers carried her father to the hearse which waited to carry him away to the crematorium and thence to eternal rest.

It was not intended he should enjoy it. Nor that she should live to regret it. She trembled with the terror of what was to come. Alexandar felt her distress and put his arm around her waist. "It will soon be over, my darling. Be strong."

Mike spoke from the heart. "He was my friend, and I miss him," he said simply. "I mourn, as do all of us who were close to him. Our memories are strong. His delight in his recent reunion with Mercedes and their daughter, Liana, was shared.

"My friend was no saint. He had a lust for life, a keen sense of humour and an explosive temper. Ron knew tragedy and was inspired to rise above it. He experienced loss and from it drew hope. He did not seek fame, but it found him. As has been said before, he sought no honours but they have at last caught up with him. I have been informed today that he has been honoured posthumously by the Royal Academy of Art, which will stage a Retrospective of his work.

"His talents raised millions of dollars for others, yet he died a poor man, such rewards as he received being given to others. But he counted himself rich in love.

"In his own words, which are inscribed in the entrance to the Church of the Children, 'I know there is a power beyond that of men, and a love which transcends all evil. That power drives the prayers of those of many faiths, for it lies at the heart of Judaism, Islam, Buddhism, Catholic and Protestant Christianity, the creeds of Shinto and Zoroaster, of Tao and Confucius. God manifests his power in many ways, for in his house are many mansions. And the special rooms in his Eternal Kingdom, are those of the children of the world.'"

"This is not a time for sadness, but for joy. At Ron's request, we will depart this place to the hymn beloved of all children, 'All things bright and beautiful, all things great and small; all things wise and wonderful; the Lord God made them all.'"

Kostas, Mike. Alexandar, Mark Hopkins, Dixie, who had flown from Australia two days earlier, and Woody's eldest son, included at his own request, took up their positions and lifted Ron's coffin. Liana laid the flowers on top of it and stepped back, following with her head low, as the bearers moved to the centre of the church. She saw the dark stranger and knew he was willing her, willing her, willing her to do what he commanded.

She glanced over her shoulder at the face of Hope, her mother's face, painted above the altar, and from it to the mural on the roof above her head. She remembered Mike's words, Ron's message to the world, and rebelled against the hatred driven into her subconscious by the terrorists.

"Be merciful," she prayed, her lips mouthing her words. And her mind was filled with a great light and a flood of happiness.

She tore the radio-device from her skin and threw it into the baptismal pool, shattering the reflected image of Christ and the children around him.

The dark stranger groped frantically for what looked like a mobile phone, pressing buttons with urgency, determined to achieve what it had been feared she would resile from.

"Sorry, sir. You can't use that in here," said the plain clothes policeman, taking the object from his hand and removing the battery. "No mobile phones. Didn't you see the notices? You'll have to get a new one. The security screen ruins them." He nodded to uniformed police near the door and muttered softly into his walkie-talkie. "Take him in for questioning."

Liana stood at the top of the steps outside the church, blinking in the sunshine, looking with astonishment at the large crowd which had gathered to honour her father.

Alexandar ran towards her and, as he reached her side, she took off her headcovering and let her halo of blonde curls spring free.

He put his arms around her waist and kissed her.

"It is better to love than hate," she said, her lips curving in an enchanting smile."

"And peace is better than war," he replied, leading her down to receive those wishing to pay condolences, ignoring angry strangers who tried to approach the mourners.

***

Chief Inspector Mark Hopkins returned to the church and joined the police who were fishing in the pool for the device Liana had thrown there.

"Dear Mary, Mother of God," he whispered, when his suspicions were confirmed. "I could smell it. I couldn't believe what my nose told me. Cordite. Bloody cordite. The coffin weighed a tonne."

"Not a word about this," his Superintendent said. "Official

Secrets Act. War may be announced at any minute. People are already near to panic. If news of this attempt got out, there could be riots on the streets."

"My God, there'd have been a bloodbath if they'd succeeded." Hopkins wiped sweat from his brow. "What will become of the man you arrested with the radio detonator? And his pals in the crowd outside?"

The Superintendent looked at him seriously. "Roman is not the only one whose remains will rest in a lonely wood," he said.

***

The End.

www.ingramcontent.com/pod-product-compliance
Lightning Source LLC
Chambersburg PA
CBHW030400180626
46812CB00005B/1855